TORPEDO JUICE

A SERGE STORMS ADVENTURE

Tim Dorsey

This edition published in 2019 by Farrago,
an imprint of Prelude Books Ltd
13 Carrington Road, Richmond, TW10 5AA, United Kingdom

www.farragobooks.com

First published by William Morrow in 2005

Copyright © Tim Dorsey 2005

The right of Tim Dorsey to be identified as the author of this Work
has been asserted by him in accordance with the Copyright, Designs &
Patents Act 1988.

All rights reserved. No part of this publication may be reproduced,
stored in a retrieval system, or transmitted, in any form or by any
means, without the prior permission in writing of the publisher.

This book is a work of fiction. Names, characters, businesses,
organizations, places and events other than those clearly in the public
domain, are either the product of the author's imagination or are used
fictitiously. Any resemblance to actual persons, living or dead, events or
locales is entirely coincidental.

ISBN: 978-1-78842-000-6

Serge Storms leaves the world breathless

"Hilarious . . . Serge Storms is, **hands down, one of the most original and just-plain-captivating characters in modern crime fiction**."
Booklist

"**I almost exploded with laughter as I read**. It's manic, hysterical, and puts Dorsey well up there with the cream of comic writers satirizing America in the 21st century."
Independent

"In Serge Storms, the convivial, schizoid torturer with an encyclopedic knowledge of Florida, Dorsey has created **a truly lovable loon**."
Birmingham Post

"**Twisted hilarity . . . a compelling page-turner** . . . a book that, if it was not funny, would be very, very frightening."
Belfast Newsletter

"Dorsey's prose scampers at a rate just this side of manic . . . **Fans of the fast-read, you have met your match**."
Tampa Tribune

"**A newer, nuttier individual is introduced on practically every page** . . . It's a sweet relief to discover that Dorsey can keep up with himself. Heaven knows nobody else can."
Orlando Sentinel

"**Irreverent and loving at the same time** … leaves the reader gasping for breath."
Washington Post Book World

Have you read them all?

Treat yourself again to the first Serge Storms adventures—

Florida Roadkill
Local trivia buff Serge Storms loves eliminating jerks and pests. His drug-addled partner Coleman loves cartoons.

Hammerhead Ranch Motel
There's a different schemer or slimeball behind every door. And then there's Serge—who has stopped keeping up with his meds.

Orange Crush
The Republicans' "golden boy" seems a virtual shoo-in for re-election. That is, until he undergoes a radical personality shift.

Turn to the end of this book for a full list of the series, plus—on the last page—the chance to receive **further updates** on Serge Storms.

For Jack Simms, Jerry Brown, and Ruth Brittin

This is funny.

—"Doc" Holliday's last words, 1887

Prologue

THEY FOUND THE body crucified upside down on the side of the bat tower.
"Cut! Cut!" said a man in a director's chair.
"What's the matter?" asked someone holding a script.
"It's starting to rain. Cover the equipment."

HOWDY. I'M YOUR NARRATOR.

In literary classes, I'm what's referred to as the "omniscient narrator." Yeah, right. Truth is, I've been drinking. We were supposed to start this book several hours ago, except the weather's been cruddy. All the big stars are back in their trailers eating catered food. But does the narrator get a trailer? What do you think?

I've been waiting it out in the No Name Pub. That's on Big Pine Key, two hours south of Miami. Actually not all the stars are snooty. Coleman's been here awhile. Whoops, I wasn't supposed to say anything. . . . Screw it. You'll find out soon enough. Yes, Coleman's back. Remember the big supporting player a few books ago? He went and pulled a McLean Stevenson and left the series when he thought he had this big movie career. Then Hollywood put that notion out like a cheap cigar, and he came back around begging for work. But his character had already been killed off. What were they going to do? I'll tell you what they did. They hatched some crazy gimmick to resurrect him, a stupid idea if you ask me, but nobody ever does. That's typical.

I've been loyal through seven books, dropping polite hints about a little on-screen time. Nothing big, just a few lines. But no, I'm "far too valuable in my current role." Then the prodigal boob comes home and they fall all over themselves writing him back in. . . . I shouldn't blame Coleman. It's not his fault. It's "The Suits." . . . So Coleman's here with me, and this is the thing about Coleman: You can't just be sociable and party a little bit with him. It's either avoid him like the plague or you end up in the eye of a complete fiasco. Like now. He's still trying to get me to take these pills. Even *he* doesn't know what they are, but he's already taken like five. We're getting nothing but glares. First he broke those glass mugs. Then he fell into the rack of cue sticks that went rolling under the pool table and he crawled in after them saying he was sorry and was going to fix everything until they pulled him out by the legs and told him to just go back and stay at the bar. . . . What's that, bartender? Another beer? What the heck, weather ain't going to clear, so there's no way they'll restart today. . . . What now, Coleman? Geez! Okay, okay! If you'll stop bugging me, I'll take one of those pills. No, not *three*—one! . . . All right, down she goes, chase it with a little brewski and . . .

. . . How much time has passed? And why is my head laying like this on top of the bar? Got to sit up straight—summon the will. Come on, you can do it. There. Mission accomplished. . . . Who's that waving at us from the front door? . . . You got to be kidding! They're actually going to start again? *Now?* . . . I am so screwed! There's no way I can pull this off. Where are my breath mints? Freakin' Coleman. He doesn't go on for several pages. They're waving for me again. *Coming, just give me a minute.* What the hell am I going to do? . . . What'd you say, Coleman? Are you sure? I just take this other pill of yours, and it will counteract the first one as well as all the beer? Damn, what a fix. . . . All right, gimme that thing. *Coming!* . . .

A-hem. So far so good. Nobody notices I'm bent. But that second pill better kick in soon. I guess this would make me what professors call the "undependable narrator," except that's usually some schizo character using first-person voiceover who's supposed to be the sympathetic detective, but in a hairpin twist is revealed as the psychotic killer dressed in drag and suffering stress-induced blackouts. *Man, am I fucked up.* What the hell was I just talking about? That second one's kicking in like a mother. I remember my place now. That undependable narrator guy? Well, that's not me. I won't steer you wrong. It's going to be hard enough as it is. This story's a mess. But it's about the Florida Keys, which means it's a documentary. And frig some fancy setup. Let's slice through that elliptical fogbank of piffle right now! Here's the conceit: And if you haven't driven down to the Keys, you'll just have to take my word on this. But you know how if you *are* driving down to the Keys, the people in all the other cars are freaks? Everyone flying down U.S. 1 for a million different reasons, and all of them are wrong. And the ones who don't look like freaks—they're the worst. Because that's the thing about the Keys: Nobody is who they seem to be. It's the perfect place to hide out and reinvent yourself. And that's the story. Got it?

What? . . . Oh, right, the plot. Okay, mixed in with all the freak cars is one very important plot car—a white Mercedes with tinted windows. That's the key to everything. Remember sea monkeys when you were a kid? Doesn't have anything to do with this book, but my brain is starting to fizz. The crew is giving me weird looks—need to wrap this up fast, get the hell out of here. So I was supposed to tell you in this prologue what balls to keep your eyes on, and I just did. Cross that off the list. There's lots of other cars and buses and boats and planes racing south, too many to count. Hey, that's the Keys. Every day the entire island chain is this Idiot's Gumball Rally. *Get used to it.* Just pay attention to that white Mercedes and you'll be fine. It all starts with this massive traffic jam on U.S. 1. Wait, no, it starts when they find a body. But right after that there's this big tie-up clogging everything. You guessed it—Coleman again. He didn't mean to cause it. Trouble just seems to find him like he's some kind of big trouble-type thing like a magnet or something. What are those twinkling lights? These beautiful bugs are circling my head. Let me catch one and inspect its bioluminescent ectoskeleton. Ho. Wha—? Blubbrsg. Shnbeb? Gfhljlsm. Lijloiejlkme . . .

Crash.

"Cut! Cut! . . . What the hell happened to the narrator? He passed out. . . . Coleman!"

"I didn't do anything. He was fine a minute ago."

"Wonderful . . . Where's the backup narrator?"

"Right here." A young man in a starched dress shirt ran over with a pack of stapled pages.

"You're on."

"I am?" He nervously rustled pages and talked to himself. "This is what you've been waiting for. Get your head in the right spot. Narrator, narrator, narrator . . ."

"What are you waiting for? This is costing us money!"

"Okay . . ."

THEY FOUND THE body crucified upside down on the side of the bat tower.

Two Monroe County sheriff's deputies got the call. Gus and Walter. The green-and-white cruiser rolled down a bumpy dirt road on Sugarloaf Key, coming around a bend in the mangroves until an old wooden tower came into view.

In 1929, a real estate developer named Richter Perky decided to make a killing on Sugarloaf, about fifteen miles from Key West. The only thing standing in the way were the mosquitoes. Millions of 'em.

But Perky had an angle. He erected a giant, gothic wooden tower covered with cedar shingles. It was hollow. Perky planned to fill the inside with bats, which were known to come out at night and feed voraciously on the insects. The tower's interior contained a series of ascending louvers coated with bat guano, just the way Perky had heard they liked it.

On the appointed day, thousands of bats arrived in cages. They were released under the tower's open bottom. And flew away, never to be seen again.

Three-quarters of a century later, the tower still stands anonymously on an isolated part of the island. No historic plaque or anything else to identify the enigmatic structure that has been described as a bladeless windmill. Now there was a guy nailed to it.

Gus parked the sheriff's cruiser near the base of the tower. The deputies got out and looked up.

"I may be ill," said Walter.

"I know him," said Gus.

"You do?"

Gus nodded. "Drug smuggler named Hendry. Indicted yesterday. Was in the papers."

"Who would do such a sick thing?"

"Who do you think? His employer. That's why nobody can ever pin anything on him. Never leaves any witnesses."

"You don't mean . . ." Walter stopped short.

"Don't tell me you're afraid to even say his name."

"No, but some people are."

"Not that stupid urban legend again."

"They say he's gone completely insane, especially since he started using that nickname . . . you know . . ."

"What?"

"Okay, I am afraid."

"That's silly."

The medical examiner arrived, along with a small fire truck, because it had ladders.

"I'll tell you something else," said Gus.

"What's that?"

"We're about to have a whole lot more bodies. There were a bunch of other names in that indictment."

Walter looked up again. "Nobody knows what he looks like. He stays hidden in that secluded place out on No Name Key. They say if you ever see him, you die."

"More myth," said Gus, helping prop one of the ladders against the side of the tower. "We've got hundreds of hermits like that way back in these islands who haven't been seen in years."

"Yeah, but this one's running a drug empire. It's like he's a ghost. How does he come and go without anyone seeing him?"

"He drives this big white Mercedes, but the windows are tinted."

Part One

1

It was another typically beautiful morning in the middle of the Florida Keys. People were drunk and people were screaming.

Patrons from the roadside bars heard the commotion and carried drinks outside to watch the routine mess on U.S. 1, the Nation's Highway, 2,209 miles from Fort Kent, Maine, on the Canadian border, to the tip of Key West.

The road was snarled to the horizon in both directions. Standard procedure: midmorning congestion, then the chain reaction of rear-enders from inattention. Now a parking lot.

Drivers honked, shouted obscenities, turned off their engines and popped beers. A Mercury overheated and the hood went up. Ninety-nine degrees.

Two sheriff's deputies stood at the window of their air-conditioned substation on Cudjoe Key. Veterans Gus DeLand and Walter St. Cloud. Drinking coffee. It was the beginning of the shift, the part where they were supposed to review the latest bulletins on all the serial killers and mass murderers heading their way.

Gus looked out the window with his hands on his hips. "We've got to do something about that road."

"I've never seen a crucifixion before," said Walter, holding a ceramic cup covered with swimsuit models. "Check out this new mug. I got it in Vegas. When you pour a hot beverage in it, like coffee, the bathing suits disappear. I don't know how it works."

The fax activated. Gus headed toward it.

He came back reading the all-points bulletin. *". . . Brown Plymouth Duster, brown Plymouth Duster, brown Plymouth . . ."*

"What are you doing?" asked Walter, holding a coffee mug at eye level.

"Mnemonic device. Possible serial killer heading this way. . . . *brown Plymouth Duster, brown . . .*"

The fax started again.

Gus came back with another piece of paper. *". . . Metallic green Trans Am, metallic green Trans Am, metallic green . . ."*

"I brought one back for you, too."

". . . Trans Am . . . What?"

"Coffee mug." Walter set it on Gus's desk. "Figured you might need it since you're divorced."

Gus stuck the mug in a bottom drawer.

"Aren't you going to use it?"

"I'm not sure it's appropriate in the office. But thanks for thinking of me." Gus held up the second APB. "Spree killings in Fort Pierce. Six dead and counting. They got a partial license." Gus began repeating a number.

Walter set his mug down on the first APB, making a round stain. "So, busy day already. Crucifixion, traffic jam and now two serial killers on the way."

"No, the second is a spree killer." Gus handed the fax to Walter.

"What's the difference?"

"One's in more of a hurry."

"They always come down here."

"And blend right in."

"How's that?"

"Just look at 'em all out there," said Gus. "Hell-bent to lose their minds in Key West. A psychopath would be the quiet one."

"But it doesn't make sense," said Walter. "They're on the run, and this is the ultimate dead end. What are they thinking?"

"Who says they're thinking?"

THE LOGJAM STARTED at Mile Marker 27 on Ramrod Key, feeding on itself for an hour. New arrivals flying down the Keys in convertibles and motorcycles and pickups pulling boats, getting closer to Key West, anticipation busting out of the cage, coming upon stalled traffic way too fast.

It quickly backed up over the Seven-Mile Bridge. People with to-go cups of warm draft stood in front of the Overseas Lounge and watched a Chevy Avalanche sail into a Cutlass, knocking the next six cars together like billiards, a half dozen airbags banging open like a string of firecrackers. Three minutes later, the audience outside the Brass Monkey saw a Silverado plow into a Mazda, the twenty-two-foot Boston Whaler on the pickup's trailer catapulting over the cab.

Sirens reached the Sandbar, a rustic stilt-top lounge poking out of the mangroves on Little Torch Key. Customers ran to the crossbreeze windows overlooking South Pine Channel and the bottled-up ambulances unable to cross the bridge. The gang at Boondocks heard a *whap-whap-whap-whap* and looked up at the runners of a sheriff's helicopter called in by the stranded emergency vehicles.

The Mercury with the raised hood had since caught fire, and the tiki bar crowd at the Looe Key Reef Resort appreciated the uncomplicated entertainment value when it reached the gas tank. A fishing guide with sun-cracked skin set his Miller on the bar. "This is worse than general. I have to make Boca Chica this afternoon."

"Why don't you call Foley?" asked the bartender. "See if it's reached."

A cell phone rang inside the bar at Sugarloaf Lodge.

"Foley here. Hold a sec, let me stick my head out. . . . No, road's clear here. Traffic's fine—" Crash. "Check that. A dope boat just rolled . . . because I can see the bricks in the street . . . Yeah, people are grabbing them and running away. . . ."

More *whap-whap-whap*. Another chopper cleared the roof of the No Name Pub, a 1935 roadhouse hidden in the banana trees on Bogie Channel.

The customers wandered out the screen door and up the road, where a helicopter hovered over the bridge. Loudspeakers cleared the fishermen below, and the aircraft set down, scattering bait pails.

The rotors stopped. One of the pilots in a green jumpsuit got out and took off her helmet.

A bar patron approached. "What's going on?"

"Car fire caught the brush on Summerland and jumped the road. Need a place to rest the engines."

Three more patrons leaned against the bridge's railing. The oldest was a well-read biker from north Florida named Sop Choppy who had relocated to the Keys under hazy circumstances. Bob was the middle in age. He operated a very seasonal accounting firm on the island and closed in the summer to run a customerless tour service with his personal pleasure craft for tax reasons. The youngest was also named Bob, a shirtless construction worker who hammered roof trusses by day and had dreams but no workable plan to become a dragster mechanic for Don Garlits. Two regulars named Bob made things complex, so the other customers called him "Shirtless Bob." He had to wear a shirt in the bar.

The trio didn't possess a single common reference point but were welded into a fragile axis of daily bar chatter by the necessities of tourist hegemony. They gazed across the water at the Spanish Harbor viaduct, where a frozen line of cars stretched down the highway as far as they could see. A tiny driver stood on his roof for vantage.

Their heads suddenly jerked back as a fireball went up in the direction of Ramrod. They sipped drinks as a mushroom of black smoke dissipated in the wind.

"Ever watch *Monster Garage* on the Discovery Channel?" asked Shirtless Bob. "Last week they converted a PT Cruiser into a wood chipper. You jam logs through the open back window and twin sprays of chips go flying up from two secret hatches in the roof."

"Why?"

"Because it's *Monster Garage*."

Barely audible in the distance: *Bang. Bang.* Followed by: *pop-pop-pop-pop-pop,* a small under-the-armpit smuggler's machine gun.

"They've got to do something about that highway," said Bob the accountant. "Too vulnerable. Least little thing and it all craps out."

Sop Choppy looked down in his empty drink, then up at the road. "Wonder how it started this time."

How It started: before dawn

THE WORLD LOOKED weird to Coleman. It was curved in a fisheye through the peephole of room 133 at the Royal Glades Motel. A single raindrop on the outside of the small glass bubble distorted the crime lights on Krome Avenue. This was up on the mainland, south of Miami, across the agricultural flats with pesticide musk and giant industrial sprinklers that were still at this hour. Coleman toked the roach beginning to heat his fingertips and kept an eye to the door. Downtown Homestead. Not a soul.

Coleman was at the threshold of forty-something and crouched against the bong-hit ceiling of eighth-grade maturity. His honeydew head was too big for his body. Coleman was never up before dawn, except now. Because he needed to make the Great Escape.

Cash was low, and Coleman had slept—make that remained unconscious—through checkout the previous day. The front desk had been phoning ever since. "Coming up in a minute to pay." "Be right there." "Eating dinner now, but immediately after that." Then knocks at the door. "No clothes on—be over in a sec." The night manager finally opened up with a passkey. Coleman lay snoring in his BVDs, empty beer cans randomly strewn around the room like spent artillery shells in a busy howitzer battery. The manager decided his salary didn't cover social work. He closed the door and left a note in the office for the morning person.

Most recently, Coleman had been living on the couch of a party buddy's apartment in Port Charlotte. Then, cultural differences. His friend had a job. And the evenings of brainless bingeing curiously began to seem like evenings of brainless bingeing. Coleman was asked to move on, enticed by some free pot for the road. His host considered it a high-yield investment.

The Royal Glades Motel was halfway back to Coleman's rusty trailer with rotten floorboards on Ramrod Key. He'd headed south on 1-75 and soon reached the edge of the Everglades at the bottom of the state's west coast.

People with a few dollars in turnpike money preferred to cross the swamp on Alligator Alley, a safe, divided, four-lane interstate with fences on both sides to keep wildlife out of traffic. Those who couldn't scrape up tollbooth change were forced to drive farther south and take the Tamiami Trail, a harrowing two-laner with no shoulders next to deep canals. Depth perception in the Everglades was always tricky. Stupidity even trickier. People were always trying to pass, and there were many spectacular head-ons.

It was worse at night.

But there was little traffic at four A.M. when Coleman entered the Glades. No light or sound either, just stars and the cool air coming in his open windows. Coleman hadn't seen anything but black marsh for fifteen miles, when he passed the silhouette of a Miccosukee Chickee hut and a peeling billboard of a falsely cheerful Indian giving airboat rides to Eurocentrics. Then nothing again for a half hour until an auburn first-quarter moon on the horizon toward Miami. His headlights bounced off a panther-crossing sign. There was a small glow to the south: something burning down one of the gravel roads to a water-filled quarry. Coleman was driving a gold '71 Buick Riviera that dripped oil. The maintenance money had been spent on the car's furry steering wheel cover and Playboy shift knob. This was Coleman's version of the economy.

The Buick passed a closed restaurant that served frog's legs, then the locks of a dam where they had diked for this road way back. Coleman was lighting a joint and trying to get something on the radio when another set of headlights made him look up. "What's that guy doing in my lane? Wait, what am I doing in *this* lane?" Ahead: A Datsun had come to a complete stop, its passenger compartment and the driver's open mouth filled with Coleman's high beams. Brakes squealed. At the last second, Coleman veered around the other car. He glanced back over his shoulder at the Datsun, then turned around to find a twelve-foot gator in the mist of his headlights. He stiff-armed the steering wheel and slammed the brakes again. Thump. The squish-grease made the tires lose traction, and the Buick slowly rotated sideways down both lanes until it completed a perfect three-sixty. Coleman came out of the spin back in his own lane, still speeding east. "This road is *way* too dangerous. I need a beer." He reached under the seat. On its own, the radio picked up a weak station fading in and out. Steely Dan. Something about a weekend at a college that went awry. Coleman imagined a wooden shack and a lone radio tower with a blinking red beacon, personally transmitting to him from an island in the middle of the swamp. He slouched and settled in for the rest of the drive. Fate. It was meant to be. God was watching out for him, Coleman thought, or he never would have made it to this age.

He couldn't have been more right.

APB # 1: the brown Plymouth Duster with Ohio plates

BACK UP THE Tamiami Trail, a light grew brighter, the one Coleman had seen down the gravel road. The fire was really involved now. An Oldsmobile with a body inside.

A brown Plymouth Duster with Ohio plates sat nearby. The trunk lid went up. Hands in leather gloves placed a metal gas tank inside and slammed the hood.

The Duster began driving out the gravel road, branches scraping the windshield. Gravel became tar as the car turned onto the Tamiami Trail, leaving behind the burning Oldsmobile with the sticks of dynamite that soon sent a chute of flame and evidence skyward.

The Plymouth continued east. The driver could make out major power lines against the moon, the first wisps of Miami. A tiny traffic light flashed in the distance. It took ten minutes to get to it. The crossroads. The Duster made a lazy right, then a half-hour straight shot south through migrant tomato fields and palm tree farms.

It turned in the entrance of the Royal Glades Motel.

2

West Palm Beach, near the airport: five A.M.

A DOZEN POLICE cars with flashing lights filled the parking lot of a small brick medical complex that looked like a strip mall. There was crime tape and a sheet-covered body. Little numbered markers sat on the pavement next to each bullet. Evidence cameras flashed. The head detective was on the phone to the home of the police chief.

"I think we just solved that tourist robbery at the motel . . . no, not an arrest, a body . . . yes, the victims just made a positive ID. . . ." He glanced toward the traumatized retired couple from Michigan clutching each other. The man had bandages on his chin and nose. ". . . No, I don't think a press conference is a good idea right now. . . . I know you're getting a lot of pressure from the mayor's office because of the tourism angle. . . . Because I don't think we know what we're dealing with yet. Something's not right. . . . Six bullet wounds . . . right, but they're all *exit* wounds. . . . No, someone didn't stick a gun up his ass or down his throat. The medical examiner has confirmed the trajectory. These are all straight through, three in the stomach and three in the back, like someone was firing a gun *inside* him. I've never seen anything like it. . . ."

A uniformed officer approached the head detective, who covered the phone. "What is it?"

The officer told him.

"Thanks." The detective uncovered the phone. "Sir, we have a second crime scene. Someone broke into one of the clinics in the medical complex. . . . Yeah, it's related. I think we just figured out those exit wounds. You're not going to believe this. . . . No, we definitely want to hold off on that press conference. . . ."

The previous evening

A LANKY MAN in a flowing tropical shirt raced down Southern Boulevard on a ten-speed ultralight aluminum racing bike. He passed the airport, a steak house, a medical complex, some gas stations, budget motels. . . . Suddenly, his senses perked up. Something was out of place. He squeezed the brake levers on the handlebars.

A RENTED GRAND Am with its doors open sat in front of room 112 of the Golden Ibis Motel. Hank and Beatrice Dunn from Grand Rapids carried luggage inside. Beatrice began unpacking a suitcase on the sagging king bed. Hank locked up the car and went in the room. He hung the DO NOT DISTURB sign on the outside knob and started closing the door.

The door flew back open, knocking Hank to the ground. A burly man with sores and crazed, crack-head eyes ran in the room. "Where's your money!"

Beatrice screamed. The man went to punch her.

Hank grabbed his arm from behind. "Don't hurt us. We'll give you everything."

So he spun around and punched Hank. He was going to do more damage, but saw the wallet and jewelry on the dresser. Then he tore through a purse on the bed. When he was satisfied he had just about everything, he turned to Beatrice. "Give me your wedding ring!"

She clutched her hand to her chest. "No!"

Hank was still woozy on the ground with a torrential nosebleed, trying to get up. "Honey, give him the ring!"

"Shut the fuck up!" The man seized Beatrice's arm and yanked on her finger. The ring didn't budge. He pulled and pulled. No luck.

"It's stuck," said Beatrice. "I never take it off. Please!"

The thug unsnapped a leather holder on his belt and flicked open a jackknife. "It'll come off now!"

"No!" yelled Hank, grabbing the man's shirt from behind. He got another punch in the face and hit the floor again. The assailant turned back to Beatrice and forced her hand down on the sink counter for a cutting surface.

He heard a click behind him and felt something cold and metal against the back of his head. A new voice: "What do you say we let her keep the ring?"

The couple was dizzy from the swing of events. First the motel invasion and now this mystery man in a tropical shirt holding their assailant down on the bed and tying his hands behind his back with the cord from the curtains.

When he was finished, Serge jerked the man up off the mattress and turned to the retirees: "I just want you to know this isn't what we're about down here. I'm very sorry about the inconvenience. Welcome to Florida!"

Serge marched his prisoner toward the door.

"Uh, what are you?" Hank called after him. "Some kind of undercover cop?"

"No, a historian."

THREE BLOCKS AWAY Serge was still marching his prisoner down a series of alleys. He had the gun in one hand and was walking his tenspeed bike alongside him with the other.

"That's far enough," said Serge. They were behind a medical complex. Serge went to work with a lock-pick set. "What's wrong with you? When I was growing up, the criminals had a code. No kids, old people or cripples. Now they're the first ones you guys go for."

The back door of a clinic popped open and Serge flicked on the lights. He waved the gun, ordering the man inside.

The man looked around, confused. Serge reached in his pocket and pulled out a handful of bullets. He raised them to the man's mouth. "Swallow these."

"Fuck you."

Serge held his hands out like scales, the bullets in the left, the gun in the right. "Your pick. Bullets are going in your mouth one way or the other."

The man didn't answer. Serge forced the barrel through his teeth. The man started yelling and nodding.

Serge removed the gun. "Good choice." He fed the bullets one by one, even fetched a paper cup of water from the cooler when the going got rough after number three.

"That wasn't so bad, was it?"

The man didn't know what the hell was going on.

"Now come over here and lie down on this table."

The man didn't move.

"You were starting to cooperate," said Serge, poking the gun in his ribs. "Don't make this go worse than it has to."

The man reluctantly lay down on the table. Serge pulled some extra curtain cord from his pocket and tied the man's ankles. The table was narrow. It was on some kind of rolling track. Serge pushed the table until the man began sliding headfirst into a tight tube in the middle of a gigantic medical contraption.

"I know what you're thinking," said Serge, pushing the bottoms of the man's feet until he was completely inside. "What the hell is this thing? Well, I'll tell you. And it's really amazing stuff. This is an MRI. That stands for Magnetic Resonance Imagery. Huge leap forward in medical diagnosis! And since Florida has so many old people, they're conveniently located all over the place, lucky for me."

Horrible screaming echoed out of the tube.

"Quiet down. I can't think." Serge walked behind the control panel and began throwing switches. "Now, how do we get this baby going? . . ." More switches and dials. "These machines use a powerful magnetic field to produce three-D X-ray-type images. And when I say powerful, I'm not kidding. This is an absolutely true story: One hospital learned the hard way it couldn't mount fire extinguishers in the MRI room. They were in the middle of scanning a patient, and the extinguisher snapped out of its wall holder, flew clear across the room and stuck to the side of the machine. That's why they can't use this thing on anyone who has metal plates or pins—rips them right out your body. . . . Okay, I think this is the right switch. . . . Are you ready? I sure am! This is going to be so great! ..."

Downtown West Palm Beach: the wee hours

A POLICE CRUISER rolled quietly toward the waterfront. A spotlight swept storefronts and alleys. There'd been numerous reports of a suspicious person in the vicinity of Clematis. He matched the description the Michigan couple had given of the vigilante in their motel room.

The patrol officer was bored. He turned at the end of the block and backtracked on Daytura, just to be thorough.

Okay, this is definitely a waste of time. He clicked off the spotlight. Just as he did, a silent form shot across the end of the street. At least he thought he'd seen it. He clicked the light back on.

Nothing.

The patrol car accelerated and whipped around the block. The spotlight scanned the street. Empty except for a skinny cat darting under a van with four flat tires.

Five blocks away, a dark form flew down Dixie Highway. It zoomed under a street light. A lanky man in a flowing tropical shirt on a ten-speed ultralight aluminum racing bike. Leaning way over in aerodynamic wedge, legs like pistons, no wasted motion.

The bike took the next corner in a graceful arc and zigzagged through a grid of streets near the train tracks. It raced south on Tamarind Avenue. Knife-fight territory. A juke joint had its door open to the street, blue light and arguments spilling out, then the next corner, two guys waiting for business. One saw the bike coming and pulled a pistol. "Give it up!"

"Buy a fuckin' antecedent! . . ."

The cyclist's voice trailed off as he sailed through the intersection; the gunman never had a shot and went back to discussing the Monroe Doctrine. The cyclist sat up in his seat as he cruised down the center line with no hands. He looked at his left arm and the checklist taped around his wrist like a quarterback's game plan. *Jupiter Inlet Light,*

Blue Heron Bridge, Royal Poinciana Playhouse, Flagler Park, Hypoluxo house where they shot Body Heat . . . All crossed off. He activated the backlight of his watch, then looked up at a red and blue sign three blocks ahead. Right on schedule.

The cyclist parked in front of the bus station. He leaned the bike against the wall and went inside, and someone jumped on the bike and rode away. Half the people in the waiting room were fighting to stay awake, the rest trying to fall asleep. The man walked briskly for the lockers. He opened one of the largest and removed a beaten-up knapsack and a guitar case, then ran out the back exit to the loading platform. The door closed on an idling Greyhound.

"Hold on!"—waving a ticket—"You got one more."

The door opened. Serge A. Storms bounded aboard.

The bus was mostly empty as Serge walked down the aisle, thinking: Where do I want to sit? Whom do I want to talk to? That's absolutely critical. For long rides, I require a stimulating conversation partner with deep reservoirs of cultural references upon which my metaphors can find purchase. . . .

Serge spoke his thoughts out loud, quite loudly in fact, as he moved through the bus, studying fellow riders who either gathered their belongings tightly or spread them out on the next seat so there was no room.

Serge placed a hand on the back of each person's seat as he passed by.

". . . No, not this woman, a disaster-in-waiting. Clothes and makeup that are only in fashion in penitentiary visiting rooms. . . . Not this guy, the bad-breath merchant keeping alive his record-breaking streak of wrong life decisions . . . Not this woman, who looks like she's running from a failed two-week marriage consisting of late-night shrieking, credit card debt and venereal disease . . ."

Serge was running out of people. He glanced toward the back of the bus and brightened. "Ahhh, that looks like a hospitable chap."

He trotted all the way to the last row and took a seat across the aisle from a late-stage alcoholic from Lower Matecumbe Key on the verge of kidney failure. The bum was sleeping across two seats with his neck bent against the side of the bus in a way that would remind him later.

Serge stowed his knapsack, then opened the guitar case and began strumming. He rattled around in his seat. He cleared his throat. He paused and looked over at the bum. No movement.

Serge reached across the aisle and shook the man hard—"Hey you!"—then quickly sat back in his seat and strummed. The him raised his head and looked around in a fog.

"Oh, I'm sorry," said Serge. "Did I wake you?"

The bum began reclining again.

"Well, since you're already up—" Serge hopped across the aisle and made the bum scoot over. "Traveling is all about talking to new people. That's the ball game. That's the whole point, travel to an exotic place, meet the people, immerse in their culture, and find out why they're so fucked up. If you're not going to spill your guts to complete strangers, why take the trip? You might as well just stay home abusing sex toys until that mishap that brings paramedics and you become the talk of the neighborhood. But communication is easy for me because I'm a listener. I love to hear people gab about themselves. Every single person is special. Everyone has great stories. Like you. I'll bet you have a million. How old are you? Sixty?"

"Forty-three."

"I'm all about listening. That's why the world is in shambles. Nobody listens anymore!"

"I, uh . . ."

"Shhhhhh! Listen," said Serge. "I have big news. I'm getting married! I don't know who yet. I'm still conducting the statewide search, in case you have any undamaged relatives . . ."

The bum began slouching and closing his eyes.

Serge jerked him upright. "I'm taking it to the next level. Marriage will force personal growth. In the meantime, I'm trying other methods. Like this one."

Serge turned forward and stared with intense concentration. Small folds twitched under his eyes until . . .

"Ahhhhhhhhhhhhhhhhhhhhhhh!"

The bum jumped. The bus driver looked up in his rearview.

"Sorry," said Serge. "I'm training my brain to look directly into the naked essence of life. Do you realize the person who lies to us most is ourself? Several times a day I stop and take a prolonged, unblinking look at the truth. . . ."

The bum started getting up. "I'd like to go to another seat."

Serge yanked him back down. ". . . It usually goes one of two ways. Horror or ecstasy. That time I flashed on the Black Death sweeping Europe in 1348. Let me try again. . . ."

Serge stared ahead and squinted.

"Yeeeeeeeeeeee-hawwwwwwwwwwwwwww!"

Serge turned to the bum. "Now *that* was a good one! I just realized how lucky I am. I could have been born a cystoblast! It's not important what that is. All you need to know is it's one of the many, many things you definitely don't want to be. It's not even an organism, just a bunch of cells, which means they don't have eyes and can't appreciate the radiant colors of God's creation. From nature: sky blue, forest green, the creamy pink of the spring blossom, the honey in the clouds at sunset. From food: eggshell, guacamole, tangerine, cranberry. From science: carbon, chrome, cobalt, copper. From women's magazines: mauve, ecru, fuchsia, taupe. Colors I dig just because I like saying the word: *gamboge, gamboge, gamboge.* Other words that should be colors but aren't, like Cameroon and DiMaggio. You're a cystoblast, you can forget about all that. . . ."

Serge hadn't noticed that the bus was pulled over. The driver stood over him. "If you keep yelling, I'll have to ask you to get off."

"Sorry," said Serge. "Can I play my guitar?"

"Do you yell when you play?"

"Not usually."

The driver was already walking back up front. "No more yelling!"

Serge cradled his acoustic and began strumming. *". . . Mama don't take my Kodachrome awaaaaaaayyyy-eeeee-yay. . . ."*

A GIANT EYEBALL rotated in the peephole of room 133 of the Royal Glades Motel. Coleman took a hit from the corner of his mouth. Still dark out there. Nothing but the sandwich shop across the street, where local teens had come along in the night and rearranged letters on the roadside marquee: 99¢ HAND JOBS.

Inside room 133, two days of Lifestyle Coleman. Fast-food sacks, roaches, matches, spilled trash cans, wet socks on lampshades, smashed potato chips in the carpet, fried chicken bones between the sheets, slice of pepperoni stuck to the mirror, bloody footprint on the dresser, pocket change in the bottom of the toilet, sink clogged with vomit, cartoons on TV.

Coleman's eye stayed pressed to the door. Paranoid. Every time he thought he'd watched long enough for a clean escape . . . second thoughts. What if someone comes out of the office in the next minute? Then he'd watch another minute, and so forth. Coleman wanted to make sure his getaway was absolutely perfect; nothing as much as a hair out of place. The eyeball scanned the street again. Drugs finally made the decision. The roach had burned out; no reason to stay any longer. Coleman stepped back from the peephole and grabbed the strap of a duffel bag at his feet. He took a deep breath.

Now!

Coleman threw open the door and it banged against the wall. He took off running. Into a metal garbage can. They both went over with a crash. The can tumbled loudly across the parking lot. Coleman pulled himself up by a car door handle, activating the auto-burglar alarm. *Whoop-whoop-whoop.* "Shit!" Lights started coming on all over the motel. Bleary people walked onto balconies without shoes. The manager emerged from the office. Coleman dove in the Buick. He dropped the keys. He hit the horn. The car finally started. Tires squealed. Coleman patched out, running over the garbage can, which wedged under the bumper and sprayed sparks. The people on the balconies winced when the Buick's undercarriage bottomed out at the base of the driveway, and they cringed again when Coleman made a hard left turn, sending the garbage can flying free and shattering the lighted roadside marquee in front of the sandwich shop.

Then he was gone. Quiet resumed. Motel guests trudged back to rooms. Some decided sleep was futile. Might as well get a leg up on driving. They began loading luggage. Two blue American Touristers went into the trunk of a brown Plymouth Duster with Ohio plates.

3

APB #2: the metallic green Trans Am

Dark and deserted on the Florida Turnpike, the part of day you can't quite put your finger on. No longer the night before, not quite the next morning. Even more off-balance if you've been driving some hours.

A metallic green Trans Am skirted the backside of Miami International, down through Sweetwater. The blackness alternated with pockets of light at the interchanges. The lights were the harsh orange shade found at businesses with barbed wire and surveillance cameras. They said: Don't exit here.

Almost five a.m., but the driver didn't know where her watch was. The strap had broken. She kept looking in the rearview. The Trans Am had a smoked T-top. Her legs had bruises.

The woman was petite, practically swallowed by the Pontiac. Twenty-eight years old, but her new skin, dimples and tiny features always got her carded.

The Trans Am passed a tollbooth sign that said to get seventy-five cents ready. A shaking hand rubbed makeup onto the bruised thighs. Her window went down. Change flew into a toll basket, and the Trans Am accelerated. The makeup compact flew into an oversized purse on the passenger seat, then she jerked the whole thing into her lap and rummaged. The handbag's organizational system was shot, the entire contents dumped out and thrown back in twice already tonight. She found a cigarette, lit it with the car lighter and coughed. She had just un-quit smoking with the pack bought back in Delray. The nicotine slowed her rampaging imagination, but it couldn't block the involuntary images: what she'd seen when she opened the bathroom door. And again at the second place. That's what really shook her, besides all the blood. How on earth did they know about the second place? It meant she wasn't safe anywhere. She looked in the rearview. No sign of the white Mercedes with tinted windows.

The Trans Am passed the Kendall exit and a blue info sign. She waited for a tanker to go by and slid over a lane.

The Snapper Creek Service Plaza was at Mile Nineteen. Nineteen miles till the end of the turnpike, then just two isolated lanes through mangroves as the mainland seeps into the part of the map with those spongy symbols before reaching the drawbridge to Key Largo.

Only a few vehicles at the plaza. An unattended Nissan with no tag. A security car with a sleeping guard in the driver's seat and an emblem on the door of an irritable eagle and lightning bolts. A Peterbilt tractor-trailer, dark in the cab but the engine still on, along with hundreds of amber running lights that traced the entire outline of the truck in a manner that said someone was getting rich on amber running lights.

The Trans Am pulled into the space closest the building. The woman forced her legs out of the car. She walked stiffly to the pay phones, pushed coins in a slot and dialed an exchange in the lower Keys. "Come on!" Three no-answers at the last three service plazas. Now ten rings and counting. The exposure time out of the Trans Am seemed eternal. A car door opened. Her eyes shot toward the sound. The night guard smiled like a sex offender.

Thirteen rings, about to call it quits. A sleepy voice answered. The woman jumped. "Don't hang up! It's me!"

BELOW MIAMI, YOU'RE on your own. Dixie Highway slants across a hot, dusty wasteland of Mad Max predators, where the famous roadside "Coral Castle" is now ringed with razor wire, and copulating dogs tumble past the doors of Cash Advance Nation. Above all this, another world away, are the elevated lanes of the Florida Turnpike. A metallic green Trans Am raced south just before dawn until the lanes ended and twisted their way down to merge with U.S. 1. Welcome to Florida City, a franchised boomtown decided by automatic traffic counters and satellite imagery. Mobil, Exxon, Wendy's, Denny's, Baskin-Robbins and a continuous row of chain motel signs indicating that the cornerstones of the white race are free breakfast and AARP rates.

A maid pushed her cleaning cart and sang a merry Spanish song. Room doors opened; Middle America herded kids into cars. Lobbies filled with people grabbing Pop-Tarts and sticking paper cups under spigots. *"The orange juice is out."* The sky grew lighter. The maid knocked. *"Housekeeping!"* The gas lanes at the food marts filled. *"Pump five is already on (you idiot)!"* College students with beer suitcases piled back into their Jeep Grand Cherokee and raced to the edge of the parking lot.

Two sedans went by, then a metallic green Trans Am. The coast was clear. The Jeep took off with a wallet on the roof and shaving cream on the back window: "Key West or Bust!"

COLEMAN CHECKED HIS rearview. No witnesses from the Great Escape. He continued through some modest new construction in the wake of Hurricane Andrew until the city of Homestead eventually dwindled out in a quilt of vacant lots.

The Buick rolled to a stop at the intersection with U.S. 1. Coleman's windows were down, letting in morning sounds that emphasized how quiet it was. A bird chirping, a far-off diesel getting a punch of fuel. Coleman opened a bag of peanuts and waited for some last cars to pass. A metallic green Trans Am and college students in a Jeep Grand Cherokee. He turned right.

Nothing oncoming for the first three miles. The sky went from dark to light blue, the world waking up. Coleman smelled salt. The sun finally broke, orange blotches of light flickering through breaks in the mangroves. Coleman popped nuts in his mouth. Formations of wading birds flew over the causeway. Then more birds on foot, vultures standing around overnight roadkill with the posture of guys loitering outside an adult video store. Every other mile: dead raccoon, dead snake, dead opossum, dead armadillo. Traffic began filling Coleman's rearview, and he was soon being passed nonstop by convertibles and SUVs and rental cars. Coleman was always being passed because the Buick couldn't go faster than fifty without vibrating like a paint shaker. Some of the other drivers leaned on their horns. Coleman didn't pay no mind. He was one of the most carefree creatures you'd ever meet, which meant he was an enemy of the state. He finished his peanuts and tossed the empty bag on the dashboard, which had become one of those trash gardens you frequently see on the highway: crumpled burrito wrappers, smashed soda cups, napkins, matchbooks, lottery tickets, coffee stirrers, dead AA batteries, Gulf Oil road map of Arkansas, intact vending-machine Condom of Ultimate Optimism, still-folded litter bag. As new layers of garbage were added, the older ones compacted into the seam between the front of the dash and the tapering windshield, where you could trace Coleman's downfall like a museum cross-section of an Indian shell mound. On the floor of the passenger side was a chewed pencil, an umbrella handle and a broken answering machine he'd found in a field. The AC didn't work.

Mile Marker 108 went by. The Buick slowed as it struggled up the incline toward the bridge over Jewfish Creek, the official border between mainland Florida and the Keys. Coleman was passed in the left lane by a Greyhound bus with some kind of commotion in the backseat.

"Wake up! Wake up!" yelled Serge, shaking the bum. "You don't want to miss this!"

The bum was having one of those fantastic drunk dreams, like if Georgia O'Keeffe did claymation of organic decomposition. "Wha—? What is it?"

Serge pulled him upright and pointed out the window. "There's the bridge! We're about to enter the Keys! It's one of those relaxing little life pleasures you should get into. *So get the fuck into it!*"

The bus rattled across the metal grating of the drawbridge. Serge threw his arms in the air like he was on a roller coaster but remembered not to yell.

Then it was over. He smiled at the bum. "Like no other place on earth. Raw natural beauty, relentless freedom, unorthodox natives. A friend told me something else about the Keys I never forgot: Down here, nobody is who they seem to be. When people in other parts of the country want to reinvent themselves, they come to Florida. But when people in Florida want to reinvent themselves, they come to the Keys. That's what I'm doing. . . ."

They passed Overseas Insurance, Paradise Tattoo and a house trailer with a hand-painted sign on the side of the road, WANTED: GRAND PIANO OR LEGAL ADVICE.

Serge began strumming his guitar again. He stopped and silenced the strings with his hand. "Got a ground-floor opportunity for you." He looked around to make sure nobody else was listening, then leaned closer. "I'm going to be the next Jimmy Buffett." He winked. "Only better . . ." He resumed playing. *". . . Oh, I'm an irresponsible pirate mixin' drinks and bein' lazy . . ."* He stopped playing. "That's an original. It's unfinished. The working title is 'Make Me Rich.' I really don't know how to play yet, or write songs, but that doesn't matter. It's about marketing. Jimmy's cousin is Warren Buffett . . ."—Serge reached in his back pocket for a computer printout and unfolded it across the guitar—". . . It's all in the numbers. I have an MBA." The printout was blank. Serge put it away. "I don't really have an MBA. I can admit that because you look like someone who doesn't care. I mean that in a good way. And we'll have to be straight with each other if we're going to be partners. . . ."

The bus pulled over at a roadside shelter. The bum started getting up. "This is my stop."

Serge pulled him back down. "You need to *stop* and think about my offer. The world is becoming too stressful. Both parents working, losing shirts in mutual funds, running to after-school functions, filling weekends with unfinishable home improvements that looked so easy on the Renovation Channel. They never expected adulthood would be like this. 'Holy shit! It's just more and more responsibility! Maybe if I work a little harder it'll start to get easier. . . . Nope, it's even worse now and . . . oh my God! I'm having a heart attack!' " Serge grabbed his chest and fell into the aisle. He lay motionless. The bum bent over. "You okay?"

Serge popped back up. "And then you're fuckin' dead! What kind of life is that?" Serge faced forward and nodded. "This is where I come in. I'll give people the momentary illusion of escaping adulthood, for a fee. The market's ripe: Everyone's become obsessed with maturity. . . ."

A gold '71 Buick Riviera drove past the parked Greyhound, Coleman hitting the nub of a joint and humming in falsetto: *"Hmm, kmm-hmm, hmm-hmm, fruit juicy. How'd you like a nice Hawaiian punch? . . ."*

Coleman reached under his seat, locating a loose beer and an empty convenience-store collector's cup promoting the Harry Potter industrial complex. He poured the beer in the cup so he could sip while driving, nobody the wiser, instead of having to hunch over and sneak with a can, because that would be dangerous.

The Buick passed a row of fiery poincianas down the median on Key Largo, then countless red and white dive flags, coral-reef murals, concrete angelfish, big plaster shark jaws for tourists to pose inside, a fish-basket restaurant with stone patio tables out front from a pool store, the famous Caribbean Club, the famous *African Queen* movie boat, a dozen famous tiki huts, a seashell gift outlet mall, Tradewinds Liquors, Paradise Insurance, Kokomo Dental, and the parking lot of a boarded-up shopping center where a third-rate carnival was working its way down the Keys. Rusty Ferris wheel, Ping-Pong ball goldfish games, mechanical crane rigged so you couldn't grab the mini-spy camera or switchblade comb. Disinterested clowns shuffled floppy shoes through the grimy midway. The clowns had gotten into substance abuse, flunked out of the prestigious Ringling Brothers Clown College in Sarasota and were now relegated to the hard-luck circuit of broken clown dreams. An audience of three preschoolers sat cross-legged on a mat. Mr. Blinky juggled a pair of balls. The children got up and left. Mr. Blinky put the balls in his pocket Another clown walked up. They watched forlornly as the children entered the computer arcade tent.

"Let's go get high," said Mr. Blinky.

"Fuckin' A," said Uncle Inappropriate.

The clowns went behind some propane tanks as a Greyhound bus drove by in the background, the last window open, a man strumming his guitar.

SERGE STOPPED PLAYING his guitar and faced the bum. "It first hit me when I was eating dinner in Margaritaville. I had ordered the Cheeseburger in Paradise. Figured it had to be the best cheeseburger in the world if Buffett was involved. You know what? The fucking thing was inedible, a gray Keds sole. And as far as accuracy, get this: no pickle. There's a pickle in every refrain in that song. I've heard it a thousand times. But was there one with my cheeseburger? They're betting on us not noticing. Well, they bet wrong! . . ."

The bum began standing. "I'd like to get off—"

Serge pushed down on his shoulder. ". . . The waitress comes by, and I'm looking under my plate. She asks if everything is okay. I say, 'There's no pickle.' I turn the burger vertical, going through it like a wallet, and the waitress says it doesn't come with a pickle. I stop and look up. 'Yes, it does.' She says there's no mention in the menu. I say I know what the menu says; lyrics overrule. Then we started yelling. Actually it was just me. Suddenly, there goes the table. Guess who they blame? So now these four beefy guys in festive shirts are dragging me toward the front door, and I'm screaming at the other customers: 'Call Jimmy! Somebody call Jimmy!' I land on my back on the sidewalk, and the cheeseburger patty hits me in the chest and they throw the buns and everything at me, just an ugly scene. . . . I have to tell you, somewhere along the line, something has gone horribly wrong in Margaritaville. . . ."

Vehicles flew by Serge's window. Jeep Grand Cherokee, metallic green Trans Am, brown Plymouth Duster, over the Marvin D. Adams cut, Tavernier Creek, Snake Creek, the Whale Harbor bridge, into Islamorada, the scuba industry giving way to rows of offshore charter boats at marinas with stuffed marlin and sea bass and hammerheads hanging from trophy hooks facing the road. A '71 Buick Riviera chugged past Paradise Pawn and a motel with a faux lighthouse, then another bus shelter and the pulled-over Greyhound that Coleman had been leapfrogging the last thirty miles. The views from the bridges began opening up, and Coleman grooved on the scenery. The Long Key Viaduct was particularly inspiring, especially on the Gulf Stream side, so Coleman hit his blinker and cut into the left lane for a closer look over the top of the parallel bridge span heading the other way. Yes, sir, this is living. He smiled and hit his joint.

Coleman began noticing a lot of pelicans on the other bridge span. Then a camping tent. And another. Several fishermen. More and more tents. More fishermen. Hold the phone, thought Coleman. That's not a parallel bridge going the other way; it's a span that's been converted into a fishing pier. Hmm, interesting. So I guess that means I'm on a two-way bridge. Coleman looked forward and saw the oncoming Camaro stopped cold, fifty yards up.

The Greyhound driver slammed the brakes, pitching Serge and the bum into the seats in front of them with the sound of scraping guitar strings. "Hey!" yelled Serge. "What the hell's going on up there?"

The driver threw the transmission back into low gear. "Some fool almost had a head-on."

The bus entered Marathon, smack in the middle of the Keys. The airport went by on the right. Small terminal, big fuel tank, Piper Cubs, biplanes for novelty rides, rows of corporate aircraft, white limo waiting at the edge of the runway.

Key West didn't allow jets for noise reasons. So if a big executive wanted to take the Lear, he landed in Marathon and rode a limo the last fifty miles, drinking the whole way. Like the man right now climbing down the stairs and crossing the tarmac in a tropical shirt and flip-flops. Gaskin Fussels from Muncie. The chauffeur ran around the car. "Mr. Fussels, let me get those bags. . . ."

Fussels was short, chubby and bald. He also reeked of money, which meant he was sexy.

The limo left the airport and headed west on U.S. 1. It was stopped within a mile. Fussels ran inside Overseas Liquors and was back in a flash with his usual fifth of their most expensive rum. The driver wondered whether he might get a better tip if he stopped in advance and had the bottle waiting. He'd done that once for another client, but the tip was the same and he'd gotten stiffed on the booze. The rich never ceased to amaze the driver. He'd seen everything. Take Fussels, for instance. Big attorney from Indiana with a second home in the Keys. Four-day work week, then every Friday morning a private charter into Marathon for another lost weekend as Calypso Johnny. Every single week. How could he afford it? Is there that much money floating around? The driver decided there was a secret world he wasn't being told about.

"No other way to live," Fussels explained as he always did, tidying the wet bar. "It's just service economy down here, so I couldn't make near the money. But I couldn't live anywhere else. Yes, sir, these flights are worth every penny. My competition shivers all weekend up north, then I come back to the courthouse Monday morning, tanned, recharged, the weight of the world off my shoulders, and I bash their brains out!"

The limo started across the Seven-Mile Bridge. What a day, not a cloud, the Gulf Stream chocked with color. Fussels settled into the middle of the backseat with his drink and stretched his legs. "Got a joke for ya. . . ."

The driver looked up in the mirror. "What is it?"

"How does a blind person know when he's finished wiping?"

"I don't know, Mr. Fussels. How?"

"No, you see, that's the joke."

"Oh . . . ha, ha, ha, ha . . ." The driver would never understand the rich.

Fussels grabbed his bottle. "Moron."

They didn't talk for a while after that. Fussels diligently got plowed. They reached Ramrod Key.

"Pull over. I need to take a leak."

The chauffeur looked up the road. "There's a Chevron next block."

"Fuck it. I wanna go here."

The rich again. The limo eased onto the shoulder. Fussels got out, walked down a mild embankment and stumbled to his knees. "Whoa, good rum." He stood and undid his zipper, not remotely concealed, children pointing from station wagons as they drove by. Mr. Fussels started feeling splashes on his bare ankles. "What the hell?" He angled his head to look around the stream. "Am I hitting something?"

There was movement in the brush. A nocturnal armadillo raised its head. What woke me up? And what's this stuff hitting my shell? The animal desired to be somewhere else and began marching toward the road.

Fussels returned to the limo. The chauffeur looked back up U.S. 1, waiting for traffic to clear. Just a couple more vehicles. A Greyhound bus and a metallic green Trans Am. The driver of the Trans Am had her radio on low, Shania Twain. A single tear trickled out from beneath dark sunglasses concealing two black eyes. She put on a blinker and swung around the Greyhound bus, which was slowing to an unscheduled stop behind a limousine.

The bus's door opened and Serge came flying out with his knapsack. He picked himself up from the dirt and turned around, spreading his arms in a gesture of innocence. "What?"

A guitar hit him in the chest. The bus drove off.

Serge noticed the limo and began running for it. "Hey! Do you think you could give me a—"

The limo sped off. Serge hoisted the knapsack over his shoulder and stuck out his thumb. "Here comes somebody. Looks promising. The car's pretty beat up, so they have a history of poor judgment like picking up hitchhikers. . . ."

The driver of the brown Plymouth Duster with Ohio plates was distracted by Serge, leaning way too far into traffic with exaggerated hitchhiking gestures. Never saw the armadillo.

Bang.

The Duster's driver looked in the rearview and watched the unfortunate animal tumble down the highway, coming to rest on the centerline with four legs in the air.

4

THE INSIDE OF the '71 Buick Riviera smelled like grease-smoke. Coleman had stopped at an independent convenience store with Citgo gas pumps out front and a glass case inside heated with red light bulbs. A Styrofoam box of yesterday's food now sat in Coleman's lap: chicken wings, chicken gizzards, potato logs, egg rolls, mozzarella sticks, crab cakes. He sipped a plastic soda cup of beer.

"Look, a drawbridge! I love drawbridges. And there's a waterspout! I love waterspouts."

Coleman was watching the waterspout and didn't see the lowering arm of the drawbridge that the Buick had just sailed under. The bridge tender quickly hit a button raising the second arm on the other side.

The gas gauge was on E when Coleman hit the Torch Keys. The needle had been pushing hard against the right post ever since the Seven-Mile Bridge, where an approach sign told motorists to check their fuel. Coleman checked it. Yep, on E.

He barely made it to the top of the Ramrod Key bridge before the engine cut out. Coleman had been here before. He threw the car in neutral and switched over to gravity power, coasting down the back side and saving money.

He saw a gas station sign in the palms a couple blocks up. Thirty miles an hour. Twenty-five. Twenty. Cars honking again, whipping around, giving him the finger. Coleman smiled and waved. Fifteen miles an hour, ten. Traffic stacking up. The gas sign getting bigger.

He rocked forward in his seat, giving her body English. Allllllllmost there . . .

Coleman noticed a discarded couch on the side of the road next to the gas station, then something in the middle of the street, a dead armadillo. He hit his blinker and made an ultraslow-motion left turn around the carcass. The Buick reached the edge of the parking lot and Coleman jumped out with the car still rolling, grabbing the door and lip of the roof, jogging alongside the Buick the rest of the way to the pumps.

He started gassing. When the pump reached five dollars, Coleman's eyes darted back and forth. He clicked the pump handle, resetting the price back to zero, and resumed pumping again until the tank was full.

Coleman went inside and began loading up. Red-hot pork rinds, red-hot pub fries, red-hot beef sticks, sixer of Natural Lite Ice. He spilled it all on the counter. The clerk stared at him.

"What?" said Coleman.

"I saw you. You reset the gas pump."

"I did?"

"Coleman!"

"Must have hit it by accident."

"You do it every time, and I just add it to your bill."

Coleman got out a credit card.

"I can't take your credit card anymore."

"Just try it."

The clerk swiped it through the machine. "Says to confiscate card."

Coleman snatched it back. "I'll pay cash." He opened an empty wallet. "Where'd my money go?"

"Coleman!"

"You know I'm good for it. I live just around the corner. I'm always in here."

The clerk glared.

"Thanks." Coleman grabbed a souvenir coolie with the gas station's name and threw it on the pile. "Can I get a bag?"

Coleman tossed his nonpurchases in the Buick. There were a number of beer empties on the floorboard. He wouldn't have minded except he remembered the time one got stuck under the brake pedal. He gathered the cans and headed for the trash. He happened to look up at U.S. 1. He got an idea. He had seen it in a poster.

Coleman walked to the edge of the highway. Traffic zipped by at a steady clip. He waited for a break, then wobbled into the street and went to work.

He giggled his way back to the Buick and climbed in behind the wheel. The car pulled away from the pumps with a loud *ker-chunk*. Coleman drove down a side street and turned up the dirt driveway of his single-wide rental. The trailer was dark orange. Had been white, before the rust. He could afford it because the landlord didn't want to lift a finger, and Coleman was one of the few people unbothered by rain buckets in the living room and kitchen.

It was a dump. But in the Keys, even dumps are magnificent. Coleman's crib was tucked in a thick grove of coconut palms, sea grapes, jacaranda and a tree with brilliant yellow blooms. Vines crawled up the sides of the mobile home, and wildflowers sprouted along the front, blocking more empties in the crawl space.

Coleman got out of the Buick. He saw a gas pump handle and a short length of torn rubber hose sticking out the side of the car.

"How'd that get there?"

Coleman threw it in the trash and went inside.

TRAFFIC BEGAN SLOWING on U.S. 1. Soon it was backed up to Little Torch, Big Pine and all the way to Bahia Honda. Rubberneckers inched past the Chevron station on Ramrod Key. Others pulled off the road altogether and got out with cameras, snapping pictures of the armadillo on its back, holding a can of Budweiser to its mouth with rigid front claws.

The gas station clerk was too busy to notice. He'd hit the big red emergency shutoff button and placed fluorescent cones around the fuel slick, according to corporate training. He ran back inside and looked up the phone number for environmental recovery.

More vehicles pulled over. Business at the gas station picked up despite the closed pumps. College students jumped out of a Jeep

Grand Cherokee and headed for the beverage cooler. A woman in a Hog's Breath T-shirt stuck her head through the door. "Disposable cameras?"

The clerk was on the phone. He pointed at a Fuji display.

The students set cases of beer on the counter. "Bags of ice?"

The clerk pointed at the freezer next to them.

Then, the first of the wrecks, a nasty rear-ender next to a SLOW DOWN—ENDANGERED KEY DEER sign. Traffic was at a standstill by the time the students came out the door. So they walked the edge of the highway, took off their shirts and plopped down on the discarded sofa. The volume went up on a boom box. Van Halen's "Beautiful Girls." Sunscreen squirted onto chests.

COLEMAN WAS FAT and happy, sunk deep into his living room couch with bad springs that he had considered swapping for the one on the side of the road. He ate and drank and worked the remote control. Outside: sirens and helicopters. Coleman surfed past something on TV. He backed up a channel. Local newscast. Live feed from one of the overhead choppers.

"Hey, that's my gas station."

The airborne camera swept to the horizon, showing U.S. 1 at a standstill over endless islands and bridges. The picture panned back down to the filling station, where tiny college students drank and smoked on a little sofa. One of the youths tossed a cigarette over his shoulder.

Coleman's head jerked back as a fireball exploded on TV, engulfing the Chevron pumps.

"Cool!"

THE GANG FROM the No Name Pub was down at the Bogie Channel bridge when the fireball cleared the trees in the distance.

"Wonder what that was," said Sop Choppy, hair blowing as another helicopter took off from the bridge.

"Let's get a drink," said Bob.

They started walking back to the pub. A pink taxi came up the road from the opposite direction. The gang reached the bar as the cab pulled into the gravel parking lot. Serge got out of the backseat with his guitar case. He pulled cash from a pocket and leaned through the open passenger window. "Sure you won't reconsider my offer? Ground-floor opportunity. I'm going to be the next Buffett."

"Hey buddy, I got another fare. . . ."

"Last chance," said Serge, handing over money. "You wanna be a fuckin' cabbie your whole life? . . ."

Serge and his guitar spun to the ground as the taxi took off.

COLEMAN SPENT THE rest of the morning taking on the shape of his couch. He had never watched one channel so long. People running all over the place at the gas station. A lone fire truck had somehow gotten through and foamed down the pumps. Coleman raised a can to his lips. Empty. He went to the fridge. Out. He pulled cushions off the sofa and collected coins.

Coleman walked three blocks to the charred gas pumps. Firemen folded hoses. Excited witnesses filled the parking lot, repeating stories for latecomers. Coleman went inside and grabbed another six from the cooler. He set it on the counter next to a windproof-lighter display showing a woman with a cigarette in a monsoon. Coleman fiddled with one of the lighters, broke the lid and set it back. He eventually realized nobody was coming. Out the front window, the clerk was giving a statement to a fire official with a clipboard. Coleman reached in his pocket and dumped coins on the glass counter. Pennies rolled off. He counted exact change for the sixer, including tax, which he knew from genetic memory.

Coleman pulled one of the cans off the ring and pushed open the front door. There were several clusters of people on the side of the road, each surrounding someone who said he "saw the whole thing." Coleman walked up behind the nearest group, sticking his head between two people in back. ". . . Then this idiot drove off with the fuckin' handle in his tank! . . ."

Coleman raised his face to the sky, chugging the rest of the beer. He popped another off the plastic ring and moseyed to the next group. The man in the middle was pointing at the road. "The armadillo committed suicide, an accident. I know all about this. They jump when startled. If they stayed put, they'd be fine, but instead they spring up and fracture their skulls under the cars. I'm from Texas."

Coleman drifted away from the second gathering and approached the edge of U.S. 1. People with cameras formed a line on the opposite side of the road. One had a picture-taking cell phone, beaming the action to his tax attorney in Buffalo. Coleman walked out into the traffic jam, picked up the armadillo, stuck it under his arm and headed home. The people on the side of the road lowered their cameras and became depressed. Cars began moving.

A HANDFUL OF regulars stood outside the No Name Pub, watching Serge jump up and down on a guitar. He crammed the pieces in a garbage can and dusted his hands. "Enough of that sad chapter."

They went inside through a screen door. The day wore on. The last helicopter took off from the bridge. Traffic got back to normal on U.S. 1. Time slid into early afternoon, the hot hours when everything stops in back reaches of the islands. It was quiet outside the No Name.

The silence was broken by gravel crunching under car tires that rolled past the pub.

A white Mercedes with tinted windows.

Part Two

5

Inside the No Name Pub

THE GANG HUNKERED atop tall stools. A stuffed bear in a Harley T-shirt hung from the ceiling. The bartender leaned across the counter toward Serge. She was flirting. "Ready for another?"

Sop Choppy drained a draft. "What was the deal with that guitar?"

"I'm reinventing myself." Serge twisted the cap off a bottle of water. "Music was just a blind alley."

A Jeep Grand Cherokee pulled up. College students came through the screen door. "We found it!" They grabbed a table in the middle of the room and began scribbling on dollar bills. "Bartender! Stapler!"

"Why reinvent yourself?" asked Sop Choppy.

"The trick to respect in this life is a robust turnover in acquaintances," said Serge. "The Keys are the perfect place to hole up and create a new mystique."

"Why's that?"

"Because nobody down here is who they seem to be."

"Nobody?"

A limo pulled up. Gaskin Fussels burst through the screen door. "Let the party begin!"

Sop Choppy's head sagged. "Not that asshole again."

"Did you say something?" asked Serge. He was rotating on his stool like radar, absorbing the contents of the pub, which originally opened as a pioneer trading post, complete with upstairs brothel. A living treasure chest of footnotes and contradictions. The No Name Pub is actually *named* after something: No Name Key, a remote island not yet touched by public utilities, where modern homesteaders rough it out with cisterns, solar panels and generators. Except the pub isn't on No Name Key; it's across the bridge on Big Pine, way, way back in the sticks, hidden by lush vegetation, possibly the worst retail location in all the Keys. That's why it was so popular. The pub had two main advertising points: great pizza. And you can't find the pub.

Serge continued revolving and smiling. The interior was intimate and dark, the decor busy. Old life preserver, mounted deer head, street signs, license plates, framed photos, newspaper clippings, Midwest police patches. And dollar bills. Thousands. Inscribed by tourists. "Made it from Colt's Neck, N.J.! Suzie." The walls had long since been covered, and now hundreds of newer bills hung stapled to the ceiling by their ends, fluttering down in the breeze from the screen door and giving the already cave-like room the additional impression of bats. The bartop also met Serge's approval, etched and worn from decades of rough living and ribald stories. If it was a person, it would be Keith Richards. Serge absolutely loved the No Name! He fidgeted and hopped off his stool. "I have to get the hell out of here."

"See ya, Serge."

The screen door slammed. Serge hoisted his knapsack and began walking up the street toward the water. It was an isolated stretch of road surrounded by unforgiving nature. Scorching, bright and still except for the electric buzz of crickets. Serge's senses were keen, outlook super-positive. This was his favorite place on earth. He told himself to slow down to appreciate the moment, and he started walking faster to appreciate it sooner. . . . Photos. I need photos!

Serge set his knapsack on the ground and retrieved camera gear. He began walking briskly again, one eye closed, viewing the world through a zoom lens. Click, click, click . . .

A photo of each living thing he saw. "All life is sacred, even algae. . . . Oooh, nice flowers, pine hyacinth, turk's cap . . ." Click, click, moving on to the insect family. ". . . Wood tick, spiny orb weaver . . ." Click, click. He noticed movement below on the street. "I'm in luck! A ghost crab!"

The crab skittered sideways across the pavement. Serge got down in a baseball catcher's crouch with his camera, sidestepping with it. A pickup truck flew by. "Get out of the fuckin' road, you imbecile!"

Serge kept his eye to the viewfinder. "Another soul out of tune with the life force."

The crab stopped. Serge lowered himself with stealth until he was belly-flat on the road, aiming the camera like a sniper.

"Photography teaches me to be observant," said Serge. "Discipline. Becoming one with the environment so I don't miss even the smallest detail."

A skunk ape crossed the road behind him.

Click. "Got it!" He stood and continued on. Trees gave way to scrub, the sky got big, water up ahead, sagging power lines and crooked palms. A loose parade of cotton-clouds drifting north, and Serge free-associated on their shapes: "Elephant, giraffe, Snoopy, Elvis, the Baltic states, chain of mitochondric enzyme inhibitors, a Faustian choice . . ." Standing against it all was a solitary old clapboard building at the foot of the Bogie Channel Bridge. White paint and white metal storm awnings. Behind it sat the dock, a neat row of identical rental boats and an above-ground fuel tank with a big red Texaco star on the side. Serge walked past a sign:

OLD WOODEN BRIDGE FISHING CAMP

EFFICIENCY COTTAGES

BEER • TACKLE • BAIT

He reached the building.

Ting-a-ling. The woman behind the counter looked up. She had a tank top, ponytail and a local's tan. "Hi, Serge . . ." She raised a hand in front of her face. "Don't take my picture again!"

"You're a living thing." Click.

The woman finished unpacking a UPS box of spoon-lures and reached for a hook on the door under the number five. "Your regular room?"

"Thanks, Julie.... Ooooo, new fishing caps!" He grabbed one off a shelf and studied the front. "Embroidered establishment name and dateline. That means I'm not allowed to leave without it."

She rang the register. "Anything else?"

"New T-shirts, too!" He held one up to his chest. "And hand-painted postcards. Gimme ten of each."

"Who do you send all your cards to?"

"Me." Serge inspected a nearly empty pegboard of Instamatic film and individual packets of Bayer aspirin. The Coca-Cola snack-bar menu board indicated Fruitopia was now in stock and pinfish were going for a buck apiece. Julie punched buttons on an accounting calculator. Serge spun a rack of sunglasses. "They shot the movie *Tollbooth* here."

"You told me."

"When?"

"Last six times you stayed."

Serge picked up a pot of complimentary coffee, smelled it and made a face. "It's a B movie, but it beats trench mouth. They chopped up a guy and stuck him in your bait freezer over there." Serge replaced the coffee beneath a mishmash of sun-faded photos covering the wall. People holding up bull dolphin and tarpon and snook. Bikinis, lobsters, smiles. Somebody's dog was wearing a bandanna.

The back door opened. A man came in from the dock, sunglasses hanging from a lanyard around his neck. "Hi, Serge."

"Hi, Mark." Click.

"Anything going on?" asked Julie.

"One of the rental boats came back trashed again."

"Which one?"

"Number seven, the businessmen." He turned to Serge. "Guys from the Pacific Rim, don't know what nationality. Every morning this week they come in and buy twice as much bait as anyone needs and take a boat out all day."

"Catching anything?"

"Apparently. Each time they come back, the deck is a bloody mess from bow to stern, but they never bring any fish to the dock. We just find all these skeletons in the bilge."

"They're eating raw fish out there?"

Mark nodded.

"What about the extra bait?"

"I think they're eating that, too." Mark snatched a compact yellow walkie-talkie off his belt. "Jim, hose out number seven. . . . That's right, again." He clipped the Motorola back on his shorts. "Staying in number five?"

"You know it." Serge adjusted the band of his new cap and left through the rear door. He walked along the dock, where someone was flushing out a boat with a garden hose, pushing squid tentacles and loose suckers along the deck.

"Noble work."

"What?"

Serge headed across the parking lot. He stopped and raised his camera. A row of tiny, white cottages from the forties. Picnic table in front of each.

The two proprietors were outside, trying to straighten a signpost someone had hit.

"Who's he talking to?" asked Mark.

"Himself," said Julie.

". . . Ah, the Old Wooden Bridge Fishing Camp!" said Serge. "Last vestige of the early days, when rustic compounds defined the archipelago, vernacular gems with wraparound verandas and plantation fans, Zane Grey lounging in coconut shade, polishing dispatches on pompano for northern intelligentsia. Then the march of progress, coming ashore like Godzilla, smashing the historic fish camps like balsa-wood pagodas . . ."

"Why is he stomping around the parking lot like that?" asked Mark.

Julie shrugged.

". . . Now they're all memories. Even the old wooden bridge itself is gone, replaced by concrete. But at least the camp is still here. . . ."

"What's he doing now?" asked Mark.

"Kissing cottage number five."

Serge stuck the key in the knob, went inside and double-bolted the door. Safe and snug. His own space capsule. Microwave, coffeemaker, fridge, stove, dark paneling and a dark-wood kitchen table bought at some place with a name like "The Wagon Wheel." There was a single small painting on the wall of a lionfish made with the bold, instinctive brush strokes of a state prison art class. Then more impressionism, a clashing 1963 avocado sofa covered with sunflowers, marigolds and violets like van Gogh's bitter, less-talented half-brother worked in upholstery. Serge jammed the window AC unit up all the way, closed his eyes and stuck his face in the freezing vent. Good ol' number five.

It was a busy hour. Serge scurried around the cabin, stowing all his paraphernalia in The Special Places. Finally, he was done, the cottage in perfect order. Serge unfolded a scrap of paper from his pocket and committed a task list to memory. He ran out the door, cutting between other units. There were no fences, just one big feral lawn with pockets of standing water that connected all the cottages and homes behind the camp like an abandoned par-three golf course. Serge ran past a car parked behind cottage number three, which he couldn't tell was a metallic green Trans Am because it was hidden under a tarp.

The curtains parted a slit on a back window of number three. Eyes watched Serge jog across the grass and disappear up the road. The curtains closed. The petite woman went back to the couch and sat bolt upright at the very edge. Full ashtray, nearly empty bottle of vodka, baggy eyes. She stared at the cell phone on the coffee table and was frustrated she didn't feel the least bit drunk. Adrenaline.

Her name was Anna Sebring. She'd been up most of the night, glands on battle stations, constantly peeking out the curtains for a white Mercedes with tinted windows. Then back to the windows again at every random sound. Toads, raccoons rattling garbage cans, dragonflies bumping into porch lights, the people four cottages up with their midnight fish fry and campfire songs. That was the problem hiding out at the Old Wooden Bridge. It was so quiet it was noisy.

A tap on the window.

Anna screamed and found herself standing on the couch.

Another tap. At least it wasn't gunfire or someone kicking in the door. And what if it was *him*? But how did he find her? The car?

Tap.

Anna slowly lowered a leg off the sofa. She made it to the window and parted the curtains. . . .

Her heart seized. Face to face. The beady eyes and narrow beak of the great white heron that the previous tenants had been feeding. Dinnertime. *Tap.*

In the background, fishermen returned to the dock, and two guys carried a green kayak over their heads.

Anna closed the curtains. "Get a grip!"

She returned to the couch and drank the end of the vodka. She stared again at the silent cell phone on the coffee table. A fast pulse throbbed in her forehead, which was running a horrible, round-the-clock slide show. Always blood.

Anna didn't want to turn on the TV in case it blocked out a warning sound. But this was getting ridiculous. She needed distraction.

Anna picked up the remote control and pointed it at the TV. She paused a moment and studied her own reflection in the black picture tube. She clicked the power button and was then looking at a photo of herself on the local news. The remote crashed to the floor; batteries rolled under the couch.

The multiple killings were all over TV, and now her photo, asking the public's help. The picture switched to a live shot, rows of evenly spaced volunteers combing a field for her body. Anna curled up on the couch and pulled her knees tight to her body.

The cell phone rang.

Her head snapped toward the sound, and she curled tighter. Three rings. *Answer it!* Her body wouldn't respond. It was like she was floating somewhere near the ceiling. Five rings. *Pick it up!* Seven rings, eight . . . She saw one of her arms reach for the coffee table.

"Hello? . . ."

Sunset, cottage number five

SERGE OPENED A thick, leather-bound book in his lap, the journal he wrote in at the end of each day. He tapped his chin with a pen and stared out the window at the fading light over Bogie Channel. He hunched over and started writing:

> *Captain Florida's log, star date 764.354*
> *Another night of vivid dreams. Found myself in Key West a hundred years ago when the lawless streets were filled with bloodthirsty smugglers and wreck-salvagers. Except for some reason I had a plasma gun, which gave me the edge. Basis for hit TV series? Which started me thinking: How the early pioneers must have lived! By the late 1800s, Key West had run out of fuel sources. So people on the other islands built giant, ten-foot-tall earthen kilns to make charcoal that they shipped down on boats for barter. Which brings us to what I did today: The Great Serge Kiln Project! It was a daunting task, but the payoff would be immense in spiritual terms. Then I got to thinking: Hey, this could also make some real money. Remember natural sponges? Sell bags of the shit all over the place. "Historic Keys Charcoal." Completely change the way people cook out, make a ransom by mass producing the un-mass-produced simpler life like Ben and Jerry. I have to admit, it was getting pretty exciting! I walked over to No Name Key and found a perfect clearing in the woods. There was much to do. Prepare the site, gather the right wood, assemble a domed superstructure, pack it with mud, then diligently tend the fire for at least a week, narrowing and expanding the chimney so the charcoaling process doesn't overheat or extinguish. And I'm standing there, staring at the ground, and I think: That's way too much fucking work. So I drive to the convenience store for some briquettes. And on the way in I pass the Dumpster, and there's that smell again. You know, the* Dumpster *smell. They all smell the same. Convenience store, Bloomingdale's, third-world deli, doesn't matter, exact same odor, like*

there's a Dumpster molecule we have yet to isolate, and when we do, we'll be able to neutralize it. No more smell for the customers. Boom! Business skyrockets! Another big money-making idea! But does the guy behind the register at Circle K listen? He just wants me to get out of the way so the line can move. I tell him it's that kind of parochial thinking that's keeping him behind that counter, and then the conversation wanders again into nastiness. But it's no surprise; lost people everywhere and none of them accepting my free maps. Then I realize something else. Fish have eyes on the sides of their heads. How do they focus? Do they get a split screen? Is this what's holding them back?

Serge took a deep, satisfied breath and slowly closed his journal. He gazed out the window at the soothing waters. "Can you feel it? Peace and solitude, nothing but tranquility in every direction." He nodded to himself. "Sometimes it's good to be alone with your thoughts."

He smiled and sat perfectly still. He jumped up and ran out the door.

6

The no name Pub's screen door flew open.

"Serge! You're back!"

Serge joined them at the bar. He sat next to one of his favorite regulars. A sensitive but self-destructive journalist named Bud Naranja, who first came to the Keys after being fired from a South Florida newspaper for writing a caption on a hurricane aftermath photo of a looter running down the street with a shopping cart. Except it was a bank president delivering relief supplies—and a major advertiser. Guards hovered over Bud in front of the whole newsroom as he packed belongings in a cardboard box and cut his giant, inflatable "news flamingo" down from the ceiling. Didn't even go back to his apartment, just climbed in a 200,000-mile Toyota and began driving with no purpose but an earnest devotion to the principle: How can I make this worse? He headed south until he ran out of land and kept going. The Toyota started smoking on Crawl Key, and Bud had to drive across the Seven-Mile Bridge with his head out the window. The engine finally took pity and threw a rod on Big Pine, and he caught a ride with a local housepainter in splattered overalls on his way out to the No Name Pub, where Bud got drunk and slept in the woods behind the building and never went back. Decided to stay and reinvent himself. He reinvented himself as a fired journalist for a Key West newspaper who now did occasional freelance for a variety of free weekly shoppers distributed throughout the islands.

"Bud, what's the matter?" asked Serge. "You look like someone died."

Bud pointed at the TV. "Have you been following the airbag murder case in Miami?"

"No."

"How could you miss it?" said Sop Choppy. "It's been all over TV for weeks. It's a big story."

"So I missed it. I've been on the road. What's the deal?"

"These mechanics reconditioned deployed airbags by filling them with sand to save money," said Bud.

"What's wrong with people?" said Sop Choppy. "How low does the bar get?"

"Not this jerk again," said Bob, gesturing at the local TV newscast, which had switched to a regular investigative segment called "Consumer Bloodhound." "I don't know who's worse, the scam artists they report on or the obnoxious reporter who chases them across parking lots and shouts questions at slammed doors."

They stopped and listened to the story about a contractor in Fort Lauderdale who tells people they need whole new roofs when they don't.

"I know that scam," said Sop Choppy. "Used to work construction. It's so common in Florida it's a cliché. They go up on top of your house and find rust on shingle nails and say everything's about to cave in. But it's so humid down here you can find nail rust in the finest roofs."

Next on the tube: *Wall Street Update* and the latest accounting irregularities at embattled Global-Con.

"Global-Con!" said Sop Choppy. "Don't get me started! Why doesn't anybody do anything?"

"A bunch of shareholders have sued," said Bob the accountant. "But no criminal indictments, probably never, because of campaign donations."

"I read in the papers where he's moving down here," said Bud. "Started building a giant mansion in Marathon."

"Who?" asked Sop Choppy.

"The Global-Con guy. What's his name?"

"You don't mean Donald Greely," said Serge.

Bud nodded.

"There goes the neighborhood."

"But how's that possible?" asked Sop Choppy. "I thought the courts froze his assets after the lawsuits."

"They did," said Bob. "But he'd already homesteaded and sheltered twenty million in construction under Florida's noforfeiture law. It's the first thing they teach in accounting school."

"That's typical," said the biker. "They seized my hog last year for one stinkin' joint in the saddlebag. Then this guy steals all those retirement accounts and there's a law *protecting* him?"

Jerry the bartender came over. Jerry was even more sensitive than Bud. He was naturally likable, with a chronic insecurity about being liked that got on everyone's nerves.

"What are you guys talking about?" asked Jerry, tipping a draft handle.

"The stock market."

"That's a good subject."

Serge looked at his watch. "How long have I been sitting here?"

"You just arrived," said Bud.

Serge hopped off his stool. "I gotta move around."

Serge was a wall-looker. Restaurant, hotel, bar, whatever—had to case the whole interior for history. Plaques and photos and clippings and stuff. He could get hung up for hours in the No Name with all the dollar bills. Serge had been coming here for years and was still only a quarter way through. He resumed where he'd left off last time behind the pool table. "The Brennans were here 11-12-02," "Tami, Dansville Mich., Try God." A red maple leaf drawn over George Washington's face: "Canadian and Proud!" Without looking, Serge reached over to set his bottle of water down. There was nothing to set it on. He turned and waved his hand through an empty space of air. "Hey, Joe . . ."—Joe was the owner—"didn't there used to be a cigarette machine?"

"Had to take it out," said Joe, writing in a book of receipts behind the bar. "Always full of dollars torn off the wall. *Betty and John's Excellent Honeymoon*. What's wrong with people?"

"The common good," said Serge. "It's not hip."

Joe nodded politely and returned to his paperwork. He liked Serge, despite everything. Besides, Joe was a fellow history buff. He had purchased Captain Tony's Saloon in Key West, then the No Name, more out of preservation than business.

"Can you take me upstairs?" asked Serge.

Joe added a column of figures. "I'm busy."

"I want to see the brothel."

"It's not a brothel anymore."

"I'll use my imagination."

"Later."

Serge pointed up at the ceiling. "Is it true you have the fifty-caliber deck gun from Captain Tony's boat up there? Back when he made midnight runs to Cuba for the CIA?"

Joe nodded.

"Can I see it? I won't touch. Okay, maybe I will. Sometimes I can't help myself, so no guarantees."

Joe exhaled in exasperation and started adding the numbers again from the beginning.

"If you won't take me upstairs, can you go get Captain Tony?" said Serge. "Everyone's met him but me. You promised."

"He's probably doing something."

"But Tony's the last living link to the Old Days. I have to meet him before it's too late!"

"Serge, he has a life. He's not some antique car I can just roll out of the garage whenever I feel like it."

Serge stared at Joe a moment. "Then can we go upstairs?"

Joe took his work into the back room. Serge resumed his circuit around the pub. More dollar bills, then a bulletin board. Church raffle, baby shower on Guava Lane, missing person last seen walking down a deserted road on No Name Key at three A.M. Serge came to a Xerox of a meeting notice. Paradise Obsessive-Compulsive Association. There were a bunch of little tabs with phone numbers at the bottom of the sheet. He tore one off. The tear did not make a straight line. So he tore off another.

Jerry the bartender walked up. "Serge . . ."

"Hey, Jerry."

"Can I ask a question?"

"Sure. What is it?"

Jerry looked around, then lowered his voice. "Do people like me?"

* * *

THE FLORIDA KEYS are home to the largest per-capita concentration of twelve-step programs in the nation. Some of the support groups meet at the municipal building on Sugarloaf Key, next to the fire station. The building has a long hallway of low-bid, peel-and-stick tiles.

The third room on the left was full of teens in defiant slouches. A court-ordered early-intervention program for at-risk youth arrested on petty charges. Two older men in sheriff's uniforms stood at the front of the room. Both were out of shape, but one more so. He held up a hand-rolled cigarette.

"This is *marijuana*. . . ."

The kids: *"Oooooooooooooo."*

Gus set the joint on a table up front. "It is what is known as a gateway drug. . . ."

A teen raised his hand. "Where'd you get that?"

"Evidence. After a trial."

"Weren't you supposed to destroy it?"

"We did. But sometimes we save a little for training purposes."

"That's against the law."

"No it isn't."

"Do you have a court order?" asked the youth.

"What?"

"I'm going to be a lawyer. There are very strict condemnation procedures for scheduled substances. Outside of that, only a few high-security federal research facilities are allowed to keep pot. Right now you're guilty of possession."

"And showing it to minors," said a girl chewing gum.

"This is just a class," said Gus. "If you'd all be quiet, we can wrap this up and go home—"

"You told us that possession of even a small amount of pot is a serious offense."

Another boy in baggy jeans pointed at a phone number on the blackboard. "Maybe we should call the anonymous tip line."

Gus turned to his colleague. "Walter, help me here."

Walter shrugged. "I've never seen the guidelines. Maybe he's right."

"Thanks, Walter."

A banging came through the wall from the next room. All the kids were talking now.

"Everyone, please be quiet!" said Gus. "We're here because we care what happens to you. Drugs aren't healthy. . . ."

A hand went up. "I saw on TV where obesity is a leading killer. You might consider a diet."

Another hand. "How are you supposed to catch anybody? I'll bet you can't get over a fence."

Gus was red-faced and speechless.

The gum-chewing girl raised her hand. "I heard your nickname is Serpico."

"What?" said Gus.

"Serpico. Is it true?"

"I don't know," said Gus. "I guess some of the guys call me that sometimes."

The girl raised her hand again. "Is that, like, some kind of joke?"

Gus's eyes narrowed. *Why, you little shits.*

More banging came through the wall.

The next room: Serge sat in the back row with folded arms. A gavel continued banging on the front table. Serge was beginning to wonder if he'd made a mistake. He'd never seen so much unconnected movement in his life, all these nervous rituals and spastic noises. Then the moderator had to bang his gavel again every few minutes to restore order before the next introduction. "Hi, I'm Sam." "Hi, Sam." And more ridiculous stories. Have to keep dusting the house. Have to keep making sure the doors are locked. One person couldn't stop washing his hands, one dreaded contact with faucets, and another had both problems and just stood at sinks a long time. Serge wasn't one to judge, but what a pack of loons!

The gavel banged again. It was Serge's turn. Everyone was staring at him. Serge didn't want to go.

"There's nothing to be afraid of," said the moderator.

"I'm not sure I'm in the right place," said Serge.

"You're among friends."

Serge looked around at all the tense, panicky faces staring back at him. Sheesh.

"What's your name?"

"It's Serge, look—"

"Hi, Serge!"

Serge checked his watch. "I'm missing *Space Ghost*." He reluctantly walked to the front of the room.

"What seems to be your problem, Serge?"

"Nothing."

"Take your time. And remember, anything you say here is privileged."

Someone kept scooting his chair back and forth. The gavel banged three times.

"Will you stop with the gavel?" said Serge.

Someone turned the lights off, then on, then off. The gavel banged three more times. The lights came back on. Serge was at the breaking point. What a crazy meeting! Actually, it was two meetings. They were in one of those double rooms with a sliding accordion divider in case a large group needed the extra space. Another meeting was under way on the other side. Someone kept opening and closing the divider. Serge caught glimpses of glazed adults in a variety of robes and talismans. The Lower Keys Chapter of People Susceptible to Joining Cults. The members attended religiously. The moderator was trying to get them to stop coming. The divider closed.

The first moderator politely touched Serge's arm. "Everyone here is on your side." Then he touched his arm two more times. Serge jerked away. "You're creeping me out!"

The divider opened. A man stood at the front of the other meeting wearing a bishop's mitre with the insignia of every ship in the star fleet. The divider closed. The gavel banged three times. Serge grabbed his head with both hands. "What the hell is wrong with you people!"

"Serge, please . . ."

"I will not 'please'! All I've heard since I've been here is a bunch of whining. *'I'm so messed up.' 'I need help.'* Guess what? The world's messed up! Deal with it!"

"Could you lower your voice?"

"Dammit!" said Serge. "I thought this was going to be some kind of cool club. Like Mensa. Special crafts and hobbies, take field trips, maybe pool our awesome powers for a shot at the Guinness book. Instead, all I hear is complaints! . . ." Chair scooted; people made crackling sounds with fingers, necks and jaws.

The gavel banged three times. "Quiet!"

Serge snatched the gavel away and banged it at the moderator. "No, *you* be quiet!"

The moderator picked up the gavel. "You have to bang it three times"—bang, bang, bang—"then set it on its special presentation stand, perfectly straight, equidistant from the four edges."

Serge picked up the gavel, snapped it in half and threw the pieces down. "There. You're fuckin' cured."

The moderator made a sucking scream. He fell sobbing into his chair with the two pieces, desperately trying to fit them together.

Serge faced the room. "Don't you understand? The answer is inside each of you! Don't follow anyone else! Be your own leader! *Lead yourselves!*"

The divider was open. The moderator on the other side had lost his audience. They were listening to Serge.

The lights went off, on, off.

"That's it! I'm history!" Serge stormed from the room.

The hallway was quiet except for Serge's footsteps. "Unbelievable." He glanced in the window of the next door. A deputy was at the front table. "Please! I'm begging you! . . ." Serge kept walking, other rooms, other agendas. People afraid of closed-in open spaces. People who love too much. People who try to get attention by staging hang-glider accidents. Serge looked in another window, a lone man tapping on a computer: People Afraid to Leave the House, telecommuting to the meeting. The next room, a sign outside: AA.

"At least it's tradition."

Serge passed the door and heard giggling. He took another step and stopped. "That laugh . . . no, it couldn't be—" He took another step and heard it again.

The AA door creaked open. The laughter grew louder. Serge poked his head inside.

Another gavel was banging, the moderator asking the man in the back row to control himself.

"I'm sorry," said Coleman, dabbing his eyes. "Just that last story—the image got to me. Guy wakes up naked on the bathroom floor with his glasses in the toilet and a bunch of shit mashed in his hair. I mean, how can you *not* laugh?"

Stern glares in response.

Coleman swallowed a final giggle. "I'm okay now. . . ."

Serge couldn't believe his eyes. "Coleman!"

Coleman turned around. "Serge!"

They ran together and hugged. Coleman held Serge out by the arms. "You've come back!"

The moderator shhhhh'd everybody: "One of our brothers has come back."

Serge turned. "What? Oh, no, you've got the wrong—"

"What's your name?"

"It's Serge," said Coleman.

"Hi, Serge!"

"Welcome home," said the moderator.

"I was never a part of your group."

"We understand. Some of us come for years before we're ever really a part—"

"That's not what I mean."

"We don't want to rush you. Why don't you just sit with your friend until you're ready. He can be your sponsor."

Serge looked at Coleman a moment, then cracked up.

"He's hysterical," said Coleman. "Must be the shock of the return."

They sat down and whispered.

"I thought you were dead!" said Serge. "I even saw your body. Your face was all shot up!"

"That's right," said Coleman. "The face was gone. That's why police got the wrong ID. It was my perfect chance to go underground. Everyone just assumed because it was my motel room, except it was actually this other dude who was visiting."

"But I recognized your T-shirt. *Save the Bales* . . . the one that was always getting you hassled by the cops."

"I met this guy at The Slushie Hut on Duval Street, and we started pounding the house special, Torpedo Juice. One part grain alcohol, three parts Red Bull. After a couple of those you're completely fucked up but on the move. The guy says we should go look for Thai stick. So we roam all over the island and finally meet a connection behind The Green Parrot and give him the money. Then back to my room to wait, which is where the drinks clobbered the guy, and he throws up all over himself, so I lend him my shirt, and then we realize the guy we paid for the dope is taking a really long time, and I head down to the lobby—"

"Stop right there," said Serge. "This is beginning to sound like some lame soap opera device to bring back a character they regretted killing off."

"Yeah, but that's just bad TV writing," said Coleman. "This is real life." He patted himself on the chest. "See? I'm actually here."

"Can't argue with that."

The old pals continued catching up in the back of the room, oblivious to the meeting. A guy at the front in a cervical collar explained how he crashed into the DUI checkpoint. Serge and Coleman finally realized that the gavel had been banging for a while. They looked up. Everyone was staring at them. The moderator pointed at Coleman. "Excuse me, but what is that in your hand?"

Coleman looked at the flask. "What? This?"

"Yes, that! Are you *drinking* in here?"

"Of course," said Coleman.

"But your recovery? . . ."

"Recovery?" said Coleman. "I'm here for the stories. This is the funniest shit in town!"

That did it.

The pair stood and headed out of the room. Serge slapped Coleman on the shoulder. "I'm not sure, but I think this is some kind of record. Eighty-sixed from AA."

Serge opened the door.

A bunch of faces in the hall stared back at him. People from the cult meeting, patiently awaiting orders from their new leader.

7

THE SUN ROSE on a viciously humid morning at the Marathon Airport. Birds walked along the fence. A lone runway worker in shorts and ear protectors was stained through his shirt. He waved the Lear in with batons.

Stairs flipped down from the side of the plane, and a short, bald man stood in the doorway with an umbrella drink. His bright orange shirt had vintage Corvettes.

"Let the games begin! Gaskin Fussels is here!"

The worker unlatched the luggage compartment on the side of the plane.

Fussels grabbed the wire handrail and marched down the stairs with thunderous steps. "Please! Please! Everyone! Hold down your applause!"

The worker glanced around the empty runway.

A limo raced up. The chauffeur ran to grab luggage. "Sorry, Mr. Fussels. Got held up in traffic."

"No harm, no foul."

Fussels climbed in the limo, and they soon made the routine pit stop at Overseas Liquors. The attorney poured a stiff double as they passed the 7-Mile Grill. The chauffeur looked over his shoulder. "Where to?"

"You know where."

They started across the big bridge. Out the right windows, a little tram dressed up like a train took tourists down the old span to Pigeon

Key. The chauffeur looked up in the mirror. "You sure are spending a lot of time at the No Name, Mr. Fussels."

"Sal, can't thank you enough for showing me that place. Best bar on earth."

"It's Sid."

"What?"

"You said Sal."

"Sal, Sid. You say tomato, I say bottom's up!"

The limo drove through Bahia Honda State Park, past the ruins of an ancient train trestle.

"Sal, got a joke for you. Salesman's in a small town, asks the bartender where he can get a hooker. The bartender says it's a small town, the only action is Willie over there, the wino at the end of the bar. The salesman says, 'Are you crazy?' Hours pass and he gets drunker and asks the bartender again, and the bartender says just old Willie over there. Finally, it's closing time. The salesman is wrecked and horny. He says, okay, okay, I'll take Willie. How much? The bartender says fifty dollars. The salesman says, 'That filthy bum gets fifty dollars! This *must* be a small town!' And the bartender says, 'Oh, no, the fifty is for me to hold him down.' Ha! Ha! Ha! Ha! . . . What's the matter, Sal? You're not laughing. . . ."

"So the wino wasn't really in on it?"

"No, you're missing the beauty of it. You see . . . forget it."

The limo arrived outside the No Name Pub. The chauffeur got the luggage; Fussels grabbed his wallet. "Sure you won't join us?"

"Got another fare."

Fussels paid in twenties. "Great gang of regulars. They absolutely love me in there!"

The screen door flew open. "Gaskin Fussels is back!"

"Not that jackass again."

The attorney hopped on an empty bar stool and rubbed his hands together. "Let's get this day started! Drinks for everyone! Of course you'll all have to pay, ha! ha! ha! . . . I got a million! . . ."

Regulars began getting off stools and heading for the pool table.

The afternoon wore on. More and more empty stools. By sundown, Fussels had the entire west side of the bar to himself. The only person who would talk to him was Jerry the bartender, because Jerry would talk to anyone. Fussels drained another beer and handed Jerry the empty glass for a refill. ". . . Of course people like you!"

Sop Choppy stood with a pool stick at his side. "We've got to get rid of that guy."

The others looked back at the bar. Fussels was showing Jerry his platinum pass to the Bunny Ranch.

Bob the accountant leaned over the table to line up a shot. "He's fucking up the whole chemistry in here. It just takes one. . . . Seven ball, corner pocket." Clack.

Bud Naranja circled the table, examining the shit the accountant had left him. "He's not that bad. Just give him time. . . . Three ball . . ."

A loud voice. The guys looked back at the bar again. Fussels slapped the countertop. ". . . 'No, the fifty is for me to hold him down!' Ha! Ha! Ha! . . ."

"He's never going to leave!" said Sop Choppy. "Been coming a whole month now, and we always end up over here playing pool. Then after he clears the bar, he walks up and asks what we're playing. It's hopeless. . . . Five in the side . . ." Clack.

Their eyes followed the ball into the pocket.

"You're right," said Bob, chalking his cue. "We have to take action. But how can we get rid of him?"

Fussels walked up with his drink, napkin stuck to the bottom. "So, what are you guys playing?"

A '71 BUICK RIVIERA cruised over the bridge at Ramrod Channel. Serge was the pilot, Coleman the waist gunner manning the radio. They bobbed their heads to the pounding rhythms of Pigeonhead from the *Sopranos* soundtrack.

"Hey Mr. Po-liceman, is it time for gettin' away? . . ."

"How do you like my car?" asked Coleman.

"Impressed," said Serge. "Didn't know you had this kind of taste. Early Rivieras are classics, jutting nose like a mako shark, tapering boat-tail rear windshield and, of course, the elegant comfort of a sophisticated ride."

"It was the only thing under five hundred dollars."

"Still counts," said Serge. "What's that gold chain around your neck? Didn't think you were the type."

"This?" Coleman pulled the chain out of his shirt, revealing a small brass tube. "It's my dog whistle."

"You have a dog?"

"No."

"I'll hate myself for asking . . ."

"This one makes a pitch they don't like." Coleman dropped it back inside his shirt. "Drives them away."

"And you need that because? . . ."

"Dogs don't like me."

"What do you mean, dogs don't like you?"

"They just don't. Always trying to bite me. Never know why."

"Like the time you were drunk and standing on that poodle?"

"This is different. I'm not doing anything and they give me trouble."

"When do I get to see this maximum bachelor pad of yours?"

"Right now. Turn here."

The Buick pulled up in front of a rusty trailer on Ramrod Key. Coleman walked to the mailbox and grabbed envelopes. They went inside.

Stuff was strewn everywhere. Pulled-out drawers on the floor. Furniture knocked over. Serge stooped and picked up a lamp. "Did somebody ransack your place?"

"Yeah, me," said Coleman, checking in the fridge. "Forgot where I hid my stash."

Serge set the lamp on a table. "Looks like some kind of fierce struggle."

"It was." Coleman came back in the room and plopped on the sofa with beer, Cheetos and mail. He began tossing envelopes in a reject pile on the coffee table. "All junk."

Serge looked at the pile. "You actually got a credit card offer?"

"No, it's addressed to someone else."

Serge grabbed the envelope. "'Mr. and Mrs. Lawrence Grodnick.' It's got the address of your trailer. Did they used to live here?"

"I don't know."

Serge tore it open and unfolded the application. "Well, they live here now." He pulled a pen from his pocket. "Let's see, how much do the Grodnicks make a year? . . ." He looked up at the armadillo on top of the TV, then back down. "A hundred thousand dollars . . ."

"Don't you need their social security number?"

"No, the pitch letter says it's preapproved, lucky for them."

Coleman popped a beer. "How long you been back in the Keys?"

"Just got into town. Can't imagine my surprise when I heard your voice in that room. . . . What do the Grodnicks like to do in their spare time? . . ." He began checking boxes. ". . . Astronomy, aviation, coin collecting, horticulture, international travel, literature, mountain climbing, oil painting—Coleman, these people are well-rounded—photography, rap music, religious studies, water skiing and 'other.' We'll fill that one in 'alpaca stud farm'. . . ."

"I've been going to the meetings a few months now," said Coleman. "Those people are fucked up, but I can't stop listening to the stories. It's like talk shows where chicks pull each other's hair. You know you shouldn't be watching, but what are you gonna do? There's this one guy at the meetings who keeps waking up in other people's houses. He's always getting loaded and going home with strangers. It's not a sex thing. It's just . . . I don't know what it is. He's woken up facedown in a pet-food bowl, another time his leg was in the oven, but it wasn't on. Once he woke up in Mexico. There's this other guy who comes each week with his face all scraped. You know the classic way drunks fall, landing gear up? Forgetting to put their arms out? That's this guy. . . ." Coleman clicked the TV remote. Local news.

"I'm going to need your help with something," said Serge.

"Name it." Coleman turned up the volume.

"*. . . This is Eyewitness Five correspondent Blaine Crease with another segment of 'Consumer Bloodhound.' We're here at the home of Troy*

Bradenton, owner of Troy's Roofing Plus, accused of ripping off hundreds of South Florida homeowners with fraudulent repairs . . ." The reporter knocked on the door. *"What are you hiding from? . . ."*

Serge began pacing in front of the couch. "The reason I came back to the Keys was to reinvent myself. At first I was going to be the next Jimmy Buffett."

"Good choice." Coleman fished a flat joint out of his wallet and lit it.

"Yeah, but you have to know music and all." Serge stopped and faced Coleman. "I have a big announcement to make."

"What is it?"

Serge smiled broadly. "I'm getting married."

"Serge! Congratulations! That's great!"

"I want you to be my best man."

The TV switched to a downtown street scene. *"This is Eyewitness Five correspondent Maria Rojas outside the Miami Courthouse, where the jury has just gone into deliberations in the infamous airbag-murder case. As you recall, four used-car dealers are on trial in the death of a Margate woman whose reconditioned airbag had been filled with sand to save money. . . . Here they come now!"* Three men in suits ran down the courthouse steps and jumped in a waiting sedan. *"Is it true you're guilty? . . ."*

Coleman reached under the couch and pulled out a clear plastic bag attached to a tube. He clenched the tube in the corner of his mouth and sucked.

"Morphine drip bag?" said Serge.

Coleman took the tube out of his mouth. "Security guard at the hospital owed me for some weed."

"What's right is right."

"Who are you going to marry?"

"Don't know yet."

"Is this going to be one of those Dennis Rodman things where you wear a gown and marry yourself?"

"No, that's weird. I'm going to find women in public places and study them from a distance with binoculars. That's the only way to really get to know someone."

"Why do you want to get married, anyway?"

"I've come to the conclusion men don't do well as bachelors," said Serge. "It's like a state of arrested development."

Coleman poured Cheetos in his lap and took the tube out of his mouth. "What do you mean?"

"All my married friends are so much more mature."

"I don't have any married friends," said Coleman. "Whenever a guy gets married, his wife won't let him see me anymore."

8

A PAIR OF Monroe County sheriff's deputies stood in the backyard of a modest ranch house on Big Pine Key. The landscaping was spare but neat. Crape myrtle, trumpet honeysuckle, jasmine. Chicken wire surrounded the flowers.

The deputies listened sympathetically as an eighty-year-old woman talked nonstop, pointing at knocked-over trash cans and garbage strewn across the lawn to where a clothesline had been snapped. She was wearing a nightgown and slippers in the afternoon. One of the deputies jotted down the high points in a notebook.

"He was big and hairy." The woman got on her tiptoes and raised a hand high in the air. "At least seven feet tall."

Gus wrote six feet, allowing for excitement.

The woman tapped the notebook. "I said seven."

Gus smiled and made a correction.

"I could smell him clear across the yard. The worst odor." She crinkled her nose, then held up a disposable camera. "Going to send these to the *Enquirer*. They pay."

Gus closed his notebook and smiled again. "We'll get right on it, ma'am."

The woman shuffled back toward her house. "Patronizing prick."

The deputies headed up U.S. 1 in their white-and-green sheriff's cruiser. Gus was driving. He kept shifting his weight. The seat had one of those wooden-bead seat covers.

"Is that thing helping your back?" asked Walter.

"Actually hurts more."

"Why do you still use it?"

"I paid for it."

Walter looked out the windshield at a tiny, white balloon flying high on a tether. It had tail fins. "Fat Albert's up today."

"So it is." The anti-smuggling radar blimp was flying in a stout offshore wind above the federal installation on the north side of Cudjoe Key. Whenever it was up, there was much less boat traffic in the back country.

"Hey, Serpico. I want to ask—"

"Walter. You mind?"

"Sorry. Forgot," said Walter. "Force of habit from listening to the other guys. Is the story true?"

"What story?"

"How you got the nickname."

"Depends on how it was told."

"It made fun of you."

"Then I guess it's true."

"It's a funny story."

"Is that what you wanted to talk about?"

"No, I got sidetracked. Gus . . ."

"Thank you."

"I heard your ex-wife is dating the lieutenant."

"She is."

Walter looked across the front seat at his partner. "It doesn't bother you?"

"No."

Walter faced forward. "That's what Sergeant Englewood said."

"Said what?"

"It didn't bother you."

They drove over a bridge.

"It would bother me," said Walter. "The lieutenant knowing all those embarrassing sex stories."

Gus did a slow side-take at his partner.

"What?" said Walter. "You do know the stories she's telling, don't you?"

"No."

"Oh, my God, they're hilarious! Apparently she's blabbing about everything. All your weird sexual quirks . . ." Walter started laughing. "There was this one time she was seriously pissed off at you, so that night she asked you to wear her bra to bed, said it would 'get her motor running.' Those were the exact words Deputy Valrico used. Except she was really just trying to humiliate you!"

Walter noticed his partner's knuckles turning white on the steering wheel.

"You did know she was just messing with you?"

Gus stared ahead.

"Gee, I'm really sorry." Walter looked down at his lap. "This is kind of awkward now."

"What other stories?"

"I'm not going to tell you. I feel bad."

"Don't," said Gus. "It's not your fault. It was a long, long time ago."

"It really doesn't bother you?"

"Not a bit."

"Okay, there's this other really great one. Remember the time she said there was something she'd always wanted to try in bed, but was too embarrassed and didn't want you to laugh at her? And you told her you'd do anything for her? So she made you lie on your back while she peed on your face. Remember that? I guess you would—you were there. Anyway, it wasn't to turn her on. She was just mad at you again."

Gus took a deep breath. "How many people know? You said Englewood and Valrico. Is that how you heard?"

"No, they told Brevard and La Belle, and somehow it got around to the second shift before winding through the other substations until it reached the sheriff. I was at a barbecue at his house, and his wife had a little too much sangria, and she sees you out the window in the yard, standing alone eating a hot dog. And she just cracks up and blurts it all out."

"Was anyone else there?"

"No. Yes, just a few guys."

"A few?"

"A lot. It started with about ten, but the crowd really swelled when word got around what she was talking about. By the end of the story I think everyone at the barbecue was jammed in that room except you."

"So that's who knows? The whole department?"

"No. I also heard them talking about it in the ice cream parlor and at the marina and the video store. I think the guy who came to work on my cable mentioned something. . . ."

"Walter—"

"I'd say pretty much the whole town. Can't believe it doesn't bother you. I'd be mortified, everywhere I go people looking at me picturing stuff . . ."

"Walter—"

"I'd quit my job and move away. Maybe change my name. Then I'd probably kill myself. . . ."

"Walter!"

"What? . . . Oh, it does bother you. See, I knew it."

"No, it's just that we're starting to dwell."

The cruiser turned off the highway and pulled up to a bright new mobile home on Cudjoe Key. The sheriff's substation.

Gus and Walter went inside with the full-occupancy expressions of men who had reports to write. The only other person was Sergeant Englewood, sitting at a desk under an air conditioner that made the whole trailer vibrate with an oscillating hum.

"Hey, Sarge," said Walter. "What's the word?"

Englewood hunted and pecked. "Someone took a bunch of plants last night from the nursery."

Gus handed Walter some papers, and they split up. Gus walked to his desk. There was a photo of a bearded Al Pacino sticking out of the typewriter. Someone had drawn a bra. Gus crumpled it and got to work.

You could honestly say Gus was one of the good guys. Nice to a fault. When Gus started at the department, he made a strong first impression. Deference, respect, dedication. Gus didn't have any connections in the department. Didn't want any. He was determined to make his own way in the world through hard work and character. His supervisors immediately took notice and fast-tracked him into the category of new recruits who needed to be kept down.

"Hey, Serpico," yelled Englewood. "How do you spell bougainvillea?"

"His name's Gus," said Walter.

"It's okay," said Gus. "B-o-u-g-. . ."

It had started as a proud nickname. And it had a nice snap. That was in the eighties, when Gus was a young stallion of a cop. Then his back went out, and he got fat. There was no exact moment in time—more of a gray transition—and the nickname gradually drifted into derision. After twenty years, it was a complete joke. Actually, it had been kind of a joke all along.

Nobody was talking in the substation, just the air conditioner and three chattering typewriters.

The front door opened. "I just heard the funniest story!" said Deputy Valrico. "This woman I stopped for speeding told me Serpico's wife once—"

Englewood cleared his throat. Valrico turned. "Oh, hi, Serpico. Thought you were on a call."

"Just got back." Gus pulled a completed report from his typewriter and walked to a filing cabinet. The fax machine started up. Gus tore the APB off the spool and walked over to Walter's desk.

"Remember those bodies up in Fort Pierce?"

Walter nodded and typed.

Gus set the fax on his desk. "Metallic green Trans Am spotted at a Key Largo gas station."

"So it *is* headed this way."

"There's more," said Gus. "See this list of victims? All named in the same indictment as the guy we found on the bat tower."

9

The petite woman sitting in the rear of the No Name Pub didn't take off her sunglasses. An untouched cup of coffee on the table. Her back to the wall.

After a few minutes, Anna's eyes rose slightly. Someone she'd been watching at the bar was coming over. He pulled out the chair across from her. "You okay?"

She nodded. "Thanks for agreeing to meet."

"Of course I'd meet you! Can't tell you how worried I was when I saw the reports on TV. What the hell happened?"

Anna opened her mouth, then crumbled into silent crying. Her shoulders bobbed. The man turned around to see if anyone was looking. The people at the bar were laughing about something. The man reached across the table and put a hand on her arm. "You don't have to say anything."

Anna sniffled and gathered composure. "No, I have to tell someone. . . ."

Two days earlier

Anna Sebring scurried around the kitchen as the sun went down. She looked up over the sink. A big yellow daisy said six-thirty. She opened the oven and took a chicken out. She was wearing a waitress uniform.

It was a duplex, a plain white rectangle with no landscaping in a sub-blue-collar section of Fort Pierce, about two hours north of Miami. It had been another sparkling Florida development—"from the low forties"—when it first went up thirty years ago. Now the yards were dirt and weeds and disabled cars, the lawns orphaned in the mid-1980s, when the neighborhood collapsed all at once like the fall of Cambodia, and the Middle Class fled for the next new development farther inland.

Anna tensed when the front door opened. She hurried into the living room and searched Billy's face for clues. She went to kiss him. He walked by.

"I made your favorite . . ."

He didn't answer. Just sat at the dinner table. It was one of those days she knew to leave quickly. Anna grabbed the strap of her purse. "I'll be home same time. . . ."

She went out the door.

She came back in.

"My car's gone." Anna grabbed the phone. "Somebody stole it."

When Billy didn't react, she knew. She put the phone down.

"Repossessed again?"

Billy stared ahead.

"But we're up on the payments this time. I deposited my check from the restaurant. . . ."

Billy took a hard breath. Bad territory.

"You didn't make the payment. You're gambling. . . ."

Crack. Right across the nose.

She stumbled, off-balance. Billy slowly pushed out his chair and stood. Anna began backing up.

Billy didn't have to knock her to the ground. She went down on her own, curling and covering everything important. Her legs took the kicks. She tried to keep quiet so the neighbors on the other side of the duplex wouldn't know. Didn't matter. Same story there, too.

Billy lost interest and went to the kitchen for a Coors. Anna stuffed contents back in her spilled purse and ran out the door.

But how to get to work? She'd be late again for sure, and she'd been warned. She looked at Billy's metallic green Trans Am in the driveway.

She had spare keys in her purse. It was the wrong decision, but there wasn't a right one.

Ten minutes later, Anna raced into the parking lot of the Sunny Side Up Café. The sign had a fried egg with a smiling yolk.

"You're late again!" yelled the owner, doubling as short-order cook after firing someone.

"Sorry . . ." Anna ran to the back of the restaurant and the employee rest room, actually a mop closet. She stuck toilet paper up her nose to draw blood. Checked her eyes in the mirror. Starting to puff.

Anna grabbed an order pad and rushed back out under the owner's glare. The customers momentarily forgot their selections when Anna rushed up to the table looking like she'd just rolled down a hill. Clothes out of line, droplet of blood peeking from a nostril.

A taxi arrived. Billy. He could have just taken the Trans Am in the parking lot and driven away, but you had to know Billy. He ran in the restaurant and started shouting at Anna again like they were still alone in their living room. Billy so wanted to club her, but then saw the much-larger owner coming over. He left quickly.

Customers started getting up. Tires screeched in the parking lot and Billy took off. Across the street, a white Mercedes with tinted windows pulled away from the curb and headed in the same direction.

Anna was sitting and crying at an empty table. The owner walked over.

She wiped her eyes. "I'm so sorry. . . ."

"So am I."

She looked up. The owner was shaking his head. "This isn't working."

"I need this job."

"I need this restaurant."

He called for Val, one of the other waitresses, to give Anna a ride. There wasn't any business now anyway.

They went to Val's apartment. A relative was there, watching her kid.

"What are you going to do?"

"I don't know," said Anna.

Val leaned against the kitchen counter and lit a cigarette. "I'd call the police."

"I can't." Anna turned quickly. "And you don't say anything either. Billy's on probation. He'd go back to jail."

"Good."

"Then we really won't have any money."

Anna couldn't believe how different Billy had been in the beginning.

"They always are," said Val, looking over at her own child in the living room.

But Billy wasn't like the others. And besides, he was in business with her brother, Rick. Anna adored Rick. He was married to her best friend, Janet, and Anna thought Janet was the luckiest woman in the world. If only she could find someone half as nice as her brother. And if Billy was good enough to be Rick's business partner, that was plenty recommendation.

The two waitresses didn't have answers. It got to be midnight.

"I need to go home," said Anna.

"You should stay here."

"Just take me home."

They drove across town and turned the corner at the end of Anna's street. Val leaned over the steering wheel. "Holy shit."

Anna's clothes and everything were all over the front lawn, the front dirt, that is. The Trans Am was in the driveway.

Val kept going past the house and drove to a nearby convenience store. They bought plastic trash bags and returned to the duplex. No sign of Billy. The blinds were drawn and all the lights off except one still burning in the back bathroom. They quietly stuffed belongings in the bags and tossed them in the backseat.

Val ran around to the driver's door. Anna stood beside the car, looking at the house.

"What are you waiting for?"

"There's more stuff."

"Forget your stuff!"

"I need it."

"You're not seriously thinking of going back in there?"

"He's probably sleeping. I'll just be a minute."

10

A '71 BUICK RIVIERA sat in the parking lot of the Winn-Dixie shopping center on Big Pine Key. The windows were down. Serge peered across the lot with a pair of camouflaged hunter's binoculars. He raised a tiny digital recorder to his mouth. "Surveillance file zero-zero-zero-zero-one. Subject: white female approximately thirty-five to forty years old, driving beige, late-model Pathfinder. Established contact outside dry cleaners, several dresses and a jacket. No visible scars or tattoos, full set of teeth, brunette hair, nicely groomed but not overly so in a manner indicating bullshit personality. . . . Subject now exiting vehicle for supermarket. Will resume report once inside and target reacquired."

Serge and Coleman pushed empty shopping carts side by side up the cleanser aisle. Serge had argued they should use only one cart for mobility, but Coleman didn't want people to think they were gay. Serge lectured him about bigotry, and Coleman said he needed his own cart anyway for self-esteem. . . . Where'd the woman go?

They ran in panic along the meat case, checking each aisle, soup to nuts . . . there she was. Serge and Coleman executed a flanking maneuver down the salad dressing aisle and hooked back into breakfast. The woman looked up as two carts skidded around the far end of the aisle and crashed into each other. Serge and Coleman grabbed cereal boxes and pretended to read. The woman resumed shopping.

Serge raised a fist concealing the recorder. "Target reacquired . . . comparing flavors of nature bars, original and new . . ."

The woman turned toward Serge; he looked away quickly.

"Coleman! Her cart's moving! She's coming this way!"

They held cereal boxes over their faces. The woman passed by. Coleman tugged Serge's sleeve. "Can I get something?"

"Of course. You're an adult."

"I don't see Frankenberry."

"They don't make it anymore, *the fuckers.*"

"There's no Quisp, either. And no Quake or Count Chocula."

"Our heritage has been raped."

"This one's got a free offer." Coleman turned a Pokemon box over. "Darn, it's one of those deals where you have to mail away and wait six weeks."

"I hate that," said Serge. "You could be a whole new person in six weeks. I want to immediately dig in the box and find some rubber-band toy that can put your eye out. She just cleared the aisle. We're back on."

They began pushing carts again.

"Remember when you used to race as a kid?" said Coleman.

"I loved that."

"Let's do it."

"Okay."

They sprinted down the aisle like Olympic triple jumpers, simultaneously leaping onto the bars between the back wheels. Serge's cart edged ahead of Coleman's.

"I'm winning! I'm winning! . . ."

Past the Life and Cheerios. "Coleman, you're veering into me!"

"There's no steering!"

"It's like wind-surfing. Shift your weight."

"I can't!"

Crash.

Serge and Coleman ran away from the cereal-strewn aisle with two carts nosed up into the shelves.

The woman took a number at the deli. Serge and Coleman arrived with a single new cart and hid behind the rotisseries.

"Look at this," said Coleman, holding up a box by the cardboard handle. "Marked-down chicken."

"I love marked-down chicken," said Serge. "It's always better. Put it in the cart."

"Cheap generic pizza," said Coleman, picking up a frozen disk. "And expired doughnut holes. I think we're in the guy section."

The cart began to fill.

"Ever put potato chips on a sandwich?" asked Coleman.

"That is the best! Then you mash it all down good. The bread ends up with a bunch of fingerprints, but the taste!"

"You can only do that when women aren't around," said Coleman. "And you definitely can't pour bacon bits straight in your mouth from the container."

"No kidding," said Serge. "Once they see that, the sexual ship sails forever."

"You know who really doesn't put up with that shit?" said Coleman. "Lesbians."

"What did I tell you about that kind of talk?"

"I'm not criticizing. I like lesbians."

"I've seen your video collection."

"That's not what I mean. They have lots of strong points."

"Like what?"

"Well, like they can install their own garbage disposals."

"Did you eat a lot of glue as a child?"

"Sometimes."

A butcher began slicing meat and cheese for the woman. Serge raised a fist to his mouth. ". . . Boar's Head, Gouda . . ." The woman glanced over at Serge. He looked away. A speaker in the ceiling: *"Cleanup, cereal aisle."* Two sun-burnt construction workers walked past Serge and Coleman's single cart. "Faggots."

"I told you," said Coleman.

"Serves you right for that crack about lesbians."

"But I was saying something positive."

"It's still against the rules."

Coleman noticed the seafood section on the other side of the rotisseries. "Hey, I just remembered something I loved to do in supermarkets when I was a kid."

"What?"

Coleman told him.

"That's a great idea!" said Serge. "I completely forgot about that!"

Serge and Coleman ran over and leaned with palms pressed against the cold glass of the seafood case, staring inside. A couple of five-year-old boys walked up and put their hands on the glass next to Serge and Coleman. A man in a paper hat wiped his hands and approached from the other side of the case. "What can I get you fellas?"

"Nothing," said Serge. "We just want to look at the fish with the heads still on."

Coleman pointed. "She's heading to dairy!"

"Let's go!"

The woman was checking calorie counts on various yogurts, opting for fruit on the bottom.

Serge staked her out from over in eggs.

A stock boy arrived with a large cart. "Can I help you?"

"Yes," said Serge. "Where are the small eggs?"

"We don't carry small," said the stock boy. "The smallest we have are medium."

"How small are they?"

"Really small." He flicked open a box cutter.

"What if I don't want really small? What if I just want kind of small?"

"Get the large. They're small." He slit open a carton.

Serge grabbed a Styrofoam container out of the cooler. "How big are the extra-large?"

"Medium."

"And the jumbo would be large?"

"Medium to large."

"Thanks." Serge put the container back in the cooler.

"What about your eggs?" asked the stock boy.

"I don't want eggs, just answers."

The woman headed for produce and placed tomatoes on a scale. Serge and Coleman hid behind the florist display. Coleman picked up a rose and sniffed it. "I've never stopped in this part of the store before."

"Neither have I." Serge picked up a bouquet and checked the price tag.

"Maybe you should buy something to have on hand, just in case."

"You're right." Serge placed the bouquet in their cart. "Nothing says 'I love you' like a dozen supermarket flowers for three dollars."

Coleman looked toward the ceiling. "They have helium balloons. The ones made of foil."

"Those are critical." Serge reeled one down and inspected the pressure. "But you have to save them for the right moment. You don't want to shoot your wad."

Coleman reeled down his own balloon. "This one's a double. It's got a red heart inside a clear heart."

"That's the most important of all. A guy only puts it into play if it's a super-special occasion or if he's fucked up big time."

"Why's that?"

"The double balloon gets you out of anything. Can't even be questioned. Like those letters of transit Peter Lorre stole in *Casablanca*."

"She's heading for checkout."

The woman got in line at register three. Serge and Coleman pulled into register four. Serge held up a *Redbook* with Jennifer Aniston on the cover. *Drive Him Totally Wild with Ordinary Household Products, Page 132.* He peeked over the top. The woman was looking at Serge; he peeked back down.

The cashier rang up chicken and flowers. Serge thought the eighty-year-old woman bagging his groceries looked familiar. She was going slow.

"Doris?"

"Serge?"

"What are you doing here? I thought you'd retired."

"I had," said Doris. "But then I got wiped out in the stock market. That accounting scandal with Global-Con . . ."

"Son of a—!"

The old woman was tired. She stopped and grabbed the end of the counter, then started bagging again.

Serge went over and gently held her arm. "Why don't you take a break. I'll bag these myself."

"No, I have to keep going!"

Coleman was reading a tabloid. "Hey, Serge, look at this article. 'Leading psychic reveals: Hitler kicked out of hell, starts rival inferno' . . ."

Serge began helping Doris bag. "You must have some money left."

"Not enough to live on." She sniffed the flowers and put them in a sack. "The worst part is that bastard Donald Greely has started building a mansion just up the road, rubbing our noses in it."

The woman at register three zipped her purse and began pushing a cart of bagged groceries toward the door.

"Doris, I want to get back with you on that."

Serge and Coleman hurried out of the store and reached the parking lot just as the woman finished loading bags in her Pathfinder. They ran to the Riviera. Serge grabbed his binoculars.

"Look," said Coleman. "She's getting back out of her car. I think she's seen us."

"You're right. She's coming over here," said Serge. "This could ruin everything. It's too premature for us to formally meet before I've had a chance to study her at the gym and through open windows of her house. On the other hand, you never know. She could be the one!"

The woman was almost to their car. Serge grabbed the flowers and got out, hiding the bouquet behind his back.

She stopped a few feet in front of him. "Have you been following me?"

Serge broke into his broadest, most charismatic smile. "Yes!"

"I thought so." The woman reached in her purse.

Serge whipped the flowers from behind his back and proudly held them out. "This is for you."

The woman pointed a keychain cannister at Serge. "And this is for you." Squirt.

The flowers hit the pavement. Serge stomped on them as he reeled. "Ahhhhhhh! My eyes! I'm blind!"

She kicked him between the legs. "Pervert!"

Coleman jumped out of the car. "Serge! Where are you?" He ran around the Buick and found his partner bunched on the ground. Coleman bent down and helped his buddy up into a sitting position. "What happened?"

"She's not the one."

11

A LOUD CRASH.

The petite woman in the back of the No Name jumped.

The man sitting on the other side of the table reached for her hand. "Just somebody dropping something."

Anna hyperventilated.

"You need a beer." The man got up and went to the bar. He returned with two drafts. Anna grabbed hers in shaking hands and guzzled till it was gone.

The man grabbed her hand again. "Jesus, easy . . ."

"I can't take this. I need Valium."

"I can get you some."

"Where was I?"

"Take a rest."

"No. I haven't told anyone yet. I have to get it all out. . . ."

ANNA CREPT TOWARD the duplex.

"Don't go back in there!" yelled Val.

Anna didn't listen.

"I'll keep the engine running and your door open. You just run right out. . . ."

Anna reached the porch. She cautiously unlocked the door and pushed it open with a creak. Stillness. She eased through the dark living room, no sign of Billy. The bedroom door was closed. That was good. The stuff she needed was in the bathroom. She went down the hall.

Anna got closer and heard water running. The door was ajar, a ribbon of light. She pushed it open.

Val leaped out of the car when she heard the shrieks. Anna stood paralyzed in the bathroom doorway. Red arterial spray over everything. On top of the sink was a box. On top of the box was Billy's head. The autopsy would later find the work had been done with a hacksaw, begun, at least, while the victim was still alive. A slim wire ran into Billy's mouth, attached to a miniature recording device—the kind police make informants wear—which was now broadcasting from somewhere near the top of Billy's throat. The box was on top of the sink so the head could look at itself in the mirror. Billy's surprised eyes, frozen open in a look of eternal terror, gazed at the reflection, where someone had written in blood, "How smart are you now?"

Anna came flying out the front door and fell to her knees with dry heaves. Val ran and met her in the middle of the yard. She struggled to understand Anna's hysterics. The message eventually got across.

"We have to call the police!"

"You're right." They ran to the car and Anna reached in her purse for a cell phone. It rang in her hands. They both jumped.

Anna apprehensively put the phone to her head. "Hello?"

It was her sister-in-law, Janet. Screaming.

"Calm down, I can't understand—"

"They killed everyone!"

"Who?"

"They shot Rick. . . ."

Her brother. A punch in the chest.

". . . I found him on the kitchen floor. And they shot Randy. And Pedro *and* his wife! . . ." Then more shrieking.

Janet's collapse somehow spurred Anna to get it together. It was the Rick in her. "I'm coming over. . . ."

"I'm not at home. It's not safe," said Janet. "You and Billy need to hide."

"Billy's dead."

"Oh, my God!"

"Just found him," said Anna. "We're at the house."

"Get away from there!"

Anna looked across the front seat at her friend. "We're not safe here."

Val started shaking and fumbling with the gear shift.

Anna opened her door.

"What are you doing?"

"Something's started that I can't tell you about. You need to get out of here. But don't call the police."

"What about you?"

Anna looked toward the driveway. "I've got the Trans Am."

Her friend sped away and nearly took out the stop sign at the corner. Anna kept her sister-in-law on the phone as she ran up the driveway, juggling her purse, digging for keys.

"Where are you?"

Janet looked around the pay phone outside a truck stop on 1-95. "Flying J."

"Don't move. I'm coming over." Anna revved up the Trans Am and screeched backward into the street.

Janet was still sobbing. "Rick told me there was nothing to worry about. Just said not to speak to anyone without a lawyer."

"What are you talking about?"

"The indictments today. Didn't you hear? It was on the news."

"Indictments?"

"We all got one. This was only pot for Chrissake! Rick promised nobody gets rough over that. Just coke."

The picture snapped into focus.

Anna vividly remembered the day it all began. It was windy down at the municipal marina. The women wore scarves. They loaded picnic lunches while the guys argued over their new knots. Rick and Billy had just bought the sailboat. The wives were against it at first, but the idea grew on them as they thought of all the time the couples would be spending together. They imagined raising kids.

That's when the strangers approached. They started talking to Rick and Billy from the pier, complimenting the vessel. The women didn't like the men, didn't exactly know why, just didn't. The guys hit it off.

After that, the other men always seemed to be hanging around the marina when the couples came back from sailing. Rick and Billy started going out for drinks with their new friends. Then phone calls at the house where Billy would go in another room and close the door. The husbands developed a sudden interest in night fishing.

Anna knew something was up, so Billy got the shoe boxes down from the attic and showed her the cash. "It's just pot. . . ."

That was five years ago. Rick and Janet got a bigger house, and another place in the Keys they rented out. Billy got a gambling habit and another lease on the duplex.

Rick changed. He became smart with money. They were living well, but not spending nearly what was coming in. Rick was putting it somewhere. Billy changed, too. Cocaine, the dog track. Then the women from the bars that Billy always swore were the very last time. Finally his temper, which steadily grew worse and spilled into phone arguments with the guys from the pier.

Rick tried talking to him, and Billy said he'd change. He changed into a liar. Rick didn't know what to do. From time to time, he passed money to his sister on the side.

Now the indictments . . .

"What are we going to do!" Janet yelled in the phone.

The Trans Am squealed around a corner. "Stay calm. I'll be right there."

"I can't take it anymore!" Janet leaned weeping against the pay phone. Truck drivers heading into the coffee shop couldn't help notice the drama. That hot little number in distress who obviously needed a knight.

A man in a Pennzoil cap walked up from behind. "Ma'am, is everything okay?"

Janet jumped and screamed. "No! Get the fuck away from me!"

"Jesus. You got it, lady. . . ."

"What's going on?" said Anna.

"I have to get out of here!"

"No, stay put," said Anna. "You're in the open. You need to be in public."

"I have to go! I can't handle this! I'll call back."

"Don't hang up!"

"I have to!"

"Okay, you know that place Rick and Billy have? The piece of land they go duck hunting and have that aluminum building where they work on their motorcycles?"

"I know it."

"Meet you there."

12

Serge combed his hair as he drove. He pulled up to a stop sign, tilted his head back and squeezed a Visine bottle.

"How are your eyes?" asked Coleman.

"Still sting a little, but I'm not blinking as much."

"She got you good."

"Was worth it," said Serge, capping the bottle. "I discovered her problem with men before we got too deep into the relationship."

Coleman lit a joint and pointed with the lighter. "Another midget deer."

Serge eased onto the brakes. "They're endangered. That's why I won't let you drive on this island."

"But they're so cute. I want to take one home. It would be neat having it roam around the trailer to keep me company. Do they make a lot of noise?"

"You can't take care of yourself."

Coleman looked at the road again, then at the joint in his hand, then back at the road. "Serge, I think I see a big dragon. Can you check?"

Serge hit the brakes again. "Iguana."

"It's huge." Coleman put his face to the windshield. "I've never seen one that size. Must be five feet."

"Closer to six." The lizard slithered into someone's azaleas. Serge stepped on the gas. "Exotic pet breed that got loose on the island. No natural predators and a plentiful food source, so they just mate and grow to unforeseen sizes. Hundreds now."

Serge drove around a bend on Watson Boulevard and pulled up to the No Name Pub. They went inside and grabbed a pair of stools in the middle of an argument.

"Flotsam!" said Bud Naranja.

"Jetsam!" said Sop Choppy.

"But the boat sank!"

"But they threw it overboard first!"

"What a great place," said Coleman, slowly looking around. "I didn't even know it was here."

"Bet it beats those weeklong benders where you never leave your trailer."

"They have their moments."

The bartender came over and automatically set bottled water in front of Serge.

"I'd like a draft anything," said Coleman. "But not lite anything."

The bartender stuck a tall glass under a tap. "What's new, Serge?"

"He's getting married," said Coleman.

"You're kidding! Congratulations!"

"Who's the lucky gal?" asked Bud.

"Don't know yet. We're still doing recon."

Sop Choppy laughed. "What about Brenda?"

"We're just friends," said Serge. "She doesn't like me that way."

"Are you kidding?" said Sop Choppy. "She's crazy about you, always coming around and asking if you're back in town."

"Not my type."

"What do you mean 'not your type'?" said Bob the accountant. "She's *every* guy's type."

"Brenda's got some great qualities," said Sop Choppy. "College degree. Big tits."

Serge shook his head. "The soul-mate vibe just isn't there."

Coleman was turning his eyelids inside out.

"You're going to freeze that way," said Serge.

Coleman flipped his lids back. The Stones came on the juke.

Serge hopped off his stool and began strutting to the music. "Can you feel it, Coleman? You're sitting in the greatest place in the world—the last frontier in America! Dig it everybody: It's the Florida Keys! We're weirdness on a stick!"

The gang: "Hooray!"

The petite woman in the back of the pub tensed up at the noise. "What's going on over there?"

The man sitting across from her turned around. "Oh, that's just Serge."

Serge strutted faster. The regulars: "Go, Serge, go! . . . Go, Serge, go! . . ."

"I'm a cold Italian pizza, I could use a lemon squeezer! Yowwww!" Serge did a split at the end of the bar, popped up and started strutting back toward them. "These islands have always attracted a ragtag, bottom-of-the-barrel cast of life-bunglers. . . ." He made a sweeping gesture at the bar. The gang smiled and waved at Coleman.

Serge stopped and placed a hand on a shoulder. "This is Bob the accountant, not to be confused with Shirtless Bob here. How's the car coming?"

"I just bored out the—"

"That's wonderful. And here's the well-read biker named Sop Choppy, a regular doubting Thomas who's in charge of debunking all the phooey that's slung around this joint, and this is Bithlo Tice, who runs an unethical towing service, and Odessa 'Odey' Goulds, same deal but with plumbing, and Trilby Mims, who's on total disability (wink), and Belle Cutler, a bouncer in the private room at the Cheetah Club who takes payoffs to look the other way on rim jobs, and Loughman Mascotte, who can never let himself get fingerprinted for some reason . . ."

"Shhhhhh!" said Loughman, hunching over his beer, holding a hand up to his face.

". . . And Darby Felsmere, who has a bunch of washing machines and doorless refrigerators marked offshore with GPS coordinates that he uses to supply the restaurants with lobster, and Ogden Ebb, who was about to lose everything in the divorce but instead talked his wife into faking his death at sea and splitting the insurance, and Noma Lovett, who's also Lawtey Pierce and Sewall Myers according to the unemployment checks, and 'Daytona Dave' DeFuniak, the one-hit wonder who had that big song back in the seventies, 'Island Fever,' which caught the draft behind the *Changes in Latitudes* album and topped out at number thirty-nine and he'll even sing it for you if he gets drunk enough . . ."

"I'm burnin' up, with that island fe—"

". . . But not now. And Scanlon Elerbee, who peddles caffeine tabs as bootleg speed over the internet to fraternities, and Yulee Richloam, who sells inferior roadbed to the state, and Perky Sneads, who signs off that roadbed for the state, and Eddie Perrine, who's in between gigs and has a job, and Bud Naranja here, who keeps getting fired from newspapers and abandoned his car on the side of U.S. 1 next to the chamber of commerce . . ."

"I know that car," said Coleman. "Some guy's living in it."

Daytona Dave raised his hand. "That would be me."

". . . And finally we have Rebel Starke," said Serge, "who eluded a massive manhunt in Tennessee."

"Wow, you're really a fugitive?" said Coleman.

"Tell him," said Serge.

"Not as bad as it sounds," said Rebel. "Was living in Knoxville at the time and got mixed up with this cult that was deep into Sartre and Kierkegaard, only it was really about door-to-door cleaning products. Anyway, I get this existential license plate for my car: UNKNOWN. A year later, they put in those cameras that automatically take pictures of drivers who run red lights. If they can't make out the license number in the photo, they manually type in, you guessed it, 'unknown.' In the first month I get like a hundred tickets. I went down to city hall at least a dozen times, and they always said they'd fix it, but I was still being pulled over two and three times a day. It was easier to just move."

There was a series of loud crashes out the back door, metal garbage cans falling over.

"What was that?" said Coleman.

"Roger."

"Roger?"

"Classic Keys story," said Sop Choppy. "You may think *we're* crazy, but you're looking at the solid citizens, the ones who bend in the wind. . . ."

"Only two social rules on this island," said Bud. "Don't mess with the miniature deer and don't steal the No Name dollars off the walls. Otherwise, anything goes. People who aren't used to the freedom lose their minds."

"Like Roger," said Sop Choppy. "Used to be a lawyer, good one, too. Then he started deep-sea fishing down here. It was the eighties, so naturally he hung out afterward with the other guys at the Full Moon and the Boca Chica. Roger didn't have a single bad habit, never even tried pot. But after three or four trips down here, he's into everything. Drinking till dawn, snorting lines of blow as wide as your thumb. One weekend, he never goes home at all. His wife starts calling the police, and they find him barricaded in a suite at the La Concha."

"He's under one of the beds screaming about giant flying snakes," said Bud. "The cops finally called animal control, and they dragged him out by slipping one of those lasso-sticks around an ankle, and he bites one of the officers, which got him ninety days in the Stock Island jail. On the seventy-fifth day, he runs away from a road detail and disappears into the mangroves, where he's been ever since. There are still warrants, but the police just want to help him more than anything. He's harmless except when he tears up the garbage cans all over the island—worse than the raccoons."

The trash cans banged around some more.

"That's Roger?" said Coleman.

Bud nodded. "The Skunk Ape."

"Man, you guys have some great stories!" said Coleman, surreptitiously peeling a dollar off the wall.

Serge slapped Coleman's hand.

"Ow."

"You haven't even heard the best ones," said Bob the accountant. "No Name Key."

"What's No Name Key?" asked Coleman.

"Right across that bridge you saw when you came in," said Rebel. "One scary island. People you never want to mess with. No sewer lines or power or anything. Just a bunch of no-trespassing signs at the ends of spooky private roads winding back to places you can't see."

"Bud," said Serge. "Remember the time you got kidnapped?"

"You got kidnapped?" said Coleman.

Bud nodded. "This will tell you everything you need to know about No Name Key. I was doing freelance real estate photography of a stilt house back up one of those roads. I go and take my pictures, no big deal. I'm heading out and this woman in a Dodge Dakota is coming the other way. She blocks me with her pickup, gets out with this big gun."

"Some crazy old hag?" asked Coleman.

"No, a real looker," said Bud. "Asks what the fuck I think I'm doing on private property, can't I read the signs? I tell her about the photos, even show her my real estate paperwork. Doesn't care, just waves the gun. Orders me to turn my car around and drive off this little sandy spur that leads God-knows-where. The road goes deeper and deeper into back country and we come to another stilt house, totally secluded in the salt flats and mangroves. Makes me get out of the car and walk around behind the house to a patio, where she makes me sit in this lounger with my back to the building. Tells me not to turn around or she'll shoot. Then she climbs the stairs and goes inside. I'm really shaking now, all kinds of horrible stuff running through my mind. You wouldn't even have to dispose of a body there, just let nature take its course. I'm about to make a run for it when I hear a door open and footsteps on the stairs. Then this scraping noise. She's dragging another lounger and sets it up right next to mine. I look out the corner of my eye and can't believe what I'm seeing. She's completely naked. And *fine*. No supermodel's got anything on her. She sets the gun on this little cocktail table on the other side of her lounger, which also has a pitcher of lemonade and one of those bottles of Jack Daniel's with a handle. Then she fires up this huge Bob Marley spliff, lays down in the sun and starts reading a magazine like there's absolutely nothing wrong with this picture."

"So did she kill you?" asked Coleman.

"No. But I didn't move a muscle for an hour. Finally she gets up, grabs the gun and goes in the house. I wait a few minutes just to make sure, then take off running like a bastard. I get around the side of the house and there she is, walking back up the road from the mailbox, still buck naked, nonchalantly thumbing through envelopes, the gun dangling upside down by the trigger guard from one of her fingers. Doesn't even look up, just says, 'Where the hell do you think you're going?' So I'm back on that lounger. Another hour goes by, and suddenly there's this crashing in the brush and some big lumberjack type in jeans and tattoos jumps out and charges at me, screaming and swinging a baseball bat. Chases me all over the yard. We make several circles around the naked woman on the lounger, and she's just reading her magazine, la-de-dah, and finally says like she's really bored, 'You wanna fool around or you wanna fuck?' She puts down her magazine and skips off into the swamp. The guy drops the bat and runs after her undoing his pants. I made a break for it, never looked back." Bud took a long sip from his draft. "And that, my friend, is No Name Key."

"Whoa," said Coleman. "Some story!"

"That's not even the best," said Rebel. "There's this drug kingpin who lives over there named—"

"Shhhhhh!" said Shirtless Bob.

"Give me a break!" said Sop Choppy. "Don't tell me you're afraid to even say his name!"

"Keep your voice down," said Bud.

"I don't even believe he exists," said Sop Choppy.

"You better," said Rebel.

13

THE PETITE WOMAN took off her sunglasses for the first time. She dabbed tears, put them back on. She turned her head in the direction of No Name Key. "I just know he was behind this."

"Keep your voice down," said the man sitting across from her. He scooted his chair closer. "Of course he's behind it. That's why we have to get you some place safe. And a new identity."

"I'm not going to spend the rest of my life looking over my shoulder."

"You need to start making plans."

"I'm still thinking about Janet."

"That's what I'm talking about."

"I never should have let her leave the truck stop. If only I'd driven faster . . ."

ANNA LOOKED AT the speedometer. A hundred and five. She took the second exit off the Interstate and raced east down a county road with cattle fencing and no street lights. Anna knew the area; she turned up an unmarked dirt road. The Trans Am had what's known as racing suspension, which means it's bad. Especially doing fifty without pavement. The uneven earth threw the car around. It seemed like forever, but the road soon dumped into a pasture. A dark aluminum building came into view at the edge of the Australian pines. Janet's car was already there. Janet waiting inside. Good. Anna pulled nose-to-nose with the other car. What was up with Janet's windshield? Those would be bullet holes. Thirty.

Headlights came on from an unseen car behind the building, two tubes of lighted fog across the field.

Anna threw the car in reverse, looked over her shoulder and began backing up as fast as she could. The rear end swished in the dirt. High beams from the oncoming car hit the Trans Am. Anna didn't turn around, just kept fighting the Pontiac's back end trying to muscle itself off the road. The other car was a quarter mile and closing, a white Mercedes with tinted windows. Anna came to the end of the dirt road, spinning backward onto the hardtop. She threw it in drive, went maybe fifty feet, then killed the lights and dove down another dirt road that she knew from memory would be there. The Mercedes wasn't far behind; they'd check down the road and see her taillights. So Anna cut the wheel and crashed into the palmettos. She jumped out and braced behind a tree.

The end of the dirt road: High beams grew brighter on the hardtop until a white Mercedes came into view. It stopped. Anna knew they were looking. She didn't breathe. An eternity. The Mercedes accelerated away.

Anna jumped in the Trans Am, praying it wasn't stuck. She hit the gas and the front end popped out of the crunched brush. The car rolled without headlights back to the edge of the county highway. Anna looked to the right. No sign of the Mercedes. She turned left and floored it.

ANNA SAT BACK in her chair in the No Name. ". . . And then I called you from the turnpike and came here."

"Jesus."

"Thanks again for meeting me like this."

"I told you, I'd meet you anywhere."

"Aren't you afraid?" asked Anna.

"Why?"

"You had that big falling-out with him. And everyone I know in our circle is dead."

"*Your* circle," corrected the man. "*We* were the ones who met *you* at the marina. It's a little different code among us."

"I remember that day. I didn't like you."

He smiled. "I could tell."

"So what happened?"

"Fernandez got too crazy."

"Is that his real name? I just heard his nickname."

"That's part of the myth. Except it wasn't all myth. The violence is mostly true. But the worst part was his stare. He has this way of looking at you—"

"When? I never saw him," said Anna. "In fact, come to think of it, I don't know anyone who's ever seen him."

"Almost nobody has."

ON THE OTHER side of the No Name Pub, Rebel Starke leaned low over the bar and spoke like a conspiracy. "Nobody's ever seen him and lived to tell. Nobody knows what he looks like. He lives right across that bridge. . . ."

"You guys are wussies!" said Sop Choppy. "That's just a fairy tale."

"I believe it," said Bud. "I know this guy he had killed. Castrated him with a sharpened melon scoop, let him bleed out."

"Who?" said Sop Choppy.

"My wife knows this woman at work. Her brother's friend heard it—"

"Exactly!" said Sop Choppy. "Someone told someone told someone else. That's how urban legends start."

"How do you explain that big house across the channel?" said Bud. "Nobody's seen the owner."

"I believe some hermit lives over on No Name," said Sop Choppy. "So what? That island's full of recluses. And as far as the dope-running . . . like that's far-fetched. Throw a rock anywhere in the Keys and it'll bounce off *three* smugglers. I'd be more astounded if he ran a tire store. Remember back in the eighties when every other phone booth around here had a number to call if you found a bale, and a van would come by in thirty minutes and give you five grand, no questions asked? They were more dependable than Domino's."

"What about the model-ship story?" said Rebel. "That one I definitely believe."

"Me, too," said Bud. "The ship story is practically legend. I've heard it from at least four different people."

"Big deal. A lot of people are telling the same rumor," said Sop Choppy. "How many times have you heard the one about the rock star who had all that semen pumped out of his stomach?"

"I heard that one," said Coleman. "It was—"

"Shhhhhh!" said Serge. "If you can't say something nice about someone . . ."

"The point I'm making is it's a physical and medical impossibility," said Sop Choppy. "Semen's nontoxic, so there's no need to pump, and as far as the ridiculous amounts in those stories, it would take like two hundred guys to produce that kind of . . . What? Why are you all looking at me like that for? *I* don't do it. I'm just saying check the facts before you go believing every stupid rumor you hear."

"What's the model-ship story?" asked Coleman.

"Don't tell that idiotic thing again," said Sop Choppy. "Everyone's heard it."

"I haven't," said Daytona Dave.

"Me neither," said Coleman.

"Okay," said Rebel. "There are only two things known for sure about the owner of that house: He's ordered the murders of more than a hundred men, and he loves building model ships—"

"I'm telling you he doesn't exist," said Sop Choppy.

IN THE BACK of the pub, Anna Sebring picked at her fingertips. "Who's seen him besides you?"

"Just a handful of the top people in Miami and South America. He actually gets a kick out of all the rumors. He's got it so half the people around here are afraid to say his name and the rest don't even believe he exists."

"What about the guys you were with at the marina?"

"Nope. None of them was ever allowed to meet him. That's the way he wanted it. Put an extra level of fear in the ranks in case someone decided to skim."

"All I know is he's an asshole," said Anna.

"That's why I had to quit. Too erratic with the violence. Didn't make business sense."

"So he just let you leave?"

"No, he had some guys looking for me awhile. To be honest, I was pretty scared. But I had some friends, too. He might take me out, but not without a war. We came to an agreement."

They stopped and looked at each other. The man squinted at Anna. "You understand the risk you're taking just by sitting here? He's right over that bridge."

"I know." She was still fidgeting with her fingers.

"You fled all the way from Fort Pierce to be in his backyard?"

"He murdered my brother." She looked up. "Will you help?"

"Don't even—"

"I'm gonna kill him. I don't give a shit anymore."

The man shook his head. "I can't help. It's part of our understanding. When I walked away, I walked away. He gets the big house and I get a crummy job, but at least I'm alive."

"You liked my brother."

"I did."

"And you won't help?"

"Anything else. You need cash? Help getting away? I'll even go over there and talk to him for you if you want."

She didn't react.

The man sat back in his chair and decided to change the subject. "Staying at your brother's vacation place?"

"I'm not going near there. He's probably got the house watched."

The man rubbed his chin hard and looked at Anna in a different way. "You actually did come down here to kill him."

Anna took off her sunglasses again and answered with her eyes.

"At first I thought it was the money," said the man. "But you really don't know about that, do you?"

"What money?"

"Your brother squirreled it away. A bunch, I hear. He was pretty smart about that."

"I don't know about any money."

"Everyone else does. They say it's in the millions, but that could just be talk. When I first heard you were coming down here, that's what I thought it was about. Get the money for a fresh start."

"Where is it?"

"Nobody knew but your brother."

"I don't care about money."

"You will."

"Sure you won't change your mind?" asked Anna.

The man stood. "Sure you won't change yours?"

She shook her head.

"Remember, you can always call."

"I know."

The man walked away from the table, past an involved story-telling circle at the bar.

". . . He builds these intricate model ships from scratch," said Rebel. "Old eighteenth-century wooden frigates and stuff. An insane perfectionist, painstaking detail. Some take as long as a year. Then he goes over them with a magnifying glass and if there's the tiniest flaw, he'll smash whole masts and riggings in an insane rage and spend weeks redoing them. When he's finally satisfied the model is absolutely perfect, he gets out a giant survival knife and carves his name in the base."

"What name?" asked Coleman.

"Okay," said Rebel. "I'll tell you his original name, but I don't want to say what they call him now because of the curse—"

"Since when is there a fuckin' curse?" said Sop Choppy. "This story gets more ridiculous every time I hear it!"

"Fernandez," said Rebel. "Doug Fernandez."

"That's not a scary name," said Coleman.

"That's why he changed it," said Rebel. "Fernandez has this way of looking at you. Very intimidating. Strong men have been known to throw up. There's this famous test he gives. Nobody is ever allowed to see him. Unless you're in his smuggling organization and about to be promoted into the highest ranks. Then you get to meet one-on-one. But only that single time; you'll never see him again. And if, during that meeting, you can look him in the eye and pass the test, you get your promotion."

"Ooooo, that's pretty spooky," said Sop Choppy. "They have a staring contest."

"*No*," said Rebel. "It's not a *staring contest*. There's conversation, too. The point is it's a mental test. They don't kung fu fight or some shit." He turned to Coleman. "Don't listen to him. This is all true. There was this one lieutenant of his, young but rising fast. He's up for the big promotion. They drive him out to No Name Key, all these limos kicking up dust down the no-trespassing road. The kid is led upstairs to Fernandez's personal office. All the goons assemble outside the door—they've all passed the test, but they're not allowed to see Fernandez again. They stare at the doorknob. The new guy gulps and grabs it. He goes in and finds himself standing all by himself in this huge room, looking across an empty, gleaming oak floor. On the other side of the office is an antique Louis-the-whatever desk with a stunning scale model of a British schooner. Behind the desk is a giant wicker butterfly chair, facing the other way. The kid isn't even sure if there's anyone else in the room. Then, the butterfly chair slowly begins rotating, and there . . . is . . . Fernandez!"

"Butterfly chairs can't rotate," said Sop Choppy. "They're stationary."

"Whatever the fuck," said Rebel. "It's a chair with a very high back and casters or wheels or a swivel base. You happy?"

Sop Choppy looked at the ceiling. ". . . Hmmm-hmmm-hmmm . . . *Bullshit story* . . . Hmmm-hmmm . . ."

Rebel ignored him. ". . . Fernandez leans forward in the chair and bears down on the young man with that glare of his. The lieutenant tries to maintain eye contact, but he can't. Fernandez sits back and folds his hands in his lap. He doesn't say anything. The young guy's really shaking now. Fernandez finally opens a drawer in his desk. He takes out a stopwatch and a gun. The new guy doesn't know what's going on. Fernandez braces his shooting arm on the edge of the desk and says in an unnervingly calm voice: 'You have one minute to make me angry. Or you die.' He clicks the stopwatch. This is the test. The kid is stupid with fear. Fernandez looks at his stopwatch. 'You now have fifty seconds.' The guy figures he better do something. He starts swearing at Fernandez, but he's stuttering. Fernandez laughs. 'I've been called worse. Forty seconds.' The guy insults Fernandez's mother. Fernandez laughs again. 'I never liked her myself. Thirty seconds.' The guy's in a complete panic, sweat pouring down his face. Fernandez flicks the safety off the gun. 'Twenty-five seconds.' The guy's head jerks around the room. 'Twenty seconds.' Fernandez cocks the hammer. 'Fifteen seconds.' The guy runs up to the desk. 'Ten seconds.' He picks up the model ship, races across the room and throws it out the fuckin' window!"

"No!" said Coleman.

"Yes!" said Rebel. "Fernandez loses it. Starts screaming at the kid: *'Out! Out! Out!!!'* I heard the guy literally jumped down the whole last flight of steps. Took Fernandez a whole 'nother year to build a replacement ship."

"The guy get his promotion?" asked Coleman.

"Yeah, he got his promotion all right," said Rebel. "Fernandez prides himself on his word. Then right after, they cut him in half with a table saw."

"A table saw?"

Rebel nodded. "Lengthwise."

"I'm telling you he doesn't exist!" said Sop Choppy.

"Does too," said Rebel.

"Then how come nobody's seen him coming or going?"

"He drives this big white Mercedes, but the windows are tinted."

14

A BIG WHITE Mercedes with tinted windows drove past the No Name Pub. Air conditioning on 65. The suspension made it feel like the sedan was standing still. It was the S600 class with the massive V-12 engine, liquid-display global navigation system and a manufacturer's suggested retail price of $122,800.

There were four men in the Mercedes. Actually five. The last one was in the trunk, pounding with fists.

Bang, bang, bang.

The driver tooted from a cocaine bullet and looked in the rearview. "He better not be fucking up the lining."

All the men in the car wore bright tropical shirts. The one sitting across the front seat from the driver cracked open a Heineken. "Why didn't we just shoot him back on the mainland? That way he couldn't mess up your car."

The driver whipped out a giant nickel .45 automatic and stuck it between the man's eyes. "I told you! Because this is just like the beginning of *Goodfellas*. I love that scene! *Goodfellas* is the second-best movie ever made!"

Not those stupid movies again. All the other men in the car knew what the Number One film was, and it was also how they finally realized that the driver had gone completely insane. The movie was what started the whole nickname business. Fernandez demanded you call him that or else.

It had been hard to tell for a while about the insanity thing. Between Fernandez's original personality and the cocaine, he'd always been a nervous experience, even when he was working his way up as a deckhand unloading pot. Now that he was at the top of the organization and had more coke than he needed, it was beyond intolerable. There was never any conversation in the Mercedes that Fernandez didn't start himself. Many trips were silent the whole way down the Keys, except for the near-constant tooting up that made them all tremble. One toot closer to pulling that big gun again.

The Mercedes crossed the bridge over Bogie Channel to No Name Key. Fernandez was leaned over snorting when the miniature deer wandered into the road.

The Mercedes maintained a steady sixty miles per hour. The guys glanced at each other. Fernandez was doing an extra-long series of toots, even for him. The man in the front passenger seat finally cracked and grabbed the dashboard. "Doug! Watch out!"

Fernandez looked up and slammed the brakes. Another car would have screeched to a halt, but the anti-locks quietly eased the sedan to a stop a few feet from the unstartled animal. It trotted into the brush. The .45 automatic was back in the passenger's face. "What did you call me!"

The passenger replayed his own voice in a loop inside his head. Shit, he'd called him Doug.

"I didn't mean anything by it," said the passenger. "Just the excitement. We were going to hit that deer."

Fernandez pressed the gun barrel against the passenger's forehead. "What do you call me!"

"I'm sorry. . . . *Scarface*."

Fernandez unconsciously touched the three-inch scar on his left cheek. "That's better." He put the gun away and hit the gas.

Scarface. Film Number One. There was a time when the guys had actually liked the movie, but none of them could stand it anymore. They were forced to watch it at least three times a week, the whole time Fernandez repeating lines along with Pacino to work on his accent. They didn't think it could get any worse until the anniversary special-edition DVD came out, and they also had to watch all the bonus material on disk two.

The Mercedes turned south on a dirt road and wound its way into the swamp, finally parking under a secluded stilt house. They got out and opened the trunk.

Fernandez sniffed the air. "Did you pee in there?"

The hostage shielded his unadjusted eyes from the sunlight. "Oh, please! God! No! . . ."

The other three yanked the man out of the car. His legs went limp, and they had to carry him up the outside staircase. Fernandez unlocked the door. They threw him down in the middle of the room.

He sat up on the hardwood floor. A large-screen TV at one end of the room; a big oak desk with a model ship at the other. Also, watercolors and oils: fly-fishing, sunset, a woman hanging laundry in Bimini. Some of the paintings hung on the wall over a two-hundred-gallon aquarium. The hostage wasn't looking at any of it because he was busy wiggling backward across the floor while Fernandez kicked the stuffing out of him.

"I didn't do anything! Please! I'm begging!"

Kick.

"You idiot! You fool!" Kick. "Billy was wired for sound up in Fort Pierce." Kick. "The feds heard every word you said!" Kick. "That's how they got all those lovely indictments!" Kick.

"I didn't know! I swear!"

"You're supposed to!" Kick. "That's what I pay you for!"

"Please! . . . I've always been loyal! . . ."

Fernandez shot a look to the other three men. They stepped forward and jerked the man to his feet. "No! Anything! I'll give you money! I'll leave the country! . . ."

Fernandez walked across the room to the aquarium. "Bring him here."

"W-w-what are you going to do?"

Fernandez didn't answer, just addressed the others in a low voice. "Give me his right arm."

The trio tightened their grip on the struggling man. One grabbed the requested limb below the shoulder and forced it forward. Fernandez seized it by the wrist.

The man was now more confused than terrified, until he looked in the tank. . . . His head snapped toward Fernandez. "Piranhas?"

"You need to be taught a lesson. Not to be so stupid."

Fernandez pulled the arm over the tank and lowered it toward the water. Fish gathered near the surface. Now the struggling really started. And the crying.

"Don't be such a baby," said Fernandez. "Take your punishment like a man."

"I'll be more careful next time! I've learned my lesson!"

"You have?"

The man nodded as hard as he could.

Fernandez released the arm, and the man clutched it to his chest. "You . . . uh . . . you're not going to stick my arm in there?"

"Nah, I've changed my mind."

"Oh, thank you. You won't regret this. Thank you! Thank you! . . ."

"Don't mention it."

Fernandez suddenly grabbed the hair on the back of the man's head and slammed his face into the tank. The water broiled and turned pink.

The rest of the crew winced and looked away but didn't dare release their grips. Fernandez began laughing. He held the head down a good while after the resistance had stopped, then let go. The lifeless body collapsed to the floor, carotid spurting.

The crew turned green, staring in any direction other than down.

Fernandez pointed at the floor. "C'mon, look at him. It's funny."

They couldn't bear it. Not without throwing up in front of Fernandez, and you definitely didn't want to do that.

"Okay, be that way. I try to have some fun with you guys. . . ." He walked around the oak desk and dropped down into the butterfly chair. He grabbed a cocaine mirror with one hand, a remote control with the other. "Go get some towels and clean up this mess."

The crew headed for the door. They heard the TV come on behind them at max volume.

"I bury the cock-a-roaches."

15

The gang in the No Name Pub gave up trying to convince Sop Choppy of Scarface's existence, and instead turned their efforts to Serge's love life.

"I still say you should try Brenda," said Bud. "She's nuts about you."

"And hot as they come," said Rebel. "My God, any guy on this island would love to be in your shoes."

Serge shook his head. "I told you. Something's missing there."

"Have you been seeing anyone else?" asked Daytona Dave.

"Thought I'd found the perfect woman this morning," said Serge. "But it didn't work out."

"What happened?" asked Bud.

"He got tear-gassed," said Coleman.

"What approach are you using?" asked Sop Choppy.

"He follows them at a distance with binoculars," said Coleman.

"That never works," said Bud.

"You come on too strong," said Sop Choppy. "What you need to do is relax, forget about marriage for the moment and just try to strike up a friendly conversation like a normal person."

"They'll see that coming," said Serge. He moved his right arm in a wide circular motion. "You have to sneak up from the back side."

"I'm going to do you a favor," said Sop Choppy. "I want you to walk up to a woman right now and start talking. This very minute."

"Where?"

"Right here."

"In a bar? Are you crazy?" said Serge. "The force fields are up. I always have the worst reactions."

"Worse than pepper spray?"

"He's got a point," said Bud.

"I don't see any available women, anyway," said Serge.

"What about her?" said Sop Choppy.

"Which one?"

"The petite number in back with the sunglasses. She's sitting all alone. I bet she'd just love for you to come up and talk."

"I don't know. . . ."

"Consider it batting practice," said Sop Choppy. "Go on now, get over there."

The others: "Do it, Serge." "Come on, Serge."

He took a deep breath. "Okay, here goes nothing. . . ."

The gang watched as Serge walked over to the table and started talking. After a few seconds, the woman jumped up and ran out of the bar crying.

Serge came back to his stool.

"Jesus," said Bud. "What on earth did you say to her?"

"Nothing. Just, 'Why the long face? You look like someone died.'"

The screen door opened. A large group of people streamed into the pub and stood silently behind the stools. Bud tapped Serge on the shoulder and pointed.

Serge turned around. "Oh, no. Not you guys again!"

They didn't say anything.

"Who are they?" asked Rebel.

"These people from the cult meeting. It's a long story."

Some in the group held tape recorders toward Serge.

"Go on now!" said Serge. "Shoo!"

They just stood there. A few took snapshots.

"Why won't you leave me alone?"

A man in the front piped up. "Because you speak the truth."

"I lie all the time. Ask anybody."

The man turned to the rest of the group. "See? Everyone lies. But he's the only one who tells the truth and admits it."

Serge made a whining sound. "Why me? Don't you guys have some guru or messianic folk singer to follow?"

"Yes," said the one in front. "But we found out they had other agendas. Wanted to screw all the women and have the rest of us put our houses in the churches' names. Or they were selling herbal supplements. But you're different. You don't have any agenda at all."

"Oh, I've got an agenda all right. I want to be left the hell alone!"

The man turned again to the others. "Doesn't even want to be followed. That means he's The One."

Serge raised his arms toward the ceiling in exasperation. "Why are you doing this to me?"

"He's calling on The Father."

"No! Stop it! It's a figure of speech!" said Serge. "What can I do to get you to go away?"

"Give us a message."

"Message? Okay, I have a message. Here it is: Do as I do. And you know what I do? I follow nobody. You got it? I follow nobody at all. That's exactly what all of you should do: Follow nobody!"

The group exchanged glances. "Follow nobody?" Then nods. "Follow nobody!"

They wandered out the screen door, chanting: *"Follow nobody. Follow nobody . . ."*

"Hey, I got an idea," said Rebel. "I know the perfect woman for you. Real outdoorsy type. Saw her fishing on the bridge when I came in here. Probably still there."

"What are we waiting for?" said Sop Choppy.

"I don't think so," said Serge. "This hasn't been a very lucky day for me."

"Come on, Serge."

The gang coaxed the reluctant suitor off his stool and out the door. They started up the road to the bridge. Serge's mood brightened. "I love the fishing scene!"

"There you go," said Rebel. "You already have something in common with her."

They passed a man with barbed wire tattooed around his upper arms, working a spinning rod, Marlboro hanging from his mouth. Then a pair of African Americans cutting bait and listening to a cheap radio.

"There she is," said Rebel.

"Where?"

"At the very end." He pointed at a tall, freckled redhead in shorts and a black sports bra, gathering up the skirt of a nylon cast net. "Her name's Daryle."

"I've never seen a babe cast-net before," said Coleman.

The woman expertly folded lengths of mesh, gripping the braided retrieval cord in her teeth.

Serge's mouth hung open.

The woman started spinning on the bridge. She took a couple quick steps toward the railing and twirled the net high in the air, lead weights evenly fanning out before slapping down in the water.

"What do you think?" asked Rebel.

"I'm in love."

The woman reeled the net back over the rail, depositing a respectable quantity of flopping fish on the bridge.

"You're up," said Bud.

"I'm too nervous. . . ."

The guys pushed Serge in the back. "Go talk to her."

Serge walked up and stood a few feet away. The woman was gathering the net again and didn't see him at first. He coughed. She looked up.

Serge was bouncing on the balls of his feet with a big smile. He tried to speak but nothing came out.

The woman wound the retrieval line. "Can I help you with something?"

". . . I-I love you! . . . Shit! . . . I mean, love cast-nets. That's an eighteen-footer, isn't it? Must have cost a hundred."

"Hundred fifty."

"Yes, sir. You have great style. Not many men can handle an eighteen-footer. That didn't sound right, did it? I'm completely behind *Roe v. Wade*. Can I try?"

"You want to throw?"

Serge smiled.

"Do you know what you're doing?"

"Of course."

The woman shrugged. "Okay, just don't get it all fuckin' tangled."

Oooooo, sassy, too! She could be the soul mate, thought Serge. Don't blow this. I'll impress her with my cast-net mating dance.

They all stood back as Serge bunched the net in a flurry of motion. Once it was ready, he counted off large steps to the opposite side of the bridge. He leaned with his back against the far railing, closed his eyes and took a rapid series of deep breaths.

"Serge," said Sop Choppy.

"Not now."

"But, Serge—"

"I'm concentrating. I have to prepare *the mental place*."

"But I'm trying to tell you . . ."

Serge opened his eyes and took off running. He reached the middle of the bridge and began pirouetting with tremendous centrifugal force like a discus thrower. Painful grunting noises, spinning faster and faster. Finally, he reached the railing, sprang up and released with a mighty *"Hiiiiiiiiiiyyyyy-yahhhhhhhhhh!"*

The net deployed perfectly, sailing higher and farther than anyone had ever seen before. They ran to the side of the bridge.

"I was trying to tell you," said Sop Choppy. "The wrist cord—"

They watched the net splash into the water and sink to the bottom of Bogie Channel with the retrieval line.

> *Captain Florida's log, star date 384.274*
> *Old Wooden Bridge Fishing Camp, Cottage #5. Today we launch a new Captain Florida feature: Serge's Word Corner. Here are a few* bon mots *on the state of the language.* Milieu, Zeitgeist, Ennui: *these belong to a group called "the asshole*

words." People who use them are compensating for something deeper. Bolt: *a simple word, except in fabric stores when it becomes a* bolt *of cloth. Can't get enough of that.* Picaresque: *always a compliment, as in, "Who's my picaresque bastard?"* Babbittry, tautology, sophistry: *All mean the same thing, and it isn't important. Skip over them when you read. . . . Any-hoo, it's midnight. Women everywhere pissed at me. What did I do? All I ask is an average relationship and in return I get burning eyes and now own a cast-net at the bottom of the sea. The gang tried to cheer me up back at the No Name before I had to rush Coleman to the emergency room after a bar bet that somehow resulted in a small seashell getting pushed all the way up his nose until it went through the hole in his skull and fell down into the nasal cavity. I didn't even know what was going on until Rebel and Sop Choppy were shaking him upside down behind the pool table. They asked Coleman if it was helping, but he just said, "I can feel it rattling around behind my eyes." The doctors got it out with these incredible probes and sent him home with a bottle of painkillers. I can't tell you how old these overdoses are getting. Back to the hospital, where they pump his stomach, yielding the medicine, some corn chips, a half pint of Yoo-hoo, five-alarm chili, small chicken bones and a shirt button. Then they told me to take Gomer home. I said his name's Coleman, and they confided a little hospital slang:* Get Out of My Emergency Room. *So they injected him with a sedative, rolled him to the curb and told me, "Good luck." Good luck indeed. Coleman is an unwieldy shape without convenient handholds, and getting him in the trailer when he's dead weight is an engineering feat. I found an old block-and-tackle behind the dive shop and rigged it to the roof of his porch. Then I got a Styrofoam cooler, cut a U-shape in one side for his neck to go through and set his head in it. I poked some airholes in the lid and taped it on, so his face wouldn't get smashed in case he rolled. I tied the pulley to one of his ankles, and everything's going as planned. The ratio is down to fifty pounds. Suddenly, these dogs that roam our neigh-*

borhood pick up Coleman's scent and start nipping his arms. I yell for them to get away, but I don't want to drop the rope. That's when Coleman wakes up and finds his head entombed and freaks out. He grabs the white block on his head with both hands and starts running all over the yard screaming, which made the whole cooler hum. You know that Styrofoam hum? That part was actually funny. Then he's trying to get that dog whistle of his into his mouth, but he can't because of the cooler and all. Anyway, the rope is still tied to his ankle, which is how the porch roof got ripped down, and he finally runs full speed into the side of the trailer, knocking himself cold. He's sleeping like a baby now, but I'm completely awake, sitting here listening to my biological clock tick. I think I need to start working out. That's it, exercise. Perfect timing, too. The big annual footrace over the Seven-Mile Bridge is this weekend. That'll be my first workout. Tomorrow's word: roman à clef.

Part Three

16

Pssst!

Yeah, you. Over here. Remember me? . . . Maybe if I take my shades off. See? It's me, the narrator. Ex-narrator actually. I'm thinking of suing. I'm at the Slushie Hut. Not the one in Key West. The one in Marathon. They've got franchises all down the Keys now. Coleman turned me on to the place, told me to try the Torpedo Juice. Knew I shouldn't have listened. So I need to hurry—I wanted to talk to you before the replacement narrator shows up. He's not a bad kid, just a little on the green side. It's totally unfair. Listen, I'm not the only one upset about how this is going. Think I've been screwed over? You should hear the guy sitting next to me. What's your name again?

"Jack Buckley."

Tell them what happened.

"I won this charity auction in Tampa. You know, to have my name used as a character in the book. Paid a bundle, but it was for the art museum. So I show up today like they told me, all ready to go. Then at the last second they say my part's been cut."

Classy outfit, ain't it?

"I want my money back!"

Good luck.

"Who do I talk to?"

It won't do any good. My advice is to let it go and move on.

"No, really. They can't treat Jack Buckley like this! You hear me? I'm Jack Buckley! . . ."

Okay, fine, now stop talking. Have another Torpedo Juice. . . . See what I mean out there? This is the kind of organization we're dealing with. But that's not your problem; you just came here to have fun reading about the Keys. Which is what I wanted to talk to you about. Rampant development isn't the only thing ruining this place. We're also being overrun by world-class jerks. But you probably already got that picture. There are some more real quality people you're about to meet. Actually you've already sort of met them. Remember some of the news reports? The used-car dealers who filled the airbags with sand? That really happened. Then there was the roofing company that tells every customer they need a whole new roof whether they do or not. That one's not even a surprise. The new breed of Florida predators. Old folks, handicapped—doesn't matter. There's no out-of-bounds with these people. They come down to the Keys to celebrate their trail of misery. . . . What's that you have there, bartender? Another Torpedo Juice? No, I didn't order one. I was just waving my arm for emphasis. But since you already poured it . . . and you might as well get another one for my new friend here, Mr. Billingsly.

"Buckley!"

Whatever. Shut up. Those roofers I was telling you about? They're here, right in this bar. This is where they enter the story. They're the four guys down at the end in the seven-hundred-dollar yachting jackets. That's right, those dolts who've been loud and obnoxious all night. . . . Hey, fellas! Yeah, that's right, you over there! Nice way to treat people! Really nice code of living, you pieces of crap!

"You talking to us?"

You see any other assholes?

"Ignore him. He's drunk."

"No, I want to know what he said. . . . What did you say to us?"

"I said you bite! What do you think about that? Huh? What are you going to do about it, Mr. Big Shitty-Roof-Job Fuck?"

"That's it!"

"Good! Come on over here! I'm not one of your defenseless victims! I'll kick your— Ow! Ah! Oooo! Ow! No, not the ribs! Ow! Shit! Ow! . . ."

"Are you his friend?"

"I'm Jack Buckley! I'm Ja—"

Punch.

A few days ago

AN UNMARKED NEWS truck rolled slowly through a fresh housing development west of Fort Lauderdale, built right up against a bermed canal that was the final encroachment barrier on the edge of the Everglades. Developers were looking for ways to jump it.

Spanking-new houses marched in tight formation down the right side of the road, all identical three-story hurricane fodder with circular drives, screened pools, minimum setbacks. The stately arches over the front doors were quick plywood forms with thin stucco. Politicians signed off on stormwater systems that couldn't handle the runoff. The houses sold like crazy because the development had great shrubbery at the entrance.

This is today's South Florida—inland sprawl, shiny, crime-free, exclusive.

Not exclusive enough.

The TV reporter huddled with his cameraman for last-second ambush choreography. The van's side panel suddenly flew open and they jumped out commando-style, running for the house with the camera rolling, capturing that dramatic jiggling footage. Eyewitness 5 specialized in reporters asking bold questions of doors opened a crack. Then more questions of slammed doors. Sometimes they started asking questions of doors before people had time to answer, so the station would have stock footage in the can.

The man inside the house this morning didn't have a care. He was on the couch reading the paper, digging his toes into thick white carpet. A high-definition TV was on a reality show where people trick each other. His wife sat in a loveseat on the distant side of the living room with a *Parade* magazine, "What People Earn."

The man picked up the sports section. "The Marlins won again."

"There's a bus driver in Cleveland who makes fifty thousand dollars."

". . . This is Eyewitness Five correspondent Blaine Crease with another segment of 'Consumer Bloodhound.' We're at the home of Troy Bradenton, owner of Troy's Roofing Plus, asking the tough questions! Getting results! Just be glad we're on—Your Side! . . ."

"Did you say something, dear?"

"No," said the man. "I thought you said something."

"Where's that voice coming from? Sounds like someone's on our front porch."

"I didn't hear the doorbell."

"Neither did I."

The doorbell finally rang. *"What are you hiding from in there? . . ."*

His wife put down her magazine. "I'll get it."

She opened the door on the chain.

The reporter was facing his cameraman. "Make my head bigger."

"Yes?" said the woman. "Can I help you?"

The reporter turned around. "Oh, didn't see you. Good morning. . . . *Why won't you answer our questions! . . ."*

"Hold on a second." She called back into the house. "Honey, it's for you."

"Who is it?" He turned a page to agate scores.

"Eyewitness Five again."

"Let the dogs loose."

"Okay."

She smiled back through the crack. "Just be a moment."

"Thank you," said the reporter. She closed the door. *"How much blood money did this house cost! . . ."*

She walked through the living room and out the back door and opened a gate. She returned and sat down with her magazine.

The man grabbed the business section. The yelling on the front lawn eventually subsided. It went with the territory. He was Troy Bradenton, owner of Troy's Roofing Plus. The Plus was the extra money you paid. Troy was one of the most respected, looked-up-to men in the local contracting industry, because he was rich.

Troy's trucks made the rounds of the day-labor offices each morning, collecting winos to canvass suburban shopping centers with windshield flyers that shouted in big red letters: "Why throw away hundreds on needless roofing repairs? That little leak could be a modest shingle replacement. Don't get ripped off! For honest, dependable work, call Troy today!" There was a cartoon of a happy homeowner counting a big wad of money.

Troy's office was manned with phone answerers and salesmen whom Troy had personally trained with a slide show and a motto: "Every call is five thousand dollars!"

The Roofing Plus salesman went up on the prospective roofs and smoked or ate a Snickers, then came down and called out to the owner, "I need to show you something. Afraid it isn't good."

"What is it?"

The salesman scampered up the ladder in a hurry. "Take a look at this."

"Do I have to climb up there?"

"Yes."

The customer was now on the salesman's turf, clinging to the rungs. Bolts were deliberately loosened so the ladders wobbled. The older the customer, the better.

"See these rusty nails? The whole thing's shot. And the trusses are probably eaten." He made notes on a pad. "I'm sorry, but the law requires me to inform the building department."

No, it didn't.

The salesman climbed down. "Luckily, we had a cancellation. A truck can be here this afternoon."

Troy's fortune swelled, and he became more respected. Even Eyewitness 5 couldn't ruin it with their exposé footage. The next Friday was the last of the month. Sales bonus day. Tennis rackets, video cameras, water beds. The top three salesmen got the grand prize. Sailing trip to the Keys. Troy didn't have a sailboat, so they all got sailing jackets and spent the weekend in the bars.

After announcing the winners, Troy packed up his black Jaguar, slipped into his blue and white sailing jacket with red piping and kissed his wife goodbye.

"Another great month," said Troy.

"You earned it," said Mrs. Bradenton. "Have fun."

The Jag drove off.

17

A TV REPORTER stood on the edge of U.S. 1. He looked at the cameraman. "We ready?"

The cameraman pressed an eye to the rubber viewfinder. The reporter raised a microphone.

"Good morning. It's another beautiful day in the Florida Keys for the twenty-third annual Seven-Mile Bridge Run. . . ."

The camera panned across the sea of runners gathering at the eastern end of the bridge, which had been closed to traffic. A sheriff's helicopter skimmed overhead. The camera swung back to the reporter. A '71 Buick Riviera pulled up in the background. Serge and Coleman got out in shorts and T-shirts.

"I still don't understand what we're doing here," said Coleman.

"I told you. Women respond to fitness. This is the first day of my big new working-out phase. I've decided to totally dedicate the rest of my life to running excellence."

Coleman filled a sportster water bottle with two beers and began sipping through a Flex-Straw. "I heard you're supposed to gradually ease into these new workout programs."

"That's for the sheep. The only correct way to do everything is dive right in the deep end." Serge sat down and untied his sneakers, then retied them as tightly as he could.

Coleman put on knee and elbow pads. "You ever play sports before? I mean for real?"

"Was on the high school football team for part of a season, before I got kicked off."

"What happened?"

"We were playing our big cross-city rival, and as the final seconds ticked off the clock, I dumped a cooler of Gatorade on our coach."

"So what? I see that done all the time on TV."

"We were losing by four touchdowns."

A silver Infiniti pulled up next to them. A tall, handsome man got out wearing a gold silk warm-up suit. The man looked at Serge and Coleman and smirked. He took off the warm-ups to reveal matching silk shorts and an ultra-lightweight, breathable tank top. He leaned against the Infiniti and began a long menu of stretching exercises. Hamstrings, groin, calves, pulling his feet up behind him, twisting torso and neck.

Serge and Coleman had stopped talking and were now staring slack-jawed at the man like they were watching someone prepare shrunken heads. Then, just when they thought the protracted ritual was over, a whole new set of gyrations on another muscle group.

Coleman angled his head toward Serge. "Should we be stretching?"

"Absolutely not," said Serge. "I'm naturally limber and you're drinking beer, which is a form of stretching." He looked down. "I can't feel my feet."

"Maybe your shoelaces are too tight."

Serge sat on the ground.

The man finally completed his pre-race routine with a series of ankle and wrist bends. He reached back in his car and came out with a blood-pressure kit. He wrapped it around his left arm and timed himself on a stopwatch.

Serge rolled his eyes.

The man finished and smirked again at Serge and Coleman. Something under his breath that sounded like *losers*.

"Hey," said Serge. "For your information, we're going to win this race."

The man laughed.

"And you know why we're going to win? Because we don't care about winning! That's the big mistake you guys make. . . ." Serge waved toward the thousands of runners near the starting line. "This thing today is about more than winning. It's about something much bigger."

"What's that?"

"A souvenir T-shirt. You should see my collection."

The man gave a final look of disdain and trotted off.

"We better get going," said Serge. "It's almost post time."

The pair walked over to the assembling runners. ". . . Excuse me . . . excuse me . . ." Pushing their way through the pack, people running in place, thousands of independently bobbing heads. Men, women, children, a rainbow of brightly colored shirts, pieces of paper pinned to the fronts with four-digit numbers, except for the shirtless triathletes, who had numbers in grease pencil on shaved chests. ". . . Excuse me . . . excuse me . . ."

"Watch it!"

"Sorry," said Coleman. He took a sip from his sportster bottle and tapped Serge on the shoulder. "Why do we have to be in the front row, anyway?"

"Because of my strategy to win this race. Most people make the mistake of trying to pace themselves. The key is to go all out from the starting gun and open up an insane lead, completely demoralizing the rest of the field, which will be flooded with confusing emotions of worthlessness and suicide. Then, before the end of the first mile, they'll all stop running and go home."

Serge and Coleman finally made the front row, wedging themselves between entrants who gave them dirty looks.

The official starter stood by the side of the bridge. "On your marks . . ."

The runners stopped jogging in place and leaned forward in anticipation. Except Serge. He was down on the pavement in a four-point sprinter's stance, grinding the toes of his sneakers into the cement for traction.

"Get set . . ."

The starter raised his pistol.

Bang.

Serge took off running as hard as he could, making an intense, teeth-clenched face like James Caan in *Brian's Song*. Soon, he was all alone with a giant lead, still running breakneck. After a hundred yards, he veered over to the side of the bridge and grabbed the railing. A thunder of footsteps passed behind him.

A few minutes later, Coleman walked up sipping his bottle and leaned over the railing next to Serge. "How's the race going?"

"That's enough running for today."

Two hours later, the road was opened back up to traffic. A '71 Buick Riviera crossed the bridge.

Thousands of runners milled around the post-race celebration area full of corporate sponsor tents. Paper cups of sports drinks covered folding tables. Big banners with the Nike swish, wireless sign-up booths. People formed lines at blue Porta-Johns. More lines of late-finishers snaked up to the race organizer's table, where chest numbers were matched against printouts of official completion times. Then handshakes, certificates and souvenir T-shirts.

There was rustling down in the mangroves behind the Porta-Johns. Moaning and pleading.

"Oh, please! Stop! Dear God! . . ."

The owner of a silver Infiniti was pinned to the ground by Serge's knees. Another punch in the face. "Gimme the fuckin' T-shirt!"

18

Old Wooden Bridge Fishing Camp, cottage number five

Serge stared in the bathroom mirror, admiring his torn and bloody race T-shirt.

Coleman stared in the open fridge. "Only bottled water."

Serge returned to the sofa and opened a notebook.

Coleman plopped next to him and turned on the TV with the remote. The Style Channel, *Fashion Emergency!* "What's the plan?"

"Now that I'm completely physically fit, we move on to Phase Two." Serge flipped notebook pages to a freehand schematic. "I've chopped the islands up into grids, just like when they do population counts of the endangered deer. If Miss Right is within these quadrants, she won't get away."

Coleman hit the remote again. "You know, most of my married friends, it was a chance meeting. They were simply going about their lives, and one day true love just fell in their laps."

"No time," said Serge. "My clock is ticking."

"What about a mail-order bride?"

"They're always running up long-distance bills to Estonia."

Coleman idly gazed around the inside of the simple cabin. "I didn't know you were staying here. I didn't even know it existed."

"The Old Wooden Bridge? Absolutely! Couldn't stay anywhere else! Just look at her!"

Coleman looked. "So?"

"So your paradigm's all screwed up. The ideal motel isn't someplace in walking distance of the strip-joint district and sports bars and flashing signs for Jell-O shots."

"It's not?"

"Check that beautiful water and sky. You need to get in harmony with life. Turn the TV off."

"But without TV we'll die."

"Just try it."

Coleman clicked the set off. He clicked it back on. "I see what you mean."

"It's like we just went to Mass." Serge stood up. "Let's rock. . . ."

The '71 Buick Riviera chugged slowly south on Big Pine Key. Serge was driving with binoculars to make sure they didn't run over any deer.

"Can you drive better like that?" asked Coleman.

"I'm not sure. It's too dark to see anything."

Bang.

"What was that?" asked Serge.

"Used to be a mailbox."

Serge tossed the binoculars in the backseat and turned in behind Eckerd drugs. The Buick parked at a small, lime green building. MONROE COUNTY BRANCH LIBRARY.

A dark van screeched around the corner and skidded up two slots down from the Buick. The side panel flew open.

"Uh-oh."

"What is it?" asked Coleman.

Serge got out of the car. "Thought I told you guys to leave me alone!"

The cult people didn't answer. They were all wearing identical custom T-shirts with a big picture of Serge's face above a quotation: "I follow nobody."

"You've got to stop tailing me," said Serge. "I'm jumpy enough as it is."

They sat on the ground and listened.

"Okay, okay. I give up. How about this: We set regular weekly meeting times at the community center when I'll come by and give a talk. But the rest of the time you leave me alone. Deal?"

They nodded.

Serge and Coleman headed toward the library.

"You're really going to go talk to them?" asked Coleman.

"Actually, there are some things I've been meaning to get off my chest," said Serge. "An audience is an audience."

They walked inside the library. Someone waved from the front desk.

"Hi, Serge!"

"Hi, Brenda!"

"*That's* Brenda?" whispered Coleman, checking out the tall, curvy blonde with killer dimples and Cameron Diaz smile. "The one they were talking about in the pub who's hot for you? She's about the sexiest woman I've ever seen in my life!"

"Just a friend." Serge started walking toward the desk.

"Holy cow!" said Brenda. "What happened to your shirt! It's all torn and covered with blood."

"Tough race."

"You were in the big race today?" said Brenda.

"Was even leading for a while."

"How'd you finish?"

"Pretty good, but those stupid race officials disqualified me."

"Why?"

"I crossed the finish line in a Buick."

Brenda laughed. She reached across the desk and put her hand on Serge's. "You have a great sense of humor."

"He's getting married," said Coleman.

Brenda lost her smile and stood upright, then hid her disappointment. "Congratulations. I'm happy for you. Who's the lucky girl?"

Coleman explained.

Brenda laughed again. "You crack me up."

"I'm ticking."

She reached and squeezed his hand. "You're not the marrying type. We're two of a kind that way. I get off in a half hour. What do you say we grab a bite at Mama's? It's really romantic at night in the back garden."

"Too busy," said Serge. "You wouldn't believe my workload. Injustice, disease, answering fan mail from Stephen Hawking . . ."

"If you change your mind, here's my number." She wrote on the back of an index card.

"Thanks." Serge turned. "Coleman, where'd you get that six-pack? You can't drink in the library!"

"He can if he's with you," said Brenda.

Serge wandered off for special collections.

Coleman came up from behind with his beer. "What on earth are you doing?"

"Looking something up."

"No, I mean back there with Brenda. She wants you."

"No, she doesn't."

"Are you blind? Didn't you see how she was leaning? Touching your hand like that?"

Serge scanned bound volumes on a shelf.

"She even asked you out for a date. What more proof do you need?"

"That was only platonic." Serge pulled down a volume and flipped through nineteenth-century deed filings. "I'm not going to punish a woman for being nice like the other men do."

"What are you talking about?"

He replaced the volume and pulled down another. "A woman can't just be courteous in today's culture. She always has to worry about striking a perfect balance. If she's too distant, she's a bitch on wheels. If not, some guy starts driving by her house two hundred times a day."

"I don't understand you," said Coleman. "You're conducting this big search, and Brenda's right under your nose."

"Not my type." Serge found an entry in the deed book and marked it with Brenda's index card. "You wouldn't know it to look at her, but she's a real party animal." He stuck the volume under his arm and headed for the Xerox. "Appears ultimately conventional in the library setting, reserved clothes and demeanor. But run into her on the weekend and all bets are off. Hangs out at the clothing-optional Atlantic Shores and gets absolutely wasted. She's got a clit ring, which she's always losing, along with her cell phone and purse. . . . Coleman, where'd you go?"

Coleman was grabbing a bookcase for equilibrium. "Jesus, Serge. If you don't want her, I do."

"She'd rip you apart."

"Hopefully."

Serge raised the Xerox's cover and flattened the deed book on the glass.

Coleman finished his beer and threw it in the trash. He pulled another off the plastic ring. "Ever Xerox your balls?"

"Let me think a second," said Serge. "Uh . . . no."

He turned the deed book over and reached in his pocket. "I'm out of change."

"I'll be at the computers," said Coleman.

Serge went to the research desk and pulled a one from his wallet. "Excuse me . . ."

He hadn't noticed her before. The demure little woman. Thick glasses, hair pulled back, wrong clothes buttoned to the neck.

"What is it?"—not looking up from the novel she was reading.

"Uh . . . Xerox . . . dollar . . ."

She made change with one hand, never taking her eyes off the book.

Serge floated back across the library to the main desk, little cartoon hearts in a conga line around his head.

"Brenda . . ."

"Helllllloooo there, stranger." She leaned practically close enough to kiss.

"Who's that over there?"

Brenda tilted her head to look around Serge's. "Molly? She's new. Just started this week."

"What do you know about her?"

"As much as you."

"Think she'd go out with me?"

Brenda involuntarily giggled. She covered her mouth. "I'm sorry. I just don't see the two of you . . ."

"She's the one."

Brenda covered her mouth again.

"No, really. I think she's crazy about me."

Brenda composed herself. "Did she even look at you?"

"Not exactly."

"She doesn't look at anyone. Barely talks."

"I sense something. A soul-mate connection."

Coleman came over from the computers. "They blocked the porn on those things."

Brenda pointed across the room. "Coleman, what do you think of her?"

"Who? That goofy chick?"

"Serge thinks he's found his soul mate."

"I'm going to ask her out."

Brenda and Coleman watched Serge stiffly approach the reference desk. Coleman popped another beer. Brenda checked her watch. Ten minutes till closing. "Can I have one of those?"

It was a short, one-sided conversation on the other side of the room. Molly kept reading her book. The discussion ended without her ever making eye contact. Serge came back to the front desk.

They were prepared to console him.

"She said yes."

"You're kidding," said Brenda.

"I pick her up Saturday at seven."

Serge and Coleman left the library and headed toward the Buick. Coleman stopped and whispered something to Serge.

Brenda flicked off the lights and went to lock up the front. Serge and Coleman were waiting outside. She opened one of the doors. "Yes?"

"Coleman has something he'd like to ask." Serge poked him in the ribs.

Brenda waited.

Coleman looked at the ground and played with his belt buckle. "I was sort of wondering if you maybe, you know, might want to go on kind of a"—his voice dropped to inaudible—"double date?"

"I couldn't hear you," said Brenda.

"He wants to double-date," said Serge.

Brenda suppressed the gag reflex. Then she thought quickly. It was one step closer to Serge. "Sure."

"Really?" said Coleman. "I mean, great! Pick you up at seven!"

19

THIS IS EYEWITNESS five correspondent Maria Rojas outside the Miami courthouse, where we've just received word that the jury has reached a verdict in the infamous airbag-murder case. . ."

The courtroom was hushed. The jury foreman stood.

"As to the single count of negligent homicide in the first degree, we find the defendants . . . *not guilty.*"

Yahoo!

People jumped up from the defense table. Hugs and high-fives. Prosecutors quietly filled briefcases with papers. Someone jumped up in the audience. *"You call this justice!"* Bailiffs grabbed the man, the father of the Margate woman who hit a retaining wall on I-95 and went headfirst into the undeployed airbag full of sand.

Pristine Used Motors made a killing fixing up totaled cars and not telling. They bought the wrecks at auction. Head-ons, T-bones, cars sheared in two. Sometimes they welded together halves of different cars. The junks were practically free, the bodywork done by underpaid wizards with no green cards. They replaced grills, straightened fenders, somehow got them running and, most crucial of all, a nice wash and wax. Out on the lot they went, under the balloons and strings of flapping pennants, big orange numbers on the windshields: *$3999!*

One of the biggest profit zones was the airbags that had opened in the wrecks and were required by law to be replaced. But that was hundreds of dollars. Sand was free. Other dealerships moved more cars, but

Pristine Used Motors was all about the margin. The owners had become quite wealthy and now drove fancy luxury vehicles purchased from reputable dealers because they wanted to make sure the airbags worked.

The odds began to hit. One fatal head-on, then a second, paramedics peeling open cars with hydraulic jaws. Prosecutors took it to the grand jury. The owners were a step ahead. They had compartmentalized the operation, assigning only one mechanic to airbag duty in a locked garage after hours. Then, every other month, an anonymous tip to immigration, and the mechanics were somewhere in Tijuana when the D.A. came looking for witnesses.

The defense: Hey, we're as outraged as you are! The mechanics were working on commission and did this without our knowledge. They skated on the first case. Prosecutors weren't allowed to introduce the acquittal at the second.

The postverdict celebration spilled down the courthouse steps, where a red BMW full of scuba gear was waiting at the curb. The three defendants had decided in advance that they were going to let off some serious steam if they got out of this one. They jogged to the street and piled in the car.

A reporter ran after them with a microphone.

"Are you guilty anyway? . . ."

The BMW headed south.

THE '71 BUICK RIVIERA neared the eastern end of the Seven-Mile Bridge. It had a newly installed trailer hitch.

Coleman fired a doobie. "Where are we going?"

"Have to start preparing for the wedding."

"You mean the date."

"That's just a formality," said Serge. "We're meant to be together."

"Aren't you getting ahead of yourself?"

"That's the best place. I'm going to ask her to marry me."

Coleman took a big hit. "Can't believe I'm actually going on a date tomorrow."

"Weddings are incredibly complicated," said Serge. "A million arrangements to be made. That's why you have to get a huge jump."

"I thought the women took care of everything."

"Are you kidding? The guy has all kinds of responsibilities leading up to the big day."

"Like what?"

"Like you need to hurry up and buy all the shit your wife would never let you get after you're married. I've always wanted an airboat."

"Hey, look!" said Coleman. "A waterspout!"

"I see it," said Serge. "Out by the Sombrero Key light. It's a big one."

"Whenever I spot one, I feel special."

"Me, too," said Serge. "I'm going to make a wish."

"You can't make a wish on a waterspout. Only shooting stars and magic wells."

"That's just politics."

"The spout's gone," said Coleman. He took a big hit. "Now I'm bored."

"Let's look for irony."

"Okay." Coleman took another hit. "Does something I already saw count?"

"If it's worthy."

"Then I'm calling it. That store back on Stock Island. Paradise Guns and Ammo." Coleman licked two fingers on his right hand and slapped Serge hard on the forearm.

"Ow," said Serge. "My turn. Let's see. . . . Over there. That Suburban with the PROTECT THE MANATEES specialty license plate."

"What about it?"

"It also has a Florida Cattlemen's bumper sticker: EAT MORE BEEF."

"So?"

Serge licked two fingers. "Save the seacows, fuck the land cows." Slap.

"Ow."

"Here's Pigeon Key coming up." Serge pointed north at the remains of the old Seven-Mile Bridge running parallel to the new span. "That gap is where they blew it up in *True Lies*, just before Schwarzenegger reached down from the helicopter and pulled Jamie Lee Curtis out the sunroof of a limo plummeting into the sea. And over there's where the van transporting a drug smuggler crashed through the railing in James Bond's *Licence to Kill*. In that same movie, then-Florida Governor Bob Martinez makes a two-second Hitchcock cameo as a short-sleeve guard when Timothy Dalton gets out of his cab at Key West International. . . . Coleman? You all right? . . ."

Coleman was giggling. "Pussy Galore . . ."

"Different movie. Low-water mark of Bondian humor."

Coleman couldn't control his snickers. "It's just too funny. Know what I mean? How do they ever think up that stuff? See, her first name is, you know, and like her last name . . . Zow! Good weed! . . ."

The Buick neared the end of the bridge and the shore of Vaca Key.

"What's that new building over there?" said Serge.

"Which one?"

"That big one on the shore. When did they start putting it up?"

"Looks like it's already up." A swarm of workers in white caps painted the outside with rollers.

"It's a monstrosity," said Serge. "It'll wreck my views from the Seven-Mile."

They came off the bridge. The Buick pulled into a strip mall on U.S. 1 and parked in front of Marathon Discount Books.

Ting-a-ling.

"Hi, Serge."

"Hi, Charley. You got the new Keys history book in? That Viele guy?"

"Right in front of you."

"Coleman, come here."

"What?"

He swept an arm over the local-interest section. History, fishing, zoology, cooking, oversized pictorials—all faced out. "Charley values tradition. Let's go to the bathroom."

Charley watched skeptically as they walked to the back of the store, squeezed into the tiny, one-person rest room and closed the door.

They came back out. "Cool," said Coleman. "Autographed literary posters while you take a leak."

"The chains don't understand anything."

Charley rang up Serge's book. 'Twenty-six, fifty-seven."

Serge tapped the counter. "Listen, Charley, do you think maybe you could put it on the tab?"

"Serge!"

"Charley!"

"No way! I was going to talk to you about that. You still haven't paid from last time."

"The only reason I didn't pay was because that motel took all my money."

"Why'd they do that?"

"I stayed there."

"That's how it works."

"No, I mean they ripped me off. All the cottages were taken so they gave me the last converted unit over the office. Except after they closed the office and turned off the AC downstairs, all the heat rose and the little window unit couldn't handle the load. It turned into a furnace. I called the after-hours number, but they refused to listen."

"Serge, you know the Keys. You *never* rent the converted unit over the office."

"I want to believe in people."

"Take the book. It's too much aggravation."

"You sure?"

"I'm sure I won't get paid."

"What about that aerial photography book. I've also kind of had my eye on—"

"Serge!"

"Okay, just this one. I'm boning up on my pioneer research. I built a kiln the other day."

"Ceramics?"

"No, the old charcoal kind they used to have in the back-country."

"Those were huge," said Charley. "Where'd you build it?"

"In my mind." Serge held up the new book. "I plan to reenact the life of Happy Jack, tracing the rum route from Sugarloaf to the Old Customs House that he and his merry band used to navigate in handmade sailboats. This book will help me faithfully re-create the experience down to the last primitive detail."

"But the route took days, even in good weather."

"That's why I'm getting an airboat." Serge casually flipped through his new history book. "What's with that humongous building going up on the north end?"

"The house?" said Charley.

"That's a *house?* I thought it was a new resort or sportsman mega-outlet."

"Donald Greely's new place."

"That's Greely's place?" said Serge. "I heard he was building, just didn't know where."

"Who's Greely?" said Coleman.

"You've never heard of Donald Greely?" said Serge.

Coleman shrugged and picked up a mini-booklight, flicking it on and off.

"You don't remember all those news stories about Global-Con? The telecom-energy conglomerate that cooked the books and wiped out all those retirement accounts?"

"No." The booklight stopped working. Coleman put it back. "Must have been watching another channel."

Charley sat down in a chair behind the counter and leaned back with his hands behind his head. "Heard it cost twenty million. Put the yacht in his lawyer's name and parked it out back."

"But how'd he get clearance for that kind of construction?" said Serge.

"Bribes. But they couldn't prove anything. Even had people come in at night and cut down mangroves. . . . Serge, your face is all red. . . ."

* * *

THE BUICK PULLED away from the bookstore and continued east on U.S. 1.

Coleman had his hand out the passenger window, flying up and down in the wind. "Where to now?"

"Get my airboat."

"I didn't know they had any airboat places down here." Coleman lit the roach he'd left in the ashtray. "Just on the mainland by the swamp."

"DEA seizure auction in Islamorada. Saw my boat on the internet."

"What are you doing now?"

Serge was looking ahead and squinted hard, stiffening the muscles in his arms. "Concentrating on life so it doesn't pass me by. From time to time I force myself to strip away all rationalization and gaze into the naked essence of existence. This is my truth stare."

Coleman exhaled smoke out the window. "I have my own truth stare. I look in the opposite direction and hope it goes away."

"Aaahhhhh!!!"

Coleman jumped. He picked his roach up off the floor. "What happened?"

"Found myself in the utter horror at the moment of birth. Let me tell you, it was no picnic. . . . Lower the roach—here comes a sheriff's car."

The Buick passed a green-and-white cruiser heading the other way. Deputy Gus was behind the wheel, popping Ibuprofen and chasing with coffee.

"Gonna eat your stomach lining," said Walter.

Gus scanned the side of the road for cars from the all-points bulletins.

"Why won't you tell me how the Serpico nickname started?" said Walter.

"There's not much to tell."

"I'll help you look for cars if you tell me the story."

"You should be looking anyway. It's your job."

"Why won't you tell me? I've heard it from the other guys."

"Then you don't need me to repeat it."

"How about just the embarrassing parts?"

GUS WAS A twenty-six-year-old rookie in 1985. Some officers get lucky and stumble over big cases. Gus had one crash into him—literally. Happened three A.M., a Saturday morning. Gus sat parked in his cruiser outside Overseas Liquors. The dome light was on. Gus filled out a report. The suspects were in the backseat on the other side of the mesh screen. Two of them, that is. The other six had already been carted away by backup. Gus nabbed them all single-handed—the "Overseas Eight," as they became known in law-enforcement circles.

Overseas Liquors has the coolest 1950s neon signs in all the Keys. Red and aqua. It also has one of the few basements, if you want to call it that. Four feet deep, hewn into the limestone; you have to stoop over the whole time. The access door is an unassuming square panel on the bottom of the wall behind the cash register that looks more like a cabinet. They keep the liquor stock down there. Once upon a time, they also used to rent cheap rooms in the back of the bar over the basement. If you go in the basement today, there's a diamond-shaped grid of bare alarm wires under the ceiling boards. The reason is the Overseas Eight.

Gus was the nearest deputy when the call came in. He found the store's front door unlocked. His flashlight beam worked its way along a shelf of vodka bottles, then across the room to the dust-covered liqueurs. Nothing. Until he looked over the counter. A facedown body hung halfway through the basement access. He pulled his service revolver and crept around the counter. He got down on one knee. The flashlight and pistol were together in his hands to form a single unit. He shined over the body and through the opening into the basement.

The dispatchers told Gus to slow down; they couldn't understand him. He was hyperventilating. ". . . Seven bodies. Maybe eight."

Squad cars arrived. And kept arriving, until the whole shift was there. The laughter wouldn't quit as the last of the passed-out burglars was dragged from the building. One of the tenants in the back of the store had sawed through the floor. Burglary wasn't intended. He didn't even know there was a basement. Sometimes he just started drinking and liked to saw stuff. Word of the discovery quickly spread on the bum telegraph. Dark figures converged from all directions. At its peak, twenty-nine people were crammed in that basement. Most grabbed as many bottles as they could and fled, but eight decided to party on the spot, like rats finding tasty poison in a fake cheese wedge.

Gus knew he'd never hear the end of it. That's why he didn't mind staying behind in the parking lot to start the report. He flicked on the dome light and scribbled to get a difficult pen to write. That's when the Camaro doing a hundred on U.S. 1 flew through the guard rail. It scattered a row of news boxes and clipped the nose of Gus's cruiser before wrapping itself around a cement light base. Gus saw the ejected driver, and jumped from the cruiser. His feet went out from under him and he slammed to the ground, sending up a fine white cloud. Gus stood and dusted himself.

The parking lot was full of patrol cars again. This time the day-shift commander was called in from home. Then an evidence team from Key Largo and federal agents with latex gloves, who collected ruptured cocaine packs that had spilled from the Camaro's blown tires.

"Of all the dumb-ass luck!"

"That idiot's going to get a drawer full of commendations for sure!"

He did. Bunches of them. Plaques and ribbons and shiny medals, one for each politician who got to shake Gus's hand in a separate ceremony for the newspaper photographers. Not that Gus's nonactions were particularly heroic, but his colleagues knew what the rookie didn't. Funding for the War on Drugs was based on volume of press clippings. Thanks to Gus, Monroe County shot up forty-seven budget positions.

After all the headlines, Gus became too valuable for patrol duty. They made him the department's token liaison with the multiagency state and federal task force fighting the war on South Florida's flank. That way they could have a local face at the press conferences to ensure all the hometown media ran the story on the great work of the multiagency state and federal task force.

And darned if Gus didn't do it again!

Everyone was thinking cocaine back then, watching for big, rusty foreign-flagged mother ships beyond territorial limits offloading to supercharged go-boats. Profits were so insane that the kingpins began sending shotgun waves of vessels at the overwhelmed Coast Guard. At least a couple had to make it. Then word came. A Liberian freighter expected off Fort Lauderdale any day now. Time to ship Gus to Key West.

He was assigned a low-probability scag investigation on the north end of White Street. This was before heroin came back. If he got lucky, he might collar a dime-bag peddler.

Gus tried all kinds of disguises but nothing worked. Sometimes suspects would smile and wave at Gus as he sat in his car outside a motel. Another time a bum walked up as Gus reclined on a bench, dressed like a tourist.

"You're a cop, aren't you?"

"No."

"The people you want are on the other side of the motel. Room fourteen."

"How do you know that?"

The bum opened a thrown-away paper sack and popped half a conch fritter in his mouth. "I'm homeless, not stupid."

The next day, a bum waved flies off a half-eaten crab cake. A red Maserati pulled up to the motel. A man in khaki slacks went in room fourteen. He came out with a pillow.

"I'll take that."

The man turned and noticed the bum for the first time. He'd never seen one before with a gun and a gold badge hanging around his neck.

Just like that. Nine ounces of heroin. Another round of commendations and photo ops. The "Serpico" business started.

Gus was promoted to the Narcotics Abatement & Deterrence Squad, an elite commando unit that went in with black uniforms, face paint and flash-bang grenades. He was the lead agent through the back door of a Mexican restaurant moving brown tar in south Miami. Gus's body armor had been rated to stop most tactical rounds. It didn't do as well when they tipped four hundred pounds of metal kitchen shelves on you. In the movies, he would have flung the racks aside and yelled, "You're under arrest!" In reality, this is what Gus said: "Ow, my back."

The publicity photos got even wider play because they were from the hero's hospital bed. Rehabilitation was slow and incomplete. They offered Gus a desk job, but that would have meant . . . a desk job. He might as well sell shoes. Gus eagerly accepted a demotion back to deputy and took an assignment in one of the Keys' smaller substations. Years went by and pounds went on. Instead of commendations, his personnel file swelled with reminders about the department's fitness guidelines. Gus never complained.

If only he could make another big case.

20

A '71 BUICK RIVIERA crossed the bridge to Upper Matecumbe and hit backed-up traffic. People in orange vests waved them into a field used for ad hoc parking.

Serge and Coleman walked across the grass until they came to a large array of flea-market tables. Stereos, computers, TVs, Japanese cameras, German binoculars, video equipment, night-vision goggles, parabolic directional eavesdropping microphones.

"I love DEA seizure auctions!" said Serge. "Coleman, where are you? . . ."

"I'm tired of walking," said Coleman, trying out a personal treadmill until Serge yanked him off. The tables ended, giving way to the big stuff in the back of the field near the water. Motorcycles, sports cars, boats.

Serge stopped and put a hand over his chest. "She's beautiful!"

There it was, like a mirage, radiating shafts of energy. Serge quietly approached and stroked it like a newborn. An eighteen-foot Diamondback fuel-injected 454 horse crate with the Stinger 2.09:1 gear reduction. "I've wanted one of these ever since 1967!"

"But you were just a kid," said Coleman.

"That's when *Gentle Ben* first aired on CBS. The coolest show: game warden tooling around the Everglades in an airboat, his son rescuing a cub from the evil hunter Fog Hanson, the bear growing into a lovable giant that helps the family out of complex situations."

Someone stepped up next to Serge. A squat older gentleman with a cattle rancher's hat, bolo tie and stubby cigar that he was more chewing than smoking.

"That's *my* airboat!"

"It is?" said Serge.

"Gonna be. I scare away the others with my bold initial bids. Leave 'em pissin' in their boots."

"No kidding?" said Serge. "I scare 'em away with my ridiculously tiny bids." He made a big grin.

The man studied Serge with tight eyes, then broke out laughing and slapped him on the shoulder. "I like you, boy!"

They looked at the airboat again.

"Mighty fine," said the man.

"Yes, she is," said Serge.

"I love the War on Drugs!" said the man. "Get more great shit since the forfeiture laws. They can take anything they want, not even due process."

"Of course there's due process," said Serge. "This is America."

"What are you, *for* drugs?" said the man. "Suppose you want proof, too."

"Proof's bad?"

"We're talkin' drugs, boy!"

Serge smacked a fist into his other hand. *"Goddam the pusher-man!"*

"ACLU technicalities!" The man removed his cigar and spit something on the ground. "But we've fixed *proof*. Here's your new proof: A dog barks. Then they take whatever they want."

"Barks?"

"This one family was ridin' through Pasco County, and they had like ten thousand in cash when they got pulled over for a busted taillight, which may have been a busted taillight or maybe they looked a little too brown. Anyway, car's clean as a whistle. So they bring the German shepherd over and he barks at the money, which may have been cocaine residue or maybe he had heart worms. Didn't matter. 'Well, we're just gonna have to take that drug money away from you folks.' Then they let 'em go. In the old days, that kind of arrangement would be called a bribe. Now it's forfeiture. And if they want their money back, they have to hire an attorney because the law says the burden's on *them*."

"Doesn't seem fair," said Serge.

The man started laughing and slapped Serge on the shoulder again. "It ain't! . . . Ha ha ha ha . . ."

Serge: "Ha ha ha ha . . ."

"Hoo." The man pulled out a hanky and dabbed his eyes. "You ain't thinkin' of bidding against me, are you?"

"Lookin' like I'm fixin' to get a hankerin' to."

A final slap. "I like you, boy." He walked away with his handkerchief.

Serge and Coleman headed over to the folding chairs in front of a small stage. They grabbed seats in the first row. Serge fanned himself with bid paddle number 142.

It was a furious auction, heated bidding, everything selling fast. Corvette, Indian motorcycle, forty-foot Scarab.

Coleman looked over his shoulder at the man in the cattle hat three rows back. "How much money you got?"

"Hundred dollars," said Serge.

"That's all?"

"It'll be plenty."

The auctioneer moved on to item thirty-two. "A beautiful Diamondback airboat. Only fifty hours on the engine. Who'd like to start the bidding?"

"Ooooo, me, me, me, me!" Bid paddle 142 waved frantically. "I bid a *big one*!"

"A thousand dollars?"

"A hundred," said Serge.

"Sir, this is a very expensive boat."

"That's my bid."

The auctioneer shrugged. "The bid is one *hundred* dollars."

Booming laughter from the rear. Another bid paddle went up over a cattle hat. "Fifteen-thousand!"

The crowd gasped. Intimidated bidders lowered their paddles.

"... Going once, going twice, *sold* for fifteen thousand dollars!"
"Looks like you lost," said Coleman.
"Got any more weed?"
"I thought you didn't do drugs."
"I don't."

Serge and Coleman hung around to the bitter end. Workers folded chairs and unplugged microphones. Winners paid with guaranteed checks.

A man in a cattle hat hung out the driver's window of a Bronco, backing up to an airboat.

"Congratulations!" said Serge. "Let me give you a hand hitching that."
"Mighty neighborly of ya."

Serge set the clasp and hooked the chains. He waved toward the driver's mirror. "You're all set!"

Then Serge walked up next to a DEA agent in dark sunglasses. He leaned his head sideways and whispered.

The Bronco started pulling out of the lot toward U.S. 1.

"Freeze!" yelled the agent. "Turn the engine off and step out of the vehicle!"

"What in cotton-pickin'—"

They brought the dogs over.

Barking.

The agent reached in the airboat. "What's this?" He held up a joint.

"That ain't mine!"

"Unhitch it," said the agent.

"I just bought it!"

"It's government property now."

"Excuse me," Serge said to the agent. "You haven't cashed his check yet or filed the title papers with the state."

"So?"

"So under Florida law ownership hasn't officially transferred. It never *stopped* being government property."

"What's your point?"

Serge raised paddle number 142 and smiled. "I was the next highest bidder. I'd like my boat now, please."

"Who's robbin' this train?" yelled the man in the cattle hat. "You sumbitches give him that fuckin' airboat, I'm writin' my congressman! . . ."

The agent watched calmly from behind dark glasses. The noisy little dust devil in a cattle hat stomped in an angry circle. "I'll have your badges! . . ."

The agent never moved. He spoke out of the side of his mouth to a colleague: "Give him the boat."

"Thanks!" said Serge.

"God*dammit!*" The man threw his hat on the ground. "You know who you're trying to screw? You're just a bunch of stupid fuckin' hired thugs! . . ."

Serge tapped the agent on the shoulder. "I think you're overlooking something."

"What's that?"

"While the airboat remained government property, it was hitched to the Bronco when the narcotics were found, which means under the forfeiture law the truck had become part of the smuggling continuum."

The agent began nodding. "I wouldn't mind driving one of those."

The man in the cattle hat stumbled backward against the truck and spread his arms like a human shield. "No! Not the Bronco!"

"WOOOOOOO-HOOOOOOOO!"

The gang from the No Name Pub was up on the Bogie Channel bridge. An airboat raced toward them.

It zipped under the bridge. They ran across the road to the opposite rail as Serge came flying out.

"Yaba-daba-doooooooo!"

". . . You should have been there," said Coleman, leaning against the bridge railing. "It was priceless. They had to pry the Bronco's keys out of the guy's hands. . . ."

The airboat made a tight turn in the middle of the pass, sending up a sheet of water. It whizzed back under the bridge.

Everyone ran across the road again. The airboat zoomed down the channel toward Spanish Harbor, Serge's shouts becoming mere peeps in the distance.

"He sure seems happy," said Sop Choppy. "Look at him go."

Serge turned her around one last time near the viaduct and came back, idling through the man-made inlet at the fish camp. The gang trotted down the embankment for a better look. Jerry the bartender ran a hand along the polished wooden propeller with steel tips. "I wish *I* had an airboat like this."

"Why's that?" Serge hitched the Diamondback to the trailer line.

"Gentle Ben," said the bartender. "Ever since I was a kid . . ."

Serge reached in his pocket. He worked a key off his chain and tossed it to the bartender.

"What's this?" asked Jerry, catching it against his shirt.

"Spare key. Take it whenever you want."

"I couldn't—"

Serge started cranking the boat onto the trailer. "Why not?"

"Because it's yours."

"Jerry, I like you."

"You do?"

"I'm not into possessions, just moments. And anyone who's into *Gentle Ben* deserves a moment."

"You sure?"

"Take her anytime." Serge threaded the trailer straps. "Don't even bother to ask. Just don't wreck it."

"All right," said the bartender. "But I have to do something to repay you."

"No, you don't."

"Yes, I do. Where are you going to keep it?"

"I don't know. Probably parked at Coleman's trailer."

"Don't do that," said Jerry. "It's a hassle every time you want to go out. You need to keep it near the water."

"I don't have a place like that."

"I do. Over on No Name Key. Bought a parcel way back. Was going to build but waited too long and construction went out of sight with the freight charges. I camp there sometimes. It's got this break in the mangroves that I smoothed out to launch my skiff. Not a proper ramp, but serviceable."

Serge pulled a strap hard. "It's a deal."

"Why don't we go out there now?"

Serge and Jerry drove off. They tied up the airboat on the edge of the flats and returned to the No Name Pub, where the petite woman in sunglasses was sitting alone again at a table in back.

A man walked over and grabbed the chair across from her.

"I got your call," said Anna. "What made you change your mind?"

"Did some thinking."

"You're really going to help me kill him?"

"I liked your brother a lot. This has to stop."

"You got an idea?"

"A couple. But I'm going to need a little time to sort this out. Until then we can't be seen together."

"What do I do?"

"Don't do anything. Just stay in your cottage until I call. And keep that Trans Am hidden."

21

Friday night, six o'clock

A WHITE JAGUAR with a blue tag hanging from the rearview pulled into a handicapped slot in the lower Keys. Four men in yachting jackets got out.

"Here we are," said Troy Bradenton, looking up at a big wooden sign with words written in nautical rope. LOBSTER TOWN.

Troy and the roofing salesmen could have found their way to the bar blindfolded.

The lounge at Lobster Town was their favorite place in all the Keys. Heavily lacquered wood with brass portholes peering into saltwater aquariums full of coral and clownfish. It was also the annex of a great restaurant, where they could order food over to the drinking side and not miss the babe action. Only thing missing was the babes. Wouldn't have made any difference if they were around. Troy and the boys had what might be termed an indelicate touch. They decided if their pickup lines weren't going to work, then they *really* weren't going to work. The construction site principle: Next best thing to scoring was impressing the other guys with how rude you could be.

The beer came in frosty mugs and soon the food. A waitress set up a folding stand behind their stools. It held a big round tray ready to collapse under their orders. Giant lobster tails with all the fixin's! They strapped on the bibs, grabbed nutcrackers and tiny forks, and went at it like pigs with thumbs. "Can we have more bread?"

Lemon mist and shell splinters filled the air. The waitress returned with an extra loaf.

"You have such lovely blond hair," said Troy. "Does the rug match the curtains?"

The waitress left quickly. The gang cracked up.

"Hey, guys," yelled the bartender. "Want another round? Happy hour's almost over."

Troy looked at the ship's clock over the bar. Two minutes till seven. "Set 'em up!"

Sugarloaf Key Community Center

ONE OF THE classrooms was full of people in Serge T-shirts. But where was Serge? This was the first scheduled meeting he'd called since they had accosted him outside the library. They quietly stared at the clock over the chalkboard. Two minutes till seven.

They heard running footsteps out in the hall. The door burst open and Serge marched to the front of the room. He dove right in, pacing and gesticulating, lost in thought like a field-goal kicker who blocks out the crowd. ". . . And then Neo took the red pill so he could see the truth. He was the Chosen One, ready to save the city of Zion. . . ."

A man in the front row raised his hand. "So we should smash this Matrix?"

Others nodded. *"Smash the Matrix!" "Smash the Matrix!"*

"What are you talking about?" said Serge.

"The army of Morpheus. We're ready to join!"

"Smash the Matrix!"

"No," said Serge. "It's just a movie. I told you that at the beginning. We're here to talk about my favorite flicks."

"Oh, that was a *movie*."

"Weren't you listening?" said Serge. "Now I want to discuss the oeuvre of Paddy Chayefsky. *Network* is one of the all-time greats, number sixty-six on the American Film Institute List. . . ."

A hand went up. "We should smash this Network?"

"Smash the Network!" "Smash the Network! . . ."

Serge banged his forehead on the blackboard. He spun around. "Everyone, shut the hell up!"

The room stopped. All eyes on Serge. "That's better." He began pacing again. "You want a Matrix? Okay, I'll give you a Matrix. There's an elaborate world of illusion out there designed to control all facets of our daily lives, but it's not made of computer codes. It's made of words. . . ."

They glanced at each other with concern.

"It's the calculated packaging of your entire life, a twenty-four-hour reality manipulation on a hundred channels. Cell phone minutes that set you free, instant stuffing that makes your thankless family sit up and take notice, deodorant soap that turns a shower into a life-affirming epiphany . . . Enough already! I say, Kill the advertisers!"

"Kill the advertisers!" "Kill the advertisers!"

"Are you nuts?" said Serge. "It's just advertising. If you can't see that, you're already toast. In fact, I *want* to be manipulated. If I have to watch a commercial, at least don't give me the same dreary heartbreak I see every day on the street. Briefly balm me with cheerful, slow-motion footage of an orange slice spraying the air with droplets of that citrus goodness, and I'm ready to face another day! . . . No, the real problem is lawyers. Scum-sucking, double-talking, soul-selling leeches with legs. Everything that comes out of their mouths is a feckless belch of duplicity, their entire culture communicating in a regional accent of velveteen, overly qualified, triple-couched, can't-nail-it-to-the-wall-like-Jell-O, circumlocutious fibbery. If you and I walked around nozzling this kind of fiction on a daily basis, we'd all be friendless, divorced and fired. But our justice system rewards their morning-noon-and-night press conferences pointing nine different directions away from the bloody client: 'It was drug smugglers, the ex-boyfriend, the "Alphabet Soup" killer, Satanists in a windowless van that was the dark shade of a light color, and I vow never to rest as I travel the globe in my personal search for the real killer!' And I'm thinking, yeah, well, you might want to save your frequent-flyer miles because I think I caught a glimpse of the 'real killer' today. He was sitting next to you at *the fucking defense table!* . . . There's only one Shakespearean solution. Kill the lawyers!"

"Kill the lawyers!" "Kill the lawyers! . . ."

"Are you insane? Lawyers are good! We need lawyers! Be more skeptical. Analyze those attorney-bashing sound bytes by multinational corporations and the harems of far-right congressmen they buy up on the cheap like dazed crack whores chanting, 'I take it in the mouth for jury-cap lobbyists.' Listen carefully when Fortune Five Hundreds say the greatest threat is runaway verdicts that only enrich *those greedy trial lawyers*. Then ask yourself: Why does every vested interest that wants us to get rid of *our* lawyers have entire floors reserved for their own legal teams? . . . No, lawyers are the common man's last defense against the deep pockets. *It's the corporations, I tell you! . . ."*

The audience was indecisive. A woman in the front row slowly raised her hand. "Except the corporations are good?"

"No, they truly are fucking evil. But a necessary evil. We're capitalists, after all, which means we benefit from man's worst instincts, as opposed to Communists, who suffer from man's best instincts. Who's *really* to blame? The media! Those self-righteous hacks with their *liberal bias*. Kudos to you, Fox News! You tell us what the 'media elite' refuses to: that we need to get all wadded up and distracted over gay marriage so we don't notice the next massive transfer of wealth scheme. No wonder the rest of the world hates us. Half of America hates the other half. The country's tearing itself down the middle, and these latter-day pimps of yahooism are swinging sledgehammers at the wedge. . . ."

In the next room, deputies Gus and Walter dismissed their class of juvenile delinquents. They were on their way down the hall when a raised voice caught their attention. They stopped and looked in a doorway.

"So now you don't know what to believe," said Serge, "and that's exactly what you *should* believe. To borrow from Firesign Theater, Everything You Know Is Wrong. Because the biggest danger is the people who believe Everything They Know Is Right. That's the key to personal growth: Identify your firmest, most self-comforting beliefs, then beat the living shit out of them and see if they're still standing. The key to stagnation? Worry about other people's beliefs. There's an invisible war of self-interest between the ends of the spectrum, and we're foot soldiers caught in the crossfire. That's why I'm a moderate, from the extremist wing. Because the middle is where the good people are. It's where hope is. And it's where the truth lies. But what is this truth? For starters, it's don't listen to someone whose only credentials are that he's standing at the front of a room. And that's the truth."

Serge trotted out the door past the deputies.

Gus looked at Walter. "There's something not right here."

22

Saturday. 5:30 P.M.

Deputy walter st. cloud arrived at the sheriff's substation for the evening shift.

Gus was already at his desk reading paperwork that Sergeant Englewood had just handed over from the day side.

Walter put a fresh filter in the coffee machine.

Englewood snapped a briefcase shut. He was thinking about mashed potatoes. "See you guys tomorrow."

"'Night, Sarge."

Walter came over to Gus's desk while the coffee perked. "What are you reading?"

"The reports both of us are supposed to read."

"Can I ask you a question?"

Gus continued reading. "What is it?"

"The stories really don't bother you?"

"I don't pay 'em any mind."

"Good." Walter rolled up a chair and sat down. "Because I just heard this great new one I wanted to ask you about."

Gus closed his eyes for an extended blink.

"A waitress told it at the Key Deer Café. I was having pie at the counter, and she was talking to these other people, but everyone was listening. It was the time you didn't know about one of the department's surprise urine tests, but your wife did because she was doing the major. So the night before she got you to let her draw on your penis. You couldn't see what she was doing because of the angle. And she draws this goofy Mr. Bill face. You know: 'Mr. Sluggo's going to be mean to me!' The next morning you hear about the test and try to scrub it off, but she used one of those indelible Sharpies that lasts for like a week. There was no hiding it from the monitor who has to witness you give the sample. And he blabs to everybody!"

"What's your question?"

"Well, there wasn't really a question. I just wanted someone to tell it to."

Gus went back to reading.

"I think it's my favorite one so far."

Gus looked up at his partner.

"You know what I mean," said Walter. "Actually it's quite terrible. I'm going to be back over there at my desk."

It was quiet again in the substation. The fax started.

Gus got up and grabbed the bulletin.

"What is it?" asked Walter.

"Remember that APB the other day on a brown Plymouth Duster? They just linked it to a charred body found in the Everglades. A witness also spotted it at Dade Corners. Ohio plates but no number."

"Heading this way?"

Gus taped the new bulletin to the wall next to his desk. "That's how it's looking."

SEVENTEEN MILES DOWN U.S. 1, two combat boots walked through a wrecked-car graveyard on Stock Island. "U Pull-It Auto Parts." The boots stopped behind an '81 Fiero. Hands in leather gloves twisted a screwdriver, removing a Delaware license. The plate went inside a shirt. The boots walked back out the barbed-wire gate to the side of the road and a brown Plymouth Duster.

One hour later

FOUR PEOPLE CONDUCTED predate rituals at four different locations in the lower Keys.

Serge was in his fishing cottage. His finest tropical shirt lay ironed and flat on the bed. He sprayed cologne and gargled and applied contingency layers of Speed Stick. The borrowed Buick sat outside. The plan was to arrive at Coleman's trailer with an hour cushion in case Coleman needed to be revived, then swing over to pick up Brenda by 6:50 and knock on Molly's door at seven sharp, to lay the reputation groundwork as a dependable husband.

Serge sang as he trimmed ear hair.

"I'mmmmmmmmmm coming up, so you better get this party started. . . ."

Molly stood rigid at her bathroom mirror, hair pulled back tight and pinned in a bun. She had a dark-blue blazer over a light-blue shirt buttoned practically to her chin. She auditioned pairs of granny glasses.

Another apartment, another mirror. Brenda threw her head forward, that gorgeous blond mane hanging down in front of her face. She flung her head back, the locks making the return flight and falling over her shoulders for that sexy tossed look. She clipped a belly-button ring in her bare midriff. That was for Serge's benefit, definitely not Coleman's. . . . Coleman! Jesus! There was no way she could face this sober. Time for date-priming. She grabbed her giant plastic Sloppy Joe's cup of rum and Coke.

Serge drove up to Coleman's trailer, pressed the doorbell. No answer.

He knocked.

Still nothing.

Serge stepped back from the trailer to appraise the situation. He noticed the soles of two shoes at the edge of the roof. He cupped his hands around his mouth. "Coleman!"

Coleman slowly sat up with disheveled hair.

"What the heck are you doing up there?"

Coleman looked around. "I don't know."

"Hold on. I'll get a ladder."

They ended up in the living room. A bong bubbled.

"What are you doing?" said Serge. "We have to get ready for the date!"

"I *am* ready," said Coleman. "See?" He opened the top of a camouflaged hunter's cooler next to him on the couch: Everclear, Red Bull, ice, cups, mixers. "Dating is cool!"

"You're going to make her Torpedo Juice?"

"Yeah," said Coleman. "But now I'm thinking of leaving out the energy drink. Don't want her too alert."

"And look at how you're dressed!"

"What?" Coleman examined himself. Cut-offs and an old T-shirt from a shop on Duval: *My other car is your mother.*

Serge paced and talked to himself.

"Man, are you nervous!" said Coleman. "Have a seat and relax."

Serge dropped onto the couch next to him. "I can't relax. Too much is at stake. Look, my hands are all clammy."

Coleman leaned over the bong. Smoke filled the cylinder.

"Will you stop smoking dope! You'll fall asleep in your food and fuck up the date."

"Have to smoke to get ready for the show."

"What show?"

Coleman clicked the TV with the remote. "Bob's coming on."

Serge perked up. "Bob?"

"Take your mind off your worries."

Serge and Coleman settled into the couch and folded their hands in their laps. A catchy theme song began; they swayed with the music.

"*. . . Absorbent and yellow and porous is he . . . Sponge . . . Bob . . . Square . . . Pants! . . .*"

"I wonder if Gary the Pet Snail's in this episode," said Serge.

"My favorite is Patrick the Starfish."

Serge heard clomping on the trailer's rotten flooring. A miniature deer walked between the couch and the television and disappeared into the kitchen.

Coleman exhaled a hit. "His name's JoJo."

SpongeBob jumped up swimming from the ocean bottom, blasting right out of his pants.

Serge pointed at the screen. "Notice how his pants are tumbling slow motion back to the sea floor. That's a deliberate reference to archival NASA footage of the Saturn V adapter ring between the first and second stages. Don't tell me something deeper isn't going on here."

Coleman repacked the bong. "When I'm high, I pick up stuff about Jesus."

They became engrossed. It was a double-header. And Gary was in the second show.

A commercial came on. Serge checked his watch. "We're late!"

Brenda was sitting buzzed on her front steps. She drained the dregs of her Sloppy Joe's cup and checked her watch again.

A Buick screeched up like a jailbreak.

Brenda stood, slightly unsteady. "Where have you been?"

"Get the fuck in the car!"

They raced across the island.

"When was the last double date you were on?" asked Coleman.

"I don't know. Seven, eight years ago? I think it was the Davenports back when we lived on Triggerfish Lane."

"I remember that one," said Coleman. "What a disaster! Enough to make you never want to go on another."

"There's no way two in a row can turn out that bad." Serge skidded up to an apartment building. He jumped out and ran around to the trunk. Inside was Serge's dating kit: a dozen roses in a four-dollar vase, set of pipe wrenches, an out-of-order sign.

A polite knock on the door of unit 213. Molly silently came out and locked up.

Serge produced the flowers from behind his back. Molly accepted them with embarrassment. She noticed a price tag.

"Whoops," said Serge, snatching the vase back and peeling the sticker. "The price-gun guy must have gotten it confused with a really cheap one. Shall we? . . ."

THE BUICK BLAZED down U.S. 1, hopping bridges in quick succession. Summerland, Cudjoe, Sugarloaf. It was dead in the front seat. Serge kept glancing over every few seconds. Molly's eyes stayed fixed ahead, hands stiff-arming the dashboard.

The backseat was New Year's Eve, Mardi Gras and Lollapalooza. Coleman had the contents of his camouflaged cooler in play. Brenda sloshed some of her drink on both of them and laughed. Coleman winked. "You cool?"

"Am I what?"

Coleman put his thumb and forefinger to his lips.

"You mean do I get high?" Brenda downed her drink. "Fuckin' A!"

Smoke curled its way into the front seat. Molly maintained her grip on the dashboard. They crossed the Saddlebunch Keys and pulled into the hottest new restaurant west of Marathon. Lobster Town. The line spilled out the door. Serge had a reservation. They gave him a coaster that would blink when their table was ready.

Coleman staggered up and tugged Serge's shirt. "I think I'm getting a little too messed up to dine 'n' dash."

"We're not going to skip out on the bill."

"But we don't have money for this kind of fancy place."

The coaster began blinking. "This way," said a waiter.

Their table overlooked the Gulf. Serge held Molly's chair. Brenda looked at Coleman, already seated and tearing open a packet of saltines.

Another waiter came by. "Would anyone care for a cocktail?"

Coleman's and Brenda's arms flew up. Serge turned to Molly. Her first words in a tiny voice: "Zinfandel." Serge to the waiter: "Zinfandel. Coffee for me, and a glass of ice on the side."

"Ice water?"

"No, a glass of ice."

"You want ice coffee?"

"No. Coffee. And a glass of ice. I have to control the temperature myself."

Drinks arrived, their orders taken. Coleman and Brenda held giant pineapples in their laps with extra-long straws. Serge spooned ice into his coffee and chugged it dry.

"Uh-oh," said Coleman.

"What?" asked Brenda.

"Serge drank coffee."

"Coffee's good for me," said Serge. "Remember when the chicks from the band Heart did those coffee ads? Before the dark-haired one got into the doughnuts? Said it picked them up and calmed them down at the same time. That's what it does for me! I love Heart! *Barra-cuda! Da, da-da-da, da-da-da, da-da-da, da-da-da, da-da-da, DOW-DOW!* . . ."

"Here we go," said Coleman.

Serge turned to Molly. "I see you're admiring my shirt. It's my favorite, the one the state's toll collectors wear. All these great old Florida scenes and postcards . . ." He touched various parts of his chest. ". . . Orange groves, beach balls, sailfish, names of famous roads and stuff. The turnpike, Sunshine Skyway, Dolphin Expressway, Yeehaw Junction. You know Yeehaw Junction, don't you? The crossroads in the middle of nowhere with the historic Desert Inn. The women's rest room has a statue of an Indian brave in a real loincloth that's rigged with this trip wire, so if you lift it, a loud alarm goes off in the bar, and everyone's laughing when you come out, and then you have to explain what you're doing as a man in the ladies' room. Only used to be able to get these shirts if you worked in a tollbooth. I wanted one so bad that I applied for a job. On the first day they gave me the shirt and stuck me in one of the booths, and when they weren't looking, I ran off into the woods."

Four lobsters arrived. The evening averaged out: Molly didn't say a word, Serge didn't stop. He pulled a notebook from his back pocket. "Okay, just a few routine questions. Nothing to worry about. Belong to a religion? Doesn't bother me if you do, as long as it's not one that says to stop thinking and be loud about it. How do you want the kids raised? Policy on in-laws? Are you a neat freak? Ever called Miss Cleo? What about Ted Williams being frozen upside down without his head?"

No answers.

More pineapples arrived.

Serge made marks in the notebook. "I'll just pencil my best guesses and we can go back later and change them if you need to. Any childhood diseases? Ever seen a psychiatrist? No big deal if you have. I've gone, but it wasn't my idea. . . ."

And so it went. The waiter finally came and laid the bill facedown on the table.

". . . One last question," said Serge. "Will you marry me?"

Molly's eyes bulged. But they had on some of the other questions, too, and Serge took it as an encouraging sign. He closed the notebook. "Get back to me on that last one when you're ready."

Coleman turned the bill over. "Two hundred dollars!"

"Plus tip."

Coleman yanked the napkin from his collar. "I have to take a leak."

Serge pushed his own chair back. "I'll go with you."

They stood at the sinks. Serge splashed water in his face. Coleman uncapped his graffiti pen. There was a sign: EMPLOYEES MUST WASH HANDS. Coleman wrote, *Why can't we wash them ourselves?*

Serge splashed more water. "I think she likes me."

Coleman went to a urinal. "How on earth are we going to pay for dinner?"

"Like this." Serge splashed water on his shirt.

"What are you doing?"

Serge kept splashing water until he was drenched head to foot. "Taking care of the bill."

They left the rest room. Serge pulled an out-of-order sign from his waistband and hung it on the men's room doorknob. "Coleman, go keep the women company. I'll just be a minute."

People cleared a wide path as Serge dripped his way to the maître d' stand. "Call the manager!"

A man in a well-fitting suit arrived. He pulled up short at the sight of Serge. "What the—?"

"You need to turn off all the water in this place."

"Who the hell are you?"

"One of your customers. I was just in the men's room. You got a main break. . . . What are you looking at? You have to shut the water off right now!"

"We can't shut the water off. This is our biggest night. . . ."

"We're still talking. You've got three minutes tops before she starts flooding, which means backed-up sewage. . . ."

People in line looked at each other and murmured.

"Lower your voice," said the manager. He waved one of the waiters over. "Shut off the water. The valve is by the main loading door. The white one. There should be a wrench leaning against the wall. . . . What are you waiting for?" The waiter ran off.

"I'm a plumber," said Serge. "I mean if you have your own, I perfectly understand. But it's pretty straightforward. I got some tools out in the car. Can have you back up in five minutes."

The man gave Serge a look like someone was trying to screw him. "And what exactly will this cost me?"

"Cost you? Oh, no, I wouldn't think of . . . well, okay. I've just had a wonderful evening here with my friends. Going to tell everyone I know about this place. Yes, sir, best food in all the Keys! Why don't you just comp our meals and we'll call it even?"

"That's it?"

"Throw in fifty for our waiter. He was incredible. Don't let anyone steal him from you."

"Deal."

"Be right back."

Serge ran out of the restaurant and returned with tools. He went in the rest room and slouched against the door, staring at his watch. Five minutes later, he emerged and removed the out-of-order sign.

The manager rushed up. "So?"

"Good as new!" Serge headed back to the table.

"What the hell happened to you?" said Brenda. "You're soaked."

"Gave 'em a hand with a plumbing problem."

"He's always helping people," said Coleman.

Serge held Molly's chair again as they got up. Brenda started getting up, too, but misjudged a number of things and took three off-balance steps backward before landing on her butt like a child in a playpen. "Whoa! Those pineapples! . . ."

"I do it all the time," said Coleman. "Let me help you."

They worked their way toward the front door, the manager shaking Serge's hand hard as they went by. "Thank you so much. Please come back . . ."

They passed the packed lounge, newcomers waiting with cocktails and nonblinking coasters. Four men in yachting jackets were halfway in the bag. Troy Bradenton buttonholed a passing waitress. "Hey, baby, ever kissed a rabbit between the ears?" He stood and turned his pockets inside out. The woman stormed off. The salesmen cracked up. One of them noticed something going by the lounge's entrance.

"Look at that soaking-wet asshole!"

"What's *his* problem?"

Serge kept walking.

"And get a load of his date! Did dork school just get out?"

Serge froze. Hair stood up on his neck. He slowly turned to face the roofing salesmen.

The quartet got off their stools to form a united front. Troy stepped forward. "What are you going to do about it, drip on us?" He looked back and smirked at the others.

Molly was standing behind Serge. He couldn't see her, but he could sense her discomfort like static electricity. He bit his lip and resumed walking out of the restaurant.

"That's right," yelled Troy. "Run away, tough guy!"

They got to the parking lot, and Serge called Coleman aside. "I need you to do something for me. . . ."

There was a tiki bar on a landing down by the water. Serge asked the women if they wouldn't mind waiting.

"What is it now?" said Brenda.

"I forgot to explain some plumbing things. And Coleman has to help. We'll just be a minute."

Brenda stumbled down the staggered terrace of railroad ties. "You said you'd just be a minute last time." She slipped on the edge of a step and went down, then popped up and wiped her kneecaps. "I meant to do that. . . . Come on, Molly, let's get a drink." Molly followed, looking back over her shoulder. Coleman was walking toward the restaurant's entrance, but Serge had split up and was sneaking around the back side.

TROY BRADENTON CALLED over a waitress. "Do you have a mirror in your pocket?"

"Why?"

"Because I can see myself in your pants! Ha, ha, ha . . ."

They noticed Coleman standing in front of them.

"Look, it's one of Jerry's kids!" said Troy. "The telethon's over, beat it!"

"I'm not sure," said Coleman, "but I think one of you dropped a whole bunch of money in the parking lot."

"What are you talking about?"

"A big pile of twenties behind a Saab. Some fifties, too," said Coleman. "Guy in a white jacket just like yours. Didn't you just come in here a second ago? . . ." Coleman stood on his tiptoes and looked around the lounge. "Maybe it was somebody else." He was acting a little drunk, except he wasn't acting. "Or maybe it was me." He patted his own pockets, then turned and started weaving back toward the front door.

Troy ran up and grabbed Coleman's shoulder from behind. "No, it was me."

"Great. I'll show you where the money is."

Troy winked at the guys. They gave him three big thumbs-up.

Coleman wandered back and forth across the parking lot. Troy grew impatient. "Where the hell is this Saab?"

"I could have sworn it was right around here. Wait, no, it's on the side of the building, just around that corner."

Troy followed Coleman into the darkness. "I didn't even know they parked cars back here."

Serge stepped out of the shadows. "They don't."

The man exhaled with frustration. "Not you again."

Another classic cultural misunderstanding. Troy had a completely different context of confrontation. Preliminary bravado, then everybody gets ready and starts boxing and the best fighter wins. You know, rules. He started taking off his jacket to teach Serge a lesson, and Serge grabbed his testicles. Troy hit the dirt so immobilized he couldn't even cover up when the kicking started.

"You mean little bastard!" Kick. "Where does that kind of cruelty come from?" Kick.

Down at the tiki bar, Brenda's head started lolling around in her neck socket. She tried lighting a cigarette by the wrong end, but the flame kept missing. Luckily, the bartender had just taken an alcohol-awareness class. He realized what was happening and rushed over to figure out how he was going to fuck her. Molly got up and went looking for Serge, tracing his steps around the back of the building. As she got closer, she heard voices. She put her hands on the wall and peeked around the corner.

"You evil piece of shit!" Kick. "Nobody talks about my Molly that way!" Kick.

She quickly pulled back. A hand went to her mouth. "Oh, my!" Molly scurried back to the waterfront, trotting in an odd sort of way that made it appear as if her knees weren't bending, like the Church Lady might run.

When she returned to the tiki hut, the bartender was doing calculus: Brenda's weight vs. the distance to his car. Molly jerked her off the stool.

Coleman squatted near the ground. "I think you killed him."

Serge was bent over, grabbing his legs and panting. "Huh? What are you talking about?"

Coleman stood up and nodded. "He's dead all right. Must have been the head kicks."

"I just wanted to teach him a lesson."

"Serge, we gotta get moving. Anyone can just come walking around that corner."

"Okay, you wait here with him. I'll get the car."

Molly kept tugging Brenda's arm to move faster. "Come on!"

"Let go of me. I need to lie down."

Molly dragged her friend toward the corner of the restaurant.

"You got his ankles?" said Serge.

"Ready when you are," said Coleman.

Troy thudded into the bottom of the trunk.

Molly and Brenda appeared in front of the car. Serge slammed the trunk shut. "Oh, there you are! We were just coming to get you." He opened the passenger door and gestured suavely.

"Your carriage awaits."

23

U.S. 1

A POLICE SIREN ripped through the starry night, island to island.

A large crowd had gathered on the side of Lobster Town. A sheriff's cruiser pulled into the parking lot.

Walter grabbed a clipboard. "There goes our quiet evening."

The deputies got the onlookers back, and Gus began unrolling yellow tape to protect the crime scene. Other units arrived. Specialists took photos and video and poured plaster to make casts of tire imprints. There was a large quantity of blood and a shoe, but no body, just drag marks up to where the tire tracks stopped.

Walter canvassed the crowd. Nobody saw anything. He found the manager.

"And you say nothing unusual happened tonight?"

"Only a plumbing leak." The manager remembered that one of his dishwashers was smoking outside by the garbage cans and heard something. "Alfonso! Get over here!"

A thin young man in a hairnet walked up. He was trying to grow a mustache. ". . . No, just crashing sounds, things breaking, shouts."

"And you didn't go look?"

"The parking lot always sounds like that."

Gus rounded up three drunk roofing salesmen he'd found staggering down by the tiki hut, calling into the night for their missing buddy. They now leaned with their backs against the patrol car for balance.

"When did you last see him?"

"Someone found a bunch of money in the parking lot and he went to claim it."

"Was it his?"

"Not really."

An evidence tech with surgical gloves dropped a muddy Sebago Clovehitch into a clear bag.

"That's his shoe!" yelled one of the salesmen.

"Don't go anywhere," said Gus. "I have more questions."

Walter was directing a forensic photographer to a just-found pattern of blood spray on the side of the building. "Right over here." Revolving blue and red lights swept across the dark wall. Gus walked up. "I think we have an ID on the victim." Walter looked at his partner, then at the red splatter. A camera flash went off. Walter started laughing.

"You find this funny?"

"No, I'm sorry. I'm still thinking about the Mr. Bill drawing on your dick. You'd laugh too if you saw the photos."

"Photos?"

"The waitress at the café had printouts. Your wife took pictures while you were asleep."

"Printouts?"

"From the internet."

* * *

HEADLIGHTS PIERCED THE fog and a salt mist that hung over the road under a harvest moon. The Buick Riviera sailed back up the Keys shortly before midnight.

Serge's face glowed green from the instrument panel curled around the steering column in that vintage Buick design. He drove casually with one hand. His right arm was over the seat back, slowly inching toward Molly, who was bunched up against the opposite door. He addressed the passenger compartment in general: "Figured we'd top off this great evening with a nightcap at the No Name. What do you say?"

Nothing from Molly. Odd sounds from the backseat. Serge looked in the rearview, but didn't see anyone. "Hey, what are you kids doing?" He turned and craned his neck for a look. "Uh-oh."

Dark islands passed beneath. Serge kept glancing across the front seat at Molly. What an angel! Almost looked lifelike with that green instrument patina on her face. Serge pretended to yawn. He stretched and extended his arm farther across the seat back. Molly made herself as flat as possible against her door, like people in a prehistoric sci-fi movie when the T. Rex sticks its head in the cave but can't quite reach them, and then, for some reason, one of the minor characters carelessly steps forward and the dinosaur bites him head first and drags him out kicking and screaming.

"I won't bite," said Serge. "Why don't you come a little closer?" He patted the vinyl bench seating between them.

Molly stayed put.

"You're going to fall out of the car like that," said Serge. "This thing's pretty old. I can't vouch for the latches."

She released her grip on the door and sat stiffly in the seat. Serge's fingers tiptoed toward her. They both stared ahead, cresting another bridge with a rhapsodic view across the night water, twinkling lights from homes along the western bank of Ramrod. Serge's hand slithered. Easy now, almost there. The sounds from the backseat grew louder. Serge peeked out the corner of his eye. His hand was now hovering over Molly's shoulder, Neil Armstrong looking for a place to land on the Sea of Tranquility. The Buick started rocking on the springs. Serge eased his hand down. Two inches, one inch. Steadyyyyyyyy . . .

Molly flinched slightly but didn't pull away when Serge's hand gently settled onto her shoulder. He released a breath of relief. *Contact light, the Eagle has landed.*

Brenda erupted in the backseat: "Oh, my God! Oh yes! Fuck me! . . ."

"Yikes!" said Serge, snatching his arm back and lunging for the radio dial. "How about some music?"

"Oooooo, love to love you, baby, oooooo, owwww, ohhhh! . . ."

Serge twisted the dial again.

"I can see paradise by the dashboard light . . ."

Another station.

"Get down with the boogie, say, 'Uhhh! Hahhh!' Feel the funk y'all! Let it flowwwwww . . ."

He turned the radio off and sat back with a nervous smile.

The Buick stopped rocking. It was quiet again. Not for long.

"Stop the car!" yelled Brenda. "Going to be sick!"

Serge skidded onto the shoulder as he'd done a hundred times for Coleman. Brenda's door flew open.

Serge turned around in his seat. "Coleman! Be a gentleman! Hold her hair!"

THE SCREEN DOOR at the No Name Pub flew open.

"Serge!"

Serge ran down the line of stools high-fiving. He turned around at the end. "Molly, this is the gang. The gang, Molly. You already know Coleman. Not pictured is Brenda, who's hanging out of the car."

Coleman and Molly grabbed a table in the pool room. Balls clacked; the seven went in a side pocket. Pizzas came out of the kitchen.

Serge went over to the juke and pushed coins in a slot. "Let's see. So many to choose from. Can't make a mistake. Have to pick the perfect tunes. Tunes are everything. Tunes affect emotions. Tunes change behavior. The wrong tunes could ruin everything. Which one, which one, which one? Let's see what we've got here. . . ." His finger ran down the glass. ". . . She's waiting by the phone, he needs to be free, she'll stab you in the back, he's cryin' on the inside, her body's a danger zone, his heart's on fire, she needs more lovin', his watch is set to cheatin' time, she never dances anymore, he wants one last chance, she's takin' a midnight train. Someone dies at the end of that one. In that song, it's always raining. In that one, it's not raining but the sun don't shine. The horn section in that one gives me the nagging sensation I've forgotten to study for an exam. That one reminds me of costly errors in foreign policy. . . ."

"Pick a song!" yelled Coleman.

"Okay, okay! There, that's a good love song." Serge hit B-12. Six times.

He rejoined them at the table and sat sideways, appreciating the layout of the room, tapping along with the music.

"Saturday night's all right for fighting . . ."

Molly studied his content profile. But all she could think about was the horror from the side of the restaurant. And just because some idiot had insulted her, like they always did.

"Yes."

Serge didn't hear her at first.

"I said yes."

Serge turned. "Yes what?"

"I'll marry you."

Everyone at the bar startled at the outcry.

"Yaaaaaahhhhooooooooooooooooooo!!!! . . ."

Serge jumped up and began doing the twist, singing along with the juke. *". . . Sat-ur-day! Sat-ur-day! Sat-ur-day! . . . Sat-ur-day! Sat-ur-day! Sat-ur-day! . . ."*

The commotion drew the owner out of the back room. "Serge! Get the hell off the pool table! What are you thinking?"

Serge hopped down. He did the moonwalk, the hand jive, the chicken dance, the Iggy Shuffle. *". . . Sat-ur-day! Sat-ur-day! . . ."* He threw imaginary dice, dunked an invisible basketball. He fell to his knees and threw his arms toward the ceiling.

"She said *yessssssss!!!!!!*"

Sop Choppy walked over to Coleman. "What's going on?"

"I just got laid."

"No, I mean Serge."

"Oh, I think he's engaged."

"No kidding?"

The already festive mood inside the pub became reckless as the news spread. People bought rounds of drinks, toasted, got loud, went by to shake Serge's hand. They pulled the newly betrothed couple out of their chairs and got them to dance. At least Serge was dancing. Molly just sort of stood there while Serge pogo-sticked in a circle around her.

MOLLY GOT UP on her tiptoes to give Serge a quick peck goodnight.

The Buick raced south on U.S. 1, Serge's head out the window in the night breeze. He came back inside. "This is the best day of my life!"

"I got laid."

"That's right, you did! Congratulations! When was the last time?"

"Last time what?"

"Sex. You have had sex before, right?"

"Oh, sure."

"When?"

"All the time. Yesterday morning, twice again in the afternoon."

"I mean with someone else."

"That doesn't count?"

"Not exactly."

"Then that would be"—Coleman began counting on his fingers—"the first."

"You're kidding!"

"Nope."

Serge slapped the steering wheel. "Hot damn! Now we *really* have to celebrate. But what can we do? It has to be extra special. . . ."

Coleman made a suggestion.

"You read my mind."

Moments later, Coleman stared through hot glass at rotating corn dogs. "What would we do without convenience stores?"

"You know who can't go to convenience stores?"

"Who?"

"Barbra Streisand."

"That's right. She's a prisoner."

They carried their haul out to the car in five plastic bags and drove back to the trailer. Soon it was spread across the floor of Coleman's mobile home. A Looney Tunes marathon came on. They toasted with Slurpee cups.

"What about Brenda?"

"That's right. We should probably bring her inside before we forget."

"Next commercial."

They each grabbed an armpit and dragged Brenda up the steps. Coleman lovingly tucked her into one of the two single beds in the back of the trailer.

He stood and smiled.

Serge pointed. "What about JoJo?"

Coleman looked at the tiny deer in the corner. "How can he sleep standing up like that?"

"The people at the post office do it all the time."

"I'm going to put him in the other bed. Someday I want to get him some little clothes."

Coleman set the deer on its side and began tucking him in.

"What's all that red stuff on the blankets?" said Serge.

"What?"

"What do you mean, 'what?' You got ketchup everywhere."

Coleman looked at his hands. "I always forget napkins." He wiped them on his pants, then smiled at Serge. Serge smiled back. Nothing could ruin this evening. They watched the beds like proud parents.

"They're so peaceful," said Coleman.

"Life is good."

24

Sunlight streamed into the trailer. Brenda's eyelids fluttered.

She rolled over and stuck her head under the pillow. "Oh, no."

One of her top ten hangovers. She remembered all of them. Her brain throbbed, her mouth felt like something had molted in it. Somehow she found the strength to raise her head. "Hey, this isn't my room. Where am I?"

Her head fell back on the pillow and her eyes closed. It gradually came to her. Coleman's trailer. Then another delayed response. Something she'd just seen.

She opened her eyes again. Over on the other bed. What the hell is that sticking out from under the blanket? Looks like a deer head.

It *is* a deer head. And the blanket has a bunch of red stains. Brenda thought it was real, a local copycat of *The Godfather*. Probably someone after Coleman for a drug debt.

"Jesus! That's some seriously sick shit." She laid her head back down and closed her eyes again.

After a moment, she realized her arm was resting against something. Her hand felt along a large form in the bed next to her.

Brenda's eyes sprang open.

Just after daybreak, a Buick Riviera sped west on U.S. 1. Serge had already been up for two hours, reading the paper, watching early news on TV, anxiously checking out the windows to see when night would end, standing over Coleman and Brenda in bed, waiting for them to wake up so he'd have someone to talk to, but they never did. He finally gave up and hopped in the Buick for a solo breakfast run.

Serge cleared the bridge on the return trip to Ramrod Key. He sipped orange juice and peeked inside the warm brown sack in his lap, taking a deep breath of McMuffin magic. The Buick made a left after the Chevron station.

Serge pulled up to the trailer in a super mood. He got out of the car with a sack of fast food and thoughts of Molly.

Brenda flew out the front door. *"Ahhhhhhhhh! Ahhhhhhhhh! Ahhhhhhhhh! I fucked Coleman! I fucked Coleman! I'm going to be sick! . . ."*

Serge smiled and tipped an invisible hat as she ran by. "Good morning."

". . . I'll never drink again! I swear to God! . . ." She grabbed the trunk of a sapwood tree and bent over retching.

Coleman was sitting up in bed with clumped hair when Serge entered the room. JoJo looked around from the other bed. Serge held out the bag and smiled. "McMuffins."

Coleman grabbed an ashtray off the nightstand and excavated for roaches. "Where's Brenda?"

"Out in the yard." Serge sat on the foot of the bed and passed a sandwich.

"Thanks." Coleman took a giant bite, chewing with open mouth. "Maybe I should get married, too. What do you think?"

"Absolutely," said Serge. He jerked a thumb over his shoulder. "If you hurry, you can propose right now before she leaves. That way, last night's memory is still fresh."

"I think you've got something." Coleman stuffed another bite in his mouth and threw the blanket off his legs.

Serge set his own sandwich on the bed and savored the unwrapping process. He heard the front door creak as Coleman went outside. He took a bite and closed his eyes. "Mmmmmm. Unbelievable! Never ate anything so good in all my life!" He opened his eyes and looked at JoJo. "That's because I'm in love. Everything they say about it is absolutely true. Food tastes better. Colors are more vivid. The air is like candy gas. . . ."

Serge and JoJo turned toward the racket coming through the front wall of the trailer.

". . . No! Fuck no! I wouldn't marry you if it meant eternal life! I renounce what happened last night as the most repulsive experience in human history! It was worse than eating maggots! I'd rather be buried alive in shit! . . .

Serge and JoJo went to the door. People were now on the front steps of trailers along both sides of the road. Brenda stood several feet in front of Coleman. She had stopped yelling and was now repeatedly spitting at him as fast as she could work up saliva. Of course she was too far away, so she dropped to the ground and began packing dirt balls with shaking hands.

Serge and JoJo walked up next to Coleman. "What's going on?"

A dirt ball hit Coleman in the chest. "I think she needs more time."

Brenda collapsed facedown in the yard and kicked her legs. *"I just want to fucking die. . . ."*

The neighborhood watched as Brenda eventually got up and staggered off down the street.

"You know, I have this weird sensation," said Serge. "Like we're forgetting something."

Brenda stopped in the middle of the road and spread her arms wide in front of a dump truck. The truck hit the brakes and drove around her. She stumbled away crying.

"I know what you mean," said Coleman. "I have the same feeling. But what can it be?"

"I'm not sure. It's been bothering me all morning."

They looked at each other, then at the sky, then over at the Buick's low-riding trunk.

A RED FLAG with a diagonal white stripe snapped in the morning breeze.

The first dive boat of the day was returning. It rode a pair of silver pontoons and had a large, flat deck for all the scuba tanks and tanned people casting aside wet-suit tops. They were pumped from the morning run, endorphins, laughing, cracking beers, holding hands apart to represent the girth of barracuda and moray eels. The boat idled down an oolite canal cut through Ramrod and docked behind the Looe Key Reef Resort.

The "resort" label was a little dated, considering all the newer, sterile behemoths that had gone up in the last twenty years. More of a raggedy old Florida roadside motel, which was better. It had survived to become the last genuine diver's joint. The back doors of the rooms opened right onto the dock; out the front doors was the tiki hut on the shoulder of U.S. 1. It was a big hut, as tikis go, and it was legendary. Every seasoned diver had done time there. The bar was always cranking, night, day, hurricane evacuation.

Three used-car salesmen climbed off the morning boat and headed for the thatched roof. They were the only ones still wearing wet-suit tops. The one worn by the chief partner of Pristine Used Motors was black and turquoise. He wore the wet-suit top for two reasons. First was the stud factor. He began sending free drinks to the women around the bar, and they began coming back. He decided to deliver the next drinks in person. He got off his stool with a rumrunner in each hand and slimed over to a pair of sorority sisters from Georgia Tech.

The women reluctantly accepted the glasses.

He hopped on the stool next to them. "Fuck me if I'm wrong, but haven't we met before?"

That was the other reason for the wet-suit top. Drinks easily washed off.

A '71 BUICK RIVIERA emerged from a side street on Ramrod Key and pulled onto U.S. 1.

Coleman looked out the passenger window as they passed the Looe Key Reef Resort. "Why don't we just dump him in the mangroves like everyone else does?"

"Getting too crowded," said Serge. "I found a better location."

The Buick flew through Islamorada and Key Largo, back over the bridge to the mainland, Coleman bugging him for food the whole way.

"You just had a McMuffin."

"I can't taste it anymore."

Serge acquiesced and hit a drive-through in Florida City, then raced straight into the heart of the Everglades.

Coleman reached in his Arby's sack. "Want a sandwich?"

"Why'd you get five?"

"It was five for five dollars."

Serge turned off the Tamiami Trail and onto a dirt road with a chained-shut gate. He hopped out with a pair of large bolt-cutters, glanced around and grabbed a link of the chain.

Coleman walked up with a soda cup. "Where are we?"

Serge leaned into the cutters. "Government research center." The chain snapped. He pushed the gate open.

The Buick drove down the deserted road. Coleman's nose twitched. "It stinks."

"It's supposed to."

The road opened into a clearing. It looked like an abandoned movie set. Broken-down vehicles, rusty refrigerators, steamer trunks, fifty-five-gallon drums, some partially submerged in a pond. Coleman saw what looked like shabby mannequins draped in a variety of positions. They parked and Serge opened the trunk.

Coleman came up beside him. "I still don't know where we are."

Serge pulled a pair of hankies from his pocket. He covered his nose and mouth with one and handed the other to Coleman. "Necro-studies."

"What?"

"The cadaver farm."

"Cadaver? . . . You mean those mannequins are really . . . Oh, gross!"

"Forensic detectives face a particular problem in Florida. Decomposition is too aggressive, so the regular textbook decay tables are useless. Had to establish a local lab to come up with their own figures. The Everglades are ideal. Perfect breeding ground for everything that can ravage a corpse. Heat, moisture, bacteria, more insects than you can count. Some with little pincers and mandibles that bore right through the skin, others that get in through body cavities. It's amazing how they know right where to go. Rodents, crabs, snakes. Oh, and birds. Don't forget them. They go for the eyes."

Coleman steadied himself against the car. "I don't feel so good."

Serge reached in the trunk and grabbed wrists. "Get his ankles."

They hoisted Troy Bradenton out of the Buick, lugged him twenty yards and set him down behind the bumper of a tireless Impala. Serge retrieved a crowbar from the Buick and began working on the Impala's trunk. "A body that lasts three months in the Virginia winter might be down to the wishbone in weeks. . . ."

Serge put his weight into the bar. The trunk popped.

Coleman jumped back. "There's already a body in there! . . . And some stuff's moving—" His hand flew to his mouth.

Serge poked the second corpse with the crowbar. He bent down and grabbed Troy's wrists again. "Coleman, give me a hand. . . . Coleman?"

Coleman was holding his stomach. His cheeks bulged.

"Stop fooling around!"

Coleman reached for the ankles. "What if somebody sees us?"

"Today's Saturday. I have the place to myself on weekends. . . . Lift!"

Coleman grunted. "Yeah, but what if someone happens to come off-hours?"

"Not a chance. This is a government operation."

The new corpse fell on top of the first. Serge slammed the trunk lid. "I love science."

They climbed back in the Buick.

"I still think the mangroves would have been better," said Coleman. "They might find him here."

"They'll *definitely* find him," said Serge, starting the engine. "That's what makes it so perfect."

"What do you mean?"

Serge began driving back out the dirt road. "They used to have one body in the trunk; now they have two."

"So?"

"Everything's backward at the cadaver farm. They may be dealing in dead bodies, but it's still a bureaucracy, which means the cardinal sin is to *lose* inventory. If they come up with a high count, they don't think they gained a body; they think they lost paperwork. And in civil service, that could be someone's ass. So they'll cook the numbers."

"What if they don't?"

"These are professionals. It's why we pay taxes."

Serge stopped and got out of the car, locking the gate behind the Buick. He jumped back in and gunned the engine, sending up a thick cloud of dust as they whipped back onto the Tamiami.

A half minute later, another car appeared out of the cloud. A brown Plymouth Duster.

The Buick neared the end of the Everglades. It flew through the flashing red light at Dade Corners and kept on going for the turnpike. Serge and Coleman began seeing evidence of western Miami. Heavy industry, quarries, refining plants, paint-sample test institute.

"Hold everything," said Coleman, watching something go by his window. "Turn around!"

"What is it?"

"Just turn around. We're getting farther away."

Serge veered off the right shoulder, making a liberal U-turn in the grass on the opposite side. "What's the flavor of this wild-goose chase?"

"We passed a medical supply depot," said Coleman. "The warehouse with the barbed wire around all those industrial tanks in the back lot. I think I saw nitrous."

"Laughing gas?" Serge slammed the brakes and the Buick squiggled to a stop down the middle of the empty road.

"What are you doing?" said Coleman.

"I'm not going on some drug safari!"

"Why not?"

"Didn't you read where those two guys in that van passed out and died from nitrous."

"Because they were abusing it."

Serge yanked the stick on the steering column. "I'm turning around."

"Not fair!" said Coleman. "We already got to do what you wanted to."

"What are you, in second grade?"

"I didn't kick the guy to death. I didn't have to come out here and help you."

Serge stewed a moment. "Okay. Since you appeal to my sense of fairness. But I'm not waiting forever."

The Buick drove another hundred yards and pulled over next to a chain-link with a red-diamond warning sign: VICIOUS DOGS.

They got out and walked to the fence. "You're right," said Serge. "These *are* medical tanks. Oxygen and nitrogen. And there's the nitrous...."

Two Dobermans galloped across the storage yard. They jumped up on the fence and snapped teeth at the level of Serge's face. "Hello, puppies."

Coleman walked up next to Serge, pulled the dog whistle from his shirt and blew. The Dobermans yelped and scampered off to hide behind a stack of empty pallets.

Four hundred yards back, a brown Plymouth Duster sat quietly on the shoulder of the road with a clear view of the tiny Buick parked in the distance. Hands rested on the steering wheel. They were inside tan leather gloves, the kind with holes cut out for the knuckles. The hands came off the wheel. The driver's door opened, then the trunk. Out came wading boots and a bolt-action Remington deer rifle. The boots started down the shoulder into the swamp.

"Where are your bolt-cutters?" asked Coleman.

"Trunk."

Serge climbed up on the Buick's roof and sat with his legs crossed, leaning forward with rapt curiosity. Coleman snipped away at the chain-link fence, the dogs repeatedly charging, Coleman dispatching them each time with another blast from the ultrasonic whistle.

A half-mile north of the highway, an eye pressed against the scope of a deer rifle. The 10X-magnification compressed the view, eight hundred yards of sawgrass and cattails, then two Dobermans, a fence and, finally, Serge, sitting yoga-style on the roof of the Buick. A finger curled around the trigger.

Serge was amazed. He had never seen Coleman put together such linear purpose. After a few minutes, Coleman had snipped a Coleman-shaped hole in the fence.

There was a faint pop in the distance. The car window shattered beneath Serge.

"What did you do to my car?" said Coleman.

Serge leaned forward and looked down at the empty window with jagged pieces of glass around the frame. "I didn't do anything."

"Yes, you did. All your weight."

"Hope you're not expecting me to pay for that."

"Forget it. I was tired of rolling it down anyway. . . ."

"Coleman!"

"What?" He turned around. The Dobermans were almost on him. He blew the whistle. The dogs ran under a forklift.

In the unseen distance, wading boots sprinted away through the reeds, back toward a brown Plymouth Duster.

Coleman stuck the whistle in his mouth, climbed through the hole in the fence and wrapped his arms around a four-foot-tall chemical tank. He returned through the fence, tooting the whistle all the way, and slid the cylinder into the Buick's backseat.

"We can go now," said Coleman. He turned as the Dobermans were almost to the car. The whistle blew. They ran back through the hole in the fence.

Serge threw the car into gear and nodded. "So *that's* why you carry the whistle."

"Dogs just don't like me."

The Buick flew south on U.S. 1. Serge accelerated across the drawbridge from the mainland to Key Largo. He looked at Coleman. "What's the matter?"

Coleman scratched his arms. He glanced in the backseat. Then scratched again.

Serge grinned. "You can't get in the tank, can you?"

"There were always other guys before. They had equipment."

"What were you planning?"

"I don't know. Maybe tap a little hole with a pick and a hammer."

"Are you insane? Those things are highly pressurized. It'll blow the pick right back through your forehead!"

"What about a really tiny hole?"

"You don't know anything about physics, do you?"

"Will you help?"

The Buick pulled into a strip mall and parked at the first of fifty scuba shops on the island. The store was empty except for a single employee behind the cash register. The nineteen-year-old salesman had sun-bleached hair, a surfer's tan and half-mast marijuana eyelids. He was totally stoked.

"Uh, listen," said Serge, lounging against the counter. "We need some valve work on a tank."

"No problem-o."

"Except it's not really a scuba tank. It's for medical purposes."

The salesman shook his head. "No oxygen tanks. I can't work on anything flammable."

"It's not oxygen. It's something else, but it's inert."

"What?"

"Why don't I just show you?"

Serge and Coleman wrestled the tank into the store.

The salesman started giggling and pointing at them. "You dudes are gonna do nitrous!"

"Shhhhhhhhhhhh!" Serge set the tank in front of the counter.

"Don't worry, dudes. I do this all the time. One of my specialties."

"How long?"

"Half hour. But it has to be cash. The owner's kind of weird about this."

Serge and Coleman killed time wandering the store. They gazed into a glass case of hulky metal wristwatches with five-hundred-foot crush depths. Coleman picked up a Speedo box. "So you're really going to marry Molly?"

"Isn't she special?"

Coleman opened the box and stretched the trunks in front of his face. "I just don't see you two together."

"There's a soul-mate connection," said Serge. "I can't explain it, but she's definitely the one."

The Speedo ripped. Coleman stuck it back in the box. "What if she isn't the one?"

"Then we shake hands, say no hard feelings, and I drop her some place with no phones for five miles. Word on the street is you need a big head start. . . ."

"Nitrous tank's ready!"

They went in the back room. The salesman beamed proudly at his art. "Okay, you're gonna love this. Easy connections, that's my trademark. Here's where your regulator goes"—he attached a rubber hose that ran to the mouthpiece in his other hand—"and this is your auxiliary port with universal mount."

"What for?" asked Coleman.

"So you can fill other tanks. Regular scuba or the minis. You can't take this giant thing to parties. Suggest you get one of those little emergency tanks we have. Fits in your pocket. Five minutes of air . . ." The salesman stuck the regulator in his mouth.

"Hey! Hey! Hey!" said Coleman. "That's my gas!" He jerked the regulator away and stuck it in his own mouth.

"C'mon. This is a quality job," said the salesman. "Gimme a bump."

"All right, but just a little."

A short while later, Coleman picked up the tank and stepped over the passed-out teen. They got back in the Buick and continued west. More bridges, Tavernier, Upper and Lower Matecumbe. They started across the Long Key Viaduct.

"Coleman, check this out." Serge wiggled his finger inside a hole in the driver's door. "I think I feel a bullet. . . . Coleman?"

Coleman was slumped against the far door with the regulator in his mouth, a puddle of drool on his shirt. Serge plucked the rubber mouthpiece from Coleman's lips, and it came out with the sound of someone popping a finger in a cheek.

A minute passed; Coleman sat up. "What did you do that for?"

"There's a bullet hole. I told you I didn't break your window. Somebody was shooting at us. It shattered the glass, traveled across the car and lodged here."

"Why would anyone do that?"

"I don't know, but I've been getting an odd feeling lately that I'm being followed."

"You're imagining things."

"How do you explain the bullet?"

"South Florida," said Coleman. "Probably a stray from all the people shooting for reasons that don't concern us."

"Think so?"

"Remember that celebration after the Miami Heat playoffs where they shot those guns in the air, and one of the slugs came down and dropped that guy sticking videos in the overnight box?"

"Guess you're right." Serge looked off the south side of the bridge. "I spy . . . another waterspout!"

"I see them all the time in the Keys."

"The conditions are just right in the Gulf Stream."

"Maybe it'll bring us good luck."

A few miles back, a brown Plymouth Duster began crossing the Long Key Viaduct.

25

The night before the wedding

SERGE WAS A wreck. He paced back and forth at a boat ramp on the northwest end of Big Pine.

The sun started down over the Gulf. A wavering orange furnace reflecting off the incoming surf. All three types of clouds in attendance. A bank of stratus burned red on the western sky. Straight and high above, wispy cirrus glowed pink from the underlight. To the east, a front of purple and gray cumulus from an approaching storm. Serge stopped on the boat ramp and raised his camera. He snapped the shutter as a lone gull crossed the center of the bright ball filling his zoom.

Serge always had to wait until the very end. Once the sun touched the horizon, it would go fast, quickly halfway down, then a brilliant arc on the rim of the earth. Finally, a last pop of light and it was gone, leaving Serge consumed with the same postcoital emotion he had after every session of strenuous sex: He wanted a pizza.

Serge had to stay till the end because he was still hoping to see the elusive Flash of Green that John D. MacDonald had written of so eloquently—an extremely rare emerald ignition over water at the exact moment of sunset. Diehard Floridians were always chasing it. Some people, like Serge, went years without success. A few old-timers said they'd seen it two or three times. There were many competing theories for the flash. Others thought it was just a fairy tale. Serge was not one of them.

On this particular evening, Serge stood beside the ramp and took the last of his photos as the sun dipped deep into the sea. Almost gone. Time to look for the flash. He let the camera hang from the strap around his neck and crossed his fingers. *"Please, please, please . . ."* He squinted at the last bit of light wavering on the horizon. It disappeared.

Serge gasped and put a hand to his mouth. "Oh, my God. I saw it! I finally saw it!" He turned and began running across the island toward the No Name Pub. "I saw the flash! I saw the flash! . . ." Serge noticed a big green spot down the road ahead of him. Serge stopped and held a hand up to his face, a green spot in the middle of the palm.

"Shit, of course. The sun was almost solid red at the end. It's just a damn reverse-image afterspot on my eyeballs from staring too long." His shoulders slumped as he trudged on toward the pub. "Now I'm depressed." He reached the parking lot and looked up at a tiny jetliner, its lengthy contrail catching light from over the horizon to form a bright streak across the darkening blue sky with a green spot in the middle.

The No Name was rockin'. J. Geils on the juke. Early *Whammer Jammer* stuff. Serge opened the screen door.

"Serge!"

He grabbed a stool and sagged at the counter. Jerry the bartender came over with a bottle of water. "Why so down?"

"I just saw the Flash of Green."

"That's great!" said Jerry. "I've never seen it and I've been looking forever. Where? On the north shore?"

"It's still here." Serge reached out with his finger and touched a point in the air between their faces. "It's just a damn spot on my eyeballs. There's no magical flash."

"Yes, there is. It's an atmospheric condition. You just stared too long."

Serge noticed a commotion at the pool table. "What's going on over there?"

"Bar bet. They're working on Coleman."

Serge looked at his hand again. "I think I've done some kind of damage."

"It'll fade."

Serge picked up his water and headed for the pool table, where three guys were gripping Coleman's head from different angles, trying to dislodge the cue ball stuck in his mouth.

Serge walked up to Sop Choppy. "How are they doing?"

"Almost got it out. You ready for tomorrow?"

"Really nervous. I don't understand it. I never get this way."

A cue ball bounced across the floor.

"It means you're normal," said the biker. "Even the toughest guys get the shakes."

"You know how to get rid of a green spot on your eyeballs from staring at the sun too long?"

"Look at the pool table. It'll blend in."

Coleman came over. "Whew. Another close one." He pulled an envelope from his pocket and handed it to Serge. "Got a piece of mail for you."

Serge checked the address through the cellophane window. *The Grodnicks*. "Perfect!" He tore open the envelope and stuck the credit card in his wallet. "Just in time for the wedding."

The screen door flew open. "Son of a bitch!"

The gang didn't even have to look. Gaskin Fussels. Sop Choppy's head fell. "Not again."

Fussels charged up to the bar and jumped on a stool. "I'm going to have to kill someone!"

"What happened?" said Jerry.

"I just got ripped off! One of those little mom-and-pop motels. Oh, they're so fuckin' sweet and countrified when you arrive. You know what they did to me? They stuck me in the last room over the office. Then after they closed up, all the heat rose and the window unit couldn't handle it. I had to check into another motel!"

"Didn't you ask for a refund?" asked Jerry.

"Of course! I called the after-hours number, but they refused!"

"That's not right," said Jerry.

"I'm going to get them!" said Fussels. "I'm going to get them so good!"

The gang at the pool table was having difficulty focusing on their game with Fussels yelling and pounding the bar with his fists. Sop Choppy concentrated on a shot. He pulled the stick back.

"Nobody messes with Gaskin Fussels!"

The five went in the corner pocket, followed by the cue ball. Sop Choppy slammed the butt of his stick on the floor. "That's it. He's gotten on my last nerve."

"We can't wait any longer," said Rebel. "This used to be a great place."

Jerry came over with a tray of drafts the gang had ordered. "Here you go, guys. . . ."

"Jerry, why the hell do you talk to that jerk?" said Bob the accountant. "You're just encouraging him!"

"What?" said Jerry. "Did I do something wrong?"

"No, Jerry. You didn't do anything," said Sop Choppy. "You're just a nice person. Bob's upset about something else."

"You're upset about it, too," said Bob.

"What is it?" said Jerry. "Maybe I can help."

"Trust me. This isn't in your area," said Sop Choppy.

"We need to figure out how to get rid of Fussels," said Bob.

Jerry looked puzzled. "Why? What'd he do?"

"See, that's what I mean," said Sop Choppy. "You like everyone. It's not your nature."

"He's fucking up the whole pub," said Rebel.

"He is?"

"Jesus, Jerry. You talk to him more than anybody, and he doesn't annoy you? All his offensive jokes? We're the most offensive people we know, and we find *him* offensive."

"You like it if I got rid of him?" asked Jerry.

"Shoot, we'd *love* it!" said Rebel.

"I know how to do it," said Jerry.

"Yeah, right."

"No, really . . ." Jerry told them what he had in mind.

"Jerry, that's awful!" said Bob. "I can't believe you said that. It's so out of character. It's perfect!"

"You really think so?"

The guys started laughing. Rebel put a hand on Jerry's shoulder. "We always knew we liked you. . . . Serge, what the hell are you doing?"

Serge was working with the wooden break triangle, tediously assembling an elaborate triple-deck configuration of balls in the middle of the table. "Pool trick. Saw Minnesota Fats do this once on TV, but not nearly so complex." He grabbed the bridge, three sticks and some chalk. Coleman was already kneeling on the floor behind the right back pocket, holding the eight ball on top of his head with an index finger.

"Serge, you're not going to knock that ball off Coleman's head, are you?"

Serge's tongue stuck out the corner of his mouth. He carefully set the last ivory ball atop the pyramid inside the triangle. "Not at first." He arranged the three cue sticks in the bridge with their ends jutting over the edge of the table. He stepped back. "Okay, here's what's going to happen. Don't take your eyes off the table because it'll be over in a blink. I'll have to go all the way to that corner on the far side of the bar because I need the biggest running start possible. Then, when I get up enough speed, I slam the ends of the three sticks. If I do it just right, the balls scatter and one will immediately fly into each of the six pockets. But that's just the beginning. Other balls will leave the table altogether, the three ball caroming off the rest-room door, the seven taking a short hop on that wall, the two skipping back, knocking the eight off Coleman's head"—Serge patted the side pocket near his hip—"which ends up right here."

"I gotta see this," said Rebel.

Gaskin Fussels banged the counter with an empty glass. "Jerry! Getting mighty dry over here!"

"Coming, Mr. Fussels!" He hurried over and stuck a frosted mug under a tap.

"Hey, Jerry, I got a new joke for ya."

Jerry poured foam off the top of the mug. "What is it?"

"Why did God give women vaginas?"

"I don't know, why?"

Fussels slapped the bar. "So we'd talk to them! *Ha ha ha ha . . .*"

Jerry set the refill in front of Fussels. "And we talk to them and then what?"

"No, you see the thing about women . . . screw it, this one's easier. Stay with me, boy. You know why my ex-wife threw away her vibrator?"

"No."

"It chipped her teeth! *Ha ha! Woooo! . . .*"

"She threw it away? What? It didn't work right?"

"Jerry, you gettin' enough oxygen back there?"

Serge passed behind Fussels, counting off paces to the far corner of the pub.

Jerry wiped the bar down with a towel. "So, Mr. Fussels . . . that motel business really got under your skin?"

"Damn! You had to go and remind me! Of all the underhanded, chicken-shit—"

Jerry worked hard with the towel on a particular spot. "Yeah, it sounds like something he'd do."

"Who?"

"The owner."

"You know the owner?"

"A total asshole."

"Jerry, I've never heard you talk bad about anyone."

"This guy's different." The bartender slung the towel over his shoulder. "Biggest jerk I ever met in my life."

"You're preachin' to the choir."

"I know how you can get even with him."

"You do?"

"Definitely. I know what he loves. That's what you attack."

"Jerry, this is a completely different side of you," said Fussels. "I like it!"

"Believe me, this will completely burn his ass."

"I'm all ears."

Serge went sprinting by in the background.

"I know where he lives," said the bartender. "He's out of town right now. What you want to do is go over to his house. . . ."

A three ball bounced across the top of the counter between Fussels and the bartender.

"Jerry!" yelled Sop Choppy. "Quick! Get me all the ice you got!"

"What's the matter?"

"We got some people down."

26

The morning of the Big Day

SERGE HAD SLEPT all night in his white tux. At the first hint of sunrise, he leaped from the couch in Coleman's trailer. There was much to do before the wedding.

He'd told Molly not to worry about a thing. Just leave the planning to Serge. He reached under the couch and grabbed a tickle stick used to catch lobsters. The sticks were long Lucite wands with a hook on one end and a scuba diver's wrist strap at the other. If you saw antennas twitching out a hole in the coral, you stuck the stick inside and "tickled" the lobster on the tail, and it would jump out into your grasp.

Coleman was dead to the world.

"Wake up! I'm getting married!"

A groan and a head buried in the pillows.

Serge poked him in the ribs with the tickle stick. "Wake up!"

Coleman swatted blindly behind him.

"Wake up!" Poke.

"Ahhhhh!" Coleman rolled onto his back and swatted wildly with eyes closed.

Poke.

Coleman reared up and grabbed the end of the stick. Serge struggled expertly with the other end like an alligator poacher. "There we go, big boy. . . . Easy now . . ."

Coleman suddenly stopped and opened his eyes. He swung his legs over the side of the bed. "I'm hungry."

They wandered into the kitchen. Coleman rubbed his ribs. "Why do you always have to use the stick?"

"Because you always swing."

"Automatic reflex," said Coleman. "From those times I've woken up in jail with some guy straddling my chest punching me in the face."

"Need to shake a leg." Serge dragged three already packed gear bags from a closet. Coleman plopped down on the end of the sofa next to his nitrous tank. He turned on the TV and grabbed the regulator.

Serge yanked it out of his mouth.

"Hey!"

"We have to get moving!"

"But the wedding isn't till this afternoon."

"I'm expecting a lot of traffic."

He wasn't kidding. It was going to be a huge day in the lower Florida Keys, and not because of the wedding. One of the largest annual community events was about to kick off. That was no coincidence. Serge couldn't conceive of getting married without a cultural tie-in. He'd approached the organizers, who loved the idea. A wedding would be great publicity. Lots of photos for the newspapers. Serge was going to get married at one of his favorite places on earth: Looe Key.

Looe Key wasn't like the other keys. You couldn't get there by highway. And even if you could, you'd be in trouble. Looe Key was submerged.

It was named for the HMS *Looe*, which sank in 1744. There's almost nothing left of the wreck, but the awash coral reef is famous for its spectacular pattern of finger channels supporting teeming quantities of angelfish, parrotfish, tarpon, snapper, eel and just about everything else. The reef sits five miles offshore to the south. Dive boats make continuous runs from Ramrod, Little Torch and Big Pine.

For twenty-one years, the locals have hosted the annual Looe Key Underwater Music Festival. Water conducts sound much better than air, and divers come from all over to feel the tunes pulse through their bones. The music is broadcast by WCNK—"Conch FM"—and pumped down to the reef with special underwater speakers from Lubell Laboratory. Some of the divers arrive in wacky costumes. They jump in the ocean with guitars and trombones and whatnot, forming string quartets and marching bands. Some dress like pop stars. Tina Tuna. Britney Spearfish.

The concert lasts six hours. The minister would arrive during the third. The vows would be exchanged under water. Serge had written them himself.

Gear bags flew into the Buick's trunk and the lid slammed. Serge checked his watch. "Still on schedule. You got the ring?"

"Ring?"

"Coleman! You're the best man!"

"What ring?"

"I gave it to you last night. I was extremely clear. I said, 'Coleman, put down the bong and pay attention. This is the ring. It is of utmost importance. Screw up everything else, but don't lose the ring. The ring is everything. The ring is life and death. Do you understand?' And you said, 'Sure,' and I handed it to you."

"Oh, *that*," said Coleman. "I thought you were handing me a piece of trash."

Serge and Coleman sorted through garbage dumped out on the kitchen floor.

A half hour later, the Buick pulled up to the tiki bar at the Looe Key Reef Resort. Serge took the ring from his pocket and wiped off coffee grounds. He handed it to Coleman. "This is the ring. It isn't trash. Do not throw away."

The gang from the No Name was already waiting under the thatched roof. Molly was there, too, sitting on a bar stool in her wedding gown. Wearing glasses. Serge gave her a peck on the cheek.

"We're not supposed to see each other before the ceremony," said Molly.

"I don't believe in bad luck. . . ." Serge pointed at the ground. "Coleman!"

"What?"

"In the dirt! The ring!"

"How'd that get there?" Coleman picked it up.

Serge snatched it. "You're relieved of ring duty."

"Thanks. That was way too much pressure."

The gang toasted the happy couple. Nothing could go wrong now. They were already in place with a full two-hour pad. Just let the moment build enjoying the company of friends.

They weren't all friends. Most of the customers in the tiki hut were divers attending the music festival. Lots of rum drinks, cans of beer, buckets of oysters and cocktail sauce and chisels. It was noisy. The loudest were the three used-car salesmen on the opposite side of the bar from Serge and Molly. They'd just gotten in from the morning dive, drinking up quickly so they could work in another afternoon dive. A definite no-no. But rules were for other people.

Serge had noticed the trio in passing, but now he happened to catch them pointing his way and laughing. Actually, they were pointing at Molly. Serge scowled at them. They looked away, made another unheard remark and laughed even harder.

Serge turned to Molly. Her head hung sadly. Laughter across the bar. They were pointing again. Serge got off his stool.

The three men were still giggling when Serge arrived in his white tux.

"Hey, look. It's Bogart!"

"Were you pointing at my fiancée?"

"Who?" The leader stretched his neck theatrically and looked across the bar.

"I'm getting married today," said Serge. "So you've caught me in a good mood."

"Oh, the one in the wedding dress." He looked back at his buddies. "Wonder how a nerd does it?"

Serge tapped him on the shoulder.

The leader got off his stool and stood up to Serge's chest. He was a lot taller than he looked sitting. "Why don't you go back to your seat before you get hurt?"

"I'm trying to be polite." Serge snapped his fingers for the bartender. "Give these guys a round on me." He turned to the salesman again. "A little common courtesy. It's all I ask. I don't want anything to ruin this special day."

"Whatever, Bogey."

"Thanks." Serge returned to his stool. He and Molly faced each other, holding hands, lost in each other's eyes. A loud remark came across the bar. This time it was clearly audible.

"My Big Fat Geek Wedding!"

Serge continued smiling at Molly. "Would you excuse me?" He got off the stool and tugged Coleman's arm. "We need to go back to the trailer."

On the way to the Buick, Serge stopped in the motel's dive shop to pick up the reserved scuba tanks for him and Molly. "I'm going to need an extra."

The pair made an express trip to the mobile home and was back at the tiki hut in under forty minutes.

Serge hoisted an orange tank from the trunk and carried it on his shoulder into the bar. He walked up to the head car salesman and set the tank down. "Sorry about the misunderstanding earlier. Free tank on me. No hard feelings."

A sheriff's cruiser drove up. Gus and Walter got out and walked through the parking lot. Gus stopped behind one of the cars and looked at the APB in his hand. "This is the one."

The deputies entered the tiki hut and made a slow circuit around the bar, studying customers.

"Uh-oh," said Serge. He held up a hand to shield his face.

Gus stopped behind a stool and checked the mug shot on the bulletin in his hand. "Are you Rebel Starke?"

"Yeah, why?"

Gus pulled handcuffs off his belt. "You're under arrest for six hundred traffic tickets in Tennessee."

Rebel jumped off his stool and ran up to Serge, grabbing him by the lapels of his white tux. "Serge! Hide me! Do something!"

The deputies dragged him off.

Serge stood and straightened his jacket. "Sorry there was a disturbance, folks, but everything's all right now. Just relax and have a good time." He offered Molly his arm. "Shall we?"

* * *

THE DIVE BOAT throttled down and moored to a special float over the reef. The minister was already waiting below. The wedding party and best man lay around the afterdeck. They would be staying topside because of safety technicalities like not having dive certificates and being drunk. Serge and Molly stood on the back dive platform with their tanks. They held hands and gazed at each other one last time, before clutching regulators to their mouths and splashing into the ocean.

The first song was "Octopus's Garden," then "Fins" and "Aqualung." The radio station had let Serge pick them out himself. Serge also gave the station a marriage script that would be piped into the water as the minister and the couple pantomimed. The groom removed the ring from a Velcro pocket in his buoyancy compensator. The theme from *Jaws* started. A DJ began reading.

> *I, Serge, take you, Molly, to be my lawfully wedded wife, to love and hold, in sickness and in health, in good times and bad, choosing you exclusively as my wife, friend, partner, airtight alibi, getaway driver, nurturing each other's growth, making fun of the same relatives behind their backs, developing a list of running gags that is the foundation of any solid relationship, doing all the cool things married people do, which is why I'm really looking forward to this: snuggling on the couch with photo albums, watching classic movies in bed with lots of snacks, making silly remarks when we fart, at least at first before it becomes contentious, always agreeing with my wife that her really hot-looking friends dress like sluts and promising never, ever to fight. And when we do, to fight fair and not take off our rings and throw them at each other or reach for hot-button secrets we confided like those kids from junior high and their cruel*

nicknames—damn them to eternal hell! Then having lots and lots of kids with normal names instead of Scout, Tyfani, Dakota, Breeze or Shaniquatella, reading them bedtime stories and nursery rhymes, singing Christmas carols, teaching them that the "special words" Mommy and Daddy use around the house can't be repeated at school because it's "our little secret." Now a moment to thank the sponsor of today's wedding. Let's hear it for Conch FM, home of the hits! And remember to keep a lookout for the Southernmost Prize Wagon! Back to live action: I further solemnly swear to adore and respect, to honor and defend, against all foes foreign and domestic, my love, my light, my life, the wind beneath my wings, the rockets' red glare, the bombs bursting in air, fourscore and seven years, in Birmingham they love the guv'nah—ooo-ooo-ooo! As long as we both shall live! Amen!

He slipped the ring on her finger.

"I now pronounce you man and wife."

The nuptials spit out their regulators and kissed to "Yellow Submarine."

The dive boat erupted in applause when Serge and Molly broke the surface. People on the other boats began cheering, too. So did some of the divers who had wandered into the ceremony and surfaced with the couple. They scrambled for the artificial bouquet that sailed over Molly's shoulder into the Gulf Stream.

There was a cake on the boat, finger food, champagne. The merriment built. People danced. Serge stomped on a plastic cup.

Before they knew it, the sun was fading and the wind had picked up. The underwater music festival neared another successful conclusion. Time to head in and continue the celebration back on land. Boat engines started; mooring clamps were unhooked. The remaining divers began surfacing.

Except one.

Down in a distant ravine between the corals heads, a diver in a black and turquoise wet suit top was acting a little strange. He stumbled along the sandy bottom with a goofy grin. The diver had logged over a thousand hours, and his experience told him something was amiss. He was too happy. He checked his watch and his depth gauge. It didn't add up. He hadn't been down deep or long enough for nitrogen narcosis, but there was every indication. He staggered and swayed in the current. A barracuda stopped and stared in that unnerving, teeth-bared way they do. The diver just smiled. He thought: Narcosis isn't that bad. In fact, it's pretty great! So this is how all the less-experienced guys get the bends or die. They're having such a good time, they forget the fundamentals. Well, not me. Have to fight it. Must think.

The owner of Pristine Used Motors forced his mind to reach back through years of underwater training. He checked the mini decompression table on his wrist, then hit a timer button on his scuba watch. Twenty minutes, then a little air in the vest and up to the next depth for another stage. The diver was executing the procedure to perfection, resisting the natural tendency to panic and shoot to the surface, which is what he should have done with Serge's ten percent mixture of nitrous oxide building up in his bloodstream.

He watched the sweep-second hand on his chronograph as it approached the ten-minute mark. The periphery of his vision slowly dissolved to darkness as Pink Floyd throbbed from a dozen submerged speakers.

Eleven minutes. The diver stared straight up. Tunnel vision. Solid black around an ever-tightening circle of light from the surface. Twelve minutes, the tube of light shrank to the diameter of a quarter. Thirteen minutes. An ultimately euphoric grin wrapped across the diver's face as Floyd built to climax.

A pinpoint of light.

". . . I-yiiiiiiiii . . . have become . . . comfortably numb. . . ."

The light went out.

27

ANOTHER TRAFFIC JAM in Marathon. The airport crowded with people. Local chamber of commerce, reporters, federal agents. A line of limos waited by the terminal. This was the day *he* arrived.

The largest private jet the airport had ever seen came into view. It touched down and used all of the five-thousand-foot runway coming to a stop.

Stairs rolled up. The door opened. People on the runway tried to surge forward but were held back by private security. A pair of executive attachés emerged first, followed by lawyers, accountants and a team of miscellaneous handlers in dark sunglasses. Finally . . . Wait, there's more. Personal guests, local politicians and a handful of relatives, including the grandmother who had to be lowered with a special lift. . . . Was that it? No, hold on. Yes-men, suck-ups, professional entourage members, two "independent" experts ready to go on CNN at a moment's notice, the unemployed celebrity golfing pal, and a woman in a bright tangerine scarf carrying a leather organizer—the highly protective traveling publicist. Okay, that was definitely it. Finally, the person they'd all been waiting for. And he comes now, confidently striding down the stairs in a lightweight gray suit tailored in Rome. Donald Greely, former CEO and chairman of embattled Global-Con, Inc.

Greely reached the tarmac and was immediately mobbed by a tight crowd that shuffled with him toward the terminal. Newspaper photographers held cameras in the air, snapping photos over the swarm. Reporters shouted questions.

"Will the company reorganize?"

"What about all the wiped-out retirement accounts?"

"Why'd you take the fifth before Congress?"

"How much did the house cost?"

"Are you going to live here permanently?"

The reporters were roundly booed by supporters from local civic organizations, who endlessly thanked Greely for his generosity. The new hospital wing, new arts center, scholarships for local teens with high SATs and the home for unwanted puppies.

With an artful and carefully rehearsed technique, the team of handlers acted in choreographed unison as a kind of giant ectoplasm, gradually elbowing, shouldering, sidestepping and jockeying the noisiest journalists to the outer rim of the crowd, simultaneously letting the most enthusiastic supporters percolate through to the inner core.

All the way to the terminal, Greely grinned and signed autographs. They clasped his hand earnestly. "Can't thank you enough for the donation!" "Will you speak at our awards banquet?" "You've been such an inspiration!"

"Just trying to be a good member of the community," said Greely. "Really, no need to thank me." He had a point. It was all being paid for by other people's life savings, routed through Caribbean shell corporations. Standard PR for controversial companies and public figures moving into town: Buy advance goodwill.

The crowd approached the terminal. The traveling publicist glowed. Everything unfolding according to plan. Lots of photos of happy residents greeting their newest neighbor.

Something caught the eye of one of the newspaper photographers. Out in the parking lot on the other side of the runway fence. The photographer broke from the pack and started shooting on the run. When his rivals noticed, they stampeded for the same picture, followed by reporters with open notebooks.

The traveling publicist noticed the crowd around her client getting a little lean. Where'd the media go? She looked back and saw her worst nightmare. On the other side of the fence was a lone picketer, an elderly woman with an expression of collapsed hope, barely strong enough to hold up her homemade sign written in a pitifully unsteady hand: I HAD TO GO BACK TO WORK.

"Goddammit!" shouted the publicist. "What did I ever do to her?"

28

THE HONEYMOON WAS a corker.

The gang gave Serge and Molly a traditional Keys send-off. They waved farewell from the dock on Little Torch Key. Serge and Molly waved back from the rear of a charter boat with aluminum cans and fishing bobbers tied to the stern, the gunwales shaving-creamed: *"If this boat's a rockin', don't come a knockin'."*

"I'm dying to know where we're going!" said Molly.

"I told you," said Serge. "It's a surprise."

"I'm so excited!"

The ferry took them on a short, three-mile hop to a private dock, and that's when Molly saw it. She grabbed Serge around the neck and jumped up and down. "I love you! I love you! Thank you! . . ."

"Easy, my neck."

Little Palm Island.

Oasis.

Tahitian bungalows riding small rolling hills, surrounded by bright island flowers and coconut palms growing out over the water. More like the South Pacific, which is why it was the movie location for *PT-109*.

A chilled bottle of wine waited in the couple's suite. Molly walked onto the veranda and drank in the aquamarine harbor. She squealed with glee and swirled in a circle.

Nothing was too good for his Molly. Serge had arranged a mega-package of romance and pampering. All weekend long: the serenity massage, seaweed body mask, volcanic earth clay ritual, Bali spice treatment, then hours together in their private teakwood Jacuzzi filled with lilacs.

And the food! An elite team of world-class gourmets kept it coming. Breakfast: avocado omelets, salmon mimosas, silver pots of coffee and fresh-squeezed juice, then a room-service lunch of chilled lobster bisque, black mussels poached in fennel, goat cheese with arugula, goose liver pâté, steak au poivre and pommes frites. Wait, leave room for dinner: petite bouillabaisse, grilled yellow snapper, pollo-sautéed andouille with hearts of palm and corn-roasted chipotle sauce. Finally, the pièce de résistance, raspberry tart with crème anglaise.

It didn't come cheap. As they say, don't forget your VISA. Seven thousand bucks. Molly read the welcome card that came with the chilled wine. *Congratulations, Mr. & Mrs. Grodnick.*

Almost forgot! The sex!

Serge had been apprehensive. He was a fairly urbane guy—didn't want to spook Molly with anything too weird right away. He brushed his teeth and walked barefoot into the room with the mahogany poster bed and gauzy white canopy. "Honey? . . ."

Something slammed him hard from the blind side and knocked him onto the mattress.

"I'm going to make you so happy! I'm going to be the best wife! . . ." She seized the front of his pants. His zipper ripped apart.

Serge grabbed her wrists. "Honey, slow down. We've got the rest of our lives."

"I'm sorry. Did I do something wrong? I did, didn't I? I'm so sorry. . . ."

"You're fine. Just don't burden yourself."

She stared down. Serge gently put a hand under her chin and raised her head. "You don't have to answer this if you don't want to, but . . . is this, uh, your first? . . ."

She tried to lower her head again, but Serge's hand was still there. She nodded.

"No crime in that. Let's start slow with the basics."

It was a precipitous learning curve. What Molly apparently lacked in experience, she more than compensated for with enthusiasm, stamina and mind-curving imagination.

Serge began to suspect he wouldn't last the night. At the two-hour mark, he tremored on the mattress. "Where'd you learn to do *that*?"

"I just made it up. Want me to stop?"

"Hell, no!"

Deeper into the night. More pioneering technique. Serge never would have guessed she was double-jointed. And just what was this she was starting to—oh, no! . . . Serge's head arched back over the pillow, his mind's eye catapulting through the Milky Way, comets and quasars zooming past. . . .

She sat up. "You didn't like that, did you? I'm sorry. Now I'm embarrassed." She put a hand over her eyes in shame. "You're always going to picture me doing that. . . ."

Serge pulled the hand away from her face and grabbed her by the shoulders. "Holy God! . . . You sure you haven't done this before?"

She shook her head.

"I want you to listen carefully and trust me on this one," said Serge. "You're incredible. You have absolutely nothing to feel self-conscious about."

"You really mean it?"

"Completely," said Serge, nodding hard. "Especially the naked-but-still-wearing-glasses part. Throws something into the mix I can't quite explain."

Molly sprouted a giant grin. "Good!" She jumped off the bed and skittered into the next room, returning quickly with a turkey baster and feather duster. "Let's try this! . . ."

Serge pitched in agony against the pain-pleasure threshold. Molly finally showed mercy and let him up for air. "How was that?"

Serge panted until he regained speech. "Where'd you get the accessories?"

"I packed a few things. Wanna see?" She ran in the other room again, coming back with an overnight case that she opened on the foot of the bed. Oils, ointments, fur cuffs, nipple clips, whip, latex mask, double-ended dildo, illustrated manuals, ball of twine, clear tubing, bungee cords and trick-or-treat costumes.

"I wasn't sure what you were into, so I got a little of everything."

"From where?"

"That adult superstore in Fort Lauderdale. The one with the shopping carts." She reached in the case. "Now hold still. . . ."

On it went, Molly's self-esteem climbing. By midnight, she had lost all inhibition and bloomed into a regular Chatty Cathy. "I have an idea. Let's . . . no, I'm going to surprise you. You like surprises, right? You still having fun? I sure am! You're going to love this one! You don't have any heart conditions, do you? . . ." She reached deep into the overnight bag.

"What's that?"

"Blindfold." Molly strapped it to his face. Her voice deepened. "Lie down, slave!" Her voice returned to normal pitch. "Is it okay I call you 'slave'? I don't really mean it. I read it in a magazine. It's just a game. I can leave the 'slave' part out if you want. I'd like to leave it in because of the story line. . . ."

"Go for it."

"Shut up, slave! Open your mouth!"

A piece of twine tied his big toes together. He heard some kind of motor start.

The next thing Serge knew, the blindfold was off and he was staring at the ceiling. Molly lightly slapped his cheek. "Honey, are you okay?"

"What happened?"

"You passed out. At first I thought I'd killed you."

"Make a note. That's how I want to go."

"You're not tired yet, are you? I'm not. I'm just getting started. . . ."

Who *was* this woman? Still waters certainly ran deep. It continued the rest of the night. Serge tried to remember as much as he could, but there was too much new data, Molly venturing far beyond her shell and into uncharted territory. Three to four A.M. became the profanity hour, which Molly executed with naughty, schoolgirl glee. She was on top, riding fast and hard. "Wow, I've never said these words before! I didn't know it could be such a turn on. Fuck! Pussy! Cock! You like that? I think I'll try it with the word 'hot.' Hot pussy! Hot cock! I like it better that way. What do you think? What about 'sweet'? Which do you prefer? 'Sweet' or 'hot'? Hey, it's kind of like mustard. Get it? Sweet and hot mustard? Did you ever think of that, you big-cock motherfucker? . . ." Right on through daybreak, Serge stretched out on his back, utterly spent. Molly sat next to him on the bed, flipping through her manual. She turned the book toward him and tapped an illustration. "We haven't done the Praying Mantis. . . ."

Serge didn't know how much more he could take, but Molly showed no signs of fatigue. "Come on up!" said Molly. "It's the 'Wallenda,' page 143," swinging from one of the driftwood rafters.

Finally, mercy. "I'm starting to get tired," she said, stifling a yawn with the back of her hand. "It's all right if we stop? I need to get some sleep. But I don't want to disappoint you. That'll disappoint you, won't it? I can tell. Okay, one more thing. . . ." She trotted out of the room again and came back wearing one of the trick-or-treat costumes from her overnight bag.

Serge sat up. "Which one are you supposed to be?"

"Buttercup."

Molly ran toward the bed for her superhero pounce. She pulled up at the last second. "Baby? . . ."

He was snoring.

Serge usually had an immense aquifer of energy, but it wasn't bottomless. Now he had to recharge. And there was no more restful place than Little Palm Island. Isolated, exclusive, utterly tranquil. It stayed that way because of the limited access. Only three ways to get there: private yacht, the seaplanes that occasionally splashed down in the harbor with a belly full of executives, and the ferryboat that docked at the landing on Little Torch Key. The landing had a small parking lot where you could leave the car overnight. It currently held eight vehicles. The last car was backed into its slot, hiding the license plate against the bushes. A brown Plymouth Duster.

SHAFTS OF BLINDING afternoon light streamed through bungalow windows on Little Palm Island.

Serge's eyelids fluttered open.

Molly was in the wooden Jacuzzi, luxuriating in exotic bath gels. She heard him stir. "Where are you, my love?"

Serge banged into a doorframe.

"Honey?"

"Right here," said Serge.

Molly cupped her hands together and squirted water into the air. "I'm in the hot tub. Why don't you join me?"

"Not right now." He stepped onto the veranda.

Molly hummed and squirted water. "Come on. We'll *play*."

"I have to go down to the shore for a minute."

"What for?"

"To die."

"I'll keep the water warm . . . *hmmm, hmmm, hmmm*." Squirt.

Serge was operating on fumes. He needed to find some place away from that woman and gather strength. He stumbled down to the beach toward one of the big burlap hammocks that were hanging everywhere between the palms. Being a Floridian, he looked up to make sure no coconuts were hanging over the end where his head would be. He clawed his way into the mesh and was snoring again in under a minute.

Molly walked out on the veranda. "Serge?"

The hammock sagged deep in the middle where Serge curled up like a baby. He'd never slept harder. After an hour, the wind changed and the hammock began taking an eastern breeze off the harbor. It was down by the dock on the southern indentation of the island, visible from the upland bluff where two hands in leather gloves parted the fronds of a saw palmetto. The hands opened a small steel case lined with foam padding. A disassembled Marlin thirty-ought-six. The hands screwed on the barrel and snapped the stock in place. The barrel poked through the branches and rested in the yoke. An eye went to the scope, a leather finger eased through the trigger guard. A hammock appeared in the crosshairs. The finger squeezed.

The first bullet grazed Serge's shoulder, an otherwise excellent shot. The elevation was dead-on, but a tiny miscalculation in windage. Serge woke up grabbing his arm. The second shot was hurried and missed altogether, smashing the support ring fastening one end of the hammock to the tree. Serge crashed to the ground just before the third shot flew through the spot where his head had just been. Serge instinctively tucked and rolled toward the cover of brush. Leather hands jerked the rifle out of the branches and deftly broke it down into the case. Serge was on his feet, running in a tight crouch against the vegetation, then into the thick of the trees, taking a long, looping fox trail around the island.

Serge finally made it back to the cottage, clearing the front steps in two giant leaps and diving through the door. Molly heard the noise and came in the room drying her hair with a hundred-watt blower.

Serge ran for the sink, blood trickling through the fingers holding his injured shoulder.

A scream. The dryer crashed to the floor.

"It's just a flesh wound," said Serge. "The bullet didn't even enter."

"Bullet!"

Serge grabbed the bungalow's first-aid kit from a cabinet and patched himself up with antibiotic cream and large bandage. "There, like it never happened."

"You got shot?"

"A little bit."

"Who did this!"

"Who knows? It's a crazy world."

"I want you to tell me right now about this consulting work you do."

"What's to tell?"

"Have you ever been in jail?"

"Where'd *that* come from?"

"Just answer the question."

"Jail?" Serge repeated. "Words are such relative things. . . ."

"I knew it!" Molly jumped up and headed for the bedroom.

Serge ran after her. She started packing.

"Baby, wait. I can explain. . . ."

"Let go of my arm!" She stuffed clothes in a bag and muttered to herself. "What was I thinking getting married so fast? Right, people do it in Vegas all the time. I'm so stupid! I don't know anything about him! . . ."

"Why *did* you marry me so fast?"

"Because you were the first man who ever . . ." She finished the sentence by cramming a bathing suit in the bag.

Serge grabbed her by the hand and got down on a knee.

"I married you because I just *knew*. When you're positive you've found your soul mate, why continue shopping?"

She pulled her hand away and kept packing.

"You're the only woman for me. Whatever I was before was *before*. Everything is all new now. I meant every word of my vows."

Her packing rate slowed. "There's just so much I don't know about you."

"Okay, I'll come clean. You're my wife and you deserve the complete, unfiltered truth. Marriage is sacred. It must be based on total trust. . . ." He paused and looked deep into her eyes. "Okay, here goes. . . . I'm . . . a social worker."

"Social worker?"

Serge nodded. "I find people with really screwed-up lives and gradually ease them back into the herd."

"Coleman? . . ."

"My toughest case. Been working on him for years."

"Oh, Serge. I'm so proud of you! That's a wonderful line of work!"

"Most of the time," said Serge. "But some of these people are pretty bizarre. That's why you'll have to understand if I'm suddenly required to go someplace in the middle of the night."

"But why didn't you just tell me in the first place?"

"Afraid it might scare you away. Some of my clients are totally unpredictable, which is why you can't tell anyone about me or where I live."

Molly released a big sigh. "I feel so much better now."

"Hey! Let's open our wedding gifts!"

"Okay."

They unwrapped Coleman's present. A porn tape. *Chitty Chitty Gang Bang*.

"Thanks, Coleman." Serge grabbed the next gift.

Molly reached for the cast-aside video. "Let's watch it."

So went the next thirty-six hours. The honeymoon finally ended but not the endurance test. Serge moved into Molly's apartment, and life turned into a Pink Panther movie. Serge would stroll out of the kitchen with a sandwich and—wham!—Molly diving from a closet, pinning him to the ground.

The staff at the Big Pine library didn't recognize Molly when she returned to work. Hair down, clothes fitting. She looked them in the eye and even talked! Good heavens, they thought, I need sex like that. The transformation was so stunning that her female colleagues involuntarily pictured Serge's manhood in scale next to a Polaris missile, an old-growth redwood and the Statue of Liberty.

29

The no name pub's screen door flew open.

"I'm Gaskin Fussels! And I rule!"

Hearts sank around the bar.

Fussels was holding a large box with both arms. He marched up and set it on the counter. "Y'all come over and take a gander at this!"

Nobody moved.

"Okay, stay where you are. I'll take it out of the box and show you." Fussels reached in with both arms and carefully extracted the contents. He proudly placed it on the bar.

The pub went silent. Mouths agape.

"I knew you'd be impressed," said Fussels. "This'll teach him to fuck with me!"

They hopped off their stools and crowded around Fussels.

Bud looked at Sop Choppy. "I hope that isn't what I think it is."

"Uh, where exactly did you get that?" asked Daytona Dave.

"Just up the street," said Fussels. He formed a vicious grin. "At the home of that dickhead who owns the motel."

"What motel?" said Bud.

"Lazy Palms. The one that ripped me off." Fussels nodded to himself with satisfaction. "We'll see about that fucking refund policy."

"Where exactly was this house again?" asked Sop Choppy.

Fussels waved an arm east. "Right across the bridge on No Name Key. Down one of those back roads."

"That's not where the owner lives," said Bud.

"What are you talking about?" said Fussels.

"I know the owner. His place is up on Cudjoe."

"Then who lives out there?" asked Fussels.

It slowly began filtering back to Sop Choppy through the haze of the other night's boozing. "Oh, no." He looked at Bob the accountant, who was just beginning to remember himself.

"What is it?" asked Bud.

Bob had his hands over his face. "Us and our stupid practical joke."

Sop Choppy looked at the object on the counter. "How could we be so dumb?"

"Because we were drunk!" snapped Bob.

"This is a major fuck-up," said Sop Choppy.

Jerry the bartender started shaking. "I-I-I thought it's what you wanted me to tell him."

Bob ran his hands through his hair. "We have to think."

They became silent again and stared at the bar.

Fussels looked around at everyone. "Will somebody tell me what the hell is going on?"

Nobody answered. All eyes on the magnificent, scratch-built model of a nineteenth-century British schooner. *Scarface* carved into the base.

"I'm starting to get pissed off!" said Fussels.

"Shut the fuck up!" yelled Sop Choppy. "You didn't steal from a motel owner. You stole from a drug kingpin. He's going to kill you, okay?"

"What are you talking about?" Fussels pointed across the bar. "Jerry said—"

"Jerry lied!"

"Why would he do that?"

"So we'd like him!"

"This is so bad," said Daytona Dave.

"We gotta get it out of here," said Bud.

"I don't understand," said Fussels. "Why would you want Jerry to—"

"Because you're an asshole!" said Sop Choppy. "We were trying to get rid of you!"

"Get rid of me? I thought we were friends."

Five guys: "Shut up!"

"He's got to take it back right now," said Sop Choppy.

"I'm not taking shit back," said Fussels. "Not until I get my refund."

"Aren't you listening? Jerry was fucking with you!"

"You really are serious about this, aren't you?"

"Yes! The guy's had dozens of people killed!"

Bud grabbed the empty box. "You have to pack it back up and return it right now before he discovers it's missing."

The color left Fussels's face. "No way. I'm not going back anywhere near there."

"You have to!"

Fussels looked like he might faint.

"Hold on," said Sop Choppy. "We might be missing something here. How do we know there's any way to connect him to this?"

"Think hard!" said Bob. "Did anybody see you go in the house? Did you leave any clues?"

"I don't know. Maybe."

"What does that mean?"

"I left a ransom note."

"You what!"

"How was I supposed to get my refund?"

"It's still okay," said Sop Choppy. "It's just a ransom note. They're anonymous."

"I sort of signed it."

"You idiot!"

"What did the note say?" asked Bob. "You'd be calling him or something?"

"No, I said I'd be waiting at the No Name Pub. Just bring my refund here."

The guys jumped back and spun toward the door.

"Oh, my God!" said Bob. "They could be coming in here any second with machine guns!"

"You have to take it back right now!"

"I can't!"

"You have to!"

Fussels's legs got rubbery. "I need to sit down."

"Jerry, get him a beer."

Fussels upended the draft in one long guzzle. The others quickly packed the ship back up and pushed the box into his stomach. "Get going!"

Fussels walked meekly toward the screen door.

"Whatever you do, don't drop it!"

"What?"

"Don't drop it!"

He dropped it.

The gang screamed. They ran over to the box.

"Maybe it's all right," said Bud. "It's a pretty tough box."

They opened the flaps. Sop Choppy pulled out a handful of broken toothpicks.

Bob held up a snapped crow's nest. "We're fucked."

"He's gotta go back and get that ransom note!" said Bud.

"That's right. You have to get the note!"

Fussels was frozen with fear. The gang picked him up by the arms and rushed him out the screen door.

"Go get the note!"

30

Scarface's office

THE COCAINE USE was clearly out of control. He'd called the crew together for a late-night staff meeting, then forgot what he wanted to say. But it didn't stop him. A torrent of disjointed, random thoughts, punctuated by lines of coke and Scarface surfing through chapters of his favorite movie on the big screen.

"I want my chu-man rights!"

The crew stood nervously on the other side of the desk, silent, hands behind their backs. They'd already had that big gun pulled on them four times. Scarface was currently nose down on his desk again for another line. He sat up and scratched his head with the gun barrel, trying to figure out why his desk looked so much more spacious.

"Hey, where'd the ship go?" He reached and grabbed a scrap of paper sitting where the model had been. "Who the fuck is Gaskin Fussels?" He tossed the note back, got out some more coke and turned up the television.

When the blow was gone, Scarface stood and pulled a large molded plastic case from behind his chair and set it on top of the desk. He flipped open the latches and nodded toward the TV. "This is my favorite scene!" He opened the case and removed a giant assault rifle complete with rocket launcher under the barrel, identical to the one

Pacino now had on the screen. The crew ducked as the weapon swept across them. "You're not watching the movie!"

The crew, anxiously glancing back and forth from the TV to their leader, who stood in the ready position with the weapon, repeating dialogue with Pacino:

"Say hello to my little friend!"

Scarface inadvertently pressed something.

Woosh.

A rocket fired.

"Oh, gee," said Scarface. "I'm awfully sorry."

The crew member in the middle had a half second to look down in surprise at the hole in his chest, before the projectile's explosive charge blew him apart, knocking the other two crew members over in opposite directions like Scarface had picked up a spare in the tenth frame.

He leaned over the desk, looking for the survivors. "You guys okay?"

"Yes."

"Why don't you get up?"

"We don't want to."

"Come on, get up! I got it pointed in the air. The safety's on."

The remaining two crew members peeked over the edge of the desk.

Woosh.

A second rocket took off toward the ceiling, blowing a massive hole in the roof of the stilt house. The crew ducked again as debris fell. Scarface looked up at open sky. "How'd that happen?" He shrugged and dumped out more coke.

Finally, Scarface told the two remaining crew members to go get something to clean up the mess. *Thank God.* They hurried for the door.

"No, wait. Except you," said Scarface. "I want you to stay behind."

The pair turned around to see which of them he meant. The one Scarface was looking at pointed reluctantly at his own chest. "M-m-me?"

"Yes, you."

"W-w-what do you want?"

"Relax. You didn't do anything. I just want to talk."

The selected crew member gulped and walked back across the room. Scarface got up from his butterfly chair and came around the front of the desk. Both turned and watched until the other crew member had left and closed the door. They faced each other again. Scarface broke into a wicked grin.

The other man reached back and slapped Scarface as hard as he could.

"Ow!" Scarface grabbed his cheek. "Why'd you do that?"

"What the hell do you think you're doing!"

"What are you talking about?"

"You've lost your fuckin' mind!"

"What"—pointing at the ceiling—"the rocket launcher?"

"All of it! You're out of control!"

Scarface continued rubbing his cheek. "But I thought this is what you wanted. You told me to pose as the head of your organization. To draw attention away from you."

"Draw attention, not go on a publicity tour. You cut Billy's head off, then posed it in front of a mirror!"

"That was wrong?"

Slap.

"Do you have any idea how much media that's getting? I tell you to take care of a guy, and I expect two in the back of the head. Instead you give me a horror show."

"You told me I was doing a good job."

"Five years ago! Before the coke started eating through your brain like termites. Your judgment's fucked. Like the upside-down crucifixion at the bat tower. What the hell was that about?"

"I was sending a message," said Scarface.

"What kind of message?"

"I don't remember the message code, but it was a strong one. Especially the upside-down part. That's never good."

Slap.

"And you're paying for my roof! I'm not standing for this—" His expression suddenly changed. He looked oddly at Scarface's left cheek. "Your scar . . ."

Scarface smiled proudly. "You like it?"

"It's peeling."

"It is?" Scarface urgently felt his cheek and pressed it back in place. "There. How's that?"

Slap.

The scar went flying.

Scarface ran across the room and picked it up off the floor.

The other crew member returned with the cleaning supplies.

Scarface pressed the scar back on and turned toward the door. "What the hell are you looking at!"

The crew member didn't want to say anything, but he could have sworn the scar used to be on the other cheek.

31

During the first few weeks of wedded bliss, Molly asked more and more questions about Serge's job. His answers became increasingly vague.

"I understand about the confidentiality," said Molly. "And it's not that I don't trust you. It's just all these strange hours and phone calls, running into the house and locking the door, then peeking out windows. If only I could see something concrete for peace of mind. . . ."

"Okay," Serge relented. "You've been very supportive of my career. I couldn't do half of this without you standing behind me. If it'll help you sleep, you can come with me next time."

"Really?"

Monday night, Sugarloaf Key Community Center

Each week, the crowd had grown, drawing on audiences from other meetings as word spread. They had to move to one of the double rooms and push back the partition, and still it was standing-room-only. Serge had a particular ability to connect with youth, siphoning down the juvenile-intervention class until it was now empty. At first, the deputies were going to report the absences to the court, but Gus suggested they sit in on one of Serge's talks to see if they could pick up techniques to help the kids.

Five till seven. The seats almost full. The deputies stood in the back of the room by the punch bowl. Serge, Molly and Coleman arrived.

Molly had a serving tray. She smiled at the deputies and peeled back cellophane. "Cookie?"

Gus took two.

Serge marched to the front of the room and grabbed chalk. He wrote across the blackboard in big letters. He set the chalk back in the tray and faced the class. Everyone became quiet. Over his head was the title of tonight's lesson: TWELVE STEPS IN REVERSE: GETTING THE MOST FROM YOUR INNER MANIAC.

This time Serge didn't start talking right away. He paced with hands behind his back, staring in accusation. Some in the audience fidgeted and averted their eyes.

"Why do you come to these meetings?" He let the question hang as he moved across the front of the room. Suddenly, he fell to the floor, flopping around and whining in a loud voice. "Because I'm a victim! Oh, please help me! I'm so fucked up! . . ."

A young girl in the front row giggled.

Serge jumped to his feet. "Did I say you could laugh?" He ran up fast until he was right in her face. "Shut the hell up! You're a child. You don't know shit! You think adults with problems are funny? You know how they get that way? They start like you, a smart-ass punk disrespecting underpaid teachers who are trying to hand you the keys to the world, thinking life's going to bloom all by itself and wipe your ass with roses! You have no idea where you're headed. But I do . . ." He began moving his hands over an imaginary crystal ball. ". . . I'm getting a picture now. A middle-aged woman with thirty-inch thighs and no health insurance working entry-level checkout, going home to a run-down rabbit warren full of *TV Guides*, pregnant offspring, paint-ball guns and a slob of a husband who can't go look for another job just yet because he has to hurry up and finish these beers before the police drop by to break up your weekly slap-dance in the front-yard, dog-shit orchard. And you go back to that cash register, year after year, your anger growing in proportion to the success of the people coming through your line. Why are *they* so happy? Because they're screwing you, that's why! You can't say exactly how they're doing it because that's part of the conspiracy. More years pass. You're switching channels after dinner and happen to hear something that finally explains how none of this is your fault. You see, you're a *victim*. You did nothing to deserve this. And you know what? They're right. You did absolutely nothing. And one day you wake up and find yourself in one of these meetings you find so hilarious."

The girl was quaking. Serge saw some of the adults nodding and whispering. "Tough love." "The boot camp method."

Serge erupted. "No! No! No! I *hate* tough love! Screw the boot camp! Are you crazy? That's the last thing you should do to children! They need love! As much as you can give!" He walked over to the girl he'd just been yelling at. "You look like you could use a hug."

She nodded with glassy eyes.

He helped her up by the hand and gave her a big squeeze. She sat back down with a quivering smile, wiping her eyes.

"There," said Serge. "Now go forth and be a nuclear physicist."

He faced the room as a whole and spread his arms. "The entire problem is this victim mentality. When did *that* start? Life's not turning out the way they said it would when you were in first grade. You're not the president or a movie star or playing center field for the Yankees. Guess what? They lied! Move on! You come from incredible stock! Immigrants who chewed through it all and spit it out with thanks: Ellis Island, Manifest Destiny, the dust bowls, Normandy, and for what? For a society that now encourages everyone to choose up excuse teams: My attention span's a little off, sometimes I'm nervous, sometimes I'm tired, insults make me sad, I was unfairly labeled slow in school when I really just didn't want to do any work, a diet of super-size French fries turned me into a human zeppelin, your honor, so I need to be given a lot of money...."

A person standing along the back wall grabbed a Styrofoam cup from the refreshment table and picked up a pot of coffee.

Serge stopped and pointed. *"Put . . . the coffee . . . down!"*

The pot returned to its stand.

"Just look at your speaker tonight," Serge continued. "I'm a complete mess. But so was every successful person who ever got off the boat and climbed to the top. Watch those cable biographies for any length of time and you realize that the most accomplished people were every bit as weird as Son of Sam. The difference? Choice. *Choosing* to harness your peculiar energies. Me? I could be home right now giving into my all-consuming urge to construct the world's largest ball of pencil shavings. But I *choose* not to. I *choose* to be here with you fine people. Sure, I've been thinking about it the whole time I've been standing up here, boxes of new pencils, electric sharpeners, the special adhesive you use, that twelve-year-old little *fucker* from Iowa who got on Leno with his pitiful five-foot ball that I'm sure had a false basketball core but just can't prove it. . . . I forgot what I was talking about. Thanks for coming."

They gave Serge a standing-O as he walked down the aisle to the back of the room, taking up a position by the door to shake hands like a pastor.

"Great talk . . ."

"Loved it . . ."

"So moving . . ."

Molly couldn't have been prouder of her husband. He was really helping people. How could she ever have doubted he was a social worker?

Serge shook more hands. "Thank you." "Thank you." "That's very kind of you." "Thank you. . . ."

Coleman walked over. "You've never said anything about pencil shavings. When did that start?"

"While I was up there talking. I realized I've never been on the *Tonight* show. . . . Thank you. . . . Thank you very much. . . ."

The audience was almost completely gone, just the deputies left. Molly swept crumbs into the trash from her cookie tray.

Gus shook Serge's hand. "Enjoyed the talk, especially how you connected with the kids."

"Thank you."

Molly came up with her clean tray, and Serge took her by the arm.

The deputies watched the couple leave the room, Coleman bringing up the rear.

"Something's not right there," said Gus.

"He *was* pretty strange."

"It's not that," said Gus. "I remember something from somewhere. Just can't put my finger on it."

32

THE NIGHT WORE on. Only a few fishermen left on the bridge over Bogie Channel. One added fuel to a camping lantern. Headlights hit him. A late-model rental car rolled slowly over the span toward No Name Key.

Gaskin Fussels came off the bridge barely above idle speed. No light except his high beams. A form appeared. Fussels hit the brakes. A miniature deer clopped across the road. Fussels's heart pounded in his ears. The rental began moving again. It was quiet the rest of the way down the long, straight dark road. Fussels slowed when he came to the end of the no-trespassing driveway. The muscles in his arms resisted instructions to turn the steering wheel. His chest heaved. The fear of *not* continuing overrode the panic instinct, and he turned onto the dirt road. The overgrowth was thick, almost forming a canopy, full of glowing animal eyes. The sedan quietly pulled around the back of a stilt house. Fussels knew he couldn't stop to think about it. He slipped out of the car and left the door ajar, creeping across the yard and tiptoeing up the stairs. He reached the sliding glass door and froze when he saw flickering light. *Scarface* playing on the big-screen TV with no volume. He cupped his face to the glass and scanned the room. Nothing. He grabbed the glass door's frame and lifted carefully. He cringed when it made a loud metal snap, but at least it was out of the track. He was in.

His skin was aflame, so much adrenaline it made a metallic taste in his mouth. He wouldn't have been able to move at all, but Fussels was on autopilot now. His progress across the wood floor was ultraslow, setting each step, then adding the weight, fearing creaks in the boards that came with every movement. Finally, good news: There was the ransom note, still sitting on the edge of the desk where the ship had been. Twenty feet away. Another step, another creak. Fifteen feet. Almost there. Ten. He wanted to reach with his arm and not risk more noise, but it was still too far. Another step . . . suddenly . . .

Fussels's feet flew from under him and he slammed to the floor with a tremendous thud. He found himself on his back in a pool of slick fluid that had caused the fall. He raised an arm; black drops fell from the sleeve. What the hell? He made his way back to his feet, concentrating on centering his weight like someone roller-skating for the first time. He was at the desk, the note easily in reach. Except he was still looking down at the floor. The fluid was dark and shiny in the moonlight coming through the giant hole in the roof. It trailed under the desk toward the wicker butterfly chair on the other side. The high-back seat was facing the opposite direction. Fussels used the desk for balance and started working his way around.

A '71 BUICK RIVIERA crossed the bridge to Big Pine and pulled up to a two-story, flat-roofed building with wasp-yellow trim. Coleman got out.

Serge and Molly had gone home after the meeting at the community hall, and Coleman went partying. Now he was lonely. He wanted to see if Serge could come out and play.

Coleman climbed the single staircase of Paradise Arms. He had a greasy white paper bag in his hand. He popped a jalapeño snap in his mouth and knocked on the door of apartment 213.

No answer.

He grabbed another snap and knocked again.

Still nothing.

Coleman bobbed his head to the memory of the last song from his car and stepped over to the window. He put his face to the glass and peeked through a slit where the curtains didn't quite meet.

"Oh, shit!"

He pulled a canceled video card from his wallet and stuck it in the doorjamb. It took a little work, but Coleman eventually tripped the angled bolt. He ran inside.

Serge was sitting in the middle of the living room in a wooden chair from the dining set, his back to the door. He looked over his shoulder. "Coleman! What are you doing here?"

Serge was tied up, his hands bound behind his back, ankles strapped to chair legs. A thick-braid nylon rope was loosely looped a ridiculous number of times around his chest like the Penguin used to tie up Batman.

Coleman rushed over and began undoing knots. "Don't worry, buddy! Have you free in a second!"

"Coleman! Get out of here! This is a game!"

"It's always a game with you!" Coleman freed the ankles. "Hang in there. Just a few more seconds . . ."

"Coleman, you don't understand—"

"I'm not as stupid as you think." Working the wrists now.

A falsely deep female voice: "You've been a bad rebel soldier!"

Serge and Coleman looked up at the bathroom door. It opened.

Molly was completely naked except for the Darth Vader helmet and toy light saber. There was a brief moment of suspended animation when everyone silently stared at each other. Then time speeded up. Shrieks of horror rattled out of the helmet. One of Molly's hands dropped the light saber and flew up to cover her breasts, the other shot down to the nexus of her legs. She ran crying into the bedroom and slammed the door.

It was quiet again in the living room except for the light saber rolling across the wooden floor with a sound representing husbands in deep shit everywhere.

Serge pushed Coleman away. "You idiot!" He finished untangling himself and ran to the bedroom. Molly was inconsolable, her head buried deep under the pillows. Serge caressed her back, but she wouldn't stop crying. He removed the pillows and helped get the helmet off.

It was no use, nothing Serge could say or do. Only more tears. He came out of the bedroom. Coleman was rummaging through the refrigerator.

"I'm new to this marriage thing," said Serge. "But I'm guessing this is the part where you need to leave."

"Let's go someplace."

"Coleman, I'm married now."

Coleman closed the fridge. "Damage is done. You'll only make it worse by staying here. I suggest you head to a bar with me and wait for this to blow over."

"You really think so?"

"Do it for Molly."

THE WIND HAD picked up again, blowing the stout beginnings of a good rainstorm. Perfect drinking weather. The '71 Buick Riviera pulled up to the No Name Pub. TV news was going in the background when Serge and Coleman came through the screen door and climbed on their favorite stools.

"*. . . A Wisconsin scuba diver was arrested just before dawn for public intoxication, burglary and other pending charges after breaking into the Key West Aquarium and spearfishing. The staff is mourning the loss of the lovable tarpon Bernie . . .*"

The owner was doing paperwork behind the bar. "Hey, Joe. How's it going?"

The owner didn't look up. "Hey."

Serge turned to the others. "He's usually in a good mood." Then he noticed the two men in dark suits. They were standing at one of the walls, writing in notebooks.

"Joe, who are those guys?"

"IRS."

"What are they doing?"

"Counting the dollar bills. It's considered income."

"*. . . Another body was discovered inside a sand castle on Smather's Beach. And from Duval Street, police are still puzzled by a Vermont man's head injuries. . . .*"

"Serge, that was a beautiful wedding," said Sop Choppy. "How's married life?"

"Molly's crying and refusing to come out of the bedroom."

"That's normal," said the biker. "What you need to do is wait it out in a bar. That's what I always do."

"But you're divorced," said Serge.

"Problem solved."

"Hey, Coleman," said Bud. "Where'd you disappear to after the wedding? We were supposed to meet back here."

"Had a little trouble when I tried to return Serge's tux," said Coleman. "Gave me shit, like, they're not for scuba diving or something."

"Get it straightened out?"

"No, I had to run away."

Daytona Dave pointed at the TV. "Look!"

A young female reporter appeared on the screen in a red rain jacket. She walked backward along a bridge railing, talking in her microphone. *"This is Eyewitness Five correspondent Maria Rojas coming to you live from the Seven-Mile Bridge where an intense human drama is currently unfolding. Authorities have blocked off traffic while they attempt to talk a distraught woman out of committing suicide. . . ."* The reporter looked up the bridge, where a half dozen police spotlights converged at the top of the span. The cameraman focused over the reporter's shoulder and zoomed in. A drenched woman had one leg over the railing.

"Check it out," said Coleman, popping a pretzel in his mouth. "It's Brenda."

"You need to call the police," said Serge.

Coleman chewed and washed it down with some draft. "Why?"

"Whenever a person is threatening suicide, they're always looking to put them on the phone with someone close."

"Get Coleman a phone!" yelled Sop Choppy.

A cell phone appeared. Bud Naranja hit nine-one-one and passed it to Coleman, who took a last quick sip and placed it to his ear.

"Hello? Yes, I know the woman on the TV. No, not the reporter, the jumper . . . Right, I'd like to help. I think she may want to talk to me. . . . Her boyfriend . . . yeah, I'd say we're pretty close. . . . I recently asked her to marry me. Sure, I'll hold." Coleman covered the phone. "They're patching me through."

"Wait a second," said Maria Rojas, placing a hand over the tiny speaker in her ear. *"The woman seems to be yelling something. Let's see if we can make it out...."* The camera zoomed even tighter on the top of the bridge. The TV station turned up the volume on the directional microphone pointed at Brenda. The wind whipped strands of wet hair across her eyes. *"I don't want to live anymore!... I can't face myself! ... I ... fucked ... Coleman! ..."*

The guys in the bar slapped Coleman on the back. "Way to go, dude!"

Coleman grinned, then waved them off. "Shhhh! I think they're putting me through!"

On TV, a police negotiator held a waterproof phone at the end of a long pole. He inched toward Brenda, urging her to take it. Brenda finally agreed and answered it tentatively.

"Uh, hello?"

"Hey, baby!" said Coleman. "What's shakin'?"

"Who's this?"

"It's Coleman! Your sugar daddy! Remember our special night?"

"Ahhhhhhhhhhhhhhhhhhhhh!"

The cameraman pointed over the side of the bridge to catch Brenda's fatal plunge into the stormy sea.

It was like a tomb inside the pub. Coleman quietly closed the cell phone and picked up a pretzel. The others stared at the floor and the ceiling. Rain pattered.

The station cut to an older man behind an anchor desk. *"We must remind our viewers that Eyewitness Five news brings you the best in live, unedited coverage and cannot be responsible for content...."* He shuffled papers and turned to a second camera, so the station could show it had a second camera. *"In other news, a suspected drug kingpin was found shot to death execution-style in his home on No Name Key. Police have sealed off the area, and aren't commenting. However, sources close to the investigation, who are those same police officers, have told us that they're closing in on the suspect as we speak.... In sports, more arrests..."*

The screen door creaked open. A soaked Gaskin Fussels stuck his head inside.

The gang jumped off stools and ran to the door. "Get in here!"

They dragged him to a table and sat him down. Gaskin closed his eyes and began weeping. "He's dead."

"We know he's dead," said Sop Choppy. "It was just on TV."

"What happened?"

"Did you kill him?"

Fussels shook his head emphatically. "I swear I didn't! He was already dead! You gotta believe me!"

"We believe you," said Bob the accountant. "But you have to tell us everything you saw."

"I didn't see anything. Just a big pool of blood and this butterfly chair facing the other way. So I crept around it and there he was, shot through the eyes!"

"They were sending a message," said Sop Choppy.

"What kind of message?" asked Bud.

"I don't remember the message code. But I think that's a strong one."

"All of you, shut up!" said Bob.

"What am I going to do?" pleaded Fussels.

"Just stay calm. We might be able to work this out. Is there any way they can connect you to this? Think hard! Did you leave any clues?"

"I don't think so."

"Okay, we need to get you out of town—"

"You mean like falling in the blood?"

"Yes, *like falling in the blood*. Did you get any on your hands?"

"Just the palms and fingertips."

"But you didn't touch anything. . . ."

"No."

"Good."

"Does the desk count?"

"Yes."

"Then the desk. . . . And the doorframe and the railing on the stairs, and the butterfly chair when I slipped again, and one of the legs of his pants pulling myself up, and on the ransom note that I dropped when I fell again and left behind in all the excitement. . . ."

The gang got up and started backing away.

"What?" said Fussels.

The screen door opened again.

Deputies Gus and Walter came in. "Is there a Gaskin Fussels here?"

They all pointed.

Gus produced handcuffs. "Gaskin Fussels, you're under arrest for the murder of Douglas Fernandez."

33

CAPTAIN FLORIDA'S LOG, star date 385.274
Starting to have my doubts about this marriage thing. Thought it was going to take me to the next level, but so far all it's been is moody obedience school. First Coleman breaking in during our Star Wars game, then more shit for going to the pub until three A.M. Didn't think it could get any worse. Was I wrong! Had a full day planned with Coleman, but Molly wanted to pick out bathroom towels. I'd already packed my gear and told her I'd be happy with whatever she picked out. Next thing I know, I'm fucked without a clue. All this negative body language and those slamming doors again. I run after her and say, 'What's the matter, honey?' And she says, 'Nothing.' But doors keep slamming. That's the thing about marriage—I haven't deciphered it yet. But I've just figured out the first thing. "Nothing" really means "something." If it actually is *nothing, they'll tell you all about it, just yap and yap and yap about the most meaningless tripe while you're trying to watch a documentary on Czar Nicholas, and finally I say—real nice—"Baby I've kind of been looking forward to this show all week. . . ." So now all of a sudden Czar Nicholas is more important than she is. Like a stupid idiot, I had to say he was— you know, Russia, dynasty, big turning point in global history. I'd tried climbing out of that hole but anything I said was just pulling more dirt down on myself. I called a married friend of mine*

in West Palm Beach and asked him what the hell was going on, and he said, "Are you nuts?" Turns out I'm supposed to pick out towels with her. It's part of the marriage bonding. I didn't know this. So I go to the department store, and she's happy again, and we're walking the aisles and pretty soon I want to cut my fucking head off. If I'm going to buy a towel, I walk in, grab a towel and buy the goddam thing. Then I wash with it. End of story, fade to black. But I find out that in marriage, the towel selection becomes some kind of introspective chick flick with Holly Hunter that lasts three hours and never goes anywhere. Molly keeps holding up towels and asking if I like them, and I nod impatiently, glancing at my watch. "Perfect. Love 'em. Let's go." And she says, "You don't like them. I can tell." And she picks up some more. "Love 'em. Spectacular." "You're just saying that." It goes on like this for twenty more towels until she finally decides on the very first ones she showed me. We go to the counter and—get this, the little hand towel in the set is nine dollars! I say, "Holy cow! In some countries you can get blown *for nine dollars!" Apparently this isn't what she wanted to hear. What am I, psychic? It's an around-the-clock minefield. Like whenever there's a bunch of blood on my clothes— automatic question time. Oh, and friends. That's another thing. I'm not allowed to have any. They're bad influences. And she really hates Coleman. Doesn't want him coming around anymore. I say he's my best friend. She says she works hard to keep a clean home and can't have him throwing up all over the place. I say, "But that's what he does." And whenever he is here, she's always calling me aside for secret conferences, like, "What's he doing?" And I say, "Drugs." Come to find out it wasn't really a question at all; it's a* rhetorical *question—another curve ball! But here's the biggest caveat: Actually, I can have a few friends, but they have to be married to* her *friends. After the towel travesty, there was this dinner at the head librarian's house where I was supposed to meet all my new, approved buddies, like a forced marriage in Nepal. Guys who wear plaid sweater vests. Jeffrey, Ronald, Ned. I tell myself, "Don't prejudge." The women are in the kitchen, and we're out back by the barbecue with glasses of Lipton having loads of chuckles, and then we go in the garage looking at tools and golf clubs and I'm bored as hell until I realize, hey, we've got everything here to make pipe bombs. In short, everyone got* way *too emotional in the emergency room, and now* I'm *the bad influence. I tell my wife, look, I didn't want to hang out with the noodle-dicks to begin with. . . . And that's why I'm writing this on Coleman's couch. Still looking for the sorcerer's key that unlocks it all. Night-night.*

34

The morning sky was threatening a slight drizzle. The local fishermen stayed in, but the tourists still went out in their rental boats, arrays of fishing poles sprouting from their holders like antennas. They wore bright yellow and orange rain slickers and fought uphill against the choppy tide in Bogie Channel with a style of seamanship suggesting future Coast Guard rescues. The weather wasn't that bad today, but tourists were known to go out even under storm flags. Vacation would not be denied.

Two people watched the bobbing vessels through the back patio windows of a waterfront ranch house on Big Pine Key. It was one of the older homes, built on the ground before flood-plane ordinance required stilts. The streets on this side of the island had names like Oleander, Hibiscus, Silver Buttonwood. The front yard was a field of little brown river rocks because fresh water was scarce for lawns. The rocks had an unintended security feature: You could always hear people driving up. In the middle of the yard was the centerpiece, a faux nineteenth-century ship's anchor. That's how visitors were given directions—"Just look for the anchor"—one of those big, three-hundred-pound jobs with a new antique verdigris finish, festooned with fishing nets and strings of colorful Styrofoam crab-trap floats. The nautical kitsch was surrounded by rings of cheerful lavender and pink flowers that had recently opened and would soon be chewed to the stems by night-feeding mini-deer. The original owner had known the bridge tender who was killed when a trawler struck the old Seven-Mile Bridge and was honored by a memorial plaque at the top of the new span that nobody could read because they were going by too fast and weren't allowed to stop. A baby-blue sea horse sat over the numbers by the door. A dark sedan was parked half a block up the street.

The two people watching the boats were sitting at the kitchen table. They had been there since long before dawn. Periods of intense conversation or awkward silence. This was one of the quiet spells. The table had a glass top with a pebbly surface and a round, white metal frame. It could be used outdoors. There were two coffee cups on the table. Bottle of scotch. Pair of dark sunglasses.

"I need another Valium," said Anna.

"You need to slow down."

"Are you going to give me one?"

The man opened his wallet and scooped out a pill.

Anna tossed it in her mouth and chased it with the contents of her coffee cup.

"It's all going to work out," said the man.

Anna set the cup down. "I feel even worse now."

The man put a hand on hers in the middle of the table. "It's over. You're finally safe. Time will heal."

"We could get the death penalty."

"We're not going to get caught. As long as neither one of us ever says anything. You can do that, can't you?"

"I knew I couldn't go through with it," said Anna. "I knew I couldn't shoot someone."

"Then what were we doing there?"

"Jesus, you shot him in the eyes!"

"I was just aiming for the head."

Anna's stomach spasmed. "I'm getting another panic attack."

"The Valium hasn't kicked in."

She poured more scotch.

"You're going to make yourself sick."

"I'm sick right now!" She fiddled with the sunglasses on the table. Her two black eyes had reached full bloom. She looked out the back window at the patio, which was the roof of the cistern. Her nose flared at the faint indication of the sulfur sticks that had been dropped in the tank for mosquitos. The man reached for her hand again. Drops of rain ran down the windows.

She pulled her arm away. "Why'd you grab the gun? Why'd you shoot him?"

"Because you didn't."

"I changed my mind. You heard him. He was ready to negotiate. And he started saying stuff about my brother that made no sense, a lot of stuff that made no sense, but you shot him before he could—"

"You think this is some kind of game? You think you can point a gun at someone like that and *not* shoot?"

"But we had his word. . . ."

"You still don't have any idea the type of person we were dealing with! He's going to say anything! He's not going to be grateful for sparing his life! He's going to come after us first chance he gets!"

"So fucking what? I was already on the run."

"But I wasn't! I tried to talk you out of this, remember? Then I'm standing there watching you lose your nerve, and I'm like, shit, that's my ass right there! Once you raised that gun, you wrote the future. Him or us."

Quiet again. No lights on inside the house, just what was coming through the windows from the overcast dawn, suspending the house in an off-balance gray. It was actually a pretty nice day to be alive in the Keys. Curl up with a book, listen to the rain, watch the weather.

"I hate this. It looks like shit out there."

"Are you going to be able to keep it together?"

"Why?" said Anna. "Are you going to kill me, too?"

The man looked down.

"I'm sorry. I didn't mean that."

"You don't need to say anything."

"No, you've been too good to me."

"I'll always be there for you. You know that."

This time, her hand reached across the table. "That's why I called the other day. That's why I called before, you know. . . ."

They looked at each other. History. Countless sobbing phone calls when Billy started hitting her up in Fort Pierce. More tears in person at coffee shops. Then, lovers.

Anna grabbed the scotch. She decided not to pour and put it down. "The Valium's working."

"Good."

She began picking at a corner of the bottle's black label. "I recognized him."

"Who?"

"Scarface."

"You did?"

"Up in Fort Pierce. From the marina. He was one of the guys who came around a couple times. But he was just one of the loaders. I don't get it."

"He did that sometimes."

"You said he never met anyone."

"Not as Scarface. Because he didn't trust anyone. But since almost nobody knew what he looked like, it allowed him to move invisibly through his own organization to make sure nobody was skimming, which they always were. A lot of guys ended up dead and never knew why."

The man checked his watch. Getting near eight. He grabbed the scotch.

"I thought you weren't drinking."

"So did I." He looked across the terrazzo of the vacation home that used to belong to Anna's brother. "You decided to stay here after all."

"With Scarface gone, there's no reason not to."

The man drained his cup and poured again.

"You're making up for lost time."

There was a purpose. He finished the second drink and let it work. The clouds finally let loose outside. Rain pounded the windows at a hard angle.

"I have a confession to make."

Anna stretched and yawned from the medicine.

"My motives weren't entirely pure."

"What are you talking about?"

"I wanted to protect you and everything. I really liked your brother. . . ."

"Yeah?"

"Remember the rumors I told you about? Rick putting money away with Scarface—Fernandez, whoever. It wasn't a rumor. I knew it for a fact."

Anna looked confused.

"For some reason Fernandez liked your brother. Or at least trusted him. Or didn't. But your brother was sharp. He knew this wouldn't last forever . . . he had to put something away. Sometimes we'd go drinking after bringing a boat in. Fernandez was always asking him questions about money. He finally let your brother know who he really was. That might have gotten him killed."

Anna's breathing shallowed. She grabbed the scotch again. Rain sheeted on the glass.

"Fernandez and Rick got some money together. I know you didn't know. It's at least three million, maybe four. I don't know where it is. Well, I do, sort of. There's a safety deposit box—"

Anna raised the cup to her mouth with both hands.

"The box contains instructions in case anything ever happened to Rick. Some of the money was your husband's, except your brother knew Billy would just gamble it. So he put it away for you. There are four names on the deposit box. Fernandez, your brother and his wife. And you—you're the only one still alive to claim it."

Anna was grabbing the edge of the table. "H-how do you know all this?"

"Your brother knew about you and me being . . . together. He could just tell. It almost made him feel better knowing I was there for you because he'd already given up on Billy. A few times he came close to killing him over the beatings he gave you. He came to me one day, asked if anything happened to him, that I'd tell you about the box. Made me swear."

Anna just sat there; too much to process at once.

"You're going to hate me for what I'm going to say next, so I'm just going to say it. . . ." He looked her straight in the eyes. "I want Fernandez's share. You can have the rest."

"Jesus, Jerry!"

"I don't like this any better. But I'm practical. We don't have much time before the police find out their guy in the morgue has a deposit box. Then it's gone for good."

"But how can you think about money at a time like this?"

"I'll tell you how! I've been sitting here for years, watching Fernandez over in his fancy house getting rich and fat while I work a shitty job fetching drinks for a bunch of tourists I have to pretend to like. That's how. I want mine! I deserve it!"

Anna pressed back in her chair. "What's wrong with you?"

Jerry the bartender poured another scotch. "You have to go to the bank."

"I'm not going anywhere!"

"Yes, you are. We're in this together now." He raised the cup to his mouth. "You *will* be going to the bank."

"But what about the murder? Shouldn't we be lying low?"

"We don't have to worry about that."

"Why not?"

Jerry reached in his pocket and set a brass bank key on the table. "I fixed it so they suspect someone else."

35

Monday evening: six-thirty

Serge was in the living room of the love nest, checking his wristwatch. Molly was in the bathroom. A car honked outside.

Serge looked out the curtains. Coleman.

"Honey! . . . I'm leaving for my meeting. Love you! . . ." He grabbed the doorknob.

"Wait a minute," called Molly. She walked into the room holding one of the new hand towels. It was dangling between her thumb and index finger like a used diaper.

"What is it?" said Serge. "I'm running late."

"Did you use this?"

"Yeah, I washed my hands."

"You're not supposed to use this."

He grabbed the doorknob again. "Right, right . . . what?"

"You weren't supposed to use it."

"It's a towel."

"You don't use these."

A car honked.

"Sure thing." He opened the door.

"You don't care."

"I do so care."

"I'm not finished talking about this."

"Can we deal with it when I get home? I've got people waiting."

"They're more important than our marriage?"

"Of course not. But the meeting starts at a specific time. We can discuss your towels later."

"What do you mean, '*your* towels'?"

"I didn't mean anything. . . ." Glancing at his watch. ". . . Come on, don't stare at me like that."

Honk.

"Shit." He stuck his head out the door. "Coleman, knock it off. Be down in a minute." He closed the door. "Okay, let's talk."

She stood there.

"I thought you wanted to talk."

Still standing there.

"Okay, see you tonight." He opened the door.

"You never liked these towels."

Serge closed the door. "What?"

"I knew it."

Serge gritted his teeth. "The towels are fine. I may eventually grow to hate them at this rate. But right now they're still okay by me. . . . Can I leave now?"

"Go ahead. Go off with your friends."

"It's a trick. That means stay."

"I want to make a nice home for us."

"And I'm all for that." He looked at his watch and emitted a high-pitched whine of anxiety. "I understand completely. I promise I won't use the towels."

"No, just the *guest* towels."

"What's the difference?"

"You don't use them."

Honk.

"I really gotta go."

Molly's silence said not to.

"Okay, you win!" Serge dropped into a chair. "Let's talk about it. Are there any other movie props around here that I can't touch or I'll get a ration of shit?"

Molly ran crying into the bedroom and slammed the door.

"What did I say?"

Monday evening: six-thirty. Sheriff's substation, Cudjoe Key

"I HATE THE night shift," said Walter. He dumped an old pot of coffee in the sink.

Gus highlighted a textbook with a yellow marker. "It's always slow on Monday."

Walter went through mail at his desk while new coffee trickled. Gus swivelled his chair and taped another fax to the wall.

Walter came over with his coffee mug. He had an envelope in the other hand. "I got a piece of your mail by mistake." He handed it to Gus. "It's from Internal Affairs."

"How do you know?"

"I opened it."

"Thanks."

"Someone filed a complaint about you having marijuana evidence that was supposed to be destroyed."

Gus tossed the letter aside and resumed reading. Walter took a sip and stared at the wall. "New bulletin?"

"They connected another possible murder to the Duster." Gus made a yellow line in his book. "And the missing woman's green Trans Am was spotted in Marathon."

"Looks like trouble."

"I know," said Gus. "They're probably both headed our way."

"No, I mean you're not supposed to tape stuff to the walls. Department rule."

Gus looked up dubiously at his partner, then back to his textbook.

"I'm just trying to help," said Walter. "You're already under investigation. Is it true you were even showing drugs to kids?"

"Walter, you were there. It was a class."

"I'll say whatever you want me to. We're partners. You just tell me what the line is, and that's how I'll testify."

"Testify?"

Walter pointed back at his own desk. "Got a letter myself from Internal. They want me to turn on you. They can stick their rules. This is about loyalty."

"Let me see that letter."

"I'm not allowed to show you."

Gus returned to his book.

Walter took a sip of coffee. "What are you reading?"

"Psychological profiles," said Gus. "I'm getting a strong feeling that something big is about to happen around here."

"Looks boring."

"Actually, it's quite amazing." Gus tapped a page. "Check this out. They've developed a written test that's ninety-nine percent accurate in determining whether someone's a potential serial killer."

"Baloney," said Walter. "If it's a written test, they'll just lie. People are going to answer the way they think you want them to."

"That's the fascinating part," said Gus. "There are a bunch of obvious questions on the test where people *will* answer like they think they're supposed to: 'If you could get away with it, would you shoot someone who slept with your wife? Stole ten thousand dollars? Got you fired?' But those are the null questions. Scattered in between are a handful of innocuous ones a person would never suspect—those are the real questions. Any answer would appear benign. But they've empirically prescreened the test, administering it to hundreds of murderers in prison, as well as people of unimpeachable character, boiling down the questions until they arrived at a short list with a ninety-nine percent mutual exclusion rate between the two groups."

"Like?"

"Like this one. A woman is at her mother's funeral and she meets this hunk of a guy. It's love at first sight. The next week the woman murders her sister. What was her motive?"

"I don't know," said Walter. "Her sister made a move on the guy?"

"No."

"The woman started dating the guy, and her sister told some horrible lie that made him dump her?"

"No."

"I give up."

"Here's the red-flag answer that says you think like a killer: She wanted to meet the guy again at the next funeral."

"But that makes no sense."

"That's why normal people don't give that answer."

"It's a stupid test."

Gus grabbed the keys to the cruiser. "We need to get going."

Seven o'clock, plus a few minutes

AN ECLECTIC BLEND of people in "I Follow Nobody" T-shirts milled around the base of the Bogie Channel Bridge, where Serge's notice on the community center's bulletin board had told them to assemble for their first field trip. They were joined by several regulars from the pub and some clowns from a local carnival who were buying pot from Coleman.

A '71 Buick Riviera skidded up, and Serge jumped out. "Welcome to the Night Tour!"

He reached in the backseat for camera equipment. "Truly apologize for being late. Hate it when people do that to me. Unavoidable personal emergency. Okay, I'm actually having marriage problems. But that's confidential; I can't reveal any details. Even *I* don't know the details. And I definitely don't want anything getting back to her in such a small town that might make it worse. So all I can tell you is I think my wife is getting her period. Is everyone ready?"

They nodded.

Serge began leading them on foot over the bridge.

". . . Observe the stars, their concentration and brightness almost like special effects this far from the light pollution of the cities. . . . And now we come to the night fishermen. Can't say enough about the night fishermen! You see them throughout the Keys, every night, all night. How can they spend so much time like this? When do they sleep? What about their jobs? . . ." The fishermen stared at Serge as he walked by talking loudly. ". . . Don't they know how to form relationships? What killed their life ambition? Keep it up, guys! . . . And now we come to No Name Key, best viewing location for miniature deer, especially at night when it's cooler and they come out to forage. . . ."

The gang walked two more miles down the straight road across the island. They saw a total of eight deer, including a doe and a fawn that slowly crossed the street ahead of them and climbed into the brush. They came to the end of the road, which used to be the ferry landing before they built the Seven-Mile Bridge. Now it was just ruins with a barricade and reflective warning sign so tourists wouldn't drive into the water.

"This way." Serge left the road and started up an unofficial footpath that led from the north side of the pavement. The gang followed. After a few hundred yards, dense trees gave way to a moonlit clearing bordered by mangroves on the bay side. Water from a rising tide splashed through a maze of exposed roots that ensnared trash. Swim trunks, fishing line, rusty beer cans, two shoes tied together, mildewed pup tent and a Clorox bottle.

Somebody else already occupied Serge's clearing. Teenagers in trench coats and stud collars and black makeup. They tended a waning campfire. A small pelt lay on the ground, blood and entrails. One of them held a stick over the fire, roasting an animal heart.

"Who the heck are you?" asked Serge.

The teen with the stick took a bite off the end. "Vampires."

Another teen with spiked palm mitts relieved himself in the bushes. "Devil worshipers."

"Which is it?" asked Serge.

"Both," said the one by the fire.

"I see," said Serge. "Overachievers."

The one at the fire stood up. He was the leader because his mother let him borrow the station wagon. "What are you doing here?"

"Holding a meeting," said Serge. "We reserved this clearing. It's been on the board at the community hall all week. I know we're a little late, but we still have the rest of the hour."

"You have intruded on the sacred sacrificial circle," intoned the leader. *"And now you must die. . . ."*

One of the people susceptible to joining cults raised his hand. "Is it hard to become a vampire?"

"*. . . We call on you, most high Satan, to strike down the unbelievers . . .*" The leader continued incantations as he walked around the group, drawing on the ground with a long stick. "*. . . I am now drawing the death pentagram, condemning your souls to the eternal bowels of hell. . . . Pardon me. . . .*"

"Oh, sorry." One of the clowns stepped out of the way so the teen could continue his line.

"*. . . Your mortal remains will be torn asunder, consumed by the seven-headed beast, your intestines devoured. . . .*"

Coleman tapped Serge's shoulder. "He's making me hungry."

"Me, too. Night Tours require munchies." Serge borrowed a cell phone and punched in a number. "Hello? No Name? Eight large pepperoni supremes. Make it an even ten. . . ."

"*. . . Oblivion awaits. I unleash the curse of the black tabernacle. . . .*"

"No, that'll be delivery," said Serge. "You know the clearing off the north side near the ferry landing? That's right, the devil-worship place. Thanks."

The teen began saying The Lord's Prayer backward. "*. . . Evil from us deliver and temptation into not us lead. Trespass against forgive . . .* Wait, that's not it. The 'trespasses' always mess me up. . . ."

"Hey, Vlad the Imp," said Serge. "Until oblivion gets here, we'll just start our meeting over there if that's all right."

They gathered round Serge's feet at the edge of the clearing. He began his trademark pacing.

"The Keys are an enchanted land removed from the continent, evolving independently like the Galapagos, a necklace of lush little neighborhoods across the Overseas Highway where the bad parts of town have *boats* up on blocks. Churches, dogcatchers, school buses, oncoming bikers low-fiving on drawbridges, art-guild galleries specializing in watercolors and handbags made from coconuts, streets like Cutthroat Lane and Mad Bob Road, a fire chief actually named Bum Farto, a mayor arrested for shaking down jet ski rentals, tourists eating mangoes out of motel swimming pools, wild roosters, feral cats, Duval merchants charging credit cards of Dutch visitors five *hundred* dollars for a T-shirt, federal roadblocks sparking the Conch Republic revolution. 'Remember the Aloe!' Then, greed. Unaffordable resorts crowding out the funk that brought 'em here in the first place. A bearded, turtle-necked Papa Hemingway reduced to a logo for Sloppy Joe's franchises like some kind of literary Chef Boyardee. The real Key West vanishing, moving toward a convergence point with the Key West pavilion at Sea World: tourists forsaking the genuine article to stumble through piped-in Jamaican music, plastic trees and misting wands, thinking they're part of the wild Key West lifestyle. 'Y'all better stand back. I'm pretty crazy. Who knows what I'll do next? Guess I'll buy me another Creamsicle.' I tried to warn them. 'Run!' I yelled. 'Run before they strap the rat cage on your face!' But nobody wanted to talk to me except security. . . ."

The audience heard a rustling in the brush. Serge stopped his speech. The head teen arose by the campfire. *"Almighty Lucifer has heeded our unworthy calls. . . ."*

The rustling grew louder. Something large approached through the mangroves.

"The sword is raised! Beg for the mercy you won't receive! . . ."

Everyone tensed and huddled together, eyes shifting nervously. The sound came closer and closer until it was right at the edge of the clearing. Whatever it was would emerge any second.

"Bow your heads for sweet death! Behold! It is Satan! . . ."

A deliveryman in a paper cap popped into the clearing. "Ten supremes?"

Serge waved. "Over here, Satan."

The gang began chowing.

"Is that pizza?" asked one of the vampires.

"Yeah," said Serge, holding up a slice. "Want some?"

"Sure!"

"Approach not the unbelievers!" yelled the leader.

"But it's *pizza*."

The two groups merged, stomachs filled, then digestion. Everyone gathered quietly around Serge by the campfire. His face glowing red as he poked embers with a stick. A number of attentive squirrels, owls and deer arrived and listened along the edge of the woods.

". . . The Keys are like Florida squared, but not for long. It's a creeping rot, inoperable gangrene moving up a limb, starting at Mile Zero and crawling east along U.S. One. Key West was the final haven of the true individual, a subtropical Greenwich Village. But it got too popular. In came shortsighted developers, cutting off their own air supply, raising prices so high that service employees can't afford to live there any longer. . . ."

A vampire raised his hand. "Is this a concurrency flaw in the growth-management plan or simply a multi-dwelling density issue?"

"It's both, but it's more. Who's heard of Donald Greely?"

Some hands went up. "Isn't he supposed to move down here?" asked a teen.

"Just did," said Serge. "But here's the worst part. He's planning a major development. Not supposed to, under the deal with the bankruptcy court. So he's fronting for some cats. It's along the protected southern shore of Key West."

"But if it's protected . . ."

"Bribes," said Serge. "Bribes and secrecy. That's the part I hate the most. I'm not a hard case. Developers have to make a living, too. Just do it in the open. But, no, it's all cigar smoke and brown envelopes slipped inside coat pockets. Secrecy, secrecy, secrecy! . . ."

"Then how did you find out about the development?"

"Can't tell you. It's a secret."

"What can we do about it?" said one of the clowns.

"Glad you asked. Greely's laying a preemptive foundation of local goodwill by giving to all these charities. The climax is this new community appreciation festival he's sponsoring Saturday. Big shindig, free food, music, blah-blah-blah—you know, the kind of event they advertise with vinyl banners over the road. The newspaper even published a schedule of all these celebrity appearances he's going to make—limbo, parasail, get on stage to sing with one of the bands—trying to prove he's a regular guy."

"But Serge, what's that got to do with us?"

The air cooled. A previously unseen cloud slipped across the moon. Serge rubbed his palms together. "I have a plan. Here's what we're all going to do. . . ."

There was an ominous rustling again out in the dark brush. Serge stopped talking. People looked in the direction of the sound. Goose bumps.

The rustling grew louder. Then a final snapping of branches before a large form appeared at the edge of the woods.

"The Skunk Ape!"

"Hi, Serge."

"Hi, Roger."

"I smelled pizza."

"A few slices left. Have at it."

"Thanks."

Serge crouched by the fire again. "Okay, here's the plan." He laid it out in detail. A role for everyone. Compartmentalized. Tight synchronization. He was just about finished when there was another rustling from the woods.

"What now!"

A naked woman popped into the clearing.

Bud Naranja jumped back in alarm. "That's her! That's the woman who kidnapped me!"

"Hi, Serge," said the woman. "Been a long time."

"I'm married now."

"Damn."

"What are you doing here?"

"I smelled pizza."

"Roger's got the last box."

"Cool."

Serge pulled a large envelope from his shirt, removing a stack of papers that he began handing out. "Here are your plans for our tactical operation at the Greely festival. Each is different depending on your mission. . . . And one for you and you, and one for you . . . Accompanying the plans is a separate homework assignment. It's a scavenger list. Right after this meeting I want you all to go on your own Night Tour and find as many items as you can before dawn. Then we'll meet at the address at the bottom for breakfast—if you make it! And one for you, and one for you . . . Each item must be touched for it to be considered an official find. Do not remove artifacts. Photos or tracing permitted. . . . And one for you, and one for you . . . Coleman, one of the vampires didn't get one."

"I see him."

Serge held up the empty envelope. "Everyone got theirs? . . . Good. Gather round." Serge put out his right arm, palm down. Everyone made a tight circle, placing their hands on top of Serge's, like a college football team before a big game. "Bow your heads," said Serge. "Almighty Father, please stop making jerks. Amen . . . Break!"

36

A GREEN-AND-WHITE sheriff's cruiser flew east on U.S. 1.

Walter had the microphone in his hand. "Ten-four, we're rolling." Gus hit the lights and siren.

A NAKED WOMAN walked down a dirt road on Sugarloaf Key. She was reading a piece of paper.

The woman approached the bat tower and placed her palm against the side. She grabbed a pen from over her ear and crossed it off the sheet. She wandered off into the darkness reading the paper.

A sheriff's cruiser rolled slowly down a dirt road on Sugarloaf Key. Gus scanned with the search beam. They reached the end of the road, their spotlight sweeping across the base of the bat tower. Walter was on the radio. ". . . Nope, no sign of her."

SERGE AND COLEMAN walked down another footpath from the clearing until they reached an opening on the water. Small waves lapped the shore. Coleman was carrying his flexible cooler. "I love Night Tours."

"Give me a hand with the airboat."

They sloshed into the water and dragged the hull off the sand. Serge held the boat steady a few yards from shore while Coleman climbed up into the high seat in back, grabbing a beer and stowing the cooler.

Serge thrust himself over the gunwale and settled into the low driver's seat up front. He started the engine. The airboat zoomed away from the island with astounding acceleration. Serge gripped the control stick hard in his right hand, cheeks flapping in the high wind. Coleman was pasted back in his seat, sucking an aluminum can, rivulets of beer that had missed his mouth trickling upstream over his forehead windshield-style.

"You buckled in?" yelled Serge.

"What?"

"Good." He made a sharp port turn around a mangrove point, catapulting Coleman into the water.

The airboat ripped across the flats. Serge tore up the channel on the windward side of Howe Key, then cut east, spraying water, making the wide pass between Raccoon and the Contents, yelling back over the deafening propeller.

". . . Always wanted to do this, Coleman! Trace the historic route of Happy Jack and his merry band, the original Keys party animals! The books of the great historian John Viele bird-dogged me to the microfilm of the original *Putnam's* and *Harper's* articles from the 1850s. What a gang! Jolly Whack, Paddy Whack, Red Jim, Lame Bill, Old Gilbert and of course their leader, Jack himself. They drank whiskey and rum on the isolated north coast of Sugarloaf. When the booze ran out, they harvested vegetables and sailed to Key West to barter for more spirits. One problem: they started drinking on the way back and kept falling overboard. . . ."

Serge tacked a gradual thirty degrees southwest, mangrove silhouettes all around. He skirted the Torch Keys, then Summerland and Cudjoe. The moon caught the white skin of the radar blimp tethered at five hundred feet. Serge opened the throttle wide for another screaming run across the flats.

COLEMAN WADED ASHORE on Big Pine and started walking up a deserted road. Headlights hit him. A station wagon stopped. The back door opened. Coleman got in with the vampires.

BIG FLOPPY SHOES slapped down a footpath on Coppitt Key. The trail led between a row of dirty headstones. Two men read checklists as they walked. Red rubber balls on their noses. Mr. Blinky stopped and fired up a joint. He handed it to Uncle Inappropriate, then bent down and touched one of the tombstones. He stood up and crossed it off his page.

The pair continued passing the joint as they strolled off into the darkness. On the other side of the cemetery, a sheriff's cruiser rolled through the front gate.

Gus panned the searchlight across the tombstones. "What exactly did the dispatcher say?"

"You know, the usual. Some clowns in the cemetery . . ."

AN AIRBOAT BLASTED across the Great White Heron National Wildlife Refuge and slalomed through the Saddlebunches. Serge was in his element. "Over there," he shouted. "Boca Chica, where the Navy jets touch and go. Used to have a historic dive. The men's room door opened to the parking lot. . . ."

The airboat straightened out and raced northeast, avoiding sandbars that were only visible on a map in Serge's brain. He heard other boats now. Distant running lights from the fishing trawlers; no lights on the smugglers. Getting closer, skimming north of Stock Island, then the naval installations on Dredgers and Fleming Keys. "Almost there, Coleman! . . ." A final cut due south through Man of War Harbor, on a dead bearing for the sparkling lights of Key West Bight.

Duval Street. Key West

DRUNK TOURISTS STAGGERED out of saloons, barefoot runaways begged on the sidewalk in front of St. Paul's. A station wagon drove north through the intersection of Eaton. Five vampires read five sheets of paper.

"Let me off up here."

The car stopped at the corner of Greene. Coleman got out. He stuck his head back in a window. "I think number eighteen is right over there. Serge takes me all the time."

"Thanks." The station wagon turned left. Coleman began walking east toward the string of bars along the harbor. All had doors open to the night air. Turtle Kraals, Half-Shell. Coleman entered Schooner's and took a seat overlooking the big dock that ran parallel behind the restaurant. He ordered a rumrunner and opened his wallet to the family photo section stuffed with bar coupons.

Coleman had just finished his drink when a deep aviation drone came across the water, growing louder and louder until a silver airboat appeared out of the night. The boat pulled sideways up to the dock as Coleman trotted down the steps behind the bar.

Serge unbuckled his seatbelt and reached down for the mooring rope. "Coleman, get up on the dock and tie us off." He turned and threw the line to Coleman, who wrapped it around a cleat.

Serge climbed out of the boat, and they headed off on the Night Tour.

In the parking lot at the end of the pier, headlights came on. A brown Plymouth Duster.

SERGE LED COLEMAN on a crooked path until he stopped and sat on a curb between the water and the end of Lazy Day Lane.

Coleman tried to get a wet lighter going. "Why are we stopping here?"

"There's Jimmy's secret studio, number twenty-two on the scavenger list. I want to see who gets it first."

"What studio?"

"That plain, white-washed building with no signs. Looks like an ice house."

"Buffett really records there?"

"Yeah, but nobody's supposed to know," said Serge. "I staked out the place two years ago when I heard they were about to start the new album. Sure enough, these fancy cars start pulling up, people looking around suspiciously before ducking inside. I recognized Fingers and Utley and Mac and finally Bubba himself. I figured that was my chance."

"Chance for what?"

"To do some session work. I've always wanted to get in the liner notes. So I grab the door before it closed behind someone. You wouldn't believe how many people are in there when they record. You got technicians and extra musicians and a million personal assistants getting coffee and Danish. People were tripping all over each other, so I tried to stay out of the way and stood in the back by the three microphones set up next to the keyboards. After ten minutes, the guy behind the mixer points me out to the bodyguards. Up till then, everyone just assumed I was with somebody else. The guards walk over and ask just what the hell I think I'm doing. I say, 'Singing backup.' So now I've got six guys on me. Jimmy was off to the side going over sheet music, but he finally looked up when we knocked over the cymbals. They had me completely off the ground, rushing toward the door. I yell, 'Fine, Jimmy. I know when I'm not wanted. And for the record, it's been an awfully long time since 'He Went to Paris.' Go ahead, put out another sonic-turd . . . Then I hit the sidewalk—"

"Someone's coming."

They looked across the street. A naked woman walked out of the darkness, reading a piece of paper. She stopped and pressed a palm against the white building. She walked away, grabbing the pen off her ear.

"I knew she'd be good at this." Serge stood up. "Let's rock."

They headed back to Greene Street and went inside a bar with a giant grouper over the door.

"So this is Captain Tony's," said Coleman.

"Used to be the Blind Pig and the original Sloppy Joe's." Serge sniffed the air. "Still reeks of history! See that tree growing up through the roof? Used to be the 'hanging tree' when they still had public executions at the turn of the century. And look over here on the floor next to the pool table."

"A grave marker?"

"Uncovered it when they were building on, so they just poured the cement around it. There's Eric Clapton's bar stool and John Goodman's and Neil Diamond's. Everyone comes to Captain Tony's! Once I was sitting in here and we see this bunch of guys march past the door in combat fatigues. A couple minutes later they march back the other way."

"Who were they?"

"Cuban military defectors. We're always getting them here, like the guy who landed his MiG at the airport. This group had pulled their patrol boat right into the harbor, completely undetected. They couldn't find anyone to turn themselves in to, so they just wandered the tourist district with fully loaded Kalashnikovs. But nobody paid any attention because everything's so weird down here. They finally came in Captain Tony's and surrendered to the guitar player."

Coleman looked up at an old photo on the wall. "Who's this?"

"A young Captain Tony fishing with Ernest Hemingway, and here's a poster from the movie they made about Tony's life. It's driving me nuts!"

"What is?"

"Everyone's met him but me. I just have to talk to the captain! He's well into his eighties now, the last living link. Done it all, running booze and guns, then this saloon, where Tennessee Williams hung out. Was even mayor for a while. You know what his motto is?"

"No."

"It's right up there on those T-shirts they're selling. 'All you need in this life is a tremendous sex drive and a great ego. Brains don't mean shit.' I disagree, of course, but still a nice sentiment."

A Skunk Ape came in reading a piece of paper and put his hand against the hanging tree.

"Tony looks pretty old in this other picture," said Coleman.

"He *is* old. But the sex-drive part isn't just cheap talk. Women still flock to him in amazing numbers. Everyone around here knows all about the phenomenon."

A PLYMOUTH DUSTER sat at the curb next to the Bull & Whistle. Combat boots climbed an old wooden staircase to the second floor, then around the landing and up another flight. The roof was a clothing-optional lounge. Except some weekdays in the summer were slow, like now. You could still go up and look over the side of the building for a bird's eye of Duval, but the bar was closed. The combat boots crossed the roof. The access door at the top of the stairs had been jammed shut with a chair. Gloved hands snapped a folding stock in place and screwed on the silencer. The end of a rifle barrel soon rested on Spanish roofing tiles at the edge of the building. Serge and Coleman appeared in the scope's crosshairs as they walked past a street artist doing caricatures. Vampires came toward them on the sidewalk.

"How many you got?" asked Serge.

"Eight," said the leader, holding up his list with enthusiasm. "Would have had nine, but couldn't catch the Hemingway cat. Wish me luck. . . ."

"Satanspeed."

Up on the rooftop, an eye stayed pressed to a rifle scope. Serge still in the crosshairs, waving goodbye to the teens as they parted in opposite directions. A leather finger curled around the trigger.

One of the vampires stopped on the sidewalk. He looked at his list, then at the Volkswagen driving by. "There's number sixteen. An insane person's car."

"Where?"

"The Beetle completely covered with bumper stickers, seashells, bingo markers and religious figurines."

They sprinted back up the sidewalk, passing Serge and Coleman. The fastest darted into the street and caught the car at a red light, slapping the fender. "Sixteen!" The slowest ran up behind Serge just in time to take a slug in the shoulder.

"Did you hear something?" said Serge.

"You mean like a yell?" said Coleman.

"Yeah. You heard it, too?"

"No."

They kept walking.

Leather hands quickly disassembled the rifle. Combat boots ran across the roof and down the stairs.

THE END OF the night. Serge's favorite time. The critical thirty minutes when the sky goes from its blackest to a tricky tease of light. Serge just *had* to be at the Southernmost Point, sitting on the seawall, legs hanging over and kicking with hope.

"My stomach's making that noise," said Coleman.

"You're not watching," said Serge.

The sky ran through a palette of grays and blues, the amorphous view toward the Gulf Stream separating into sky and water. A rooster activated in the distance. Serge stood and stretched. They began walking again, starting to see people, someone on the curb weaving five-dollar hats from palm fronds, someone else setting up a table of conch shells.

Serge picked up one of the largest shells. "May I?"

"May you what?" said the man behind the table.

"I'm going to be in that big conch-blowing contest next month," said Serge. "I'd like to practice my chops."

"Just don't drop it." The man began unloading another box.

Serge held the shell an inch from his mouth. "Okay Coleman, this is the winning entry for sure. I've been polishing it all year. Joe Walsh's guitar solo from 'Life in the Fast Lane.'"

"I love that song."

"Here goes . . ." Serge pressed the shell to his lips.

Coleman tapped his foot to the catchy tune. Serge blew relentlessly into the third and fourth measures with big Dizzy Gillespie cheeks. The man behind the table looked up. "I've never heard anyone play that fast."

"It's 'Life in the Fast Lane,'" said Coleman.

"His face is purple."

"It gets that way."

"Do his eyes roll up in his head?"

"Serge!" yelled Coleman.

Serge was still playing, reeling sideways off balance until he crashed into the bushes.

Coleman ran over and shook him. "You all right?"

Serge sat up and blew the spit out of his shell. "They might as well start engraving that trophy."

They were on the move again, past the Southernmost House, the Southernmost Inn, the Southernmost transient, back around Simonton Street and up to a building that opened in 1962. On the roof, a suntan lotion sign with a dog tugging a little girl's bathing suit.

Serge opened the door. Most of the gang was already seated around the U-shaped lunch counters of Dennis Pharmacy, comparing lists, spearing sunny-side yolks. Serge and Coleman grabbed stools and menus.

The front door opened again.

"Serge!"

"Joe!" Serge then noticed the eighty-seven-year-old man standing next to the owner of the No Name. "You actually got him to come!"

"I told you I would."

The old man appraised Serge. "You look like a fucking tourist in that shirt."

"I know. Isn't it great? All the toll collectors wear them." Serge faced the gang at the counter. "Can I have your attention? Our dysfunctional klatch is honored this morning by the presence of the one-and-only Captain Tony! Number thirty-seven on your lists."

"*That's* Captain Tony?" They quickly formed a line, one by one touching him on the shoulder.

The pharmacy window opened; Coleman was waiting behind a young woman with multiple piercings.

". . . I'm telling you," said the pharmacist. "I've known this doctor all my life and this isn't his handwriting. . . ."

"Yes, it is," said the woman.

". . . And he never gives fifteen refills for painkillers."

"I'll take one."

The pharmacist picked up the phone. "You can either leave or be here when the police arrive."

Two hungry sheriff's deputies got out of their cruiser and walked toward the pharmacy.

"I thought you told me this was going to be a quiet night," said Walter.

"I've never seen anything like it," said Gus. There was a piece of paper stapled to the telephone pole on the corner, a photocopy of a penis with a Mr. Bill face. Gus tore it down and crumpled it into a ball. "I'm just glad it's finally over." The front door flew open and smacked Gus in the shoulder. "Ow." A young woman took off down the street.

The deputies went inside and walked past the pharmacist, who smiled at Coleman. "Now, how can I help you?"

Coleman slipped a prescription back in his pocket. "Uh, where's the rest room?"

The deputies headed for the breakfast counter.

"Hey, there's Captain Tony," said Gus. "The legend."

A naked woman put her hand on Tony's shoulder.

"He's still got it," said Walter.

Serge saw the deputies and energetically waved them over. "Join us!" He turned to the gang. "Some of you make room for hardworking law enforcement."

"Serge, please," said Gus. "I don't want to take anyone's seat."

"Nonsense. You're heroes."

The deputies grabbed stools, and Gus opened his textbook.

Serge turned to the captain. "I was just telling my friend about your hanging tree."

"Almost cut it down," said Tony.

"What!"

"Didn't know what it was. This was decades ago. The thing was wrecking my roof. And this old-timer says, 'You can't cut that down. It's the hanging tree.' He tells me that when he was a little kid, he saw them lynch a woman. Except she didn't die right away, tongue sticking out and wiggling and everything . . ."

Walter made a butter pool in his grits, then pointed at his partner's textbook with a fork. "You still on that psychology garbage?"

"I'm telling you, the test works."

Walter salted his hash browns. "It's a stupid test."

"What's a stupid test?" said Serge.

"We've been having an argument all night," said Gus. "Maybe you can help us."

"Name it. Always ready to help the police."

"It's not a big deal. Just a riddle."

"Tell me."

"A woman goes to her mother's funeral and meets this hunk, and she's smitten. The next week she kills her sister. What's the motive?"

"What else?" said Serge. "She wanted to meet him at the next funeral."

"There!" said Walter. "There's your great test! You've asked one person so far. One hundred percent failure rate."

"I don't understand it," said Gus. "They backed it up with all kinds of research. Less than one percent false results." He looked at Serge. "How on earth did you know that answer?"

"What are you talking about?"

"That answer is supposed to indicate someone who thinks like a serial killer. . . ."

Serge laughed unnaturally. "Ha, ha, ha . . . Oh! Those tests! . . ."

"But how *did* you get the answer?"

"Well, I, uh . . . read a lot of murder mysteries," said Serge. "That's it. It was in one of the plots."

"I rest my case," said Walter. "Unless you want to arrest Serge . . ."

37

CAPTAIN FLORIDA'S LOG, star date 736.973
Molly! The woman's driving me crazy! Remember those tiny little doubts about marriage I mentioned? They're now a full-blown crisis of faith! To the news: I leave the apartment to go see Coleman, minding my own business and checking what's in the Dumpster like I always do. I notice trash from our apartment, and I can't believe my eyes. She's thrown out my favorite tennis shoes! There they are, under the Maxi-pads. I fish 'em out with a stick and the poor things are full of soggy corn flakes. I'm on the verge of tears. I march right back upstairs and confront her. I figure this time she's the guilty party so I'll be in control of the debate. Know what I learned? Women are ninjas! Suddenly I'm back on defense! Says she's embarrassed to be seen with me in those shoes. I say, "But they're my favorite shoes." The silent treatment again except for all the slamming. I didn't know the apartment had that many doors. I call my married friend in West Palm again, and he says, "Are you crazy? You have to hide your favorite tennis shoes." I say, "I didn't know." He suggests the wheel well of the car. I get off the phone and say, "Okay, honey. I want you to be happy. I'll throw the shoes out." Guess what? She catches me! The trunk lid was up and I didn't see her coming. So now I'm dishonest in the relationship, which I was informed is worse than bad shoes. I say,

"Time-out! I'm just trying to retreat here. Now I can see how marriage turns the most honest men into sneaks." Whoops. That didn't lead anywhere I want to visit again. Speaking of which, I was right about her period. We discussed it, and come to find out, she's not responsible for anything she says or does three days a month. I ask if I can have three days, too, and she says, "No." I suggest we at least put a calendar up on the refrigerator and mark the days so I have time to dig a foxhole. Holy shit! Can that woman throw! Didn't even see her pick up the flowerpot. I call my friend again, and he says, "Are you nuts? You can't ask her to post her period on the fridge!" I say, "Why not? I've never lived with a woman before. I'm going through my first one and, Jesus, can you believe those fucking things? How can husbands everywhere be going through this and there hasn't been anything about it on the news?" He just said, "Welcome to family life." I decide to drive to the supermarket and get a balloon to buy a fresh start. I come home and she's got a wooden box in her hands. My matchbook collection! I say, "What are you doing?" She says I'm a pack rat! Ladies and gentlemen, this could be the deal-breaker. I grab the box out of her hands and call my friend again in West Palm. There's screaming in the background on his end. He says I have to stop calling—his wife overheard our last conversation. I say it's important. I've lost all domestic territory except a little corner in the closet, and now that's under siege. If I give it up, I'll have to start walking around the house with a backpack all the time. He says the last piece of turf is important, and he wishes he still had his. Do I have a garage to hide stuff? I say, "I don't." He says, "You're screwed." Then more screaming on his end and the line went dead.

The phone rang. Serge put down his journal.

"Hello? . . . Coleman did what? Of all the stupid—Yes, I'll be right there."

Serge ran out the door.

MOLLY LOOKED UP at the wall clock in the branch library on Big Pine. Quitting time. She stood and hoisted a purse strap over her shoulder.

Her colleagues at the front desk waved goodnight as Molly walked past the flowers under Brenda's memorial plaque.

She drove to the apartment and opened the door. "Serge, I'm home! . . . Honey? Are you here?" Molly took the purse off her shoulder. Something on the coffee table caught her eye. "What's this?"

She picked up the journal.

38

Sheriff's substation. Cudjoe Key

THE FRONT DOOR opened. Walter looked up from the coffee machine. "Gus, what are you doing in that suit?"

Gus walked toward his desk. "Have a meeting in Key West."

"Oh, that's right," said Walter. "Internal Affairs. The pot business."

Gus looked surprised. "It's a confidential proceeding."

"They're going to suspend you."

"Where'd you hear that?"

"The coffee shop."

Gus grabbed some papers from his in-basket and headed out the door.

"Maybe you can say you have glaucoma."

"Later, Walter."

A STARK, WINDOWLESS room in Key West. An uncomfortable metal chair under a bright fluorescent light. Gus was in it.

There was a desk in front of him and two men in dark suits and thin black ties. The one sitting behind the desk was known as R.J. The one leaning against the side of the desk with a leg hitched over the corner was J.R.

"Serpico," said R.J. "Why are you sweating?"

"It's hot in here."

R.J. turned to J.R. "I'm not hot. Are you hot?"

"I'm not hot."

"This is ridiculous," said Gus. "The pot was part of an official presentation. The department does it all the time."

"Don't worry about the pot," said R.J.

"But I heard you were going to suspend me."

"You *heard*?" said J.R.

"You've been snooping around?" said R.J. "Interfering with an internal investigation?"

"That's a serious crime," said J.R.

"No," said Gus. "I mean my partner mentioned it in passing—"

"Turning on your partner?" said R.J.

"Breaking the Blue Wall of Silence?" said J.R. "There's a name for cops like you."

"It's not a nice name," said R.J.

Gus looked confused. "So you aren't going to suspend me?"

"We already did," said R.J.

"But we suspended the suspension," said J.R.

"I don't understand," said Gus. "Then why am I here?"

J.R. handed a sheet of paper to R.J., who held it up in front of Gus. "Is this your dick?"

"Where'd you get that?" said Gus.

"A guy was passing them out with restaurant flyers on the corner of Southard," said J.R.

"I'm not believing this," said Gus.

"He hasn't answered the question," said R.J.

"Why won't you answer the question?" said J.R.

"Look," said Gus. "There's a very simple explanation. . . ."

R.J. produced a coffee mug from Las Vegas. "Is this yours?"

"What?"

"Don't try to deny it," said J.R. "We found it in your desk."

"The bathing suits disappear," said R.J. "The lab boys tested it numerous times under a variety of conditions."

"Inappropriate material in a government office," said J.R. "That's a serious offense."

"But I was going to take it home," said Gus.

"We get the picture."

"No, you don't," said Gus. "I didn't even want it. That was a gift."
"Who from?"
"My partner."
"Oh, still trying to give up your partner?" said J.R.
R.J. held up the Xerox again. "Is this your dick?"
Gus wiped sweat off his forehead. "I can explain that piece of paper."
"By all means."
"It's not what you think," said Gus. "I wasn't involved."
"But this *is* your dick?" said R.J.
Gus nodded.
"And you weren't involved?" said J.R.
"Yes, no, I mean it was done without my knowledge."
"Someone drew on your dick without your knowledge?"
"No, I agreed to the drawing part."
"That's all the questions we have for now," said R.J.
"Wait, I have to explain."
"You have a funny way of explaining," said J.R.
"The more you do it . . ." said R.J.
". . . The worse it gets," said J.R.

ANOTHER OFFICE IN Key West. This one had windows and diplomas. The marriage counselor flipped through the pages of a handwritten journal.

From time to time, his eyes bugged. He solemnly closed the book and looked up at Serge. "I want to thank you for allowing me to read this. It shows a commitment to making your marriage work."

"Why not?" Serge said in resignation. "I'm worn out."

Serge and Molly were sitting as far apart on the couch as possible. Molly was all scrunched into herself at one end, trying to occupy minimum space. Serge was at the other, lounging with legs spread, tapping a foot. The counselor sat across from them in a padded chair. He wore a toupee that was too black. He patted the cover of the journal. "I think you subconsciously wanted her to find this."

"That wasn't it," said Serge. "I had to run out. Coleman ended up in the emergency room again after a bar bet trying to uncap a beer bottle with his eye socket."

"Coleman!" blurted Molly, folding her arms tight and looking away.

"Who's Coleman?" asked the counselor.

There was a quick knock at the door, then it opened. A man with an eye bandage stuck his head inside. "Are you going to be much longer?"

"What are you doing?" said Serge. "This is a private meeting."

"Yeah, but I have to go see *the guy*."

"Excuse me, sir." The counselor gave the man a stern look. "Do you mind?"

"Sorry." He looked at the empty beer in his hand. "You have a place I can throw this?"

"There's a wastebasket in the lobby."

"Thanks." The door closed.

The counselor looked at Serge. "Coleman?"

Serge shrugged. "What are you gonna do?"

The counselor opened a file in his lap. "Okay, who wants to start? Serge?"

Serge stared at his watch. "This wasn't my idea."

"But you *did* come," said the counselor.

"I buckled. It was like a land-for-peace swap."

"Molly?" said the counselor. "How about you?"

"I made him a sandwich last week, and he took off the top piece of bread and added potato chips. He's not the man I married!"

"I need my space," said Serge.

The counselor looked at him with concern, thinking, You never make the potato-chip sandwich around your wife. "Let's talk about your space—"

"His *space*!" said Molly. "So he can write more mean things about me in that evil little book of his?"

"She's completely unreasonable," said Serge. "I even gave her the double balloon—the one with the heart balloon inside the clear one. That's supposed to get me off the hook. You know the rules. Tell her!"

The counselor took a deep breath and wrote something in the file. "How about we start with intimacy? How's that going?"

"Sex?" said Serge. "Exhausting! The woman's a machine! Molly may look like a wallflower, but she'll suck you dry! Half the time my testicles are like little walnuts...."

"Serge..."

"... The closets are filled with all these costumes and props and this plywood thing she built with leather straps. Then there's her incredible Tibetan muscle control that'll make your hat spin...."

"Serge!"

"What?"

The counselor had his hand up. "Details aren't necessary." He made a notation in the file. "Intimacy not a problem." He looked toward the other end of the couch. "Molly, what would you say the problem is?"

She stared away.

The counselor read his file. "You told me you got engaged and married almost immediately. You had to expect some surprises."

Still silent.

"Molly, since it was your idea to come here, I'm going to need your help. You have to open up."

She hesitated, then turned her head. "I need a quieter lifestyle. I'm scared all the time. I never know what's going to happen next."

The counselor got a new expression. "Has he ever struck you?"

"Oh, no, no, no. He'd never. That's not what I'm talking about."

"What *are* you talking about?"

"His job. I . . . I can't take it anymore."

The counselor glanced at the file. "What's wrong with social worker. It's an honorable profession. You must learn to support his career."

"I thought I could. I was proud at first, watching him talk at the meetings. All that respect. But then the other stuff started. Strange phone calls. Clothes always ripped like he's been wrestling. Sometimes he stays out all night. Then he rushes in and hides something and tells me if anyone asks, he wasn't here. Once I saw him digging a hole behind the apartment building."

"That's the business we're in," said Serge. "I'm sure you have your own unorthodox methods."

"I just want it to stop," said Molly. "I want a safe family, dinners at home, maybe children. But his insane rhythms are making me a wreck."

"Rhythms?"

"Everything's crazy all the time. When he isn't running all over the place, there are souvenirs and gadgets spread all over the bed. Or he gets into his books and suddenly decides we're going to live like the pioneers and only allowed to eat roots, so I try to be understanding and eat roots with him for two solid weeks until he jumps up from the table and says he's always hated roots and he's going out for tacos, and I don't see him until the next morning when he's covered in mud and cleaning a claw hammer in the sink. Then there's his best friend, Coleman. He's there all the time, almost like he's living with us. . . ."

"I thought you liked to entertain," said Serge.

Molly's head snapped toward his end of the sofa. "Having some drunken oaf break all our shit isn't entertaining!" She turned to the counselor and began enumerating on her fingers. "He broke one of the dishes that was part of a matched set, a lamp, the TV remote, a glass picture frame on the wall, a leg on the couch. I found a spaghetti sauce handprint on the bathroom ceiling. Oh yeah, he broke the toilet roll holder, snapped the shower rod out of the tiles, and I had to throw out one of our guest towels because it looked like he had—I don't even want to know. . . ."

Serge's head fell back against the wall. "Those fucking towels again!"

Molly spun toward her husband. "What is your stupid friend doing using the guest towels in the first place!"

"He was a *guest*!"

"They're the *guest towels*!"

Serge threw up his arms. "To this very day I don't understand the towel rules!"

Molly turned to the counselor. "He said my towels cost more than blow jobs."

The counselor raised his eyebrows. "You did?"

"In certain countries."

"Coleman's an idiot!" shouted Molly.

"He is not!" Serge shouted back.

Another knock at the door. It opened. "Where's the rest room?"

"Down the hall on the left," said the counselor.

"That's what I'm talking about," said Molly. She folded her arms, gave Serge a look, then stared away and refused to talk.

"There!" Serge pointed at Molly. "She's doing it again! What the fuck *is* that?"

"Serge, please calm down—"

"No, I want to know what the hell that is. An amazing spectacle of nature. Lasts as long as a week. I'll wake up in the morning all happy at the prospect of another day of life, then she'll walk through the room and shoot me that look. Uh-oh, almost forgot: Shit's still on! Where do they get that kind of endurance? I mean, check the frost in that body language! Plummeting toward absolute zero degrees Kelvin, where all life ceases to exist and electrons refuse to orbit their atoms . . ."

"Serge, I don't think this is help—"

". . . If I have something on my mind, I say it. But if she's got an issue, it's the sixty-four-dollar question. Did I forget an important date? Did I not compliment you on dinner? Did I track dirt in? Did I leave the seat up? Did I look at one of your girlfriends the wrong way? Did you think I was *about* to do something? For the love of God, just please tell me, *what the fuck did I do this time? . . .*"

"Serge, it might be better if—"

". . . She wants to know why I spend time with Coleman?" He extended an upturned palm toward Molly. "Exhibit A. Men don't do that. We just hang out and watch the game and not harbor festering shit. Of course, we're responsible for almost all the homicides, so I guess there's a tradeoff. But in between the murders, it's really quite pleasant. Women, on the other hand. . . . Watch out! Have you ever heard them talk about their friends behind their backs? Pick, pick, pick, pick! . . ."

The counselor looked at the clock on the wall.

Molly was crying in her hands. Serge made a hissing sound and clawed at the air like a cat. ". . . They'll rip you to pieces!"

A woman shouted in the hall. "Look out! You're going to break that!"

Crash.

The counselor closed his file and smiled. "Same time next week?"

39

Dawn broke over the Florida Keys. It began like any other day. But by sunset, the TV people would have the footage of a lifetime.

It started with unusually heavy traffic on U.S. 1. A giant vinyl banner hung across the road:

> FIRST ANNUAL DONALD GREELY COMMUNITY
> APPRECIATION JAMBOREE

Small print underneath:

> Paid for by The Committee for Fairness to Donald Greely

There was much to do. People busily handled festival preparations at a variety of locations.

A car pulled up to the sheriff's substation on Cudjoe Key, Deputy Gus arriving for overtime security duty at the festival.

He opened the door and walked to his desk. There was a cardboard box on top of it. All the APBs and photos that he'd taped to the wall were inside.

Walter strolled over wearing an orange traffic vest. "Sorry to hear."
"Hear what?"
"You getting fired."
"I was?"

"Actually it's not till Monday," said Walter. "It's a secret."

"They're really going to fire me over those Xeroxes of my—?"

"No, you just got probation for that," said Walter. "They compromised with the union under the new tolerance for sexual deviants. Remember the precedent with the undercover guy who had the vagina surgery?"

"What? A transsexual?"

"No, he kept his penis, too. Then he started dating himself. The union argued you were just as weird."

"How'd you find out?"

"Newspaper called me for comment."

"Wonderful."

"Don't worry; I took your side. Told them you made a valuable contribution to law enforcement, despite your lifestyle choice."

Gus began removing APBs from the cardboard box. "I don't understand. Then why are they firing me?"

"Taping stuff to the wall. I warned you about that."

"You're joking."

"Wish I was. Internal Affairs just left after taking it all down."

"They can't fire me for that."

"They can under the new Three-Strikes Rule. First pot, then your dick. I'm afraid this is going to be our last shift together."

"But it's only taping stuff to the wall."

"The Three-Strikes Rule has a Zero-Tolerance Policy."

A FINGER PRESSED the doorbell button on Coleman's trailer. The button fell off. A hand knocked.

Coleman had the stereo up all the way, watching a *Girls Gone Wild* tape to AC/DC. Serge gave up knocking and walked around the side of the trailer, scooting down the narrow, overgrown space between the mobile home and a chain-link fence. Empty bottles, damp leaves, mosquito larva in a tire. He banged on the window.

Coleman looked in various directions, trying to place the noise. More banging. Coleman turned around, kneeled on the couch and opened the curtains. "Serge . . ."

"Open the door!"

"What? I can't hear you."

"Open the door!"

"Can't hear you. Meet you at the door."

Coleman opened up. Serge came in with his knapsack. "You idiot."

"What are you doing here?"

"What do you mean? Aren't you ready?"

"For what?"

"The Greely festival!" said Serge. "Our big operation. The one I've been talking about all week."

"That's today?"

"Yes!" Serge pulled a pair of walkie-talkies from his backpack and handed one to Coleman.

"Cool."

"Get your stuff. We have to move out." Serge raised the walkie-talkie to his mouth and keyed the mike. *"Tango Zulu, come in . . ."*

A VAN SAT in the parking lot of Paradise Transmission. On the side, a smoked bubble window and an airbrush mural of a Yes album cover. The back of the van was full of people crouched on the shag carpet like a S.W.A.T. team.

The walkie-talkie on the dashboard squawked. *". . . Tango Zulu, come in . . . Tango Zulu, are you there? . . ."*

Sop Choppy was behind the wheel. He turned to Mr. Blinky in the passenger seat. "Are we Tango Zulu?"

The clown passed a joint back over his shoulder. "I don't know."

". . . Tango Zulu, where are you? . . ."

Sop Choppy grabbed the walkie-talkie. "Are we Tango Zulu?"

"Who is this?"

"Sop Choppy."

"Yes!"

"Tango Zulu here."

"Is everyone ready?"

Sop Choppy looked back. "Yep, they're ready."

"You got the oxygen tank?"

Sop Choppy glanced at the metal cylinder Mr. Blinky was holding between his legs, Coleman's old nitrous tank that had been refilled with O_2. "Check."

"Let's do it."

A METALLIC GREEN Trans Am rested under a tarp in the driveway of a waterfront home on Big Pine Key.

Anna Sebring was alone inside her late brother's vacation place. She sat at the kitchen table, gazing out the back windows at the fishing boats filling Bogie Channel. The weather was perfect.

Anna looked down at the table. A big brass safety deposit box key lay in the middle.

She looked at her watch and took a deep breath.

"Now or never."

She stood and picked up the key.

THE SOUTHERN SHORELINE of Key West was crammed before noon.

South Beach, Higgs Beach, Rest Beach, Smathers Beach, wall-to-wall cabanas, bikinis and umbrellas sprinkling the sand with bright primary colors. Two cocker spaniels chased each other through a volleyball game on Dog Beach. The swim areas were full of happy, splashing bathers dodging Jet Skis. Farther out, an ocean highway of pleasure craft. Bowriders, cabin cruisers, sailboats and catamarans that bobbed in the wakes of cigarette boats, which in turn were passed by giant hydroplanes and open-sea racers in paint schemes for Budweiser and Little Caesar's pizza. Beyond that, on the horizon toward Cuba, fleets of shrimp trawlers with boom-arrays extending from both sides. Overhead, news helicopters, parasailers, an ultralight with pontoons and six circling Cessnas pulling banners for drink-till-you-drop specials in Old Town. Atlantic Boulevard and South Roosevelt were jammed with parked cars, traffic at a standstill, convertibles and rentals and VW microbuses with competing music. Matchbox Twenty, 50 Cent, Third Eye Blind.

The sun approached zenith, but it was only ninety degrees with a light breeze that smelled of salt, tanning oil and hot dogs cooking in a relentless line of sidewalk stands. Also, Sno-Kone stands, cotton candy stands and stands with battery-operated blenders serving alcohol-free daiquiris and piña coladas that were openly spiked. Standby ambulances sat at strategic intervals, paramedics already running stretchers back and forth across the beach in front of the concert stage. Passed-out exposure victims burned down one side of their bodies, a college kid who tried to stand on the seat of his jet ski, the ultralight pilot who crashed into the giant inflatable Corona bottle.

Nothing would stop the party. And what a party it was. Donald Greely was paying for it all with his own personal money, which used to be other people's personal money. He wasn't supposed to have the money under the court agreement, so it was filtered through judgment-proof combinations of lawyers and Caribbean accounts. It wasn't cheap. Ten thousand free hot dogs, gallons of soda, city overtime, insurance, upcoming concert by the Beach Boys tribute band and, finally, after sundown, the big offshore fireworks extravaganza. Total bill: thirty grand. Greely had gotten the idea from the block parties John Gotti used to throw in Queens after each acquittal.

All that was missing now: the big entrance.

A corporate jet helicopter skimmed over the breakers.

"Almost there," said the traveling publicist. She rechecked her organizer, a full schedule of photo ops synchronized to the minute.

TV cameras clustered as the helicopter swooped in from the Gulf Stream and gently touched down. Greely, in a tropical shirt, got out, waving both arms Nixon-style. A crowd surged forward.

The publicist checked her organizer. "Eleven thirty-seven. Hot dogs."

The mob moved with Greely toward one of the food stands on Rest Beach. An aide fitted a chef's hat on Greely's head as he grinned and tonged wieners into buns. People shouted from the back of the crowd.

"We love you, Donald!"
"We're behind you all the way!"
"You da man!"

The traveling publicist had paid them each twenty dollars and told them to wait till the cameras were rolling. Picking crowd-shouters was always an imprecise science, especially at events with alcohol.

"Don't take no fuckin' shit from those assholes, Donald!"

Another wave from Greely. "Just trying to be a good neighbor."

Greely's expensive smile filled the field of vision in Serge's binoculars. He and Coleman were down by the shore, where a large contingent of Greely's personal security team and local police had sealed off one of the docks and was giving a parasailing boat the thorough going-over. Serge continued surveillance with the binoculars and raised his walkie-talkie. "Tango Zulu, whenever you're ready."

"Roger."

Greely had picked the southern shore of Key West for his festival because it was so magnificent. The perfect place to ruin. A cartel of financial backers had already been meeting for a year. If everything went according to plan, this stretch of real estate, from the Southernmost Marker to the salt ponds to Cow Key Channel, would sprout a solid wall of condos.

That's why Greely needed their love. He was planning to parlay goodwill into city council fiat. A couple more of these parties and he could pack any council chamber with an audience of enthusiastic, poster-waving local supporters who would swear until the end of the universe to vote against any politician who didn't give Greely his rezoning. The financiers had asked Greely to be their front man because of his rare talent. He could make people smile while he fucked them.

Of course it wasn't all greed. He was going to give back to the community. The blueprints included a provision to donate a portion of the land to descendants of the first Native Americans in the Keys, because the backers also wanted a casino.

The publicist snapped her leather organizer shut. "Eleven-fifty-one. Limbo."

An assistant removed Greely's chef's hat. A van with a Yes mural inched past the hot dog stand.

Sop Choppy monitored the second hand on his wrist-watch. *"Readyyyy . . . readyyyy . . . Now!"*

The side door of the van flew open. Mr. Blinky slapped each person on the back as they jumped from the vehicle. *"Go! . . . Go! . . . Go! . . ."*

The team hit the ground, angling off in the different directions for their respective stations. When the back of the van was empty, two clowns grabbed the oxygen tank and advanced on the beachhead.

THE BANK WAS a fortress. Built like a German pillbox on the Atlantic Wall.

It wasn't for robbers. It was for hurricanes.

The bottom of the building was the truncated base of a pyramid. It rose above the storm-surge plane before a tiny slit opened where people and money went in and out. On top of that, another huge concrete slab that displayed an iron sculpture of the island chain as seen from orbit. A metallic green Trans Am sat under a tarp in the parking lot. A black sedan pulled up six slots away.

Anna couldn't stop fidgeting in the glass office of the bank vice president. A woman smiled at her from the other side of the desk. Anna smiled back, wearing dark sunglasses, picking her fingernails, hyperventilating with alcohol on her breath, just like everyone else in the Keys who comes to check safety deposit boxes. The vice president examined Anna's driver's license and looked something up in the computer. She pushed her chair back and stood. "Follow me."

A guard opened the vault. The women went inside and simultaneously stuck keys in a drawer like a missile launch.

"Call if you need anything," said the vice president. She left Anna alone.

Anna looked up at the wall of brushed metal boxes, various sizes. She felt her heart beating in the still room. The wall seemed to tower. What was going on in the other boxes? Were they all like her brother's—debris from life wreckage? This being the Keys, the answer was yes. If Anna had X-ray vision, she would have seen pornographic detective photos, bloodstained packs of hundred-dollar bills, serial number–filed pistols, ledger books entirely in code and recently drawn maps of backyards with Xs over flower beds. Anna pulled her box from its slot and lifted the long metal lid. One item inside. Polaroid photograph. Anna immediately recognized it.

THE CLOWNS HAD been busy. They finished filling a hundred elongated balloons with oxygen and twisted them into parrots and monkeys and dachshunds. The balloon-animals were tied together, forming gigantic bouquets that the clowns carried off in opposite directions.

A small child walked up to Uncle Inappropriate. "Mr. Clown, how much for one of the balloons?"

"Fuck off."

The traveling publicist checked her schedule. "Twelve-thirteen. Schoolchildren bury you in sand."

A personal assistant lifted the limbo bar. Serge's binoculars followed Greely over to a group of first-graders vetted with background checks. Greely lay down on the beach. Children began digging with plastic shovels. The binoculars panned across the shore. Everyone was in position. Serge raised his walkie-talkie. "Get it going, Dave."

An emcee climbed the steps of the concert stage and grabbed the microphone. "Let's kick this off with a real treat! We have with us today the legendary 'Daytona Dave' DeFuniak, singing his mega-hit 'Island Fever,' which appears on the new album 'One-Hit Wonders of the '70s: The Rehab Collection.'"

Dave walked out and waved to a smattering of applause. He turned to the band and snapped his fingers. "A one, and a two . . . *I burnin' up with that island . . .*"

Mr. Blinky and Uncle Inappropriate glanced at each other from opposite sides of the beach and simultaneously lit cigarettes.

In another direction: demonstrators in Serge T-shirts ran toward Greely, shouting and waving picket signs, STOP DONALD'S DEVELOPMENT! FIGHT THE RESORT-IFICATION! WHERE'S MY LIFE SAVINGS!

The traveling publicist turned toward the noise. "Where the hell did they come from? . . . Security!"

The head of Greely's security team barked into his own walkie-talkie. "Get him out of the sand! Now!"

The TV cameras swung from Greely to the demonstrators. A shoving match broke out between the protesters and the bodyguards. The security detail at the parasailing boat was called in as reinforcement.

From the concert stage: *"It's always good to have that Island Fever . . . Uh-oh—"* Dave fell writhing onto the stage.

"Daytona Dave's having a seizure!"

Cops and paramedics rushed over.

Two clowns taped their cigarettes to long sticks and raised them toward the balloon bouquets.

Bodyguards pulled Greely from the sand and hustled him from the melee. At opposite ends of the beach, balloon-animal fireballs exploded into the sky. People ran screaming, crashing into each other—"Look! The Skunk Ape!"—a full-scale, multidirectional stampede. Sop Choppy's biker associates arrived and joined the fray with the bodyguards, now spilling into the street. The remaining cops at the parasailing boat abandoned their posts and ran to help.

Serge and Coleman climbed aboard the vessel. "Hey!" yelled one of the parasail's two operators. "You're not supposed to be here!"

Serge produced a gun. "Down in the cabin. Both of you."

The traveling publicist shuddered at the PR carnage. TV cameras pointing everywhere except at Greely. Ten reporters interviewed a naked woman. The publicist ran over to the head of Greely's security team. "We have to save this." She opened her organizer. "Twelve-forty-nine. Parasailing."

ANNA RACED AWAY from the bank and parked behind the nearest gas station. She ran to the pay phones and dialed. The man at the next phone was on meth. Anna sprang up and down on her legs. "C'mon, answer!"

A dark sedan rolled up to one of the gas pumps.

Then, shouting. Anna jumped. The man on the next phone slammed the receiver. It bounced off the hook and swung on its metal cord as he stomped away. A click in Anna's ear. "Hello?" She turned and burrowed into the phone booth. "I got it . . . no, just a photograph . . . you'll understand as soon as you see it . . . right, I know the place."

* * *

THE OFFICIAL ENTOURAGE whisked Greely down to the dock. The publicist grabbed a couple of TV cameramen along the way. "There's nothing worth shooting over there. . . ."

They arrived at the parasailing boat. One of the deckhands reached over the railing. "Let me help you aboard."

Cameras filmed as twin three-fifties throttled up. The boat blasted away from the dock.

The deckhand fitted the ex-mogul into his Coast Guard—rated life vest and parasailing harness.

"Have to make sure this thing is good and tight," said Serge, yanking up hard on the strap between Greely's legs.

"Ow!"

"You're all set," said Serge. "Let's get you back to the launch area."

Greely stood in position on a specially welded platform and grabbed the chest-high safety bar in front of him. Serge screwed down the metal O-rings attaching Greely's harness to the parasail, ready for deployment in its cradle. He bunched the little drogue chute in his hand and threw it into the wind, pulling the main sail out of the holder. It quickly inflated, yanking Greely a few inches off his feet. Serge grabbed the handle on the winch.

"Okay, I'm going to start unreeling you."

Greely immediately popped up to an elevation of ten feet. Serge turned the handle faster, letting out more rope. Twenty feet. Greely pointed at the boat's driver.

"Is he drinking beer?"

"A few." Still unspooling. Thirty feet.

Greely had to shout now. "How much experience do you have?"

"Tons," Serge yelled back. "Oh, you mean parasailing? This is our first time."

Fifty feet. "I want to come back down!"

"What?" yelled Serge, still cranking.

Greely's shouts grew faint. Serge finally tied him off at two hundred feet and went up front with Coleman. They made a swing by the dock. Greely saw the TV cameras and figured he better stop screaming and start waving.

He stayed up a half hour without incident, starting to relax, numerous happy passes by the dock for the cameras. "This is more like it," said the publicist.

The parasail began swinging side to side, only slightly at first, then more and more until Greely was whipping across the sky horizontally.

"My turn to drive." Serge pulled the steering wheel away from Coleman, hard to the left.

"You just had a turn," said Coleman, pulling back to the right.

"But you had an extra long one. That counts as two." Serge pulled back.

"You're making up rules." Coleman pulled back. Serge pulled. Coleman. Serge.

Greely was flying all over the place, then an upside-down loop. *"Ahhhhhhhhhhhhhhh! . . ."*

The TV people on the dock zoomed in. "I didn't know he could do tricks."

Greely finally leveled off after Serge and Coleman struck a truce, each steering with one hand, snarling at each other.

Another pass by the dock, the publicist checking her watch, growing puzzled.

Serge checked his own watch. He released the wheel. "It's all yours. Happy?"

"My turn anyway."

Serge walked to the stern and picked up a megaphone. "Ready to come in?"

All he heard was faint shouting. Serge grabbed the winch's handle and began reeling. When Greely was halfway down, Serge could make out words. ". . . I'll destroy you! You're finished in this town! . . ."

Serge stopped cranking and raised the megaphone again. "I'll bring you in under one condition."

"Condition? Fuck you!"

"Give back the money."

"What money?"

"The money you stole. Sell your house and give the money back."

"Take me down this instant!"

"As soon as you give back the money."

"I'll have you arrested! I'll put you out of business! I'll take your boat!"

"This isn't my boat," said Serge.

"It isn't?"

"No, it belongs to the two guys tied up down in the cabin."

Greely paused. "Who are you then?"

"Shareholders."

"You had stock in my company?"

"We have stock in *America*!"

"You're insane!"

"Give back the money."

"Help! Help!"

TV people back on the dock: "He's yelling something."

"What's he saying?"

"I think he's just whooping it up."

Serge pointed the megaphone. "Give back the money."

"Not a chance!"

"You stole. It's wrong."

"I didn't steal anything. They made bad investments. Nobody put a gun to their heads!"

"Old people had to go back to work. It's caused premature deaths." Serge produced a scuba knife and placed the blade against the rope.

"What are you doing?"

"Disconnecting this call. All I'm getting is static."

"You wouldn't—"

Serge started sawing through the rope. He yelled up front to Coleman. "Swing toward land."

The boat made a slow starboard arc until it was in line with the dock.

"Stop!" yelled Greely. "I'm ordering you!"

"You're not the boss of me." More sawing.

Greely looked up at the dock, then down at Serge again. "What are you planning?"

"These parasails are incredible. One guy accidentally broke loose and was dragged a mile over land. Nothing stopped him, concrete benches, cars, fences. They said nearly every bone in his body was broken."

"Okay, I'll give back the money."

Serge stopped sawing. "You will?"

"Absolutely!"

"What about your Key West development project?"

"Dead. I'll kill it. Anything! Please!"

"Promise?"

Greely nodded urgently.

Serge thought a moment, then shook his head. "I don't believe you." Sawing resumed.

Greely screamed all the way in to shore. Serge was three-quarters through the rope. The dock closed rapidly.

"Oh, my God! Coleman! Look!"

"What?"

"Over there! Turn the boat around!"

"I see it." Coleman swung the wheel hard in a tight one-eighty. Greely whipping directly over the dock. "Help! Help! They're crazy!"

The cameramen pointed straight up. "I didn't catch that."

"I think he said, 'I'm wild and crazy.' "

The cameras kept filming, gradually lowering trajectory as Greely neared the horizon. That's when one of the cameramen saw it. "Holy mother! Look over there!"

Greely saw it, too. He began crying. "Oh, please! Don't! I'm begging you!"

Serge went up front. "I'll need to take the wheel from here. It's going to require expert driving."

"You can have it," said Coleman. "This is out of my league."

The boat raced across the Gulf Stream, a smile spreading over Serge's face. "This is what I'm talking about, Coleman. Life's a crapshoot. But just keep fighting the good fight and sooner or later it turns your way."

They were on a direct bearing for the Sand Key lighthouse, five miles southwest, but they wouldn't need to go nearly that far.

"Are you sure about this?" asked Coleman. "I mean, I've never heard of it being done before."

"Because it hasn't."

Back at the dock, pandemonium. "Doesn't he see it?" "Why isn't he turning?"

The wind picked up. Serge and Coleman's hair flew around, needles of rain hit their cheeks.

Serge had to squint to see. "Come on, baby, just a few more seconds . . ."

"Pull back!" Coleman grabbed the port railing to keep from being thrown over the side. "We're too close!"

"Here we go . . . almost there . . . *Now!*"

Serge cut the steering wheel all the way starboard, closing the angle around the vortex and going into a tight circle, drawing the parasail into the cone. A final scream from Greely and the rope snapped.

Serge and Coleman looked back as they accelerated away—the parasail going up, up, up into the waterspout, the end of the rope whip-snapping as it was sucked in like a piece of spaghetti. Then nothing but colorful silk shreds jettisoned from varying heights.

"What a horrible way to go," said Coleman.

"It's the Gulf Stream," said Serge. "Has a nasty way of creeping up on you."

The dock was silent. A leather organizer slipped from a hand and fell in the water. The boat disappeared over the horizon.

40

A sheriff's cruiser returned to the substation on Cudjoe Key.

"What an insane day," said Gus. "I've never seen an event like it."

"I don't know. Fantasy Fest gets pretty out of hand."

They went inside. Walter found a film of burnt coffee bubbling in the bottom of the pot. "Did I leave that on?"

The fax started up. Gus grabbed it. A mug shot. "Oh, no."

"What?"

"I should have known! A serial killer right here under our noses!"

They ran out the door and jumped in the cruiser.

Walter radioed for backup. They told him the nearest unit was in Marathon.

"That's at least twenty minutes," said Gus. "Can't wait that long. We have to find Serge before we have another body on our hands."

"Where do you think he is?"

* * *

A '71 Buick Riviera pulled into Coleman's driveway. Serge stepped on the brakes, but nothing happened. The Buick hit the trailer at low speed, buckling the bedroom wall.

"What the hell?" Serge got out and shimmied under the car.

"What is it?" asked Coleman.

Serge crawled back out and looked at a hand covered with hydraulic fluid. "The brake line's leaking."

"Did we hit something?"

"No, it looks like it was cut. That's strange."

"Just great. I don't have money for a repair."

"Don't need any." Serge opened the trunk and held up a gray roll. "Just wrap it in a lot of duct tape." He crawled back under the car. "Of course you have to do it again every twenty miles, but this is about value."

Coleman headed for the front door. "I'm pooped."

Serge crawled out from under the car and followed him inside. "Boating does that."

AN EMPTY QUART bottle sat in the road. A tire rolled. Pop.

The tire belonged to a brown Plymouth Duster. The door opened. Two black combat boots swung out and settled onto the ground. The driver wore gloves. One hand had a plastic bag of dynamite sticks and blasting caps. The other, copper wire and tools.

The driver walked a short distance and went to work. The explosives were soon taped under a driver's seat, the one where Serge often sat. Copper wire was routed out of sight and up to the back of the ignition switch, just behind where the key was inserted.

A SHERIFF'S CRUISER raced into the parking lot of an old apartment building on Big Pine Key. Gus and Walter jumped out with guns drawn. They ran up the stairs and knocked on the door of unit 213. No answer.

Walter tried kicking in the door but only hurt himself. Gus shot the lock. They ran through the apartment, swinging around blind corners with guns in outstretched arms. They shoved open closet doors. Gus started going through a dresser.

"We don't have a warrant," said Walter.

"Look what I found."

GLOVED HANDS FINISHED twisting copper wire to the ignition posts. Two black combat boots walked back to the Plymouth Duster and climbed in. The door closed. The Duster pulled away. Molly looked up in the rearview, making sure her hair was in place.

THE SHERIFF'S CRUISER raced back down Key Deer Boulevard.

Walter was driving faster than he had in years. Gus grabbed the radio again.

"What about that Coleman guy he hangs out with?" said Walter. "The one we met at the community hall?"

"What was his last name?"

"Don't remember."

"I'll have the dispatcher look up all utility records with that first name."

Walter hit the siren and swung onto U.S. 1. Gus radioed in his emergency request and started pulling on a bulletproof vest. Walter looked over at his partner. "This is your last shift. You sure you want to do this?"

"The fax mentioned the car in the Everglades had been wired with explosives, and we found blasting caps in the dresser." Gus pulled the strap tight on the side of his vest. "She may have already rigged his car."

The dispatcher came back. No records under Coleman.

"Must be a nickname," said Walter.

"Wait. He had this cool car. An old Riviera," said Gus. "Early to mid-seventies." He got the dispatcher again and asked for a trace through Motor Vehicles.

A METALLIC GREEN Trans Am raced over the Bogie Channel Bridge to No Name Key. Anna held her purse to her chest. She stopped near the end of the street and checked a scrap of paper with directions. She looked at her watch. Early. She turned onto a dirt road.

Nothing but bumps and brush as she drove north until she ran out of island. The Trans Am entered a small clearing with an ad-hoc boat ramp, just a space in the mangroves and a dirt incline to the water. She got out and walked a few yards to the shore. No sign of anyone yet. Just something silver flashing through the branches. An aluminum hull.

The quiet was freaking her out. That's when she heard the other car. She didn't recognize the dark sedan, but it was raising a major dust trail flying down the road.

She ran for the Trans Am. The other car skidded to a stop. A man jumped out and sprinted toward her. Anna dove in the car and locked the doors. She stuck her key in the ignition.

"Anna, stop!" The man slapped an open wallet against her window. She saw a gold badge against the glass.

"Open the door, Anna. DEA, Agent Wilson."

The badge looked real. It looked fake. She didn't know what to think anymore or why she opened the door.

The man grabbed her arm. "We have to get you out of here!"

Anna pulled away. "I'm not going anywhere with you!"

"Your life's in danger."

"Now I recognize you! You're that asshole from the pub, what's-his-name. . . ."

"Gaskin Fussels."

"You're supposed to be in jail, but . . ." She pointed at the badge in his hand. "What's going on?"

"Explain later. We can't stay here." He stepped forward to take her arm again. "I know about Scarface . . . Fernandez's murder."

She jumped out of reach and started walking backward. "You're lying."

"We don't have any time," said the agent. "He'll be here any second."

Anna just kept backing up. She reached the water's edge.

Wilson could see she was on the brink. She'd bolt, even if it meant swimming. He decided to talk fast.

"I've been watching Fernandez for a long time. I also know about the safety deposit box. I followed you from the bank."

Anna stopped backpedaling.

"Listen to me. You were used. I can help with the judge, even if you pulled the trigger—"

"I didn't!"

"We just want the head of the organization. I'll need you to testify."

Anna gave him the weirdest look. "What do you mean? Fernandez is dead."

"Right."

"What are you talking about?"

"What are *you* talking about?" said the agent.

"Fernandez was the head of the organization. And now he's dead. So why do you need me to testify?"

"Oh, my God!" said the agent. "You really don't know, do you?"

"Know what?"

"The head guy is the one you've been having all those meetings with at the No Name. You spent the morning with him at your brother's vacation place. I saw him go in. I was parked up the street."

"Jerry?"

Agent Wilson nodded. "The bartender."

"But if he's the top guy, what's he doing bartending?"

"That how he stays off-radar. It's a historic stratagem. Since ancient times, generals have been known to dress as common foot soldiers to avoid assassination. . . . It's also a great way to gather intelligence. If you want to know what's going on in these parts, there's no better place than behind the counter of the No Name."

Anna felt faint. Flashbacks streamed through her head. Jerry talking about how Scarface liked to move anonymously through his own organization, pretending to be other people, really talking about himself.

"Then who was Fernandez?"

"His first lieutenant. He was hiding money with your brother. Jerry wanted it. That's why he let Fernandez continue living, even though he was on the indictment with the others."

"I'm so stupid!" said Anna.

"Unfortunately, Jerry knew your name was also on that bank box. Then you phoned from the turnpike . . . we had his phone tapped, and just like that"—he snapped his fingers—"Fernandez's death warrant was signed."

"But why involve me? Why didn't he just shoot Fernandez himself?"

"Leverage. He needed you to go to the bank. He's going to kill you right after you give him the contents."

Anna's world started to swirl. Wilson ran down to the water and grabbed her by the arm. "We have to go!"

They ran for the agent's sedan.

Anna felt his hand come off her arm. She looked back.

Wilson was down, a fatal head wound.

Jerry stepped out of the woods with pistol and silencer.

Anna took off for the water. Jerry tackled her in the muck and began punching her in the face. Birds took flight. Nobody to hear her screams.

"Why!" Struggling under his weight.

He hit her again and began going through her pockets. He found the Polaroid. He started laughing. "I don't believe it. Right in front of us the whole time!"

He slugged Anna again, then pulled a pint of cheap vodka from his pants. He took the first swig before jamming the bottle into Anna's mouth. Jerry was just too strong and heavy. Her gums bled from struggling against the glass lip of the bottle. A lot of the booze was going down her cheeks, but enough was getting in. When the bottle was empty, he whipped it aside into the bushes.

"On your feet!"

Anna stayed curled on the ground. Jerry stuck his gun in his pants and grabbed her around the waist. He took a few big steps and threw her out into the water. Anna stood back up, coughing and clearing hair from her eyes.

Jerry pulled the gun again and sloshed out into the shallows. He shoved Anna. "Move!"

She stumbled forward. He shoved her again. It went like that until she was a hundred yards from shore. But being the flats, the water was still only to her knees.

"That's far enough!"

* * *

THE SHERIFF'S CRUISER flew down U.S. 1. The dispatcher came on the radio. She had a '71 Buick Riviera registered to an address on Ramrod Key.

Gus grabbed a cell phone and dialed. "It's ringing."

Walter glanced down at the seat between them and the latest fax, the one that had finally put a mug shot with the unsolved murders down the west coast. "She looks so harmless."

"Pick up the phone!"

"I can't remember the last time we had a female serial killer."

"Aileen Wuornos."

"That's right," said Walter. "They got some kind of memorial garden to her at a bar in Daytona."

"It's still ringing."

"Two islands to go."

"Answer the phone!"

SERGE AND COLEMAN climbed back in the Buick for a chow run.

"I'm telling you, Coleman, I think somebody's trying to kill me."

"You're crazy."

"What about the cut brakes?" Serge stuck the key in the ignition. "And I could swear I'm being followed."

"Hold it," said Coleman.

Serge took his hand off the key. "What is it?"

"I think I hear the phone ringing."

"I don't hear anything." Serge grabbed the key again.

"No, I'm sure it's the phone."

"Probably your landlord," said Serge. "Let's get going."

Serge began turning the key. Coleman grabbed his hand. "But what if it's weed? I have an order in. I'll bet that's what it is. It's hard to get hold of the weed guys. You usually only get their beeper or voicemail. You have to take the weed calls when you can. Otherwise the order goes to someone else, and you have to start all over calling their beeper and waiting. That's why you can never miss a weed call. I'll bet it's the weed guy. . . ."

Serge was banging his forehead on the steering wheel.

Coleman opened the passenger door. "I'll be right back."

ANNA'S EYES STAYED locked on the gun in Jerry's hand. A hundred yards from shore, alone in the open, expecting a bullet any second. The alcohol started doing its thing, and she stumbled sideways and fell again. She pushed herself back up. This was the moment. Her head told her to make a break for it. She'd probably still get shot, but she wasn't going without a fight. Readyyyyy . . .

Just as she was about to spring, Jerry started walking backward toward shore, still aiming the gun.

"Now stay there!"

A SHERIFF'S CRUISER leaped the bridge to Ramrod Key. It skidded around the corner at the Chevron station and sped up the block.

"I think I see the place," said Walter. "There's the Buick."

"Oh, no. Someone's already in the driver's seat!"

COLEMAN TROTTED OUT of the trailer and jumped back in the car. "Okay, let's go."

"Who was it?"

"They hung up."

"You moron." Serge grabbed the ignition key.

A loud whoop from a police siren. Serge glanced in the rearview as a sheriff's cruiser screeched to a stop, blocking the driveway. Deputies jumped out.

"Take your hand off the key! Get out of the car! Now!"

Serge momentarily thought about the gun in the glove compartment, then sighed. "I guess the jig is up."

". . . Out of the car! Out of the car! . . ."

They opened the doors.

"Step away from the vehicle!"

They stepped away. Serge laughed offhandedly. "I'll bet you want to talk about all those murders."

Gus looked at Walter, then Serge. "You know?"

"What are you, a comedian? If anyone knows, don't you think I would?"

Gus had a confused expression. "You're taking this awfully well."

"I try to keep an even disposition," said Serge. "Do you really think we're talking the death penalty?"

"Afraid so."

"What if there's cooperation?"

"Could help," said Walter. "But we can't promise anything."

"Sure would appreciate it."

"You don't mean you actually still have feelings for her."

"Who?"

"Your wife. Some guys would get pretty sore if they found out their spouse was trying to kill them."

"She was?"

"That's what we're here about," said Gus. "We came to warn you your car might be rigged."

"She's a serial killer," said Walter.

"Just got the mug shot this afternoon," said Gus. "Murdered her last four husbands or boyfriends. All after extremely quick courtships."

"Oh, *those* murders," said Serge.

"Yeah. Why? What murders did you think we were talking about?"

"Uh . . . the same ones." Serge smiled to himself: So that's why I got the soul-mate vibe.

JERRY KEPT WALKING backward through the water until he reached the mangroves. His hand found the side of a flat-bottomed aluminum hull.

The airboat. So that's it, thought Anna. The reason for the alcohol. He's going to stage a boating accident. She looked down into the shallow water. The flats. Not enough room to dive under anything.

Jerry jumped up into the captain's seat in one motion. Anna's heart seized on a strong beat. The moment froze; sound dropped out. Her eyes stayed straight, her mind thumbing through the final details. The roseate spoonbill on that branch. The tarpon fin to her right. The perforated mangrove islands across the horizon. The sound came rushing back in her head with a tremendous roar, and she found herself running.

Jerry enjoyed himself watching her pitiful escape attempt, high-stepping with awkward splashes, falling down over and over. He was mildly aroused. His empty eyes saw all the vectors. Her distance and slow progress, then the future path of the airboat that would cut her down well before shore. He turned the ignition key. Twelve volts of DC current zipped to the blasting caps on the sticks of dynamite duct-taped under the airboat driver's seat.

Anna was knocked down in the water by the force of the explosion. The demolition was over-engineered, at least three times the TNT needed for the job. Jerry's ballistic path was almost straight up, still strapped in his chair like an F-16 pilot bailing out at altitude. Except he was on fire.

Anna watched him sail higher and higher before arcing over and coming down headfirst in the muck. Just legs and seat bottom showing. It took a full minute for the last of the flaming pieces to flutter down and hiss into the water around Anna as she splashed back to shore.

EVERYONE ON THE front lawn of Coleman's trailer turned toward the sound of the explosion.

"That was dynamite," said Gus.

They looked northeast. A black cloud rose from the horizon in the direction of No Name Key.

Gus hopped back in the cruiser and stuck his head out the window. "Walter, stay here until the bomb squad arrives and clears their car."

"Be careful."

The cruiser took off. It jumped islands in quick succession. Traffic on U.S. 1 heard the siren and halted at a green light as Gus made a squealing left on Big Pine and raced up the long, straight road that would eventually lead to No Name Key.

Soon, a single car appeared a mile in the distance, coming toward Gus through the road's shimmering heat waves. The car grew larger and larger until Gus couldn't believe his eyes. A metallic green Trans Am. He hit the brakes and turned the wheel. The cruiser skidded to a sideways stop, blocking both lanes. The Trans Am ran off the road into a palmetto thicket.

Gus jumped out and drew his gun. The driver's window rolled down. Gus immediately recognized Anna from TV, the missing woman presumed dead. He holstered the pistol and ran to her door.

"Ma'am, are you okay?"

"Let's make a deal."

TWO HOURS LATER, an otherwise quiet lane on Ramrod Key was jammed with gossiping neighbors. The trailer and yard were wrapped in crime tape. Serge and Coleman chatted with Walter while demolition experts crawled everywhere.

A member of the bomb squad came over. "The car's clean . . . except for this unregistered gun I found in the glove compartment."

"Must have been my wife's," said Serge. "You think you know someone. . . ."

Another bomb technician emerged from the trailer. "Clean inside . . . except I found this." He held out an ashtray. "At least twenty roaches. There are four or five more just like it."

"She also turned out to be a burglar—and a drug fiend," said Serge. "Constantly breaking into Coleman's trailer and smoking joints."

Walter made a dismissive wave with his hand. "Don't worry about it."

The bomb squad guy dumped the ashtray in his pocket and walked off.

Suddenly, more explosions. Bright bursts of light in the sky over Key West.

"Look," said Serge. "The fireworks are starting."

Walter checked his watch. "I wonder what's taking Gus so long."

COLORFUL FIREWORKS REFLECTED off the windshield of a sheriff's cruiser parked down by water's edge on Big Pine Channel.

The people in the front seat weren't watching them.

"Tell me again about the money," said Gus.

"We split it fifty-fifty," said Anna. "There's at least three million. We get the hell out of here and start over. You'll have to quit your job, of course, but how much can that be paying?"

Epilogue

THE QUIET TIME just after sunset in the Florida Keys. Scarlet hues burning through the mangroves. Strings of headlights on U.S. 1.

The incoming tide quietly lapped the northern shore of No Name Key. A ring of seaweed formed. Another soft wave carried a six-pack ring. Some of the water washed over a Polaroid photo in the sand. It had singed edges. Another wave came in and the photo began to float. It was a picture of a house, the typical kind you'd find in this part of the Keys. One of the older ranch deals. The front yard was made of smooth landscaping stones. In the middle was an old ship's anchor. Another wave came and carried the photo off.

A METALLIC GREEN Trans Am sat in the driveway of a vacation home on Big Pine Key. There was a long gouge through the stones in the front yard—from the crab-trap floats to the driveway—where Anna and Gus were dragging a heavy anchor.

The pair got the thing to the lip of the trunk. But between Anna's petite frame and Gus's back, it was hard to tell who was having the worse of it. An old-timer watched from the porch of the house next door. He had a white T-shirt, suspenders and bedroom slippers. When Gus and Anna dropped the anchor again on the third try, the old man came over.

"Let me give you a hand."

It went in with a thud. "Thanks." Anna tied the trunk lid down with string.

"Heard about the owner. You related?"

"His sister."

"My condolences."

"Appreciate it."

"Only saw him a couple times," said the neighbor. He caught Anna looking down at his slippers. "You reach a certain age, you just don't give a damn anymore. I don't know why."

Anna smiled.

"You gonna be selling the place or coming back?"

She put her hands on her hips and looked around in the twilight. A miniature deer hoofed across the street. "Don't know yet."

The animal began gnawing on one of the flowers that surrounded the anchorless space.

"Go on, now," said the old man. "Git!"

"No," said Anna. "Let him eat."

The man pointed back at his own property, where all the plants were circled with chicken mesh. "You have to use the wire."

Gus climbed in the passenger seat. Anna went to the driver's side.

"You're lucky if you already got property in the Keys," the man told Anna across the Trans Am's roof. "Too expensive to buy in anymore. I could sell my house and get a giant place in Lakeland. I got brochures."

Anna climbed in the car. The old man came around to her window. "Let me know if you decide to sell. I know people. Actually, I get a kickback, but we can split it."

"I'll keep it in mind." She buckled her seatbelt. "Thanks again with the anchor."

The old man looked up at the sky and scratched his whiskers. "There's a big storm coming."

Anna started the car. "There is?"

"No. That's something this old guy tells Linda Hamilton before she drives away at the end of *The Terminator*. . . ." The man began walking back to his house. "I just like to say it all the time."

The Trans Am backed out of the driveway, the rear end riding low from a three-hundred-pound solid-gold anchor painted with marine primer and verdigris stain.

Stuart. Florida

A SMALL TOWN, but, as they say, a great place to live. It's up on the east coast. Jensen Beach to the north, Hobe Sound to the south. Beautiful beaches, arts, health care, the rest of the state's problems another world away. The best part is the neighbors. Always saying hello in the supermarket, the bank, the library. Particularly the library.

Today, the library's parking lot was mostly empty, but that was because of the hour. Didn't open for another thirty minutes. Just a few cars in the employees' section. Red Nissan, black Mazda and the vehicle of the library's most recent hire, a brown Plymouth Duster.

The staff was gathered inside for an announcement.

"May I have your attention," said the library director. "I'd like you to meet Pam, the newest addition to our staff."

Pam's makeup was rosy, her hair down. She grinned wide, crinkled her shoulders and gave a spunky little wave. The director urged everyone to drop by their new co-worker's desk and get acquainted.

Shortly after noon, a couple of young professionals came in on lunch break to return books.

"Hey, who's that new girl over in fiction?" said the first guy.

"Don't recognize her," said the second.

"What do you think?"

"Too conservative."

"Those are the ones you have to worry about." He started walking in the woman's direction. "I'm going to ask her out."

A '71 BUICK RIVIERA left the Florida Keys and headed west through the Everglades.

Windows down, bright sunlight.

Serge had weighed their investment options and advised Coleman to skip out on the rent. He grabbed a radio knob and turned Moby up loud.

"*. . . Extreme ways are back again . . .*"

The swamp air was sticky and thick, the horizon low across the sawgrass.

"What'd you say?" asked Serge.

Coleman cracked a Schlitz. "I didn't say anything."

"Yes you did. About swamp air and the horizon."

"Wasn't me."

"You're stoned." Serge faced the road again. A snowy egret swooped low over the Tamiami Trail.

"There," said Serge. "You're doing it again."

"Doing what?"

"You mentioned an egret."

"I didn't say a word."

"Well if you didn't—" Serge turned around and saw a grinning man sitting in the middle of the backseat. ". . . Who the fuck are you?"

Narrator.

"Narrator?"

Ex-narrator, actually.

"What are you doing here?"

Kept telling them I wanted a little screen time but they just strung me along. Now that I've been fired, what can they do? I'm taking matters into my own hands.

"More power to ya," said Serge.

"Want a beer?" asked Coleman.

Sure. The narrator accepted the can and popped it open. He tapped Serge on the shoulder. So, you don't mind if I continue?

"Knock yourself out."

Thanks. Serge accelerated and whipped around a slow-moving tractor. Coleman chugged the rest of his beer and grabbed another. The Buick continued across the Tamiami, past the cadaver farm, where a civil servant stood at the open trunk of an Impala, glanced around, then erased a number on his clipboard.

A Note on the Type

The text of this book was set in a face called Kartonia Linotype, a style first developed by a guild of radical underground printers in seventeenth-century Luxemburg, whose audacious use of kerning almost ended the monarchy and . . . A NOTE ON THE TYPE IS TEMPORARILY CLOSED. PLEASE COME BACK LATER.

KEY WEST, Fla. —A joint federal and state strike force launched a coordinated predawn raid at a local Note on the Type, uncovering six kilos of cocaine, $280,000 in cash, 120 illegal lobsters, 23 prize-fighting cocks, and 17 undocumented Haitians living in subhuman conditions and forced to fact-check for the equivalent of eight cents a day.

Contacted out of town, the author who owns the Note on the Type said he had no knowledge of the activities on the premises but plans to reopen in the future, possibly as a preface and epigraph clearance outlet.

Preview

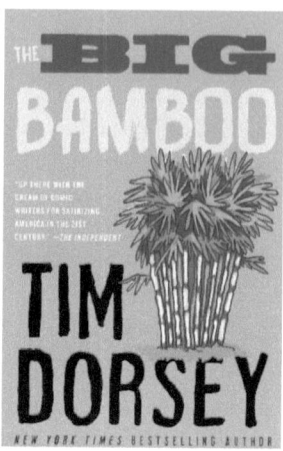

The world's most lovable serial killer is back. During this latest cavalcade of nonstop felonies, Serge Storms finds time to resurrect his obsession with movies, particularly those showcasing his beloved Florida. And he wants answers! Why aren't more films shot there? How come the ones that are stink so bad?

Naturally, Serge, accompanied by his substance-sustained sidekick, Coleman, must immediately hop a transcontinental flight to straighten out Hollywood once and for all. But his mission is sidetracked by perpetual detours to irresistible celluloid landmarks . . . and intrigue.

Welcome to Tim Dorsey's slice of America – where nobody gets out unscathed and untanned!

The next Serge Storms adventure

About the Serge Storms series

Part spree killer, part local historian, Serge A. Storms and his human narcotic partner Coleman have carved a trail of destruction and marijuana roaches through Florida, and he's just getting started.

Warning: If you sight this man, please contact the police immediately.

Further titles in the series—

Florida Roadkill

Hammerhead Ranch Motel

Orange Crush

Triggerfish Twist

The Stingray Shuffle

Cadillac Beach

Torpedo Juice

The Big Bamboo

Electric Barracuda

When Elves Attack

Pineapple Grenade

The Rip Tide Ultra-Glide

Tiger Shrimp Tango

Shark Skin Suite

Coconut Cowboy

Clownfish Blues

About the Author

Tim Dorsey was born in Indiana, moved to Florida at the age of 1, and grew up in a small town about an hour north of Miami called Riviera Beach. He worked as a reporter and editor for the Tampa Tribune from 1987 to 1999, after which he left to write full time.

He lives in Tampa with his family.

Acknowledgments

Gratitude is due once again to my agent, Nat Sobel, and my editor, Henry Ferris. I also owe another round of thanks to Michael Morrison, Lisa Gallagher, Debbie Stier, and David Brown.

Note from the Publisher

To receive updates on next releases in the Serge Storms series, sign up at farragobooks.com/serge-storms-signup

www.ingramcontent.com/pod-product-compliance
Ingram Content Group UK Ltd.
Pitfield, Milton Keynes, MK11 3LW, UK
UKHW042000230426
12048UKWH00009B/447